THE
Odessa Stone

C C CHAMBERS

STEP THROUGH BOOKS

The Odessa Stone Copyright © C C Chambers 2003

Published by Step Through Books

Cover and illustrations © C C Chambers 2003

The right of C C Chambers to be identified as the author of this work has been
asserted in accordance with the Copyright Designs and Patents Act 1988.
A CIP catalogue record of this book is available from the British Library.

ISBN: 0-9545953-1-9

Printed and bound in England by Bookmarque Limited

For things that aren't there.

29/12/2003

To KATHLEEN

BEST REGARDS,

X

X

X ⊔

X

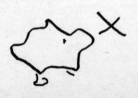

CHAPTER ONE
Strange Looks

The girl stumbled onwards, almost blind through the grim streets of a town near Odessa. Or maybe it was far from Odessa? That wasn't important to her. It was the second stop on the railway line just like the dice had shown, and that was all that mattered, that was all she could deal with. Her gaunt features were shrouded by her long, rain-soaked hair, and her head rocked slightly with each vague and unsteady step. Her joints screamed at her to stop moving, to stop right now and curl up and sleep for a while, sleep forever, sleep would make everything better.. but she couldn't. Something wouldn't let her.

She looked up at the not-quite-a-bird as it frantically dived at her over and over again, screeching as if it was possessed by the devil and wickedly intent on tormenting and bullying her. But somewhere deep within her mind she could make sense of its noises, in a way.

"Linda! Keep listening to me! Don't fall asleep again! You have to keep going.. please Linda, keep going a little further that's all, and I promise we'll be safe!"

The girl barely responded. Her eyes were so heavy and the daylight hurt them so much, and her feet seemed to weigh more and more with every laboured step. The pain in her joints ebbed away a little, and took more of her senses as it went.

A woman stood across the road, patiently waiting for a bus. For no good reason at all, her attention was suddenly drawn to a girl who was close to her own daughter's age. She sighed with despair at yet another bad sort who was throwing her life away, and tutted at how the world seemed so full of them these days. She watched the bird screeching and charging at her, and raised an eyebrow at the ugly black cat acting nervously around the girl's feet. The vile thing seemed to be scratching at her ankles. The woman sighed again, blew her nose for the hundredth time that day, and threw the tissue into the gutter.

"See that girl, Olya? What a waste, what a waste.. if she was mine,

I'd be as angry as the bird," she commented to her friend standing next to her. Olya nodded her agreement, and wondered why Galina was talking about a bird. She couldn't see a bird, but she did think there was something very odd about the girl's cat. Galina and Olya both looked away, preferring to stare down the road for their bus. The girl stumbled on.

Tarkovsky's unrated hostel occupied the entire corner block at the end of the street. With vicious encouragement, the girl managed the three stone steps and kept on moving all the way to the reception window.

The clerk didn't like being stared at, and especially not by scruffy low-life. He looked at her with contempt while she clumsily cast a wad of notes onto the counter, and he grimaced at the blood left on the money - and then shivered when he saw the masses of bite marks on her hands. And on top of all that, she'd brought a wretched bird into the place with her as well.

"How long d'you want?" he grunted, waiting a few seconds until he realised that she wasn't going to answer. He gave her a key with a cracked 18 hanging from it, which was for a filthy room on the second floor - one entirely appropriate for her sort. He watched as she attempted to make her way up the stairs, and decided to leave a note for whoever was on the next shift to check on her early in the evening, just in case a mortician needed calling - there was no way someone like that was going to be his problem. He carried on watching as her disfigured black cat clawed its way a few steps ahead of her, where it paused to look back as if making sure that she was still following. He sighed and went back to his tv.

She turned the corner, crawled up the second flight and somehow managed to half-stand at the top, trying to fight her way through the blurred and distant world around her. She had nothing left. No energy, no idea where she was, no understanding of how or why she was anywhere.

"Linda! Come on, just a little more! I'm begging you, a little more that's all! We're nearly safe!"

Somewhere she could hear the voice shouting and shouting at her, drifting deep in and out of her head and turning her mind upside down. She carried on following it, unable to even wonder if she was actually moving.

The clerk hurried up the stairs and changed her key to the one for Room 22, which was up on the next floor. There weren't any other people on that level, and it would be far better for trade if nobody knew that someone like her was there. He tried to brush the bird away, but it stayed obstinately close to the girl as he helped her up the next flight of stairs. Eventually he guided her to the bed where she would hopefully sleep off whatever she'd taken, but she just stood beside it as if she had no idea it was even there. He gave her a nudge and she toppled forwards across the horsehair mattress, lying face-down as if she had been knocked unconscious.

"Stupid kid.." he muttered, figuring that her position would be a little suspicious if a doctor had to be called later on. She needed to look as if she'd simply fallen asleep and not woken up, and that way he could claim that she had seemed fine when she arrived. He moved her around until she looked almost natural, and then rooted through her pockets to find some extra money for his time and effort.

"Damn it! What the.."

His fingers touched something far down in her inside pocket which made him wince and stifle a yelp. Whatever was nestled in there amongst the wrappers and biscuits had sent a sensation through his heart that made a cold sweat break out over his entire body. He grabbed at the roll of banknotes which had edged out from a side-pocket, dropped one or two for the girl to keep, and made a quick guess that he was holding at least four week's wages, maybe five. The cat suddenly lashed at his other hand, almost missing as it toppled from the bed.

"Oww, you miserab.." he cursed, and looked at the small, clean scratch. He hurried to the door, pausing at the room's only table to throw an ashtray and an old mug towards the vile creature. The cat didn't move or even blink as both brushed past its fur.

Perhaps it was just his overactive imagination, but even before he had reached the stairs, the small scratch was becoming quite raw and irritable, and was probably going to be a lot worse than the burns on the fingers of his other hand.

"Burns? Where the.. where've they come from?" he wondered. He swore back at the room, and staggered down the stairs.

The bird had flown to the far window at the end of the corridor, where it perched on the sill to look out. The street was almost empty except for a few cars and even fewer people going past. That was good. No soldiers, no anyones. Its wings beat loudly as it traversed the corridor and dived into the girl's room before the door could swing shut. In mid-flight it changed effortlessly into another winged creature, a glowing doll-like figure who darted anxiously around the room, struggling desperately hard not to let go of a small silvery pouch. She seemed to be losing the battle.

She looked down at the girl lying on the bed, who had started breathing in shallow and weak gasps. Her eyes were blank and stared straight upwards into nothing, straight past the not-a-bird-anymore. The cat nervously looked from the girl up to the faery, who fluttered down to hover inches above the girl's face.

"Linda! Linda! I'm still with you! You have to listen! Can you hear me? Lindahhh!"

She turned to the cat.

"Oh they've done something bad this time, really bad haven't they? What do we do now? What do we.."

She flew in panicked circles around the room trying desperately to remember her best Adapted Healing Song, but was quickly thrown into a dive by the wild movements coming from the pouch. She couldn't hold it any longer. She pulled the golden cord from her waist and raced up to the safety of the ceiling to watch the silver bag drop in a slow, irregular spiral to the floor. It settled near the cat who immediately jumped up onto the bed and stood protectively on the girl, digging her claws into the denim jacket, arching her back and hissing down to where the pouch had landed.

But nothing happened. An ominous silence fell over the small room, broken only by the sound of weak gasps as the girl struggled for another breath.

A thin trail of dense grey mist ventured out onto the floorboards. Small fingers of vapour spread out from its sides, pausing after just a few inches. Another emerged from the pouch, much denser and thicker, moving like a snake as it disappeared under the bed. Another joined it, quickly followed by another, and then another. More and more raced free of the pouch, soon covering every inch of the floor in a dark, writhing mass of misty tendrils which grew deeper and deeper, easily reaching the very top of the mattress. The cat hissed and dug her claws further into the denim as the sheets became lost beneath the impenetrable murkiness. Every strand of her jet-black fur bristled with fear and devoted, protective aggression. The sea of mist rose defiantly higher, edging around the girl's body.. and then it fell, flowing backwards in waves as it returned to the small pouch. Silence reigned for the briefest of moments, before darkness engulfed the room.

Suddenly a storm of anger roared upwards in an explosion of raging, twisting columns of shadows and light, writhing like thousands upon thousands of snakes, entwining, merging and separating in a wild frenzy until they became one single, powerful entity. Within seconds the mist, the dust and the burning light began fading away, drifting somewhere far beyond the confines of the room to leave a tall, dark haired woman standing beside the bed. She glared across to the faery, who trembled and tried to fly even further away.. and then she turned her jet-black eyes to the girl.

A cold and callous smile spread across her face.

CHAPTER TWO
A Few Days Earlier

Friday 13th June 8.57am

Linda Beaufort was not 13. If anyone asked, she was either 14 or maybe 12, but she was never, ever 13. Especially not 13 years and 13 weeks. Not that it mattered. No-one ever asked, or was ever really likely to, but if by chance anyone did.. well, she was ready for them.

She sat at her desk beneath the small windows in the antiquated Room 106, and stared at the clock above the blackboard. Its long hand took another slow clunk nearer to the moment of doom. There were now just two more clunks to go. Linda had watched the previous eight, which meant that by the time the final one arrived she would have scored a near-perfect ten consecutive clunks, which was twice as near to being totally perfect as her previous Personal Best of five uninterrupted clunks. The Unofficial Personal Best was nine, but she had blinked on three of those clunks which meant they didn't really count. All things considered, ten clunks would be a pretty safe start to the day.

She kept her eyes firmly fixed on the dial and moved her head as far over to the left as possible, and then down a little, and then over to the right. That way, the others in her class wouldn't think she was staring again. They'd think she was looking at all kinds of things instead. For the millionth time in her life, she found herself wondering why no-one else understood anything about the important things in life. There were a myriad of seemingly minor things that could be done in order to swing the balance away from misfortune and all the way over to good fortune, or maybe just to a place somewhere in the middle, into a safe haven of compromise where nothing bad would happen and no-one would get hurt. But in all the years that Linda had been at Miserable Saint Teresa's Miserable School Of Abject Misery And Miserableness, hardly anyone had ever tried to understand anything important.

The rest of the class carried on being loud, chattering their excited chatter and bouncing along through life as if they hadn't any cares in the world. Ignorance really was bliss, for them.

The final clunk triggered the nine o'clock bell to fill the entire school with a chaotic din, and Linda felt as if it shook the entire building. The day had officially started, time had run out, and her ten consecutive clunks had come and gone. But now she didn't feel like they'd have much influence at all. She stayed motionless, pretending to be oblivious to all the noise around her in the classroom, but secretly wishing she was part of it. And this time she almost managed to convince herself that she was glad to be glad that she was glad that she was never, ever part of it. Or something like that. Friday mornings were never good for brain-straining, especially ones where a fate worse than death was lying ahead.

For a fraction of a second, she thought Mrs Fellner was standing by the door. Mrs Fellner was the nice one, the kind of teacher who worked well past retirement and was as much a part of the school as Saints Days, assemblies, dubious meals and echoing corridors. And she always had so much time for Linda, and even a hug once when things were going particularly badly. The chances of her being there were very slim considering that she had died over a year ago, but Linda still found herself looking to where she possibly, maybe, might just have been standing. But she wasn't there. Nothing was there of course, and her attention was dragged back into the real world by a ball of paper embedding itself in her hair.

"Hey Loon-da? Snap out of it! There's a whole bunch of rooks outside who are looking for you - isn't it time for one of your soothsayer mystic verses?" mocked Brenda, a tall and thin girl with an overactive mouth who had been a constant source of irritation since the age of seven. Her friend Emma was even worse.

"No Bren, she whistles at rooks - it's magpies who she sings to. You have to get it right, or else you get cursed by the evil crows.."

Dumpy Trish joined in. She still had absolutely no sense of humour, despite years of practice at everyone's expense.

"Steady on you two, don't talk like that or a passing witch will get you! I actually saw one last night because Ms Beau forgot to sprinkle pixie dust on uh.. a leprechaun's rabbit's foot.. while standing on one leg. Thanks Linda, thanks so much! We're all doomed cause of you!"

Linda grinned back to them and gladly let a few waves of not-brown-but-not-black hair fall even further forwards around her face. The same old jokes, the same old jokers. She imagined herself turning around to face them, with her hair bouncing on her shoulders like in a shampoo commercial, and then delivering a barrage of ego-blasting put-downs which they'd never forget. And then she would march confidently over to the door, tell Brenda and her Living Laboratory Experiments to get out for ever, and then everyone else would be cheering and she'd..

..Linda's daydream ended abruptly as Ms Wrenchburn's heavy footsteps echoed through the corridor, announcing her arrival long before she walked into the classroom. A nervous and respectful silence immediately fell as she opened the door. Absolutely everybody was nervous and respectful when the volatile Head of History was around - even the other teachers were on their very best behaviour whenever she was near. She had a voice and an attitude which perfectly matched her squat, robust shape and Linda suspected that she might even be part bulldog. In fact, if bulldogs wore lipstick the resemblance would be unnervingly close.

She stepped up onto the raised teaching platform and stood behind her impossibly tidy desk, then carefully placed the pile of marked History papers in the centre. She looked despairingly down at Linda and took out the Registration Book.

"Morning, Form 2F. Sit!" she snapped, and the class obeyed as one. She began calling out the list of names, and sighed before dropping her voice to utter the fifth - which happened to be Linda's.

"Oh no.." Linda sighed, resigning herself to the fact that something even worse than 'horrendously awful' was coming up. A new world-record for embarrassment lay ahead, certainly a St Teresa's all-comers record and at the very least a raising of the bar, which would undoubtedly mean a humiliating weekend was going to follow.

"That's not entirely ideal.." she thought, and began nervously tapping her feet on the floor more or less in time to the chorus of Super Trouper, her current Number One in the ever-changing Abba Top 100 Chart.

She silently counted the 32 names. That was an important thing to do, and regrettably one that she knew was highly unlikely to become public knowledge, or ever gain her any thanks. Today was a Friday so she included her own name, which made 33. A nice round 33 to end the week, as always. That was also an important thing to do. She wasn't entirely sure why it was important, but it just was and it made her feel better about whatever the next week might have in store. Ms Wrenchburn closed the blue book and spoke loudly as if she was addressing someone in another classroom.

"I have in my hand your History papers, and we will spend the first two lessons of this morning going through them. Generally it was very good and I'm pleased to say the class average was high - and it would have been the highest of the entire Second Year but for one slight problem.. child."

A low murmur drifted around the room, and Linda heard her name being moaned and whispered. She shifted uncomfortably in her seat as Ms Wrenchburn walked between the rows of desks handing back the papers and awarding compliments to a privileged few. After six perfectly-observed clunks from the clock, she arrived next to Linda.

"..and so to Miss Beaufort. You wrote your name correctly, even your class correctly.. and then proceeded to get the date wrong. A bad start on a History paper, don't you think?"

Laughter filled the class, and the sick feeling in Linda's stomach spread to the rest of her body. Her heart was already racing far too quickly, yet still managed to raise its tempo even higher. Ms Wrenchburn remained stony-faced, and turned the top sheet over.

"The first three sentences of your paper offered a slight improvement regarding factual accuracy and recollection, but then.. there is no more. Why is that, Linda? Do tell me - no, tell us all why you chose not to answer any more questions. None of the Multiple Choice, none of the Short Answers, none of the Essay Questions. I have no doubt we're all very interested."

Linda looked at the crescent moon she'd drawn deep into the wood of her desk during the course of the school year, and answered very quietly.

"It ran out."

"It ran out? What ran out? Your knowledge or your pen?" said Ms Wrenchburn, to an appreciative audience.

"My biro," Linda told the desk.

"Well didn't you have any more? Adequate spares were available on the supervising teacher's desk, so why didn't you request a replacement? Enlighten us, do."

Linda knew she had to get all of this out of the way as quickly as possible. She couldn't manage a deep breath so she took a light one instead, shut out everything around her and started speaking.

"They weren't the same kind as the one that ran out. They were all different to the one I started with."

More laughter and expressions of amazement filled the room, and Ms Wrenchburn folded her arms, creasing the remaining papers in the process. Linda stayed hidden somewhere beneath her hair.

"And that's important? What possible difference does a change of biro make to anything? Why should that bother you, or anyone?"

Linda knew she was wasting her time, but had to carry on. It would take her one step closer to anything better.

"Changing biros.. would break the continuity, and that's wrong. When that gets interrupted it's like inviting problems into your life. Bad ones. But I wrote with the empty pen for the rest of the first question so if you rub a pencil over the page you can see the words. And I answered some of the others as well.. and most of the multi choice.. I can show you - it's best with a 4B."

The class dissolved into hysterics and Ms Wrenchburn threw the papers towards her desk. The blank pages spilled onto the floor, and Linda began the humiliating task of picking them all up, wondering why these idiots couldn't understand her reasoning. After all, she knew that she was completely and utterly right. The front page lay at Emma's feet, showing a big red 0%, underlined three times.

"And she survives, she lives to yawn another day.." Linda thought to herself while ignoring whatever Emma was saying, "..and now things can improve, heaps."

A knock at the door made Ms Wrenchburn bring order to the class, and a nervous First Year scurried in. She quickly handed over a note and left following a dismissive flick of the teacher's hand.

"Well well," she mused in a flat, nasal tone, "It seems today is quite a day for you, Miss Beaufort. Your presence is requested by the Headmistress at once. Perhaps you'd like to take your History papers as well? That's not a suggestion, it's an instruction."

The others found that to be far more amusing than it really was, but Linda was quite relieved. She could escape for a while. Apart from an unavoidably dismal exam result, she couldn't think of anything else that she had done which might drop her any deeper into hot water, so the prospect of facing Sister Mariephred didn't concern her too much. However, anyone summoned to Scary Mary's office was usually in serious trouble and invitations were very rare indeed, so there was a pretty good chance that the day might get a whole lot worse - but not yet, not for a few more minutes.

She put the exam papers into her bag and eagerly headed for freedom and the short journey to the Main Building. But before she left, Jeanette discretely beckoned her over to her desk near the door. Usually she was a pain beyond belief and could occasionally be even worse than Emma, but just for once she actually looked sympathetic. She quickly handed over a folded piece of paper and tried to look completely innocent.

Linda wandered the entire length of the corridor and stood at the top of the stairs before opening it up. A crude drawing of a black bird stared back at her, with the words 'Spooky Raven' written thirteen times around it. Jeanette's idea of a joke was pretty weak, but the consequences of ignoring a raven were too awful to think about, and Linda shivered. Superstitions and countless unwritten natural laws were no laughing matter, and she anxiously patted her hand against the banister rail while weighing up the pros and cons of what to do with the drawing. After all, Jeanette knew nothing about ravens apart from the small amount Linda had told her a few months ago, so was this really worth bothering with?

"I can ignore this, it's just a useless drawing.. it doesn't bother her so it shouldn't bother me.. I can ignore it.. I can.. I can.. no I can't.. oh no I can't.."

She sighed a long sigh, and knew that it had to be dealt with properly. A newspaper headline sprang into her mind.

"Lindagate: Hopeless Schoolgirl Disrespectful To Raven - Prime Minister Eaten By Satan's Hounds!"

Potential newspaper headlines had been something that had plagued Linda since her father really was a front-page headline a few years earlier. He was a rising star of the political scene, a politician who took no prisoners and was revered by almost everyone - especially Linda. However, his notorious short-temper got the better of him on a live tv debate and he put a brash opponent and a cameraman in hospital, which left his career languishing in the doldrums as a humble Under Assistant Secretary to the Minister Of Defence's Secondary Advisor. And he was never, ever encouraged to do any interviews.

The possibility of the Prime Minister encountering any of Satan's pets was pretty unlikely, but that didn't matter to Linda. Jeanette's humourless drawing needed disposing of properly.

"If only people weren't so stupid, jokes like this wouldn't happen," she thought, half whispering it to herself as she folded the paper into a star shape.

She soon left through one of the school's many side-entrances, pondering whether or not it might be a good idea to write a cleverly-worded letter to Sister Mariephred suggesting a few new subjects for next year. Lessons about Natural Harmony and Basic Karma instead of dull ones like Chemistry or Maths could only be an improvement.

Linda decided to make a detour on the way to the Main Building. She crossed over the playground, went around the tennis courts and then further along to the all-weather hockey pitch. There were just too many cracks and lines to avoid on a day like this, so instead of hurrying over it she took the long way around and eventually found herself on the far side of the playing fields, at the foot of the large alder tree. Its branches had once cast a shadow that looked just like a witch riding a broomstick, give or take a bit, and in Linda's opinion that made it a very safe place to dispose of a drawing of a raven - even a badly drawn one. Piece by piece she tore the sheet into dozens of tiny paper flakes and recited her usual verses for dealing with such bringers of bad luck, and then repeated them twice more. After all, today was the 13th of the month and it was a Friday as well - and that was bad news in anyone's books, especially hers.

"Farewell Raven
Be on your way,
Leave no misfortune
Behind you this day.

Take troubles with you
To cast in the night,
For harm comes to no-one
When you are in flight."

And that made Linda feel good - really, really, exceptionally good. The sun was shining brightly and the day was already becoming very warm, and the trees seemed to be whispering their approval to her in the gentle breeze. This was so much better than being cooped up in a horrible classroom with her horrible friends, and she took a few moments to simply enjoy being outside on such a wonderful summer's morning. Far off in the distance she could see a few heads jumping up at the windows of Room 106, and she couldn't care less as to whether they were laughing at her or not - well, not at that moment, anyway.

Her hair swept across her face over and over again as she made her way back to the playground. She loved that feeling of the wind all around her, gently pushing her this way and that. It was like a friend who was always nearby, always waiting to rush out and greet her again.

She opened the arched door leading to the school's reception area and stood on the brush-mat to have a seriously good think and carefully plan her next steps. She hated the reception floor. In seven years she had only gone into this part of the school on three or perhaps four occasions, and had managed to avoid it completely for the last two years. So this visit was going to be even more tricky than all the others put together.

Ahead of her lay a sea of diamond-shaped white tiles, each of them only slightly larger than her shoes. That meant there were roughly one billion different lines to step on and interrupt, not to mention the awful black tiles that were just waiting to cause trouble. Another newspaper headline sprang into her mind, this time complete with a picture of herself being arrested by an angry group of large policemen.

"Lindagate: Dimwit Schoolgirl In Black Tile Fiasco - Small Caribbean Island Sinks!"

According to Linda's extensive research, the many Rules Of Tile Traversal were complicated, but really just common sense. She once told them all to a friend and even thought of a few brand new ones while she was talking, but that friend didn't stay a friend for very long afterwards. The top five rules all involved the Dreaded Black Tiles, because they were the dangerous ones. If she stepped on a black one (or on a line directly linking to a black one) with her left foot, the next tile she stepped on absolutely had to be black and with her right foot. A mere connecting line wouldn't be good enough - only a tile would do. But the black tiles were a little smaller than the white ones, so the cracks and tile-borders were more difficult to avoid, especially considering a small leap was needed to go from one to another. That was a total nightmare, and the reception floor had earned a Heebie Jeebie rating of 100, which was the worst possible and was practically worthy of being on the Nine O'clock News.

Fifteen long and very fraught minutes later, Linda triumphantly arrived on the broad stone panel outside The Nun Pit, or as it was more reverentially known, Sister Mariephred's Office. There hadn't been a single problem with any tiles, except for one which didn't really count. If there had been a Tile Jury watching, they'd be debating that one for a long time to come.

She put her shoes back on and knocked twice on the door's right panel and then twice on the left panel, for a nice balance. Linda hated doors, and reckoned that most doors seemed to know it, and they probably hated her right back. Sister Mariephred's sharp voice carried through the glass, and as expected, the door didn't open on the first attempt which obviously meant that bad news lay ahead. The next attempt was the important one so she held the brass doorknob more firmly, twisted much harder and this time it opened. In Linda's mind the first failed attempt was balanced out, so at least the bad news wasn't going to be too bad.

She swung the door open without letting go, and very carefully stepped over the metal strip which separated the reception floor from the carpet in the office. She made absolutely sure that her left foot on the grey stone panel was an equal distance from her right foot inside the office - and therefore the news should only be moderately bad, rather than plain old 'bad' bad. She didn't lose contact with the door until it had closed behind her, and therefore the news would be perfectly okay. Suddenly, Linda felt ready for it.

The elderly Sister watched with perplexed intrigue. Linda was well known to her, mainly due to the tales of her neurotic obsessions recounted by any member of staff during the past few years. She had suspected that it was just a passing phase that a disturbed young girl was going through, but with each year the quirks seemed to get more bizarre and deep-set. There was no place for any un-Christian behaviour involving superstition or other such nonsense at St Teresa's Full & Part Time Boarding School For Young Ladies, and she resolved that one day soon Linda would be put firmly on the right track. But not just now. She spoke in her customary cold and emotionless voice.

"I sent for you over an hour ago, Mzz Bar'fort, Form 2F. There is a phone call from Westminster for you, and the obstinate individual responsible is still waiting on the line. Considering the nation's taxpayers are picking up the bill for this I suggest you approach my desk faster than you approached my office."

Linda tried to step from the centre of one carpet tile to the next, without giving the impression that she was doing so. Sister Mariephred ignored her performance, and secured a tissue around the ear-piece of the phone before handing it to her.

"Hello? It's me here, who's this there?" said Linda, nervously rising in pitch. Whoever was at the other end of the line sounded as if they were eating a biscuit while drinking a coffee at the same time, and had completely forgotten they were waiting for someone.

"Whuh.. yes? Hold on.. yes, hello yes, now. Is that Linda Elizabeth Beaufort?"

"Oh, hi Constance, yes it's Linda here, how's things in.. oh, my middle name isn't Eliz.."

"I'm afraid you hesitated. Kindly put down the phone and bring Linda Beaufort to the vicinity, henceforth. I will call back in precisely six minutes."

"But this is already me here! You really ought to change those nicotine patches more often, Constance, they're not doing you any good at all. Is everything okay? Is dad alright?"

Sister Mariephred gave a hard glare, so Linda put on a more formal manner. Speaking to her father's Departmental Secretary (with the emphasise on 'mental') was never easy, but was even harder when a lethal nun was within striking range.

"Constance, I don't have long. This is Sister's phone."

"Your middle name please," insisted Constance.

"Oh for Heaven's sake.."

Sister Mariephred glared harder and Linda went red. She dropped to a self-conscious whisper.

"..it's Meredydd, okay? And you still haven't told anyone have you? Don't you dare tell anyone!"

The line went silent for a few seconds. Either Constance was re-re-checking a name that she already knew, or she was finishing off the coffee.

"Identification proves positive. Good morning Linda, and I hope you are well. Now then, your father and various colleagues are to represent the British Government on a goodwill visit to Ukraine in order to observe a new co-investment sanitation plant, followed by a walk-around of one or more sizeable nuclear reprocessing facilities in or near to Odessa. You don't need to know precisely how many, where they are or when you'll be at each one. Neither do you need to know who you'll see or where you'll be located, or who else other than Mr Beaufort will be accompanying you on the venture."

"That's nice."

"But I am able to impart the tour's duration, should that be so."

The line went very quiet while Constance waited for Linda to make a formal request, and Linda waited for Constance to speak like a normal person and simply finish the sentence.

"Are you still there, Constance?" she asked, after a minute of almost complete silence.

"Yes, I have no other appointments at this moment. I had said I was able to inform you of the duration, as it's within my authority to offer such detail, regarding the duration. Of said visit."

"Ohh," said Linda, remembering that protocol was Constance's middle name. "How long will I be there, then? And why me?"

"Aha. The visit is scheduled to last ten days, and we believe your presence would lend a family-friendly atmosphere for press photography purposes. Have you understood so far? We need to boost the public perception of the safety of these ventures, and your being there would help to emphasise certain key phrases such as.."

Linda heard the sound of shuffling papers and a mug breaking on the floor.

"Here they are.. 'family-friendly, safe, happy nuclear world, future generations, the way ahead', and so on and so forth. Does that appeal? Technically speaking, you'd be working for the Government and therefore serving your country, no less!"

Linda wanted to jump at the chance of escaping from school and visiting somewhere that was far away, but needed to check at least three of her Lunar-Phase Charts and the very important Piscean Bio-rhythm Projections first.

"Umm.. when is it? School isn't over for another month.."

"Look out of the window. There should be a black car parked approximately in the centre of the open area between the science blocks, secondary hall, and the long-side of the junior school - can you see it in the playground?"

A large black estate stood where Constance had said. The driver waved to her, and she nervously waved back.

"Uhuhh.."

"Excellent. That will leave in.. let me see, precisely 32 minutes from now. Traffic permitting, you'll be home at 12.10pm, have 48 minutes to pack for six formal events, three smart-casual ones and five outdoor photo opportunities. You will then be taken to rendezvous with your father, that's Mr Beaufort, at an unspecified Heathrow terminal for 2.40pm today."

"Six formal? And there's smart-casual as well? I don't have things like that! I haven't even been home since Christmas and I've probably outgrown everything that's there in the last six months. I've hardly got anything to w.."

"Ah, yes you do, fret not. You have some very sensible items. I have personally selected fashions for yourself from the Miss La Vie catalogue which are ideal for a young lady representing her country. They were delivered to your home doorstep at 9.07 this morning. We have a security person making sure they stay there.. called Harold, I believe. He also signed for everything."

A sense of dread washed over Linda. The day had suddenly become a lot worse than she had ever imagined.

"Not the Miss Lavvy catalogue? That's a billion years behind the times! Big horror story.."

"You might be pleasantly surprised. I was!"

Linda sighed and couldn't think of anything good to say.

"Okay, okay. Is there anything else I need to know, Constance?"

"No. Well, yes, I suppose you have to know. It's your father."

"What.. what about him? Is he.."

"Mr Beaufort's grown a beard since you last saw him. When you see him, I suggest a compliment along the lines of 'What a nice beard father', or maybe, 'It is very nice, you have a nice beard', or something similar, perhaps.. whatever you think of at the time, specifically regarding his beard. I'll repeat those if you'd like to write them down?"

Linda's head was in a spin. Everything was happening so quickly, and she couldn't begin to imagine what her father looked like with a beard. Had he gone mad?

"I'll come along then.. but first I need to ask Sister Mariephred if I can go."

"She's already given clearance, faxed in handwriting. She seemed quite keen, actually. In fact, she says you needn't come back till September, but I think August or perhaps late July makes much more sense, and we do like making sense, don't we?"

"Yeah, great joy. I'll go and pack.. bye then."

Linda had spent the conversation edging along the desk, keeping safely ahead of a shadow cast by the vertical lead strip in the middle of the window. But now that she'd put the phone down, she realised how uncomfortably close she was standing to Sister Mariephred, who was pointing towards the door. This didn't feel like the right time to explain that deliberately allowing a window-shadow to pass over you was like inviting the Angel of Death in for a cup of tea and a chat about how horrible you'd like your death to be.

Instead, Linda hurried to the door and stepped on the edges of so many carpet tiles that a shiver of abhorrence shook her even before she was halfway across. The reception floor wasn't such a problem this time, because she didn't care how many lines or black tiles she stepped on or slid over. The damage had already been done and she needed to race back to her room, find her Friday Dice and start rolling some sixes pretty quickly before anything bad could happen.

She ran all the way back to the imposing St Catherine's Dormitory building as if a million demons were chasing her, and had to force herself to stop at the foot of its broad steps to try and regain some composure before tackling them - this was definitely not the time to risk even more trouble by missing any out.

The building was quiet and probably deserted, which was good. That meant there was no-one who might ask why she was in such a hurry. It wasn't that she didn't want to tell anyone, she just didn't want to waste any time explaining all the reasons to them. That could easily take up the best part of an hour, and someone on Government Business with plenty of Bad Luck Thwarting to do first simply didn't have that kind of time to waste. She carefully skated across the slippery foyer, hurtled past the kitchen and St Catherine's lounge, and turned around by the study room to hurry back to close the awkward kitchen door properly before racing back. She stood at the bottom of the stairs, trying to remember whether or not today was a left-foot-first day. It probably was, and even if it wasn't she could just roll an extra six really soon. She hurtled up the three flights to her floor without missing a single step - except for the ones which had cracks or small bits missing, of course.

The bedroom door gave its reassuring click as it shut snugly behind her, and she leaned with her back against it until her heart stopped pounding. After a few minutes she felt able to take the transparent blue Friday Dice from the dressing table and roll it until ten sixes had shown up. She gave a small cheer once the dire consequences of such awesome line-infringing recklessness had been counteracted. Now she felt on top of the world, and her life could return to normal.

Linda's room was large, far larger than she really needed it to be. In fact, she had three beds and three wardrobes all to herself, and certainly made the most of them. Unlike everyone else at the school, she didn't share a bedroom with anyone, and none of her previous room-mates had managed to last very long. Eleven complete weeks was the Official School Record, and Claire Something-Surname even had a certificate to prove it, courtesy of Brenda of course. Bizarrely, the other girls seemed to find that her obsessions made their lives unbearably difficult, rather than infinitely better. Back in September her last room-mate, Peggy Strange-Name, had hidden under the far bed and only emerged after her parents had spent an hour talking to her, and the school nurse had given her some Smarties-that-definitely-weren't-Smarties. She woke up much later in the school's St Jude Hospital Wing, still convinced she was going to die because she'd filled up a glass of water without having first emptied out the inch or so that was already in it. Not only that, but she'd changed hands while drinking it, and as if that wasn't bad enough, one of her socks was up and the other one was down at the time, which trebled the number of consecutive three-four-fives that she needed to roll.

And since then, Linda had been on her own and over the months she had found that it wasn't really so bad, all things considered. For a start, all the wall-space was hers and each side of the room had steadily become covered with posters and pages from magazines, some chosen for what they were of, but more often because their colours flowed from one into the other. And that wasn't easy to do. The only exception to this rule was her favourite wall, the one with the biggest window. It was adorned from top to bottom with Princess Diana and Abba, and Linda was extremely proud of it.

However, having three beds tended to make life complicated, because sleeping in a room with permanently empty beds was practically a cast-iron guarantee of a lonely life ahead. So to avoid that happening, the bed near the door was used on Mondays and Thursdays, the middle bed was for Tuesdays and Fridays, and the end bed near the small windows was for Wednesdays and Saturdays. Sundays had to be catalogued, indexed, and done in a strict rotation. This would have been fine if she was allowed to have three sets of bedsheets, but the Dormitory Head, the evil Mrs Pitt-Bulle, wouldn't allow that so Linda had to completely make up a new bed every day of the week. And on top of all that, every single morning she had to move her things from one wardrobe to the next as well.

"But not for at least another few weeks! Yay! Abbatastic!" she whispered to herself as the best cd in the entire world spun itself into a blur and the opening bars of Dancing Queen filled the room. She had the building to herself, so she dared turn it up a bit more.

Suddenly the entire world felt wonderful, and being able to leave school so much earlier than everyone else made her feel even better about everything.

"Special Ambassador Miss L M Beaufort, on serious Government Business for the.. entire British Government.. formal visitation to somewhere.. havin' the time of your life.. oohoo-hoo.. see that girl.. watch that scene.. diggin the Dancin' Queen.. me-eeee.."

Even though she knew that playing the part of a happy daughter and merely smiling at anyone who might have a camera was a pretty lightweight job, at least she was important enough to have a car waiting where everyone could see it. And everyone included Brenda, Emma, Trish and in particular Ms Funny herself, Jeanette. Plus, she was actually going to be flying somewhere, and best of all, after six long months of being stuck at school watching everybody else leave for their weekends and holidays, she was finally going to see her home again - and her father. Her very busy father.

And at long last, she would have something to tell her penpal Andie about, and she decided to write to her as soon as she reached whatever that foreign place was called. Hopefully they'd have stamps and all that kind of thing over there.

She lined her suitcases up on the middle bed, careful to make sure they were parallel to the bed's sides and would both open towards the biggest window. She started filling them with life's essentials along with all the things that she didn't want anyone to 'borrow' while she was gone. Top of the list was her one and only picture of her mother, which had pride of place on today's bedside table, as always. It was the first thing to be moved every morning, and was the first thing to be packed to go home every.. now and then. In the slightly-faded photo her mother was holding a very small Linda in her arms, in the same way that all loving mothers hold their children. It was taken the day after her first birthday. A few weeks later, when according to Linda's calculations she was thirteen months and thirteen days old, she and her mother were out shopping on an ordinary afternoon in late April.

The story goes that her mother was pushing her along in a trendy new pram, with one or two shopping bags hanging from the rear bar just like in the tv advert, and their entire world was perfectly normal. And then it changed for ever.

One of her mother's friends waved from the entrance of Billings Butchers over on the other side of the main street, and Mrs Beaufort responded with her own wave, plus one on behalf of her daughter. Her friend laughed and gave a joke-wave across to Linda, who was asleep at the time and looking particularly adorable, apparently. So Mrs Beaufort stepped out into the road, not giving a second thought to the fact that some new cars were a lot quieter than others, and could sometimes appear as if out of thin air, especially amidst the hustle and bustle of a noisy town centre. And one did.

As a dozen witnesses all said, the poor woman pushing the pram did very well. She saw the car in time to launch the pram just far enough for the shopping bags to cushion the impact and leave Linda lying in the road just a few feet away, shaken but unhurt. Her mother wasn't so lucky. Fortunately no-one had ever described the scene in any great detail to Linda - and she'd never, ever wanted them to.

It wasn't anyone's fault, it was just one of those things. Bad things could happen to anyone, and nobody would ever be able to really say why. However, in the twelve years since then, Linda had always suspected that actually some things really did happen for very definite reasons. In fact, absolutely everything probably happened for all kinds of reasons. Some reasons were big, but most were small and almost insignificant. Actions, numbers, objects, colours, repetitions - everything influenced everything all the time, maybe not immediately but certainly somewhere along the line. If you could crack the code and follow the rules, life would be fine and the bad things didn't need to happen. Ever.

Various aunts and uncles (not real ones, just family friends going back a while) all agreed that the change in her father started to happen sometime after that event. Instead of enjoying the intellectual duelling and wordplay involved with politics, he developed a tendency to lose his temper, get angry and inadvertently become a 'personality' before the public. He was often in demand on tv chat shows, which was good for his ego but bad for his blood pressure. Meanwhile, the young Linda was passed around to anyone who would take her, until she was barely old enough to start at St Teresa's. And now seven years later she spent pretty much all of her time there, but as Constance always pointed out, that was entirely understandable because her father was an ambitious man trying to recapture an important career - for the good of the country.

So the picture of a smiling young woman with very loving eyes who was holding a sleepy baby girl meant a lot to Linda. She wrapped it up using her two thickest jumpers to make sure it would have a safe journey, and tucked in a small branch from an elder tree, because woolly jumpers could only be relied on up to a point. A couple of books about Spiritual Balance and Harmonious Living that Andie had given her for Christmas sandwiched it for that little bit of extra protection.

By the time Linda had finished singing her heart out to the sixth Greatest Hit, her suitcase was locked and the room was in a fit state to be abandoned. Her carriage was waiting, and she didn't want to keep it waiting any longer. After all, her job was hardly the most important one on the trip and the taxi might decide not to hang around, and that would be so embarrassing. She pushed Aggy (her cumbersome-but-favourite long-suffering bear) into her shoulder bag so that her neatly-brushed head poked out, and then locked the door and hurried downstairs. Then she hurried all the way back up for her suitcases, and then started to head back down again, before heading back up to triple check that she'd locked her door.

The taxi driver was still waiting in the centre of the playground, and was being stared at by hundreds of First to Fifth years as they went from one class to another. Linda felt like someone very, very special as he held the door open - and he even put all her things into the boot for her as well. It wasn't quite Princess Diana level, but it was a whole lot nearer to it than she'd ever been before. The driver, Mr Mac-Surname, seemed pleased to finally see her and didn't mind dropping her off outside the Dormitory so that she could rush back in again and fetch her Abba cd's. How on earth she had managed to forget them was stupid squared - or maybe even cubed - because life without Abba would drag beyond belief.

CHAPTER THREE

Departure

Apart from all the sunshine and the complete absence of snow, the house looked much the same as it had done when she last saw it. A pile of boxes stood in two columns blocking the front door, and Linda dreaded finding out what was inside them. Constance was not regarded as a fashion guru - she was a 50-something who's most daring outfit revealed both ankles.

She stepped inside and immediately knew there was something different about the place. The hallway was tidy.. but that wasn't it, because the cleaner could have done that. There were flowers where there never used to be any.. so maybe the cleaner had done that as well? She wandered from the hallway into the living room, and stood for a moment trying to work out whatever it was that didn't feel right. Her eyes scanned the room for clues.

The cushions on the settee were new.. the tv guide was now the celebrity gossip variety.. and the tv was a new widescreen one.. a few ornaments were gone.. new glasses in the cabinet.. but nothing else seemed out of order. The new things would all have a rational explanation if she felt like trying to find one, which she didn't at that moment because there was still a huge pile of frightening boxes that had to be confronted. The phone rang at precisely 12.10pm.

"H'llo?"

"Ah, good, good, good! You're already inside, which makes you a full two minutes ahead of schedule, and that is an excellent start.. I'm just ticking that off your list, here.. and also off your driver's list as well. Now do note that you're allowed one suitcase, a smaller one and another smaller one, and one item of hand baggage. Some identifiable travelling cases were delivered last Thursday and are on your bed, you can't miss them. I shan't delay you, so for now I say goodbye and enjoy!"

Linda sighed and put the phone down, feeling incredibly sorry for Constance's husband. The rest of his entire life was probably already planned out, minute by minute right up to his funeral. All his friends probably knew him as Mr Constance.

She carried the first of the boxes upstairs, and froze as she arrived in her room. A pyramid of three pastel pink suitcases stood on her bed, crowned with a pale blue hold-all. Her name was written with flourishes on the side of each one. This was too much. In some countries anything so nauseating would be made illegal, or at least the owner would need a permit to take them outside the house.

The clothes from Miss La Vie were at least ten steps down from being terminally dull, and could easily bring about the complete destruction of London Fashion Week. If they weren't so mind-numbing, they would have been laughable, in a cathartic kind of way. Linda lifted up one Great Unwearable after another and soon gave up. She sat on her bed to try and decide what to do, and took out her Friday Dice.

"Okay, Even numbers mean throw myself out of the window, and Odd ones.. they mean throw myself out of the window as well," she thought, and watched it bounce away before rolling underneath the wardrobe. A compromise was called for. She decided to take her usual two suitcases from school, fill them with her own clothes which she'd wear regardless of what anyone said, and throw in a selection of the least coma-inducing death-rags so as not to offend Constance. Perfect, or as near as she was likely to get.

"Perfectly imperfect," she declared.

She was packed within half an hour and took a proper look around the house, partly for old times' sake, but also to make sure that the doors were either all open or all closed. The entire house had to be one or the other, and definitely not a combination of the two. As she walked around trying hard not to feel like a stranger, she started to notice that quite a lot had changed. There were new curtains at most of the windows, almost no pictures hanging up, and nothing was casually lying around.. and that was very odd.

Back upstairs she opened the door slightly to her father's room and immediately closed it again, suddenly feeling like the nosiest intruder on the face of the earth. A headline appeared large in her mind, alongside a picture of herself in an electric chair looking horribly distressed.

"Lindagate: Thickie Schoolgirl Opens & Closes Door Without Going Through - Tidal Wave Due In Japan!"

She opened it again, and poked her head inside. Her father's bedroom was a bomb site. The bed was unmade, clothes lay strewn across chairs, and not all of them were his - unless he'd taken to wearing lacy underwear and a bright yellow dress, all of which were a few sizes too small. She walked around to the other side of the bed, where a row of framed pictures had been lined up along the floor, neatly out of sight. An unknown woman grinned a big cheesy grin from the front one, while a stubble-chinned Mr Beaufort planted a kiss on her cheek. Linda's worst-ever feeling of loneliness washed over her. She looked more closely at the picture, and then the one behind it. And then the one behind that, and then the next.. before feeling too numb to see the rest.

The woman was at least half her father's age, had short bottle-blonde hair and a grin so big that it closed her eyes. Mr Beaufort appeared in a few others, mainly somewhere sunny and exotic, and with his hands all over her. Or perhaps the woman's hands were all over him, not that it mattered. And then Linda realised why the year had been so horribly quiet, why he'd been on so many trips, and why these pictures weren't hanging up. He didn't want her to find out yet, and maybe he didn't want her to ever find out.

She went and sat down in the bathroom, determined not to cry and hopefully not be sick, and failed on both counts. After a while she rested her head against the cool mirror on the cabinet door, which promptly clicked itself open. It had been crammed with a huge variety of fragrant bottles and creams that certainly didn't belong to her father. In a daze she put them out on the glass shelf where they had probably been standing just the day before, feeling her heart sink further with each one. There was no need for him to hide things. That was so deceitful.

The taxi driver gave three loud beeps for her to get a move on, and Linda made a final effort to look as if she hadn't been crying. She sat in the back for the trip to the airport and wondered what to say to her father.. and then wondered why he hadn't treated her like his daughter, and then how he could ever think of replacing her mother with someone like that ten-for-a-pound empty-head. She gave up wondering and put her headphones on instead, and tried not to think about anything.

At 2.40pm, right on track with the schedule, she walked past the Terminal Desk towards her father's important group of people and watched him answer his mobile. He glanced briefly at her and nodded, deep in conversation with whoever. Linda figured Constance was checking with him that she'd arrived. And that was the reason Linda wouldn't have a mobile - Constance. Every minute of the day, even if Constance didn't have a schedule for her, she could still make sure Linda was precisely where she ought to be, doing precisely what she ought to be doing. Having no phone was a worthy sacrifice.

His dark brown beard was even worse than she had feared - it even reached down and covered the knot of his tie. It looked like a worn-out fuzzy paintbrush that had been used for varnishing a dozen huge barns, twice each. Linda stayed cool and calm as she approached him, but then suddenly a huge sneeze shook her - and maybe the entire airport as well. Three more followed making a very distressing and very rare four consecutive sneezes. That meant the plane would crash. But even worse, the first sneeze had happened in mid-stride when she had one foot well and truly off the floor, so the plane would therefore crash while she was choking to death on her in-flight meal. This was really, really bad. Linda had to restore some kind of harmony and ran through what she needed to do in her mind.

"Right thumb against left forefinger, left thumb against right forefinger.." she thought to herself, oblivious to the rest of the world looking on, "..four times to cancel each sneeze, annnd.. roll the dice until a four appears.. wahey, first go! And then two sixes to repair the broken continuity lines on the floor.."

Two stress-filled minutes after sneezing, she picked up her shoulder bag and carried on walking towards her father, calm and collected as if nothing had happened. Strangely, he looked a little less pleased to see her now.

"When are you going to stop all that? You're growing up Linda, and you need to act like you are - but anyway, it's nice to see you again. How's school going? Haven't heard from you for a while so I figured it was all hunky dory and blingy, or whatever way you kids say things nowadays?"

He looked as if he was going to shake her hand so she stepped up for a kiss instead, despite the beard. That really wasn't a good idea. A handshake would have been far preferable to having that wirey mass of whiskers pushed against her face. It made her skin crawl, and she vainly tried to pretend a shiver wasn't running all the way down her spine - and she would have succeeded if only it hadn't run all the way back up.

This didn't feel like the time for being false and pleasant, and she couldn't bring herself to pretend to be overjoyed to see him. She quickly glanced around for the new 'interest' in his life, but she was nowhere in sight. Maybe it was all over, and normal service had been resumed, and.. maybe a pig would be flying the plane.

"So, you've.. you've gone all hairy like an old yetti, dad - you could've asked my opinion first, couldn't you? Besides, beards don't have to be like Biblical ones, you're allowed to have them trimmed quite short these days. London has some of the best Beard Doctors in the world, and they can.."

He ran his fingers through it and Linda had to look away.

"Oh, the beard.. yes, I wondered if you'd notice. It's my new, new image! The PR agency and the Media Focus Group at Central Office have come up with some priceless research figures. Get this! A change of suit influences voter favourability by up to 15%, hence this sharp Italian number. See? And a poorly-maintained beard will improve my chances of a triumphant return to the political spotlight by 20% or even 23%, assuming I shave it off for charity at the start of a campaign! Add that to this trés signifiquant voyahhge, and my rating hits the magic 50% and ba-ba-ba-BINGO! I should be back with the pack and frequenting the Commons inside a year! Old Morty's standing down soon, and the shortlists for his patch are being drawn up next month! And if I lose a little weight here and there.. but enough about me, how about you? Is that a new haircut? It looks.. windswept, nature's hairdryer, very dramatic."

Linda despaired.

"No it isn't new, not since October," she replied and tried hard to think of something to say, but the only thought running through her mind was that he had never felt more like a stranger to her. And he'd actually said 'ba-ba-ba-bingo' which was practically unforgivable. Perhaps he was an impostor? Maybe her real father was tied up somewhere, kidnapped by the Government's evil Opposition Party and being forced to divulge all kinds of important Government Information. But then again, maybe he wasn't. Maybe that really was him behind the beard, the all-new him with an all-new girlfriend taking over his life. Linda knew deep down inside that she just needed to spend some time alone with him, and then he'd remember her mother and how much he had loved her.. and how much he loved Linda as well, because there was a very good chance that he might have been forgetting recently. A moment of awkward silence fell.

The Flight Announcer came to her rescue, and they all moved off to the Flight Gate. She followed the thirty or so very important

Government people along the gleaming corridors and soon found herself being ushered on board, and guided to a seat on the large charter plane. She sat alone, watching the rows fill up with nameless people who all seemed to know each other. Her father eventually arrived, checked his seat number and edged along the row in front of her. She leaned forwards to tap him on the shoulder and get him to come and have his correct seat next to her, but sat back in stunned silence as the very young female-woman-girl, the nothing-like-mum person from the pictures, arrived in a bluster and received a cheer from the in-crowd as she hurried down the aisle. She planted herself next to him, sneaked a peck on the lips, and kept touching him while she spoke excitedly. After a few minutes the plane started moving and Mr Beaufort turned around in his seat. It was about time he explained himself, Linda thought.

"So Linda, how were the exams? Are you off to stay down at Andie's this summer?"

"Bad, and yes. But I haven't asked her yet. Who's been staying at home? There's new things lying around."

"New? Oh, you haven't met Dee, have you? Well, well! I was going to mention her to you, but doesn't time just fly?"

Linda stayed cool, and made steely-eye contact with him.

"That depends on what you're doing, doesn't it? I've met her laundry and re-arranged her bathroom things. Let me guess - the beard was actually her idea?"

He exchanged a mischievous glance with Dee, and Linda felt like going back to St Teresa's.

"You know, I do think it was Dee's idea, yes. Let me explain this properly. Dee was part of the PR agency and I was her 'project', but now she works under me at Central Office."

"I'll bet she does. That must keep you both busy. Let's hope the colour of her fancy stuff in your bedroom isn't an indication of the way she votes," replied Linda, curling her voice to match the sarcasm of the last few words. She awarded herself a silent round of applause for such a quick put-down, and another one for managing to keep a look of indignation on her face.

Dee snorted a laugh, and pushed her John Lennon specs back up her nose. Linda decided that she must be about 23. And a half.

"Ooh Belinda, you and me are going to be such mates, I can tell. You're just like your dad, he's sharp as a button too! And just look at you - you've got his nose. Be careful with it 'cause he'll want it back one day!" she squealed, and Mr Beaufort laughed as well.

Linda sat back, closed her eyes, and lost herself in the first cd which came to hand. The plane flight took forever and was rounded off by everyone having to move their watches forward when they landed. She trudged through whatever airport they were in, and felt the rain begin as they were shepherded outside to a fleet of black State Limousines. She watched in silence as the world became wetter and darker on the lengthy journey to the hotel.

Her room was a long, long way up - and absolutely enormous. The porter placed her bags just inside the door, said something that wasn't in English and then left to sort out a disagreement in a room across the corridor. Linda didn't put the lights on or even bother unpacking. The room was bathed in moonlight and looked just right. A bed that was even larger than all three of her school ones put together stretched out towards the balcony door. She sat on its edge and watched the rain patterning the windows, making the lights of the world outside seem to dance.

Her mother's picture looked out from the small table by the bed, and Linda spent a long time sitting nearby, absently feeding the fine chain of her necklace through her fingers. Her mother's necklace. She hoped the loud laughter and noises coming from the couple in the room above weren't being made by her father and Dee, as she turned the angular oval gem around in her fingers. It was only the size of a fingernail, but that didn't matter. She loved the way its colour seemed to play in different light, and moonlight was the best of all. Moonlight was always perfect.

By the time the rain had slowed and then eventually stopped, tiredness was quickly catching up with her so she rolled her newly-named Official Overseas Visitation Dice. Odd meant she ought to go to bed now, and Even meant unpack first. Nice and simple. After the best-of-three, Linda started unpacking some of the most horrendous crimes ever committed against fashion, and figured that she would have to leave them firmly shut in the wardrobe for the entire ten days, and then maybe forget to pack them at the end. They looked even more dull when they were all hanging up, so she changed her mind and packed them away again and hid the suitcase behind the settee. The wardrobe didn't deserve them.

As soon as Aggy had taken up residence on the small chair, Linda kissed her mother goodnight and crawled into bed. She lay quietly settling into the soft sheets for almost an entire minute before noticing that the moonlight was casting a huge cross onto her bed from one of the window frames. A verse sprang to mind, and she sat bolt upright.

"A cross on your bed -
 By morning you're dead,
 In shadows are shown
 Where Spirits have flown,"

Closing the curtains wasn't an option because the consequences of doing that on a moonlit night were too awful to think about, so she allowed herself a brief moan and got up to try and move the bed away from the window. It weighed at least three elephants and a hippo, and wouldn't budge an inch. Or maybe it was attached to the floor like the middle bed back at school? Either way it wouldn't move. She despaired and gathered up the sheets and the pillows, took them over to the safety of the settee and eventually settled down on that instead. Then she quickly got up again because she had a sneaking suspicion that not all of her shoes were lying on their sides in the wardrobe. And she was right. One pair wasn't so she turned them over and left them facing the back of the wardrobe - no spirits were going to step into those tonight.

As so often happened, her preparations for going to bed had left her feeling wide awake so she sat over in the large chair by the writing desk and decided to start a letter to Andie. She managed two long pages all about her mad father and the vile school, drew a few portraits of Dee so that Andie knew exactly how awful she looked, then scrumpled them up and successfully lobbed them into the bin on the third attempt. She was still wide awake, so she tried writing out a few half-remembered Abba lyrics instead and eventually went back to the settee where she curled up and quietly listened to a cd, waiting to fall asleep. Abba nearly always did the trick.

CHAPTER FOUR
Souvenirs

Sunrise brought Linda a warm and glowing Odessa welcome, and made the room look as wonderful as it felt. Her gloom from the night before had disappeared with the early dawn mist, and she swung the balcony doors wide open. This was a beautiful start to the day, and was worth a fitful night's sleep in order to be awake early enough to see it. She could think of two people who might sleep right through, but that wasn't going to spoil the moment. She stretched away her stiffness from having spent the night in too many strange positions, and stepped into the sunlight.

"This is how a Saturday should be," she whispered to herself, and leaned against the rail.

The buildings far below had looked grim and uninviting just an hour or two earlier, but they now seemed friendly, bright and full of character. Odessa looked like a nice place, and Linda watched for a while as her part of the city slowly began to wake up. People, cars and trams steadily emerged from here and there, going about their business and bringing all the morning's noises with them. The phone rang somewhere back inside the room.

"Dobrayeh utra, Lindaskaya."

"Constance? Did I see you on the plane?"

"Of course not, there's far too much to be done here at Central Office. As I was saying, Good Morning Linda, this is your wake up call so I can't be conversing for too long because I still have another eight of the group to awaken. Now then, you're due in the Perun Dining Hall on the Ground Floor in 32.. no, 31 minutes at 07.45 Odessa Time for breakfast, and then.."

Constance rattled through the plan for the entire morning, and left Linda's head in a whirl. Luckily she wasn't involved in much of the day's events. She dressed in her usual weekend clothes, put her sheets back where they belonged in a way that would look as if she'd actually slept where she was supposed to, and casually walked down eighteen flights of curved stairs to meet her father outside the restaurant. He was armed with Dee, and judging by their expressions they were in the mood for business.

"Right Linda, good morning and all that. We're meeting their version of the Environment Minister over breakfast, or rather his Assistant and his underlings, anyway. You smile, we all get some photos for the local papers and then us grown-ups go off to our meetings, which leaves you in the clear till at least the late afternoon, and according to Constance we might not need you even then - how about that? Who's a lucky girl? Some of us have to work for a living!"

He grinned, but with such a beard he just made himself look sinister. Linda shrugged and looked past him into the restaurant, and grimaced at the orange decor. Dee had a thought, and felt compelled to share it.

"Maybe after breakfast you could do something with your hair, like buy a hat or something? Or maybe there's a good Ukrainian hair salon out there somewhere.. or if there isn't, I have some string off one of the suitcases and we could tie it all back with that, 'cause it might help, mightn't it?"

Dee smiled and raised her eyebrows in a hopeful manner, which suggested to Linda that she wasn't being sarcastic - she simply had no brain, and people with no brain couldn't be sarcastic. Linda nodded and smiled back, oozing sarcasm.

Two hours, many photographs and no breakfast later, the dining room was almost empty. Formal visits seemed to be remarkably informal, and up until now Linda had never realised that for some people champagne could be more popular than tea, coffee or even food to start the day. Odessa was becoming an odd place. A voice on the hotel tannoy called her to the reception desk, making her wonder what she could possibly have done wrong already.

She stood beside a bonsai tree at the end of the long desk and watched some very smartly dressed young women doing all kinds of important-looking things.

"Hello?" she said, anxiously, "I'm Linda Beaufort.. I think someone called me a minute ago? Linnndaaah. That's me."

A receptionist with a very long name on her badge handed a phone to her, and Linda found a familiar voice on the end.

"Is that Linda Veronique Beaufort?"

"Oh hi Const.. uh, no, not with a middle name like that it isn't. It's me here, bright eyed and everything."

"Very good. It's most unlikely you'll be needed until this evening so I suggest you go for a wander and take in the sights, or at least a few shops. You ought not return to your room right away because according to the staff rota.. which I have here.. they won't have made your bed, cleaned the bathroom, replaced towels and replenished generic bathroom products and so on and so forth.. until at least 11.30am which means that you'd be in their way. Now then, write down the names of these streets - they're safe."

"Safe?" she exclaimed, and almost knocked the bonsai onto the floor. A receptionist hurried over and moved it out of harm's way.

"They're monitored by CCTV. I never go along any foreign street unless there's some kind of surveillance. You can never be too careful. Oh, and we've also got some security personnel posted around - incognito, as it were."

"What, all secret and undercover? Is it that dangerous here? It looked so nice from my balcony.."

"No, it's not dangerous at all, Odessa's a wonderful place. We've just got a few of our security personnel with the group that's all. Standard practice. It's so much better to be on a street where people can keep an eye on you, rather than being vulnerable on your own. That makes sense, and if there's one thing we like.. oh, and I now have the name of a hairdresser who'll give you a generous discount.. just give him your name and say 'Today is again poor weather for ducks' and he'll reply with 'Yes, but I have never heard one complain yet' and then you can have a wash, intense trim and three-minute blow-dry, but anything over and above that is full price, I'm afraid."

"Huh?"

"..and I also have the name of the owner of the souvenir shop which has a mannequin dressed like a fisherman outside. It has some charming souvenirs, or so I'm told, and I'd like a small 'Battleship Potemkin' in a bottle please, if you see one. They're on the third shelf down, left hand side as you go in. I asked Dee, but honestly, that girl.."

Linda wondered if there was anything that Constance didn't know, or couldn't find out.

"Okay.. I'll bring you back some Odessa rock as well - the real sort. Is there anything else, Constance?"

"Have you any money?"

Linda checked in the trouser pocket that wasn't full of tissues.

"Umm.. I have.. some pound coins and a 50p with chewing gum on it, but I expect you already know that."

"Hmm.. consider it noted. Now check your inside pocket."

Linda unfolded her baggy denim jacket and opened up the velcro tab. A neatly bound wad of notes lay snugly tucked away deep in the inside pocket.

"This isn't my.. where did all..?" Linda squealed.

"Excellent. During breakfast a colleague made a deposit for you. There are roughly eight Hryvenas to the Pound Sterling and you're not supposed to spend your funds beyond essentials, and what you don't spend must be returned to me. Oh, and you simply must keep any receipts. What you have there is intended as your financial security for the duration of the visit."

"How much security have I got here?" she asked, looking around to see if anyone dodgy was watching her and planning something awful. Apart from the receptionist who was still tutting and watering the bonsai, nobody had really noticed her.

"You have about £481, give or take a few tiny Kopecks.. and you should have 85 of those. They're loose change, good for tips. That bundle should cover you. As I say, try and stay on the streets where we have our security.. they know exactly what you look like."

Linda was sure most of Odessa could hear her heart pounding. Luckily the hotel walls weren't shaking with each beat as she propped herself up, and she gave a nervous 'bye bye' to Constance.

She fanned out the array of notes. Even though it was foreign money, it was still real money and she'd never had so much of it before. There wasn't too much call for spending-power at school, and her trips into town weren't very common. The town never, ever seemed to change, and the novelty of going in had worn off quite a long time ago. Besides, it wasn't always easy to find someone to go in with. But life was different now, and Linda felt like a walking cash dispenser, someone with an entire city to navigate and billions of new shops to explore. And of course she had a big responsibility - no, it was a Diplomatic Obligation - to support the Ukrainian economy. And ten whole days to do it in.

She stood in the hotel's palatial doorway looking out at the wide streets around her and felt very, very excited. With the tiniest degree of trepidation she stepped into the bright sunshine and followed the long tree-lined road which lead towards the tall buildings of the town. Gaudy buses striped in red and yellow wheezed and trundled by, cars darted past intent on getting wherever they were going as quickly as possible, and rickety trams rattled and dinged the way ahead for her. This was just brilliant.

Linda didn't pay too much attention to the street names. Her meandering was entirely governed by other more important factors mainly to do with shop windows and what was in them, and also to do with surfaces. Pavements of tight brickwork were definite no-go areas, as were cobbled streets. They had too many lines to interrupt, too many gaps to bridge, too many everythings. She did find plenty of streets which were safe by her definition of safe, and fortunately they were absolutely crammed with all kinds of amazing stores, statues and weird buildings.

With so much going on around her, she didn't feel particularly alone even though she was by herself. Somehow being abroad allowed her to take a step away from her usual feelings and actually enjoy wandering around. She tried to notice everything about this new place, and made an effort to smile at everyone from behind her hair regardless of whether they noticed or not. She took the time to look into most shop windows, even the boring ones, sometimes only to listen to the strange voices and peculiar music coming from inside.

She even dared go into a few, but didn't stay inside for too long - there was always a danger that someone might speak to her and find that she was a real dimbo of an idiot who couldn't understand Ukrainian or Odessananianish or whatever the language was called. So Linda started along yet another unpronounceable street firmly clutching her pocketful of unpronounceable money, on the look-out for a guide book with some much-need phrases in it. Ones like 'Can I try this on please?' and 'How much is this, it's fab?' would be ideal. But then, as she neared the traffic lights, she felt as if she had turned to ice.

Was that her mother's picture she just passed? She stood outside the display window of a small store selling cameras, convinced that one of the portrait pictures looked exactly like.. but then it was gone. In the tiny split second needed for her to take a second look, the picture was back to normal. Happy, smiling people who were unrecognisable to anyone but their friends were still grinning out at the world, and Linda wasn't even sure which picture had caused her to stop. Her heart was pounding and the inevitable burst of adrenaline raced up from somewhere inside, and she leant heavily against the glass. That was altogether too weird. She sighed loudly to herself, figuring that at long last she was finally cracking up, which was an okay thing to do because she'd had so much practice at cracking up already.

"Hmm.. a session or two with some head-doctors is way long overdue - ask anyone. Talking to myself, talking to myself. Stop it, stop it. Sing instead, that's not crazy. People do that all the time. Okay.. dooh-daaa-dooh.. Friday night and the lights are lowww.. looking out for a place to go-wwwuh.."

By the time Linda reached the chorus she had made absolutely, positively, definitely sure that the pictures were only of nameless someones and anyones, and she was feeling a whole lot better for it. Billions upon billions of shops still surrounded her and they all needed exploring thoroughly. The whole incident was quickly pushed completely from her mind and by the time the traffic lights had changed colour and allowed her to cross the road, she had even forgotten which song she'd been singing.

By late morning Linda had bought a pair of the world's slimmest, blackest sunglasses ever created and was walking around feeling very, very chic. Her stomach had started growling loud enough to get her deported, so she wandered along a sidestreet full of cafés and chose the only one with dark red window shades - dark red was obviously the best colour for offering protection to unwary diners in unknown dining places. The café was a huge improvement on the Perun Dining Hall. There was absolutely no orange anywhere, for a start. It was light and spacious, with narrow black chairs, oval tables and walls made of small stone panels. And best of all, apart from a huge man on the far side, it was empty.

She sat down at a table by the window, feeling very cosmopolitan indeed and ready to start watching the rest of the world go by. After a moment's thought, she decided that chic globetrotters living la dolce vita would definitely tap only one foot if they were listening to some catchy foreign music on a radio in a café. So she did. A solitary waiter emerged from somewhere behind the counter, placed a small floral display in the centre of her gleaming white table top and looked down at her as if he somehow knew that she wasn't from these parts. He lightly drummed a biro against his order pad.

A few minutes later he brought out a white cup brimming over with frothy coffee, and a kind of apple-pastry-honey strange-thing which he thought she had been pointing at. Linda sipped at her coffee with her little finger extended high in the air in a bid to look refined and elegant, as if jet-setting around Europe was something that she did whenever she wasn't jet-setting around the rest of the world. For a few seconds, everything was fine - but then something caught her attention.

She stared at the saucer, or more precisely the chipped part of the rim. This was bad. A chipped saucer with an undamaged cup was a match made in hell. She checked all around the cup twice, hoping for even a tiny crack or sign of damage to balance out the saucer. Nothing. This would almost guarantee that something bad, vile, painful and probably fatal would happen. She covered the saucer in a serviette and took it along with the cup back to the counter. The waiter glanced over, and stopped trying to fix the till's drawer. He sighed and looked tired which made Linda feel bad, but at least he'd understood that she wasn't happy about something. He took the saucer through into the kitchens and Linda took the coffee back to her table, making sure not to put it down anywhere. It was burning her fingers and thumb terribly, but that was okay - a cup in use without a saucer was an incomplete pair, and therefore a powerful magnet for misfortune. A little burning was nothing compared to what might happen if she dared put it down directly onto the table. A headline appeared from nowhere.

"Lindagate: Jellybrain Schoolgirl In Saucerless-Cup Scandal - Plague Wipes Out Europe!"

She concentrated hard on the pleasant-but-crackly music coming from the radio, to take her mind off her hand while she waited. And waited. And waited. After a lifetime the waiter emerged rubbing a new saucer against the sleeve of his shirt. He put it down in front of her and smiled with a hint of insincerity before going back to his newspaper by the till. Linda caught her breath. Now he'd made things even worse, and a bad situation had turned into a Cataclysmic Nightmare, almost a fully-blown Armageddon Incident.

The saucer was dark green with a flowery pattern on it, and the circular groove was almost three miles too big for the white cup. It didn't match, and wasn't even close. How could he not have noticed? He didn't look like a total thickie, but apparently he must have been. Perhaps things would be fine if she could go into the kitchens herself and have a look for a good white one, and then the waiter wouldn't be cross because he wouldn't have had to do anything - and then life could get back to normal. But that wasn't likely to happen. Maybe in English it could, but not in Linda's highly individual version of tourist sign-language.

She placed the saucer on the opposite side of the table so that it couldn't be regarded as hers, and looked around to see if there was a white one that might have been left behind on another table. Fortunately there was. Unfortunately it was by the fat man, way over on the other side. And even more unfortunately, it was underneath his coffee cup.

He appeared to be engrossed in his voluminous newspaper, and Linda picked at the skin of her palm. Was it worth the risk? Was the radio on loud enough to hide the sound of her movements? Maybe she could roll a few fours and not need a saucer.. no she couldn't. A perfect white saucer for a perfect white cup, and that was that. The man put his paper down, drank a little, and went back to the sports pages, completely blocking out most of the café from his view. That was a good sign, and she had to make her move.

Linda edged off her seat and crouched down, cup in one hand, saucer in the other. She silently made her way to the next table and sat very nonchalantly, just passing the time, just seeing if it was a nice table, that's all. And then she moved to the next. And the next.

The waiter watched the weird English girl from his safe vantage point behind the till. He didn't know what to think - for some bizarre reason she looked as if she was approaching Mr Korolev, the recently-retired chiropodist. He watched for a little longer and realised that yes, she really was closing in on him. The waiter moved to stand just behind the cappuccino machine, and stared as she kneeled in front of Mr Korolev's table. She delicately placed the green saucer onto the table just inches away from him, and then almost in slow motion reached across and moved his cup onto it. And then she actually took his white saucer. The whole procedure was done with all the stealth, nerve and precision of.. someone genuinely deranged. At that point, the waiter decided there was a chance that she might be dangerous, so maybe if he didn't charge her for the coffee or the speciality pastry she might just go without causing any problems. Hopefully.

He carried on watching her as she made her way back over to her own table, following the reverse route exactly. She nervously glanced around occasionally, and like the waiter, she probably thought that nobody was watching her. But somebody else was watching - and watching her very closely.

An old lady with a tray of souvenirs stood in the open doorway, but the waiter didn't see her standing there. He had every reason to notice the old lady in her black smock, and the peculiar double-shadow that she cast far into his café, but he simply didn't see anyone blocking the entrance. He noticed the people out in the street beyond her, and he also noticed that none of them were coming in. Many of them looked as if they wanted to, but for some strange reason, not one of them did. Even the regular customers unwittingly went into other cafés on that particular morning.

Linda noticed her, but only in the frustrating way that she noticed a lot of things.

She had settled down at her table again, the triumphant captor of an unblemished white saucer, and finished her coffee before it went completely cold. She waved at the waiter, asking for another one using make-do gestures appropriate for the Hard Of Thinking. It had to be simple in order to make herself abundantly clear that the next coffee had to be poured in the same cup and served on the same saucer, but only after a very good wash. She looked out of the window and down along the busy street, enjoying all the hustle and bustle everywhere even though most of it was being caused by other tourists. And suddenly there was a silhouette again, appearing for the briefest split second, this time in the café's doorway. Almost perfectly clear, almost there long enough to be recognisable.. and then gone. Linda had seen something similar two or three times that morning and tried her best not to think too much about it.

How many times in her life had she seen things in the corner of her eye? Too many times. Ever since she was a small girl, there was usually something just at the very edge of her vision, waiting until her attention had moved elsewhere before deciding to appear. And very annoying it was too. The feeling was nearly the same as the feeling she'd get on the phone whenever the other person had said 'bye bye' and put their end of the line down. To move the phone from her ear and all the way down to the receiver was a real trial. Countless times she'd heard, or thought she'd heard, someone start speaking as the phone crossed that point of no return, the wrong side of that tiny fraction of a second that took it out of range. Of course, by the time she had brought it back up to her ear there was never anybody there, only the monotonous droning of a phone that was off the hook. Sometimes she could try to put the phone down over a dozen times before making herself leave it alone - and then quickly rolling a six of course, and maybe a four as well, depending on how unsettled and messed up she'd made herself feel.

So this fleeting silhouette was nothing new, and after some serious contemplation Linda figured that there might even be a genuine reason for it being there. Odessa was obviously full of shadows, which was perfectly understandable considering it was in a different country and probably on different lines of latitude and longitude to St Teresa's, which obviously meant that the sun would affect things in different ways here. Linda liked Geography, but only when it suited her.

She dismissed the latest Corner Of The Eye Encounter and sipped her well-earned vanilla cappuccino, gave her new pastry a prod to see if it was another warm one and then settled back to watch the Odessannanians walking by. Then suddenly a shadow passed over her. It came from nowhere and felt as if it passed right through her, and she was sure it even shivered just before it left her. And that made her shiver. Twice. And a third time. She rolled three fives to cancel out the three shivers, and after a few seconds carried on with people-watching and fashion-spotting. Three fives were very good, especially consecutive ones, and Linda decided that Odessa was definitely her kind of place.

Eventually it was time to go, and the waiter wouldn't take any money at all. He just smiled and waved goodbye instead, and gestured towards the door.

"People in other countries are weird," she thought as she drifted back towards the main street.

She didn't fancy going down too many roads and alleys without a map, so she settled for finding out how far the main one went on for - and it went on a long way. Twenty minutes later the shops were becoming few and far between, the hotels were narrower and the crowds had thinned. Well, they had thinned on her side of the street, at least. She fancied crossing over and taking a good look around a sprawling outdoor marketplace, but as she waited for the little green Ukrainian man to start bleeping and flashing on the pedestrian lights, a silhouette flickered somewhere in the shadows of the trees surrounding the market's entrance. Silhouettes were becoming so annoying for her, today. Linda stopped for a moment while the other people crossed over, and tried to decide whether or not to keep to her side of the road instead of going somewhere that might be full of irritating Half-There things. She looked over at the marketplace for a while, and figured that it was probably unbelievably interesting and packed full of good stuff.

An elderly woman stood at the dusty entrance. She was dressed in something black that must have looked old even when it was new. She was small, hunched and rather pitiful, really. Everyone ignored her and her tray of whatevers, except for one or two people who gave her a brief glance and then carried on regardless. Linda felt very sorry for her, and stepped out onto the road. A van launched a volley of beeps, and she jumped back with her heart in her mouth. The market could wait for another time. If there was one thing Linda hated above everything, it was careless traffic-moments like that, because they were just too close to home for her. The woman looked over, and Linda offered her a small wave.

"I'll go and buy something if she's there when I get back.." she vowed and waited for her heartbeat to get back to normal.

A few minutes later the road ended in a huge multi-laned junction. A fantastic building with turban-topped towers lay straight ahead, and a million tram lines criss-crossed the broad roads in front of it. Linda trod carefully as she navigated the heavy lines and cracks, and was only beeped at twice before entering the grounds of a place that in her opinion must have been 'really, really important once'. It was crawling with masses of tourists and looked far too crowded and noisy to bother with. A tall church spire loomed high above the fir trees further off to the left, and would probably have fewer colour-clashing sweaty people milling around, so she wandered across the grass to have a look. Being a tourist was so easy.

She soon found herself on a wide and almost deserted path leading up to the church. The lack of people wasn't too surprising, now that she had a good view of everything. The building wasn't particularly impressive, and its bizarrely distinguished neighbour made it look even less so. Most people were wandering along another path which lead into dense masses of oak and birch trees, so having come this far she decided to follow them. A few minutes later she took her turn at the front of a scenic out-crop of rock and had a look at a vast stretch of water. It might have been the Black Sea, but for all she knew it could easily have been the Atlantic or maybe the Mediterranean.

"No big wow.." she mused, and decided that it was definitely time to go. The shops were calling and there was no way she'd allow herself to wander the entire length of any more roads. Well, not for a while at least. She went back through the trees, humming a random medley of Abba songs to herself and idly following the sounds of the tourists ahead, and soon found herself well off the beaten track, standing at a weather-worn redbrick wall. And very alone. The bricks were covered in ivy and minute red flowers, and she followed it along until the quietness around her became far too apparent.

"Well done thickie.. why not spend the whole day here," she whispered to herself, realising that she'd gone wrong somewhere. She followed the wall back for ten whole minutes and still couldn't see anyone else or even the path she had come in along, and began to feel that shouting out for some help would be a good idea, even if it meant getting embarrassed. But then she came across a narrow door in the wall, almost hidden under layers of entwined greenery, which was in desperate need of an enthusiastic gardener's attention. There were only a few rough marks where the handle should have been, so she gave it a hopeful push. The door gave way with a sharp squeal, opening just enough for her to step through.

"Yay! That's yay to the power of a billion! Cubed!"

The church lay only a short way off to the left, and the site entrance was a long way beyond, exactly where it should be.

The old woman stood just a few yards away, holding her tray and being ignored by dozens of new people. Even though she seemed untroubled by their complete lack of interest, Linda felt a lot of sympathy for her.

"Nobody likes being treated like that.." she thought to herself, and decided it was time to make the lady's day.

The woman didn't turn her head as Linda approached, and just kept staring towards nothing in particular. Maybe she had become too used to standing around and being treated like part of the scenery. She really was exceptionally old, and Linda wondered how she had the strength to be out and about trying to sell things - or not selling them, really. The woman finally turned to her, smiling in a way that merely re-arranged some of her wrinkles, and held her decrepit tray a little higher for Linda to inspect.

It contained a collection of hideously awful rubbish, but Linda pretended to be spoilt for choice. Strips of carved bone, worn out and faceless wooden dolls, pictures too pale to recognise, ugly hat pins and the filthiest beaded jewellery Linda had ever seen. Everything was so old that she could almost feel its age. Thinking quickly, she pointed at the absolute worst thing on show, to an item that the old lady would never, ever be able to sell. It was the one thing that made the rest of the junk look like excess stock from Harrods.

A small cluster of flowers were wedged right at the back. They were bone dry, varying shades of dirt-beige, and bound with a piece of frayed string which looked almost ready to turn to dust. Linda smiled at the old lady and pretended to have found a real bargain, and kept on smiling even when she saw the woman's horribly gnarled hands rummaging near the flowers. The woman held up a shining crescent-moon on a chain. It sparkled in the sunlight and looked so out of place, so.. so utterly must-have, but Linda couldn't bring herself to take it. She drew out her own necklace from under her hair, while shaking her head.

"No, no, I have one already, see? One is enough, really it is," she said slowly and clearly, knowing the old lady would easily be able to sell the moon some other time.

The woman was unimpressed with Linda's mother's necklace and gestured sternly for her to put it away, waving her hands aggressively until it was back out of sight. She held the crescent up again, but this time nearer to Linda's eyes, and began speaking softly. Despite her prune-like appearance, she had a clear voice which was young and totally inappropriate for such a body. Her dark eyes widened with zest and vitality as her strange words took on a rhythm all of their own, and Linda marvelled at how anyone could ever understand such a strange language. Mme Kiberlaine, who was the school's genuinely-French French teacher, had often said that English and Gibberish were the only languages Linda would ever get the hang of, and moments like this supported that theory.

So Linda pointed at the flowers again, shuffled around in her inside pocket and handed over a few notes which added up to the Ukrainian equivalent of £127. Linda suspected it might have been a lot, but wasn't really sure and didn't mind anyway. The lady probably had nothing much in her life, especially if this bric-a-brac was all she could sell, so she obviously needed the money a lot more than Linda did. The woman moved her hands away, holding them up and gesturing wildly again. Her expression, which probably wasn't friendly, was lost deep within her face-map of the Himalayas.

"No, no, you don't need to thank me. Me English, me here on Government business! Plenty money! Here, have some coins as well. From the Prime Minister and his Cabinet! Bank of Ennngland, yes!"

The woman shook her head and became more agitated, and Linda felt sure people would be looking at the scene the old lady was creating. It was very, very definitely time to go and from now on she decided that shops were the only places to spend any money, because old ladies were too much trouble. She dropped the notes onto the tray, picked up the hideous flowers, smiled and nodded nervously - and then hurried into the church while the woman carried on calling out after her. Hopefully the crazy old lady might go away.

In fact, the crazy old lady went away a lot quicker than Linda could ever have imagined.

Linda always felt welcome in churches. She felt close to her mother in a church, and any church was just fine. When she was younger she felt that St Mary's (the one where she would lay flowers on her mother's grave) was a bad place. It was the place that wouldn't let her mother come home, the place that held nothing but sadness, heartbreak, huge questions and absolutely no answers. But during the last couple of years in particular, Linda had realised that a special kind of comfort was found there, a comfort somewhere within the shared feelings of all the other people who were all looking for their own answers. She liked to think that one or two people even found them, maybe. But everyone, just like her, was there because they believed there was somewhere better, maybe a place where accidents didn't have to happen, a place where impossibly difficult questions would be answered, and a place where love was all that mattered. And Linda liked that.

She sat on the back row, leaning against a reassuringly old pillar that reached all the way up into the pinnacle of one of the ceiling's domes. She closed her eyes and imagined her mother sitting beside her, her never-ageing mother who always looked exactly as she did in the picture. But this time she was heavily-loaded down with all kinds of gifts and souvenirs, and she was full of things to say about Odessa. Linda sighed to herself, and hoped that somehow she really was with her in this far-away place, sharing all the new things she was seeing and.. well, just being with her.

The small flowers eventually dropped from her hand, and brought her back into the real world. They lay on the floor looking pathetic. How could anything be as dead as those? She picked them up and the stems felt like a million splinters, and she quickly dropped them again. They needed dealing with, properly.

She walked out into the early afternoon sun, and found the day was hotter than ever. This was something else to tell Andie about, she thought to herself while looking around for an appropriate place to leave the flowers. An elder tree sprawled amongst the overgrown wooded area a few yards beyond the church. That was good. Elder trees were like a natural guardian that could ward off all kinds of evil spirits and bad witches, or so it said in one of her many essential books. The chapter on Nature's Hidden Helpers also said that they had been revered for centuries, and that the grounds of a church were the best possible place to find one - and that meant the one in front of her would be ideal. She unwrapped the flowers from her handkerchief, placed them near the tree's roots, and then completely covered them in leaves and grass. Then she took a moment to think of an appropriate farewell.

"Take these flowers,
  Dry, dulled and weary,
  Bring back their colour,
  And.. uh.. make them all cheery."

Ceremonial verses (or poetry of any kind) weren't really Linda's strong-point, but at least the right sentiment was there. The church bells rang out a tuneful descent and soon fell silent again, which Linda appreciated even though there was a good chance they weren't doing it for her benefit. Anyway, lunch was calling louder than the bells ever could, and she'd earned herself a good one.

The marketplace was even busier on the way back, and she made a real effort to hurry past. Its appeal had completely worn off, in no small way because the barmy old lady might have gone back there. She put her hand into her pocket to find her Odessa Café Dice in order to decide where the best place for lunch would be. The first side of the dice that her fingers touched was very likely a five, so she ran her middle finger over it a few times to make sure. The side opposite felt like a two, so yes, it was definitely a five. Therefore, she would be best off by ignoring the first four cafés that appealed to her, and should go into the fifth one. Simple.

"Oh no.. why me?" she moaned to herself.

The sales assistant from hell crossed the road, as oblivious to the traffic as the traffic was to her. Linda pretended not to notice her and carried on walking, but the woman soon caught up and spoke horrendously loudly while flicking Linda's money off the tray. Linda picked all the notes up off the pavement and put them back, this time securely underneath a filthy book and some very dusty wooden animals. She smiled to hide her unease, then self-consciously gave a wave goodbye and started walking away again. As far as she could tell, the old lady seemed rather cross with her for paying far too much for some flowers which she didn't even appear to have kept. In a way that was understandable, but Linda didn't really want to find out for sure so she kept on walking and walking, going a little quicker with every step until she was back in amongst the safety of the crowds again. She only dared sneak a look over her shoulder as she went into the correct café.

The place was air conditioned, not quite half full, and certainly met with approval. Lots of pale earthy shades, plenty of light, and a good array of plants, which qualified it as a fine choice. She settled down at a table that was far away from the windows, and hid behind a very tall menu which she could safely peer around every now and then. The clock on the wall opposite her was about to reach 2pm, and Linda knew she had to see the hour arrive. She really, really had to. If she watched the long hand until it reached the art deco twelve, the old lady would cause no more embarrassing trouble, ever. After all, two was on the opposite side of the dice, and now it was two o'clock. It all made sense.

The long hand slowly made its way through the first of the final two minutes, and a waiter arrived at her table. She ordered a coffee without looking at him, which lead him to think that she must be blind. He took the unopened menu from her and began reading it out, quietly for her. The final minute wasn't the time to risk taking her eyes off the clock, so she slowly moved her head from side to side, and said every form of 'No' that she could think of. One of them worked, and he hurried off to fetch her coffee. He made it extra frothy and gave it a good sprinkling of chocolate powder, added a cylindrical biscuit and decided that the strange, foreign blind girl could have a free one.

At long last, 2pm arrived. The clock chimed, chimed again, and then chimed for a third time. Clocks that didn't chime properly were such a bad omen, and Linda didn't know if she ought to stay or leave immediately. She stayed for the coffee, to be polite, and then stood up to leave. Much to her surprise, the waiter rushed over and escorted her to the door, and then just like the mad lady and the man in the other café, he wouldn't take her money either.

"If they're like that in the clothes shops.. I could live here. And the cd ones too," she thought as he cheerfully gave a Ukrainian goodbye.

Back in the sunny outdoors there was no sign of the old lady, but plenty of signs above classy shops. That was good, and Linda felt reassured that Hour Watching was such a worthwhile trick to know. A slow clock high up in a tower somewhere began chiming and soon reached four. Nobody else seemed to notice, which annoyed Linda. Why didn't it bother anyone else? Maybe people in Odessa were as happy to be ignorant as the ones she'd left behind in England. And where was the clock anyway? She turned around, looking up to find where the noise was coming from, but soon gave up - it could have been anywhere.

She turned around again and almost jumped out of her skin.

The old woman, now with her shawl drawn almost entirely across her face, stood before her. Her eyes were narrowed, dark and piercing. Linda took a step back, ready to set a new world record for the Scaredy-Cat Mile, but the woman wasn't cross anymore. She waved a hand over her tray of much-improved shining trinkets, and for a moment Linda almost chose something. But she couldn't do it. If this poor sun-dried wrinkly person could have one extra thing to sell, then that was fine by her.

"No, non, nada, niet, nowt, zippo, nothing for me, thanks muchly. I'm happy with the flowers, really I am. Me hap-eeee."

The woman sighed, then gave a frightening dog-like snarl that wouldn't have been much more frightening had it come from an irate Rottweiler. She glared up at Linda and reached behind her tray to the place where an inside pocket would be, if those Old Lady Smocks actually had any inside pockets. She paused motionless as if deep in thought while the clock chimed three more times. Her eyes widened and she seemed to look deep into Linda's as she held out a Matryoshka doll to her. Linda felt certain that the lady was smiling behind the veil, but dismissed such a stupid thought straight away.

She stared at yet another one of 'those' dolls. Odessa was full of Matryoshka dolls. Wooden ones, plastic ones, funny ones, historical ones, all decoratively painted in colourful patterns and topped with happy faces, as were all the smaller dolls inside each one. Quite clever and also a little bit weird, in a way. Even the airport had an entire shop full of them, just in case any tourists had somehow managed not to buy one during their stay. However, the one being held in front of her was very attractive. The face was pretty without being too cute, the colours were rich blues and yellows and more importantly, the doll looked clean, especially considering who was holding it. If this would make the lady go away, then so be it.

"Thank you ever so! I-will-give-it-to-the-Prime-Minister!" she said, as clearly and firmly as possible. The woman growled and muttered something, and pointed a craggy finger more or less at Linda's neck. She gestured as if she wasn't too concerned what Linda was going to do with the doll, and walked around the corner into a side street, still mumbling and maybe even laughing. Laughing? That thought lasted no longer than the suspicion about her smiling. Anyone that old and creepy would never do something like that.

Linda looked around herself, relieved that nobody seemed to be staring in her general direction. It was almost as if their encounter had passed by unnoticed, and that was a major cause for a celebration, even on a small scale. She crossed over the road to find somewhere for a late lunch, and after consulting her dice she sat at a table outside the third attractive café, and stood her new Matryoshka doll next to the table's central parasol. It was a little taller than her Coke bottle, and at least three times as wide, and its icy-cold varnish shone brightly even in the shade. She gave it a shake, and all the dolls inside rattled.. and rattled.. and rattled. It was a nice enough doll, in a this-part-of-the-world kind of way, and it would be a good souvenir for her room back at St Teresa's - plus it was something else to tell Andie about, who would probably quite like to have one as well. Linda decided to pick one up for her later on - but not quite so expensive, perhaps.

She finished off a bizarre sandwich (which hadn't been a chicken one, despite her mime for the waiter) and decided to open up the doll and give the smaller ones a breath of fresh air. She gave it a good twist but the two halves wouldn't move, so she gave it a thorough shake and tried again, but it still wouldn't give way. The other dolls would have to stay inside for the time being, rattling and rattling..

The pavement on her side of the long road back was far too riddled with cracks to allow any hurrying, and she trotted up the entry steps at the hotel much later than planned. It didn't matter though. Mr Beaufort's important afternoon meetings with the Ukrainian Defence Secretary's Assistants and Important Others hadn't quite finished. The reception area was filled with muffled singing, which according to a porter was coming from one of the Secure Conference Rooms on the first floor. Linda prayed for all she was worth that the racket wasn't anything to do with her father, and hurried over to the lifts to go up to her room - and hope that they had all forgotten about her. The lights showed both lifts to be somewhere up in the clouds, and despite hammering on both of the Down buttons twenty times each, neither lift would move. Moments later, a boisterous mob poured down the stairs and into the wide entrance hall, where their singing and rowdiness took on a deafening echo which all of them found greatly amusing. A bearded idiot supporting a giggling, red-cheeked dimwit waved and stumbled towards her. The female half spoke in a very squeaky voice.

"Awwright Bel? One of us is all tiddly.. can't take him nowhere, can I? He's a one, inneee just?"

Dee performed one of her snorted laughs, and dissolved in a fit of giggles. Linda's father laughed as well, and finally thought of something to slur.

"Aft'noo-oon L'nnnduhh! Where is it you've been to all this time today now you're here?" he beamed, and his breath hit her like a speeding juggernaut.

"So that's what death smells like.." Linda thought to herself, wondering if she would ever breathe again. She was surrounded by an alcohol-soaked mixture of garlic, strong cheese and presumably some kind of over-cooked alien life-form. It could easily knock a horse out. Linda hid behind a handful of tissues and pretended to blow her nose, hoping her eyes wouldn't start watering.

"Hey, evee'one.. evuhree-wohnnn!" he called, and waved an arm in the air to attract the mob's attention, keeping his other arm wrapped around Dee's waist. Linda knew what was coming up, and wanted to crawl under the hotel.

"Hey ev'body! This's Linda, my son jus' here come to see us! No, daughtuh.. yes. Say hello to Linda, Linda.. go on.."

The air filled with high-spirited versions of 'hello' in English, Russian and that wordless, global language understood by all drunks, and Linda managed a smile in return. This was one of the most embarrassing moments of her entire life, even worse than when she threw up on live tv. She was only five at the time, but the 'Morning Britain!' presenters made a big joke-laden deal out of it because it happened while her father was discussing a new Government Health

Initiative. But this seemed a lot worse, and it wasn't helped by Dee's presence. Linda stared up at the bearded troll-man, who carried on speaking at her.

"So you been buying stuff then?" he said, looking at the doll and then leaning close to stare into her new shades on the top of her head, until his damp beard brushed her nose.

"And you been doing.. more other girl things? Well we've had to be doing all our work.. for.. His.. no Her.. no, it is His, Her Majelsties Guvanunt, no, Guvelmuhnt.. uh, working ahlll day long anyhows.."

"Yes, I'd guess that you started just after breakfast," she said, inching further away, "Why not have these meetings in the bar?"

He grinned inanely and looked very pleased with himself before Dee flicked his tie up into his beard, bringing the conversation to a painful death. Someone took a picture of the three of them, and then another, and Linda was quickly introduced to the vast collection of middle-aged, self-important, and thoroughly sloshed men and women, all of whom insisted on having at least one picture taken. Her skin crawled more with each one.

A fleet of cars pulled up outside like a row of knights in shining armour, ready to take some of the dignitaries away. One of the lifts gave a muffled 'ding' and its doors slid open, but Linda ignored it and made her escape via the stairs instead. The prospect of getting into a lift accompanied by any of those charming Government Officials was even less appealing than entering a lion's den wearing Eau de Zebra perfume - while dressed as a zebra.

She hurried breathlessly for flight after flight up to her room on the Billionth Floor, the one with a view that overlooked Mars. She only used the even steps, and vowed to take the odd ones next time she had to go down. As she reached each new floor she stopped by the windows to catch her breath and also to make sure the political packs were definitely leaving. By the time she reached her floor, the eighteenth, she needed a new pair of legs, a heart that actually worked and perhaps some new lungs as well.

After what felt like a lifetime she locked the bedroom door behind her. She left her Matryoshka doll next to her mother's picture by the bed and started her all-time favourite Abba cd playing on the wall hi-fi before running into the bathroom. The door shook with the slam, but Linda didn't care. She needed to wash her arms once for each person who'd been holding her, then wash her face at least once for each slobbered drunken kiss, and also roll a one before drying after every wash as well. That way there would be no trace left of them, either on her or around her. At all.

An hour later she sat outside on the balcony, lost in her headphones and feeling much better. She was nice and clean, all-new and vastly improved, and happy to be watching the sun sinking ever lower as the afternoon began slowly drifting into evening. The city was looking wonderful again.

Room Service had brought her a huge tray of tea and goodies, and had it not been for a phonecall from Constance regarding the evening meal, she would have stayed out there for a very long time. She had enough cd's to keep herself in a good mood and would probably have finished her letter to Andie, which was proving to be a very long one. This time there was just so much to say. And not only that, she even managed to fix the dodgy clasp on her necklace without too much trouble at all. It had fallen off again a little earlier (luckily making a noise as it landed on the bathroom tiles) because it really needed a new fiddly bit. That was the problem with wearing it all the time - the second most important part tended to wear out.

The evening wasn't too bad though. It didn't rain, which allowed Odessa to look attractive and elegant for longer. Best of all, there were only a dozen of her father's colleagues (and their Ukrainian counterparts) to put up with at a smart restaurant near to the shore of the Black Sea - and even better than that, Dee had ended up on a different table. She was so far away that Linda had even waved to her. There were plenty more pictures taken as the night wore on, and hopefully one would show the Government reps mixing with the locals without appearing to be too inebriated. The chances of that were very, very slim though.

But something was bothering her, and as the evening wore on it began bothering her more and more. A few times on the journey to the restaurant, in the midst of the groups of people walking by, she was almost sure that she kept seeing the old lady, but only for the briefest of moments each time. She might have been in the restaurant twice, and then near the small park beyond the outside dining patio. But as always with silhouettes and frustrating Half-There's in the corner of her eye, Linda couldn't be sure. She'd have to roll a whole load of fours to get a 'yes' on that one.

CHAPTER FIVE

Avalon

As soon as they arrived back at the hotel, Linda claimed one of the lifts (along with two elderly ladies and a porter) while the rest of the party were deciding whether or not to have a few nightcaps in the bar. The doors eventually opened to reveal Floor 18 and she drifted along the silent corridors to her room, enjoying the civilised quietness around her. The restaurant had been a big, noisy zoo and she was glad to be away from it.

It was getting late and she felt thoroughly tired by the time she had converted the settee from being a very stylish item of furniture into a kind of night-time medieval torture device. She remade it a few times in a hopeless bid to make it more bearable, before giving up and just settling down for the night instead. The room looked brighter and even more like a black and white photograph than the previous night, which meant it wasn't really ideal for sleeping in. She put her headphones on and shuffled around until she was almost comfortable, and after only six or seven tracks the music was starting to take effect. And then somewhere in the room, something buzzed. Maybe.

Linda turned the cd player down even quieter, and sat up. Her mind did tend to play the most devilish tricks on her especially when she was over-tired, so this could easily be one of those Let's Annoy Linda moments. She waited for it to happen again, and watched the digital clock change until it showed 11.57pm.

And there it was again. Definitely a buzz, a low, resonant buzz and it was coming from somewhere near the bedside table, over by her mother's picture.. somewhere near the doll.

She clambered across the bed and opened the drawer, and saw nothing in there that shouldn't be in there. A few hankies, her lucky tennis ball, a brush and a narrow can of wasp-spray. There weren't any other drawers to check, so she picked up the doll and held it in the moonlight. She gave it a gentle shake and pressed it to her ear, but it didn't make any noise at all. There wasn't even a rattle, and certainly no buzz.

"Weird, weird.. who's a weirdo.." she whispered.

She made herself comfortable on the real bed, keeping well away from the shadow-cross, and tried for the millionth time to open it. It was as firmly set as it had been all day. Just her luck to have the only Matryoshka doll in Odessa that wouldn't work. No wonder the old lady was giving it away. She sighed and tossed the doll onto the mattress, and decided to buy a proper one for herself and also one for Andie, definitely the next day. Maybe even one for Constance as well. And that final thought made her realise that her brain wasn't working properly and it really was time to go to sleep. The green digits on the bedside clock behind her flicked around to midnight, and she started giving one of the biggest yawns of her life. But midway through, she stopped.

The doll had twisted a little, all by itself. Linda stared at it. Did she really just see that, or was this a Let's REALLY Annoy Linda moment, with no questions asked? She reached forwards and picked it up again to convince herself that nothing had happened, but the patterns on the top half no longer lined up with those on the bottom half, and it even felt a little loose. This was bizarre, but then again, it might be perfectly okay. Maybe the jolt of landing on the mattress did something to it? Maybe there hadn't really been a few seconds between the doll landing, and the doll twisting?

That wasn't worth worrying about at such a late hour (plus a time-zone difference, of course) so almost without thinking she started opening it up. The two halves of the first doll soon lay by her knees, followed by the second doll, and then the third. They looked unbelievably similar, not just in their designs but in their sizes as well, and it didn't really feel like it was getting any smaller at all. The fourth soon joined all the other pieces, and then the fifth and sixth.

"This could be a long night.." she thought with a sigh, and she just wasn't in the mood for one of those.

And then Linda held the seventh doll, the final one. It was unpainted and felt unnaturally smooth for wood. No moonlight reflected off its contours, and there didn't seem to be a narrow groove around the middle. She held it up close, disappointed that it didn't look good, didn't weigh much, didn't rattle at all and was probably empty. But there was something strange about it, something that wouldn't allow her to let go. She turned it the right way up again.

A shallow, zig-zagging crack silently appeared around the shoulders, which made her wonder if it had been there all along. The top came loose very slowly, and she twisted it a little one way and then the other as she worked it along a deceptively intricate path. And then it was off, and rolled itself into the pile with all the others.

She peered into the remaining section. A faint mist with the vaguest hint of blue swayed an inch or two below the jagged rim, and the hazy moonlight made it seem even more ethereal and strange. The clouds outside cleared, allowing the full light of the moon to fall onto it. Now the swirling form wasn't so eerie, and didn't look a million miles away from being something she had seen all her life. Or not seen, to be more accurate, because this kind of vague and shapeless mass was precisely what had always appeared just out of her vision, always in the very corner of her eye. And somewhere far, far below her conscious mind, perhaps deep inside her heart, there was a flicker of recognition. She was holding a Half-There, the kind that she'd seen, dismissed and forgotten so many times that they barely even registered these days.

But Linda didn't know that. She peered into the mess and wished she could see it more clearly to figure out what it was, but there was no chance of that happening. It was late and she was tired, which was a bad combination even under normal circumstances, but throw in some difficult light and a Very Weird Thingy, and suddenly she had all of the four essential items needed for getting herself completely and utterly bewildered.

The mist became a little fainter as if it was evaporating, leaving nothing behind. Linda reached in, tentatively prodding the silky-smooth vapour, and trying to feel if there was anything there. For a few seconds it was cool and yet warm at the same time, and then suddenly began growing denser. She quickly took her hand away causing slow grey waves to rise and fall, which seemed to deliberately hold back from reaching the very edge of the container.

The languid swirls steadily grew faster and rose higher and higher before calming, and then dropped as if a small plug had been pulled. Within seconds they had revealed some very definite shapes, but in the shadows and the moonlight it was hard to tell quite what was left. Linda stifled a yawn and tipped whatever was there out onto the bedsheet, where the light was at its brilliant best.

"Aahh!" she whispered to herself, pleased and surprised with what she had found. It was another doll, and a very thin one at that. It wasn't the rounded Russian variety, it was more conventional, and if anything, it was far more like..

"..Fabergé Barbie? How gorgeous," she murmured, noticing the silvery glints and flecks of light appearing and disappearing across her, as if the moon was fleetingly catching millions of minute diamond-tips. And then they all gradually faded, leaving her with a faint grey and silver-white colour. Her long legs had been tucked under her chin, and even though she seemed to be very firmly curled up, she lay in the moonlight looking a little big for where she had come from - but after midnight thoughts like that didn't bother Linda for long. Instead, she had another yawn and looked down at her new doll for a while.

She was exquisitely made and so, so attractive - and well worth a closer inspection, maybe even with the room's lights on.. although she didn't want to raise the curiosity of other people in the hotels over the road. The lights could stay off.

Linda took a moment to decide which part was least likely to break, and picked her up by a small foot. The doll weighed almost nothing and hung upside down loosely swaying in a breeze that Linda couldn't feel. If she didn't know better, the doll sounded as if she was moaning in a soft and dizzy kind of way.

"Her batteries must be getting as low as mine.. I wonder where they go.." Linda thought to herself, pondering whether she would take a watch battery or one like those in the tv remote control.

Seeing her now, her legs looked very badly designed - they were long and elegant, and probably very fragile, but far longer than they ought to be. Linda dropped her onto the mattress. Despite weighing less than a feather, there was a gentle-but-definite 'flummf' as she landed, and she lay in the moonlight on her side. Her long butterfly wings, which until now had been flat against her body, unfurled like two delicate fans to become almost as long as her legs. They shivered open, at once becoming translucent and sparkling, and Linda watched spellbound by such a beautifully crafted work of art. A feathery wave of light began at her toes, ran up and across the chiffon-like material that she was draped in, and seemed to disappear somewhere near the very tips of her wings.

The faery-doll lay perfectly still, wrapped in a faint blue glow which made her look as if she was sleeping beneath a neon veil. And then Linda looked a little closer. Was she breathing, or were tired eyes just playing tricks? This was so very, very weird.

And then she moved. She definitely moved. Her small hands opened and closed at least twice.. and then her eyes blinked open.

She shook her head, yawned as if she was never going to stop, and slowly pushed herself up into a sitting position. She turned to face the moonlight, which seemed to make her neon blue become stronger and brighter until it was replaced by a pure white one, with just the tiniest hint of sky blue remaining at its edges. She shook her entire body into a blur, rather like a wet dog shaking itself dry, and reappeared in a constantly shifting battle between being blurred and being sharply focussed. Clarity soon won. She closed her eyes and stretched, while speaking to herself in a very weak and breathy voice.

"Ooh my head.. ooh my everything.. ooh.."

This was too surreal for words. Linda thought of her mother. That was always the best way to get out of crazy dreams and practically all nightmares. But this time she didn't wake up. Either this was a very, very bad one, or.. or maybe it was really happening? She kept on looking at the talking faery-doll, who had stopped talking and moving, and was now looking straight back up at her. The faery blinked and squinted, rubbed her eyes and then tried to stay completely motionless. Linda moved closer so that her head was just a few inches away from the faery-doll-freaky-thing.

"Hello?" she whispered, immediately being hit by a headline. In the picture for this one, she was wearing a straight-jacket and a dunce's cap.

"Lindagate: Barmy Schoolgirl Thinks Doll Is Real - Entire Universe Has Huge Big Laugh!"

The doll stayed perfectly still. Linda blew softly, and watched her hair and wings wave a little. Her silvery eyes blinked rapidly, and she appeared to be holding back a sneeze. She was definitely real. But she couldn't be, could she?

"Hello.. again?" Linda breathed.

There was no response, so she decided to pick her up once more. Anything so lifelike, so beautiful - and so incredibly weird - was worth a really, really close-up look. As her fingers ventured near enough to take on a silvery glow and almost come into contact with her leg again, the doll's eyes widened with horror and she darted straight up into the air. She flew quickly from corner to corner around the room, wavering and whimpering, then hid behind a lampshade before flying off in a desperate search for a better hiding place. She could stop even more quickly than she could start, and visited every potentially-useful part of the room at least twice.

Linda's heart was pounding. This was it, this was the moment where the nice people in white coats would come and get her and put her somewhere safe and warm where there weren't any weirdy flying things to talk to. But they hadn't arrived yet, so until they did she stood in the centre of the room turning around and around watching where the not-a-doll-anymore was going next.

The faery flew at top speed across the room towards one of the tall balcony windows and hit the glass with a light half-thud, pausing momentarily in mid-air before dropping somewhere behind Aggy's chair. She lay on the carpet, very dazed. Linda knew a bump like that must have hurt, and quickly moved the chair away. The faery slowly and dizzily flew along the floor towards the corner of the room, dragging her feet behind her. She didn't stop, and collided with the skirting board, where she moaned and lay curled up for a moment. Linda kneeled in front of her and leaned forwards, down close to the carpet and let her hair sway nearer.

"Hello? I'm not going to hurt you.. uh.. nice fairy type you.. I.. I promise I won't. I'm Linda.. are you alright?" she whispered.

The faery gathered herself again, and backed into the corner as far as she could possibly go. She looked up at Linda, and shook herself into another blur, emerging as a full-size wolf which would have scared the living daylights out of Linda, if she'd been able to see it. The wolf lasted for roughly one blink. The faery lay on the floor breathing deeply. She shook herself into another blur, and became a large, snarling Alsation for almost long enough to finish the first snarl. Linda knew she ought to be scared, but something inside wouldn't let her. The faery gave herself a final weak shake, emerging as a whimpering puppy with huge, sad silvery eyes. Even that didn't last long and she became herself again, lying exhausted on the floor.

"Don't be scared.. I won't harm you.. your safe, really you are.." she whispered and moved closer to her, but the faery darted upwards, flicking Linda's long fringe on the way, and hovered near the ceiling.

"Oh okay.. be like that then. I really am a loon like everyone's always told me. Loony Linda. I'll wake up tomorrow and pretend it's just another rotten dream and then be alone again in the middle of nowhere just like always.." she said to herself, and felt her eyes starting to fill with tears.

She stood up, opened the balcony door, and held the folds of net curtain to one side. This wasn't a good moment, and she was painfully aware that her weak grip on reality was now undeniably non-existent. She looked up to the bright, shining faery and whispered to her in a voice that wobbled and faltered.

"You can go now.. if you're sure you're not hurt or anything.. just remember to be careful, okay? And.. I really am sorry if I scared you.. I didn't ever mean to.."

The faery stayed where she was, and kept her eyes fixed on Linda. They were quite big eyes, as out of proportion as her legs, and had become even more silvery. Loonda Beaufort, the newest resident of Mad Town and perhaps a future Mayoress of Crazyville, felt they were really pretty. That, she decided, would be the last rational thought she would ever have.

The faery smoothly fluttered down to be level with Linda's head, just over an arm's length away. One of Linda's arms, that is.

"Avalon," she said, in a voice that wasn't a high-pitched or squeaky kind of faery voice at all. It was a warm voice with a soft edge, and sounded as if it was inside Linda's head.

"Avalon?" whispered Linda in barely more than a breath. The faery nodded, and ventured a little closer.

"Avalon. Name. Me. Avalon. You can call me Avalon. Why can you see me?" she said. Her glow dimmed and she unintentionally dropped a few inches.

"Careful, Ava.."

"Feel so weak.. need Lunaressence.."

She fluttered in an elaborate arch over to the bed, and settled in a long rectangular panel of moonlight. Linda stood and watched, totally unsure of herself yet all too aware that she must be either completely barmy or the luckiest person in the entire world ever. She hoped it was the latter, as that would make a very welcome change.

The light radiating from Avalon began to steadily grow stronger and purer, and she soon patted the bed for Linda to come and join her. Linda lay on her front near where the pillows should have been, with her face a few inches away from Avalon - who immediately fluttered a safer distance away.

"Feeling better now. Been stuck in there a long time. Nearly a quarter moon-cycle. Very dark in there," she said, looking scared and pointing to the foot of the bed where the Matryoshka dolls had been scattered - and only one remained.

"Wh..where are they all? There was more.." stumbled Linda. Avalon tried fluffing her hair before answering. Its length changed with each attempt.

"All back together again.. they'll be gone soon.. not real. Why can you see me? What kind of Spiritae are you?"

"Huh? I'm not a spirit, I'm just me. Linda. Just a Linda. An old lady gave that doll to me, and it started opening itself a few minutes ago, and you were inside."

Avalon nodded, as if that was completely understandable.

"Midnight. Full moon. I was free to go. They don't normally take invisibility from faeries though, that's so cruel. She'll be in trouble for that."

"Who? The old lady?"

Avalon seemed distracted for a moment, and rubbed her nose. Nothing happened. She rubbed it again, and still nothing happened.

"She's a Ved'ma."

"A vedmer?"

"No, a Ved'ma. She's a bad Spirit, a kind of Demon. Her name's Mörrah, and she's horrid. She hates everything, and traps my kind for fun. But Ved'mas hold the Waters Of Life and the Waters Of Death too, which gives her kind loads of power so we have to put up with them."

Avalon yawned another of her huge yawns and then looked up expectantly. Linda hadn't a clue what to say.

"The waters of.. I'm crazy.." she thought, or maybe said.

"No you're not, you're Linda, and you might be nice. Not like nasty old Mörrah. She's had so much practice at being bad because Ved'mas live for ages and play tricks with minds and they're good at it. She made me think I was.. nearly where I should be.. but I wasn't, and then I was stuck in that Containment instead, but only for a few days until the full moon, which isn't so bad. You know what? She kept my friend Frahelle for ages and then had to use the Waters to avoid being in more trouble than you can ever imagine.. that's Alexandryite isn't it?"

Linda was finding it difficult to keep up with Avalon's rate of talking. She seemed to have moved imperceptibly from sleepy to wide awake in no time at all. And now she was pointing at Linda's necklace.

"This? I don't know.. it was my mum's."

Avalon began reaching for it, but changed her mind mid-way. Linda rested it further out on the bed, where Avalon could have a better look in complete safety. She nervously drew closer to it.

"Uhuh, Alexandryite. It's very pretty, isn't it? Mörrah would have hated that. Ved'mas can't ever go near Alexandryite. Bet she didn't lay a finger on you, did she? And her eyes would sting rotten every time she even looked at you! Was it sunny?"

"Mmm-hmm, lovely," Linda nodded, and Avalon giggled at the thought of the shining alexandrite causing Mörrah a dreadfully bad headache. Linda moved the gem nearer to her new friend, who poked it with her foot.

"Why did she pick on me, Avalon? I only arrived here last night.. what did I do wrong?"

Avalon had a think, and finally sneezed.

"Nothing wrong, you didn't need to. You must be Gifted. When her kind grow old - and she is a really, really old one, they get weak and need more greed and bad feelings to feed on. And when they're weak, hardly any of your kind can see a Ved'ma, otherwise the whole world would be full of Ground Crawlers with rotten luck and there'd be lots of really strong Ved'mas living for ages everywhere."

"She did look ever so old," whispered Linda, nodding.

"But she's not really an old lady - she looks however she wants to look. I thought she was.. well anyway, she trapped me in that doll which was a horrid thing to do."

"Hmm.. I'd hate that," she agreed, sounding sympathetic. Avalon responded to the tone of her voice and nodded.

"Why was she here though?" Linda added.

"Well.."

Avalon began preening her wings while thinking of the simplest way to explain, and didn't answer for a moment.

"..see, this is part of her territory and she would have been looking for trouble to feed on. That's what they do, they look for trouble all the time. And she found you. If you'd been looking for trouble as well, ooh you'd have found it."

"Trouble? She was only selling things, like rubbishy stuff no-one would ever want."

Avalon shuffled nearer. She seemed to be enjoying knowing so much, and being able to show it.

"She wasn't selling, she was giving. It looked yuk because she's so old. You were supposed to choose something from her, and then you'd be stuck with it for a few moon-cycles, bringing you really bad luck. You could throw it away every day and it would still turn up again. Very bad. And everything that goes wrong for you would make her a little stronger. That's how it works. Isn't she awful?"

Linda hummed her agreement. Avalon nodded again, gave a

small shiver and then held up three fingers on her hand.

"That's Step One. Step Two is she offers you something that looks like it's better, so you get greedy and have something which brings even worse luck."

"Really?"

"Uhuh," she said, and held up four fingers on her other hand, before raising a foot. She toppled over sideways, and gave up trying to show numbers.

"Step Three is where she won't take any money from you, so you leave thinking that you out-clevered an old woman. And that's greedy. She thrives on Ground Crawlers' greediness. It's like food to her. And she likes lots of it. Lots and lots. Greedy Mörrah."

Linda tried to put her brain back on track. Talking to a faery was getting in the way of anything resembling a sane thought or sentence. Speaking slowly for her own sake as much as Avalon's, she recounted what she had done.

"I chose some horrid flowers from her tray, but only because they were so horrid I thought no-one else would buy them. And then I wouldn't change them for a really nice silvery moon. And I gave her loads too much money 'cause she looked like she could do with it, and I wouldn't take any of it back. Oh, and I left the vile flowers in a churchyard, under an elder tree.. and made up a verse for them but it wasn't a very good one. Then she followed me around and did seem cross that I hadn't got them anymore - and when I wouldn't take anything else, she gave me the doll thing and.. well, you."

Avalon clapped with excitement.

"Ooh.. you know lots don't you? That's why she got so annoyed. That's so funny. You did a Selfless Act, so by Spirit Law she had to perform a.. umm.. Re-demp-tion Debt, and giving up a trapped faery like me was the most pain-free nothing-thing she could do. You won, I think. That is so funny! Hardly anybody ever wins - I hope all her friends find out!"

Avalon giggled, and shuffled closer. She didn't seem to be in the slightest bit nervous anymore and picked up the small alexandrite crystal from in front of Linda's fore-arms, careful not to touch the fine chain. She gazed into it, and held it up to the moonlight. A myriad of warm rainbow colours passed over her, and her white glow seemed to absorb them all, growing even purer and reaching out a little further.

"Lovely.. not scared anymore.." she said, and smiled up at Linda, turning the gem around in her hands.

"That's ever so good, I'm pleased about that, Avalon. I thought you were just a doll when I lifted you out of that last Matryoshka.."

Avalon froze, and her good mood disappeared. Even her glow dimmed a little and she dropped the alexandrite.

"Lifted.. you touched me? Oh you didn't.. oh no.. I bet she knew you would.. oh.. she's so bad.."

Avalon stared up at Linda, her silvery eyes suddenly wide and large, with a look of absolute dread on her face.

"Say you didn't.. please say you didn't?"

Linda felt very sick.

"Was it wrong? I didn't know it was wrong.. I thought you were a doll? Inside a doll, inside a doll.. you know.."

"That's why you can see me so much.. oh no.. I have to go now, find out if I can go back to.. I don't.. you really, really touched me?"

Avalon's voice went very high and wavery, and sounded as if she was holding back a sob. She clapped her hands twice. Nothing happened, and she stared at them in disbelief. She stood up and drifted towards the edge of the bed, where she looked up into the full moon. Her delicate lace wings opened and closed a few times before she turned back to face Linda, and she breathed deeply.

"You'll.. you'll still be here if I come back, Linda? You promise you'll still be right here won't you.. at sunrise, for me?"

Linda nodded, and Avalon drifted to within an inch of her eyes.

"Will you.. will you promise me?" she added, weakly.

"Yes, I promise you.. I'll be here.. anywhere for you.."

Avalon flew smoothly to the wrong window, remembered just in time and then followed the gently billowing folds of the net curtain through the open balcony door instead. Linda waited a little before following her outside, and wondered where something so bright could have gone. All she could see was a solitary bird flying in and out of darkness towards the moon. She leaned against the curved stone rail and watched for a long time, feeling the fragrances of summer blowing around her, as much in her heart than in any other way, and only when they had gone did she begin to think about going back inside.

Eventually she went indoors and switched the tv on, feeling very confused. Two actresses from a sunny American soap were having a badly dubbed argument on a beach. The language was probably Russian, and she couldn't understand a word of it. So how had she just been speaking to a Ukrainian faery that had been trapped in a Matryoshka? She turned the volume all the way down and covered herself in blankets on the settee-bed, and wondered how hopelessly cracked her mind had become.

Maybe she wasn't even supposed to be in Odessa? Maybe she'd imagined everything, and there wasn't really anyone in the hotel who she knew? Maybe she'd gone completely mad and wasn't even in Odessa and was actually in a hotel near St Teresa's and maybe St Teresa's staff would be wondering where she was? But then again, what if she was actually lying in a coma on the floor of her room in England, trapped in an unreal dreamworld inside her head? Or worse, what if..

..she blocked out the difficult questions with some music. Her headphones immediately confirmed that she still loved Abba and that she still knew all the words to SOS, Dancing Queen, Chiquitita, and The Name Of The Game. That was a relief. And the noises on the tv had confirmed beyond any doubt that she still couldn't understand Russian. That was also a relief. Her back ached because she was curled up on an uncomfortable settee, which meant that she still wasn't capable of lying on a bed if it had a shadow-cross on it, and that was yet another big relief, as well. Therefore, her mind wasn't too far gone yet. Maybe she was just in the middle of her all-time weirdest dream ever? She could stay where she was, all safe and snug, getting reassurance from familiar songs while watching the curtain swaying a little in the breeze. Soon the night would be gone, and it would be time to wake up and get up, and then in the brightness of the day's sunlight..

CHAPTER SIX
Sunrise

..Linda felt something brush against her face. She stayed wrapped in the warm blankets and soft pillows, more unwilling than ever to find herself back in the world beyond them. Something very fresh and very cool brushed against her again, this time even closer to her cheek. She opened her eyes as little as possible.

"Ohhh, toooo early.." she moaned to herself.

The room still carried more darkness than light and Linda wasn't in the slightest bit interested in ushering a butterfly or moth or whatever it was back outside. That could wait till much later, when she'd pushed the craziest dream of her life out of her mind and replaced it with a much better one. Her eyes stayed shut, and her cd player randomly chose another quiet track. And then it happened again, only this time someone was speaking. The voice was pitched somewhere between a whisper and a hum, and something about it was vaguely familiar.

"Wake up Lindaah.. Wuuu-yake-up! Wuuuuuuuuuuu-yake-up!"

Linda didn't have too much choice, and found herself looking at Avalon, who was hovering a few inches in front of her face. Her big silvery eyes looked sore, and she rubbed them again while humming to herself. She perched on the armrest at the far end of the settee.

"You've come back?" whispered Linda. She was amazed and pleased, not just because last night had really happened, but also because Avalon had chosen to return to her. Avalon nodded and rubbed her eyes again.

"Are you.. okay then? Try not rubbing them, or you'll make them worse. You can tell me what happened or where you went.. if you'd like to?"

Avalon took a huge dramatic sniff.

"I wanted to go back home to Hesperides which is where all my kind come from, but I couldn't. I didn't find a single moonbeam, and it was a full moon as well. Moonbeams let me get home.. but there weren't any. Not even one. It's so nice there.. and nearly all my Magics have gone as well.. look.."

Avalon flew to the other armrest and settled near to Linda's head, and clapped her hands three times. Nothing happened. She clicked her fingers a few times, quickly. Again, nothing happened. Then she spent a while making shapes in the air, and only stopped when she started crying again.

"I can hardly do anything.." she sobbed through her shining tears. "I'm so sorry.."

"I know they won't miss me.. nobody wants a low faery anyway, hardly any use. I bet you're ever so useful. I'm not. Even those pollen-brained Flower Faeries have a role in life. All I do is count and look for.. oh what's the point? I don't know you at all, you might be horrid and I'd be alright if it wasn't for.."

Avalon blinked away two huge tears that nearly wouldn't fall, and Linda had absolutely no idea what to say. Maybe honesty would do.

"Well, umm.. I didn't know I'd be messing things up for you, I mean I'd never, ever have picked you up.. but without me that Ved'ma might have locked you in a new set of dolls or done something worse, but she didn't and at least you're free again.. and I'm glad you're with me now, and there's a whole load of nice reasons I'm pleased you came back.. but if you think I'm useful and my life's marvellous you're wrong."

Avalon looked up into her eyes, examining one at a time, as if she was reading Linda's feelings. She seemed to prefer the left one.

"Can't you do Magics anymore, either?" Avalon squeaked, and stopped crying.

"Me? I couldn't in the first place. What I meant was that I'm a bit like you, I don't really have a home to go back to. I'm the only one who lives in a big miserable school all the time, I never ever knew my mum, and my best friend's so far away she can only ever write to me! And she's got a boyfriend now, and so's my dad except his is a girl of course, and I don't know where to start about that. So I'll be alone at school for years and years with people who couldn't care less about me and they all think I'm weird and I'm glad I've met something like you.. and now.. I'm really going to.."

Linda couldn't hold back. Even vaguely mentioning one or two of the things that were hurting her was a huge step. She had never actually spoken to anyone about what had been building up inside her for so long, and now she simply had to let go for a while. If Avalon knew a thing or two about crying, Linda could show her a whole lot more. Avalon reached across and picked up a length of her hair, and stroked it.

"You're Mother.. not anywhere ever? Oh no.." she wailed, "..oh no that's the worst thing ever that I've ever heard ever, ever.. and all your friends hate you too.. and your Father's married to a school as well.. that's just awful.. and your best friend won't speak to you.. it's all getting worse and worse and worse.." she cried, burying her head in her hands and shuffling behind more of Linda's hair.

A few minutes later, the room was becoming much lighter and Linda was feeling a lot better. She needed to make Avalon feel better as well, and started by handing her the small alexandrite gem. Avalon sniffed and smiled, and held it like a trophy. The sunlight, or maybe Avalon, made it glow and change slowly through soft bands of every colour.

"Well we've got each other haven't we, Avalon? I won't leave you, and I don't think for a minute that you're useless."

"Really honestly?"

"Uhuh. Promise."

Avalon gave her eyes a final wipe and hugged the side of Linda's face. She felt like a million tiny, warm feathers against her skin.

"I can still cast Glamours!" she said, straightening Linda's hair back into place.

"Glamours?"

"Glamours. You know, Not Me's!"

She fluttered onto a large fold in the duvet and briefly turned into a small hamster, a potato and then a leaf. Linda applauded, and Avalon looked proud of herself. She flew forwards until she was standing just in front of Linda's chin.

"Creatures are hard to do.. never been good at them.. and look.." she said, holding out a small silvery pouch that was loosely tied around her waist.

"I still have some Medicamentum left!"

"Medic.."

"It's the only Faery Dust I'm allowed, and it's not really much use. It's good for fixing the odd thing, if you tend to break things. Or maybe if you nearly killed something, but there's nowhere near enough of it for fixing that. Besides, I haven't accidentally killed anything for ages.. what's that smell?"

"Hmm? I can't smell anything."

"Can I smell Hazelymits? Have you got some Hazelymits?"

Avalon suddenly reached the Very Happy end of a mood swing, and she darted over to the wardrobe where Linda's denim jacket was hanging up. She scratched at the brass door handle in an attempt to open it.

"In here.. in here.. in here.." she called, very excited.

Linda clambered over the settee then hurried across the room and unlocked it, not sure what to expect. Avalon dived into one of the larger pockets on the jacket, and emerged tugging at a bar of NutzyFruit chocolate. Linda put it on the table.

"Oh, you like chocolate? Help yourself."

Avalon wasn't too bothered about the chocolate. She devoured the hazelnuts one after the other, her jaws moving too quickly to see, while chocolate and bits of silver foil slowly spread across her face and arms, and then the rest of her body. She managed to hum happily all the way through, and gave another good wet-dog shake when she finished. The chocolate completely vanished from her skin and the light swathes of gossamer.

"Love Hazelymits. Lovely Hazelymits. Haven't eaten for so long! Have you got more Hazelies? And see here - I left all the chocliate for you!" she said, beaming at Linda while holding up two sticky blobs of melting chocolate which soon oozed down to join the rest of the chocolate on the table.

The phone rang and Linda looked over to the clock. It was 6.45 and zero seconds precisely, and there could only be one person in the entire world calling her up at that time of the day.

"Zdrastvuyte, Lindaskaya!"

"Yeah's me here, hi Constance. How come you don't need my middle name? You didn't ask yesterday either."

"Aha! Perhaps you're wondering if I'm really Constance? That's very good, it shows you're thinking! Quite unnecessary, but still very good. I don't require your proof of identity because Security assure me you haven't left your room all night. We have a few operating as staff in your hotel, and one or more sited in and around the buildings opposite. Just a precaution. Did you know your television was left on throughout the night? That's not terribly civilised and we must always try to be so civilised on overseas business. To the best of our knowledge Princess Diana never ever left a television on all night when on foreign trips, apart from once.. in Rome, if my memory serves me.. but she was rather unwell at the time. I believe it was the prawns. Now then, today's schedule's been altered.."

Linda paid no attention at all to Constance. She was far too pre-occupied watching Avalon fly around the room, stopping at the things that interested her and pushing, pulling and occasionally nibbling them. Faeries found the most peculiar things completely fascinating. Constance kept rattling off times, events, names and places, and Linda agreed whenever she judged the pitch in Constance's voice was calling for agreement, and hummed replies when she didn't know what to say. The phone eventually began to sound like it was off the hook, so Linda gladly put it down and went over to the hair-dryer. Avalon was switching it on and off, and giggling to herself.

"I'm not sure what to do now, Avalon. I have to be back here this afternoon for some boring old cutesy-family publicity photos, once my dad's lot have finished whatever meetings they've all got this morning.. but I have to go down for breakfast in a few minutes. Will you be okay up here? I don't think the rest of the world is ready to see.. you know.."

Avalon set the fan blowing three more times and then changed into a songthrush. Using a hairdryer without having a genuine reason for using one would normally have driven Linda mad and caused all kinds of headlines to fill her mind. But Avalon did exactly what should be done. Three on-and-offs before putting it down were just what Linda always did, except Linda tended to do them even if she really had been drying her hair. It seemed so normal that she barely gave Avalon's actions a second thought. The songthrush hopped nearer.

"Look at me, see me now? This is my Other Me, which is still a Not Me but it's my Natural Not Me. What do you think?"

She spread her wings and turned around twice, leaving small scratch marks with her claws in the table's varnish.

"Very nice.. uh, what are you on about?"

"This is a Not Me. It's how Ground Crawlers see me if I'm not being invisible, and I can't be invisible any more, can I?"

"Right.."

"And a Natural Not Me stops me getting confused because I don't have to think about turning into one. You see, sometimes my kind need to be seen by your kind, so we get disguised in all sorts of ways.. and even then some of your kind still can't see us at all.. but imagine if I was being normal everyday low faery Me Me and someone comes along - but I choose the wrong Not Me and turn into a flying melon again? Everyone would be looking at me, wouldn't they? A melon hovering way up in the air doesn't look right, no matter how good I do it. I haven't done anything that embarrassing for ages and ages. Don't worry."

Linda tried not to look too stupid while she thought very carefully to find the next words.

"So.. you mean you're stuck being visible to just about everyone because of me and that Ved'ma, but I see you as the real you, and everyone else sees you as a bird or whatever else you want them to see you as?"

"Uhuh. That's it, pretty much."

That made sense in a bizarre way, and raised a question.

"Why me?"

"Same reason you could see Mörrah. It's because you're Gifted, aren't you? It'd be really bad if you couldn't see Me Me, I'd be so alone.. so that's good then, isn't it?" she said enthusiastically, turning back into her faery form and spinning around.

"Good? It's completely Abbatastic! Maybe we could have a look around today, and if we find Mörrha she can help figure out how you might get back to Hups.. Hersi.. your home? She owes you that, at the very least."

"Yes! And if we go outside, you could buy a hat. That would be really good, too."

"Huh? Oh, my hair.. alright, I'll have a cut if it looks that bad but I like it long and.. I just don't like people touching it, that's all. But I'll go and have it tidied up if you'd like.."

"Hair? No, shade! Too much Solaressence isn't good for me, especially my wings.. all of them. If you had a hat that was really wide, I could stay with you instead of looking for shady places all the time. Unless you want me to get hotter and hotter and maybe all burned up like sticks after a big fire.. you wouldn't want THAT, would you?" she said, with a hint of surprise in her voice.

"No, no way, I'd never let that happen. We'll get the widest and shadiest hat of all time ever, and I'll be like a walking eclipse. A squashed crab underneath the Titanic has got more chance of getting a sunburn than you have!"

Linda liked how this was going. Barmy things were starting to seem okay, and life was starting to look like being fun. Totally insane, but fun none the less.

"But in the meantime Avalon, I have to go downstairs now for breakfast or else my dad and everyone will probably think I've been taken hostage by terrorists or invading Martians, or something worse."

With Avalon taking an extremely keen interest, possibly in the hope there might be some more Hazelymits somewhere, Linda rummaged through her wardrobe for something appropriate to wear for breakfast. She wasn't exactly spoiled for choice, but did find a few things that were more or less okay. And then inspiration struck.

"Big huge brainwave! While I'm downstairs I'll leave you with the best cd ever which I really, really like, and then by the time I get back up here you'll know me a whole lot better! You'll love this!"

To avoid Constance accusing her of risking an international incident by willfully leaving the wall hi-fi playing while not being in the room, Linda retrieved her portable cd player from under the settee's blankets and laid it out on the dressing table. Avalon stood in the circle made by the headphones, looking puzzled. She hovered at a safe distance a few feet above as the first track started playing, and steadily dared herself closer and closer until she was back in the middle again. By the third track Linda was singing along and heading for the door, while pointing out that it was her favourite song ever and that she'd be back as soon as possible.

She ran down the stairs, nowhere near patient enough to wait for the lifts, wondering how amazing it would feel to be able to fly down instead. Or up, or anywhere really. Linda entered the restaurant with the world's biggest grin on her face, having no doubts at all that Avalon would be discovering something new and completely, utterly, fabulously brilliant. A bit like she just had, really.

Breakfast dragged. The few waiters were painfully slow, everyone was talking loudly and once again the champagne was flowing early, but at least this time she managed to get some food. She kept an eye trained on the bay windows just in case a songthrush appeared, and after a very, very long while, one did. It drew her attention by chirping a chorus which Linda vaguely recognised, and she hid a laugh behind her hair. She stared between a couple of tables over to her new friend, and tried to to make herself see the real Avalon, rather than the songthrush. But the more she stared and concentrated, the less it worked.

"I can do this.. I'm gifted.. Avalon says I am," she told herself, and after a little while she realised that the less she tried, the easier it was becoming.

"..like trying to fall asleep, only different.." she figured, allowing the Not Me songthrush to almost fade away, revealing Avalon waving and singing.

An ageing speech writer (who looked like he belonged in a mortuary) kept commenting to the Head Waiter about the wretched noisy bird on the ledge of one of the restaurant's open windows. He even threw a crusty roll at it, narrowly missing. The bird flew away so Linda threw a roll at him, narrowly missing his glass eye and catching him fully on the fading stitch-marks along the side of his head. She felt her point had been made. Her father didn't agree, but so what? If he was capable of making a proper judgement about anything these days, he wouldn't need to comb his face every morning - and he wouldn't let a little madame like Dee bimble into his life, and he wouldn't hide things from his one and only daughter, and he certainly wouldn't leave her at that rotten school all the time, and he wouldn't be forgetting about all the other important things in their world, and he..

Linda made a huge long list in her mind while his lecture continued, and watched the window to see if Avalon came back, but she didn't. Other birds did, but they were only the usual bird-type birds that were everywhere.

"..and then we go to.. Linda, are you listening? You must try to listen while I'm talking to you - this is important, okay? We're moving to a new place tomorrow, in order to visit the first of the nuclear reprocessing plants and therefore we'll be at a new hotel so you'd better pack tonight okay? I hope to God the new place is better than this one. And do remember the photo-shoot this afternoon - there might still be tv cameras around so you could even get on a news programme or two if you're lucky! How about that, eh? You could tell all your friends when you get back. Dee's team suggest a reported appearance on Eastern European tv will elevate you in the eyes of at least 60% of your current scholastic colleagues to being 'phatly phundamental' if not 'the bomb' which apparently can only be good for you. I bet you'd like that? We're assuming most are the 12.4-13.6 age group and of familial social grade C2 through B, and perhaps two or three from A?"

Linda nodded rather than look blank, and tried to give the impression that she was vaguely interested in being within a million miles of any kind of camera. Anything to simply shut him up.

"And Linda, Dee was hoping.. well, we.. I.. we would hope you'll wear something better than whatever you had on yesterday, could you? Dee says it was so plain that she was embarrassed.. for you. And maybe you could get all that mess trimmed or have a perm done or something? She mentioned 'High-lights' and 'Low-lights' which means nothing to me but apparently you girls understand all that. She only wants to help you, so just do as she says, because it's only difficult if you decide to make it diff.."

He was really on form today. Linda thought about putting her shades on to look seriously cool even in the middle of breakfast, but she decided not to because this ignorant collection of apes and near-apes simply wouldn't appreciate style.

"..and before then you'd better go and apologise about that bread nonsense to Mr Bengts blah blah blah do it now, before his morning medication kicks-in blah blah blah.. and what's more.. blah blah.."

He just kept on talking and talking and talking. Linda nodded and hummed like she had done with Constance, while quickly finishing her plate of strange European breakfast things. She hurried out to the lifts, waving her apology back to Mr Bengts, who looked at her disdainfully. She raced across the reception area and squeezed into a crowded lift just as the doors closed, willing to put up with the horrible wall-to-wall people in her rush to get back to her room. The frustration of stopping and starting at almost every floor proved too much for her to deal with, so she ran out at Floor 7 and decided to take the stairs. Even tackling them one at a time would be quicker than the lift.

By the time she reached her room, she had remembered that it was an extremely bad idea to tackle the stairs. Trying to climb Mount Everest with a grand piano and a whale strapped to her back while coaxing a stubborn donkey along would have been both easier and a whole lot quicker, and she stumbled into her room feeling fit to drop.

"Hello.. Aval.. whuh.. uh.. are.. you here?" she called, recovering against a side table and wondering where Avalon could be. She anxiously started checking the wardrobes, the bathroom, the obscure places that she might have flown into, and began to wonder if she might have been scared away by that ancient idiot's bread roll.

However, just as she was becoming scared that Avalon had gone forever, she noticed that her random collection of crystals had been moved from on top of the tv. They had been rearranged in some kind of order in a circle around the cd player, except for the dark blue one which was balanced at a very strange angle on the lid. The silver foil from the hotel's Goodnight Mint lay perfectly smoothed-out between the ear pieces, and the chocolate square lay nearby, covered in small handprints, a strange squiggle, and one tiny bite.

"Maybe she's settling in?" Linda hoped to herself as she admired Avalon's handiwork before heading for the balcony. Avalon wasn't there either, and a sick feeling began stirring deep inside. Maybe she'd been hurt in the hotel's gardens next to the restaurant? Perhaps that senile old fool had actually hit her with.. she couldn't finish the thought, and raced out of her room, tearing along the corridor and barging past a hung-over dolt from the night before, and forced herself to slow down enough to only use the odd steps. She hurried into the lift on Floor 7 to balance out her previous journey up, and pounded the '0' button continually. Jabbing like a demented woodpecker was bound to make the lift go quicker. The doors opened and she ran out into the underground car park, and only just managed to get back in before the doors closed. The '1' took the worst hammering any lift button had ever taken.

She eventually ran past the reception desk, tossing her key-card to one of the receptionists on the way, and stood at the top of the entrance-steps, looking around for the way to the gardens. A songthrush settled on her shoulder before she could even wonder where to start looking.

"Here you are, Avie! I was worried," Linda whispered, ready to explode with happy relief.

"That was a nice man! The bread had Cinneymon all in it. You know nice types, don't you?" she said, finishing a handful and then shaking flour and red dots of cinnamon from her hair. Linda agreed, rather than change Avalon's view of the world.

An hour later the sun was filling the day with glorious warmth, and Linda had finally found the perfect hat for a fashion-conscious jet-setting faery-protecting kind of Government Representative who was heavily involved with Overseas Business. It was white with a narrow black ribbon which not only held it safely in place but also happened to make it look particularly classy. It even went with her new sunglasses, plus it was wide enough to keep the sun off at least four elephants. Well, maybe not four, but Avalon was happy with it, and that was all that mattered.

They wandered around everywhere that Linda had been the day before, keeping a very sharp look-out for Mörrah, but they found no sign of her at all. No double-shadows, no silhouettes and not even one Half-There. Both cafés gave her free coffee again, although the waiter in the one with dark red awnings insisted that she sit near the door. He served her a cappuccino in a perfect white cup and saucer, and couldn't help but notice that today she had a bird on her shoulder, surrounded by her hair. He kept an eye on them both as he served at a few other tables, and saw that she was talking to it at times. The world was going mad, and he figured the best he could do was to go along with it. He handed her another perfect white saucer with some of the previous day's cake on it for the bird, went back to his paper by the till and sighed again. It was such a shame that someone so young could be quite so unhinged, and judging by the glances she was getting off the other customers, a lot of other people had already drawn the same conclusion.

The search for Mörrah soon became a uniquely-slanted tour of Odessa courtesy of Avalon. As they drifted away from the shops in no particular hurry to go anywhere, she flew around an austere bronze bust which gazed out to sea from the top of a marble plinth. Linda played along.

"Who's this then, Avie? I bet you know all about things here?"

"No. Yes. Let's see.. this one.. this is a statue of a man.. who had no arms or legs or even a body. Just a head, that's all there ever was. Everyone felt sorry for him, so they made this statue of him and then he felt pleased. Isn't that nice? And over here.."

Avalon flew to a small metal bar poking out from an old-fashioned street light.

"..are these tall things, each with a light at the top which shine at night to keep the bad spirits away, and it works because there's hardly ever any around here, sometimes. They're a bit like stars, but they're attached to the ground by these tall things.. which real stars aren't. Real ones stay up by themselves."

Linda nodded and pretended that she had at last found out what they were for.

"And over there," Avalon continued, gesturing out to the millions of tiny points of sunlight shimmering on the sea, "..that's where stars go in the daytime. It's called the Black Sea because at night time it really is one, but in the daytime it isn't black at all - and today it couldn't be less black if it tried, could it?" she said, and waited for Linda to shake her head before flying off again.

They wandered along the endless promenade and eventually took refuge from the midday sun in the gentle shade of some pine trees, overlooking the water. A warm breeze lazily drifted by.

"Avalon, I was wondering, what do fairies do?"

"Faeries," said Avalon, trying to straighten a cluster of small white flowers which someone had trodden on. Their heads soon waved lightly in the air, and her attention moved on to a spray of clover.

"Oh, okay. What do faeries do?"

"Well I.. uh.. there's High Order ones like Rhaedlin who do loads. She's a Primary Sylph AND she's my friend. Or was, maybe. Anyway, she helps to guide the breezes everywhere, like that one just now. And that's not only what they do."

"Really? What else do they.."

"I'm not sure. But if you hear the wind anywhere, that's her. Or maybe one of the other Sylphs because they all love singing. Audlyn's my other best friend and she's an Undine, don'tcha know.. she's something to do with water and that means she's important. Ever so important."

"Any others?" Linda asked, pulling up a long blade of grass to wave through the breeze.

"Hmm.. don't know any Devas, they're all too scary. They look after nature, like bringing thought-things into the world. I don't understand that, not one bit."

Avalon paused for a moment, looking deep in concentration. She sneezed and then carried on with the list, counting on her fingers.

"Then there's Nymphs, Dryads and Oreads, Naiads, Oceanids, Nereids.. they're always fun.. Elves and Tree Spirits. Oh, and then you're down to Floranaies."

"Floor-rahn-ayz?

"Flower Faeries. I'd love to be one of those. The Devas sort out what they do and where they do it. They make sure that flowers are the right height, in bloom when they should be and uh.. make doubly sure they're pointing the right way. Very, very, very important."

"And that leaves you?"

"Not yet. There's a load of troublesome bad ones who I don't like talking about but they aren't really part of the Faery World. They're bad. Bad like a Ved'ma and some are even worse, really they are. And now that leaves me."

"Ahaa.. and that makes you.."

Avalon shrugged, and then hummed a few notes to herself while absently prodding at a stray leaf with her foot.

"Just a low faery. No capital letters or anything. When any of the others need help doing things, they call on my kind. Well, they call on the ones who are a bit higher up than me. They're proper helpers and they help whoever needs them. They're really nice. And there's Kupula! How could I nearly not mention Kupula? She's really important, higher than almost anything and she's my Matriaere, so when she needs me, I go to her. Doesn't matter what I'm doing, I always go. Well, I used to. But she never actually called me that often. Hardly ever, really. Twice, maybe.."

"A Matri-what? Who's.. Cup-yewlaa?"

"Don't you know? All faeries have a Matriaere. She keeps an eye on me, talks to me if I'm sad, important things like that. She's lovely. And she's the Goddess Of Water, and.. uh.."

Avalon quickly turned around, reappearing holding a mauve-covered book with a peculiar, slender symbol on its front. The neatly bound volume was perhaps two inches long, an inch wide and almost an inch thick, and already open to the right page. She lifted the sheet out and held it up into the sunlight.

"..she's Goddess of Water, Sorcery and Herbal Lore. That's right. I thought I'd forgotten but I hadn't really. That's everything. You know absolutely everything that there is to know, now."

The page re-attached itself, and the book closed with a small 'whumf' sound. Avalon looked very pleased with herself. She spun all the way around again, and the book was gone.

A long cruiser slowly motored past, looking very sleek and expensive. The sunlight sparkled on its chrome and all across the small peaks of water left trailing in its wake. Linda waved to the people on board, and was pleased to see that they waved back. She figured it was better for them to see her waving and being normal than to see her talking to a bird.

"What's that book, Avalon?"

"That's not a book, it's a boat. Bow-tuh. I have to go. You wait for me here, promise?"

"Promise.." she said, puzzled.

Avalon flew out from the shade of the tree and became a songthrush even to Linda, once she was a few yards away. She landed on the cruiser's white canopy and flew down inside. Shrieks and a few screams rang out, and two very flustered people ran up to join their friends on the deck, spilling their drinks on the way. Linda was more bemused than she'd ever been, which by her current standards was quite an achievement.

After a couple of minutes a man armed with a large towel went down to remove the unwelcome guest, but the songthrush hopped out of a small black window at the front, took to the air and raced all the way back to Linda. Before her claws had even touched the ground she became Avalon again, and landed with a light step as if she was walking.

"What was that for?" asked Linda.

"Just having a look," she replied, casually.

She fluttered up into the branches of the tree, and came back down again a few seconds later.

"Why did you go up there?"

"Important things. That's why."

"Like wh.."

Linda's heart jumped. For the briefest second the old lady was somewhere in the shaded depths of the other trees, laughing and looking straight at Linda. Or was she? Maybe it was just a shadow, or maybe just a nothing. Suddenly Linda felt it was time to move on, and fortunately, according to her watch, it really was time to go. Confronting the Ved'ma could wait until Avalon had told her more about who and what they were, and how on earth to deal with them. This was not something to be treated very lightly.

CHAPTER SEVEN

The Visitor

"Coo-eeee, Bel!"

Linda cringed at the reception desk. If only there had been more staff on duty, she might have been given her room's keycard straight away and been able to make her escape upstairs. Instead she tried her best to ignore the over-excited person who was bounding across the lobby with all the enthusiasm, exuberance and dignity of an eager-to-please puppy.

"Oooh Belinda! You bought a heeeyoooge hat! Good for you!"

She arrived in a bluster, and pointed backwards over her shoulder.

"Me 'n' your dad's over in the conservatory with everyone, and there's tv cameras as well.. so we need you to just hover in the background and look happy. Do you understand what you have to do? Hover in the.."

Ignoring Dee wasn't easy, not just because of her penetrating voice, but mainly because of her habit of prodding to emphasise her important words. Linda gave in, and stared at her heavily made-up face, and tried not to laugh - or even wrinkle her nose.

"..so pretend you've got like a small part in a Hollywood movie, and you're a character in the background looking happy - isn't that exciting for you? You could be Happy Girl Number One!"

Linda wished she could fly up to her balcony, like Avalon had done.

"Now don't get worried, I'll tell you where to stand 'cause there's a live interview going out in eight minutes from.. three.. two.. one.. now! How about that? Honestly I'm so glad you turned up. Faces and ages, faces and ages, superrrb! That always works so well on the screen. You're going to be in Telly Land - I bet a squillion quid all your mates back home will be dead jealous!"

Linda shivered as Dee grabbed hold of her hand. That was a definite no-no, and would need at least a couple of fours rolling later on. She was lead quickly along a wide corridor and into a large and ostentatious room. Portraits hung on the walls, a long white piano stood in the corner, and the tv cameras were pointing to the centre at some high-backed chairs and a settee, which wasn't too different to the one in her room. If anything, it looked as if it might make a better bed than her current one, and she tried to think of a good excuse to have it swapped. Five people sat in an arch spreading out either side of an interviewer, who was occupying most of the settee and shuffling his notes on a gold-trimmed table in the centre of the set. The final touches were being made to his age-defying appearance. Linda's father was part of the group, but he was being far too professional to acknowledge her presence.

"Over here a bit Bel.. no.. I said.. yes.. little more.."

Dee positioned Linda immediately behind the settee and the stars of the show, and in a straight line with the cameras. She stood next to a smartly-dressed old man, a fat woman who understood no English at all, a man who should have been driving a taxi at that moment, and one of the star-struck receptionists. Other members of the Official Government Entourage filled up the spaces in the background and tried to look relaxed and completely sober, as if they genuinely just happened to be in the room at the time. The taxi driver soon tapped his watch and insisted that he really had to leave, and handed his glass to Linda as he went past. It smelled of something very strong indeed, probably the stuff that fuelled Space Shuttle, but it looked so very elegant and civilised that Linda decided to keep hold of it.

"Trés chic," she thought, and tried to hold the long stem in the way that Princess Diana probably would have done, if she had ever found herself in a similar situation.

After a few minutes of waiting and feeling far more self-conscious than the people around her obviously were, Linda started to notice just how hot the room was becoming. There were four strong spotlights pointing right at her, and they were all switched on which was making her feel like she was in a sheik's greenhouse during a particularly sunny spell. And that wasn't too pleasant at all.

She tried taking a step or two backwards, but the Director shouted something foreign and waved his arms wildly at her, so she stayed put - right in the middle of a decorative square on the patterned carpet. This was bad. If she was going to make a move, it had to happen before all the talking started, and it had to be a proper step somewhere because small shuffling ones would mean breaking a very heavy line an awful lot of times. The only alternative would be to move just one foot onto the neighbouring square, but that was a different colour entirely. Two feet in two colours - that couldn't be good. She took a well-aimed step to the side, and messed the move up completely thanks to Dee joining in with the Director's protests. Apparently they felt she was completely fine exactly where she was, and really ought to stay there for the next nineteen minutes or so.

Despite the intense heat, Linda was glad that she was wearing her hat. The brim made it too difficult for her to even dare try and look up, which meant that she couldn't find out if she was standing directly underneath one of the five white beams which ran the entire length of the room. If she was under one of them, she would have to move straight away and that would really annoy everyone around her. And what if they asked her to explain herself, right there on live tv? The Embarrassment Factor would be off the scale.

The Director gave a short countdown and the interviewer started talking to the cameras at precisely the same moment that Linda's head decided to go for a swim, and she diagnosed herself as feeling rather woozy.

The interviewer spoke in Ukrainian to his guests, then a glamorous translator on the settee filtered it, and Mr Beaufort jumped in for the first reply. And then it all started getting confusing, because Linda couldn't figure out who was talking to who, or how anyone could make sense of anything in so much heat. They were all so lucky to be sitting down, and even more lucky not to be wearing any hats. Being seated and hatless would be incredibly perfect, and a long cold drink would make it even more incredibly perfect. Perfectly perfect, in fact. Instead, she struggled to decide how perfectly imperfect it was all becoming, and began trying to remember what exactly she was wondering about.

And then the ground started moving, as if there was an earthquake or perhaps one of those inter-planetary collisions taking place, the sort that happen every few million years. One way or another, Linda managed to stop herself from keeling over twice, but the third wave of dizziness was the big one and she vainly tried to support herself against the back of the settee. She missed it completely and sprawled in a less-than-lady-like manner between the interviewer, the translator and the Ukrainian Minister for Social Welfare. Her glass shattered on the floor and the elegant coffee-table toppled over, throwing water, glasses and important papers everywhere. The translator's wig was lost in the mêlée as Linda made her debut on the country's most respected political programme.

A few seconds later the presenter's face loomed very large in front of her as the world came back into focus. She was nearly upside down, and he was holding her head away from the righted table for some bizarre reason. The last of the waterfalls from the large jug trickled and splashed onto the floor beside her, and she could feel someone flicking water onto her face.

"Who's he.. an' why's he doin'.. that?" she wondered through a dizzy haze. And then she became vaguely aware of herself saying something to him about Dee being a moo-cow-Ved'ma, at which point the Sound Recordist and a Make-Up lady started trying to carry her away. The cameras were still rolling, and nobody seemed too impressed with her, least of all her father - he only had sixteen and a half minutes left to score as many career points as possible.

Someone gave her a glass of ice cubes with no water, and she sat on the floor in the conservatory's large doorway waiting for her legs to wake up. The interview droned on and on and on until the replacement translator drew it all to a close. That seemed to please everyone, because the replacement had known even less English than the previous translator.

The speech writer from breakfast peered down at Linda and politely suggested she might like to keep a low profile for the afternoon. She nodded, feeling rather sorry for herself. Not only had the past half hour been pretty dreadful, but to make matters worse she'd spent much of it actually sitting in a doorway. She wasn't in the room, and she wasn't out of the room, and that had to be bad, definitely bad, but this wasn't the place to start rolling dice or counteracting anything.

"You can be a real disappointment at times, you know that? I thought this trip would do you some good, but no, I was totally.."

Her father didn't even stop to be cross with her. His lecture began before he reached her and continued as he marched out of the room. Incredibly, Dee nearly tried to offer the case for the defence, but to no avail. Linda knew she was in Old Beard Face's bad books and there wasn't much anyone could do about it. For a while she felt terrible, and waited until long after his voice had faded away before standing up. She was soon ushered into the corridor by a porter so that the film crew could leave.

Linda kept her finger pressed on the '18' button until the doors of the lift had shooshed together and left everyone behind. She was back in her own world now, and that was becoming a very strange but wonderful place to be. It crossed her mind that the people of Odessa were now fully aware of her opinion of Dee, and maybe her father was too. And maybe even Dee as well, which would be a major victory in its own way and worthy of a villainous laugh. Her attempt at a Vincent Price Thriller-voice didn't turn out too well, so she tried a normal one instead - and that felt really good.

This was the first time she'd been in one of the hotel lifts properly on her own, and she took the opportunity to check how she looked in the huge wall-mirrors. She looked a bit pale, which was entirely understandable, her hat was soaked all over one side which was also completely understandable, and her jacket had worked its way further down one arm than the other. But apart from that, she wasn't too appalled with herself. The lift slowly trundled upwards, giving a slight wobble every now and then while she rummaged around in her pockets to find her sunglasses, to check that she still looked seriously cool in them.

She slipped them on and stood further back from the mirror, noticing that she was being reflected in the mirror on the other side of the compartment as well, and that the reflected reflections went on for at least another million times more. Somehow this didn't feel too good at all, but Linda couldn't find a single reason as to why. If she was contravening a rule, it would have to be an unbelievably obscure one. What possible law of balance, harmony, continuity, fortune or even luck was she crossing? Nothing sprang to mind.

She moved her head from side to side, trying to see how far away the other Lindas went on for in the two mirrors, searching for the best angle to see her identical.. whatever a million identical twins were called. No angles were much good really, so the novelty wore off very quickly. The lift trundled on, and very, very slowly passed the fifth floor. And then maybe she was wrong, maybe it was a remnant from having fainted, but she was almost sure the other Lindas briefly stopped moving. Perhaps the lag was only a billionth of a second until they caught up, but there was a definite delay.. perhaps.

And then the lift stopped.

"Oh great," she muttered to herselves and nervously looked for the emergency phone. This was nothing to panic about, and she took a deliberate moment to think of the time when something vaguely similar happened in a large store in Bournemouth. On that occasion she'd been given a voucher for the toy department afterwards, so with a bit of luck if this was to drag on for a while, she might get to keep the wall hi-fi in her room.

The steel-panelled unit with a line-drawing of a phone on its front was shut tight. There wasn't even a handle left on it, just two holes where flattened, bent screws poked out slightly. The inevitable sick feeling swept over her and she leaned with her back against the side of the compartment, knowing that this wasn't very good at all, and in fact this.. she froze in mid-thought.

The reflections had stopped following her again. This time there were no question marks and no doubts at all. They really had stopped - all of them. Linda stared across the lift at the mirror, hardly daring to blink. For a timeless moment she held onto the sliver of hope that she was wrong, and that as soon as she stopped staring at the girl staring back, the girl staring back would also stop staring back and simply do whatever Linda would do. But somewhere inside, Linda knew that she wouldn't.

She moved barely an inch to her right. The reflection kept staring back to where Linda had been. There was no new reflection, just the old one, and a million more behind it, all in the wrong place. Her skin crawled as she realised that the reflection behind her, the one she was just a panel of glass away from, would have frozen as well. She sank to the carpet and crawled over to the back wall, where she sat with her arms wrapped around her legs and buried her face in her knees. She was too scared to dare wonder what was happening.

"Linda.. Linda.. Lindaaa.."

A distant, dreamy voice echoed through the lift, travelling up and down the shaft, becoming faster and louder before focussing itself in her head. The echoes faded away and then quietly started again. It sounded like her own voice, full of insecurity and self-doubt, carrying all the same desperate longings and weaknesses. There was a certain something within it which wasn't quite right, but Linda's mind was nowhere near able to try and figure out what that was, or even why. Her name came nearer and nearer, teasing her over and over again as it grew in strength and malice. The solitary row of lights flickered at the precise moment that she forced herself to open her eyes, plunging her into impenetrable darkness. A chill fell over the compartment, intensified by the creeping icy coldness in the mocking voice.

After a lifetime the lights stuttered and came back on, bright enough to bleach everything in the lift. Suddenly Linda found herself looking up, helplessly drawn by the calling of her name, squinting through the pain until the lights dimmed to a level that barely allowed her to see across to the lift doors. Her eyes widened as every single reflected image of herself ran across the compartment, a river of blurred and very real figures running from one side to the other. Scornful laughter chased each one as they rushed in terror from something that was all around them, and all through them. As Linda sensed their fear and panic, they began growing clearer and louder, shaking the floor with their pounding steps, and within seconds they all began screaming her name, over and over into a barrage of white noise. And then acting as one, their attention turned from whatever was tormenting them, and they pointed fingers of accusation at Linda as they ran by, filling her with their fear and guilt as she buried her face again.

She tried desperately to think of her mother, but couldn't hold any thoughts in her mind. And then the distant Lindas, far off to the sides of the lift began to fade, and soon even the ones running before her grew fainter and fainter, taking their screams away into the shortest of echoes. And then they were gone, leaving nothing but heavy silence.. and the lights grew a little stronger.

The lift gave the tiniest tremor, as if it was trying to shake itself back into life, but Linda ignored it and tried to think of nothing but her mother's picture. It shook again, and felt as if it might possibly have moved a little, or maybe that was just her desperate optimism. She touched the necklace and managed to think of everything in the picture, concentrating hard to pick out as much detail as she could. And then she imagined Avalon there as well, beside them both, and started to feel safer. The lift shook with a longer pulse this time, and definitely moved up or maybe down by at least an inch or two, no doubt about that. She opened her eyes and stared at her knees for a minute, terrified that the lights might go out again.

Her heart practically stopped as she sensed that she wasn't alone anymore. Without looking, she knew there was something a few feet in front of her. Her eyes edged upwards and she felt paralysed with fear as she watched a twisting, shapeless shadow forming against the doors, slowly refining itself into a tall silhouetted figure of a woman before effortlessly floating towards her, coming away from the brushed steel. A heartless laugh rose deep within its darkness, reaching far into Linda as if it was mocking her from within her own mind. The figure changed from being slender to hunched and contorted, giving Linda a tantalising half-glimpse of the old woman. As this thought crossed her mind, the figure froze and became even more intense and dark, shaping itself back into the slender woman, and then stretching to become far too tall for the compartment. It loomed across the ceiling and leant over her, a figure made of nothing but darkness, trying to reach into every part of her life, everything she had ever done and everything she would ever do.. and then it began fading away into.. into.. nothing, or maybe into everything, because Linda couldn't tell the difference. The laughter gradually followed the darkness, and finally she was alone again. The lights flickered once more, and came back on at their usual strength.

Linda's head began clearing and she slowly stood up and steadied herself against the narrow hand rail. She felt unbelievably shaky and more than a little queasy, and wondered if she'd fainted again, because she had no idea at all why she had been down there on the floor. She fumbled with the thought that maybe it would be a pretty good idea to take things easy during the rest of the afternoon.

She wondered what floor was coming next, and looked around for a panel. The numbers across the top of the lift doors showed that she had only reached Floor 6, which immediately became Floor 7, and that felt rather comforting. If she had really fainted again, then at least it couldn't have lasted long and besides, she was very nearly halfway home. Lifts were such a tedious drag. They were even worse than a double Maths lesson.

She checked herself in one of the huge mirrors. Understandably for someone who'd definitely fainted once and perhaps even twice, she looked paler than ever. She picked her hat up off the carpet and was pleased to see that it was already nice and dry - and that meant it was made of a good material, probably. She put it on and tied the black ribbon elegantly, and couldn't help but notice that her shades looked so smoothly cool with it. They were both an exceptionally good investment of funds from her Overseas Fashion Budget, and her nation's tax-payers would thank her for it. Perhaps.

The doors made their strange shooshing sound to reveal Floor 18 and for reasons known to absolutely no-one, and least of all herself, she raced faster than a sprinter away from the lift and didn't stop until she reached her room.

CHAPTER EIGHT
Avalon's Quest

Room 18/86 was bright with afternoon sunshine, and she was glad to close the door behind her. She locked it immediately and gave it a hefty push and pull just to make sure, and stood with her back to it for a moment, hoping that nobody watched those boring political programmes, and therefore nobody would be talking about her and having a good laugh right now.

The window above the balcony door was open and had allowed Avalon into the room quite some time ago. She was over on the dressing table, dancing in the centre of the headphones again. In her deeply considered opinion, Linda's magic was huge fun. Songs and music that made the ground tremble.. all from nowhere. Avalon knew it was too much to even try and understand, but it was definitely huge fun, that was for sure.

"Had your.. dah-dah-daaah.. pictures taken?" she sang, keeping in perfect time with the fading chorus of a song.

"You could say that. Didn't go too well though.. I give up with me at times, I really do."

Linda rolled a six on the floor, and then after a few more goes she managed another one, and then landed two consecutive fours to remove Dee's hand-grabbing, and a couple of fives soon afterwards. Her Special Dice, which was only ever resorted to if she was feeling particularly out of sorts, showed the Queen Of Hearts, which was a rare achievement indeed. Avalon seemed impressed.

"What's.. dah-dah-dee.. all that.. ladada-dadaa.. dah-dooh.. for?" she asked, matching the rhythm of the next song's opening bars.

Linda wasn't entirely sure what to say. Every time she'd ever mentioned this kind of thing to anyone, the results had been a little disappointing.

"I stepped on a few lines downstairs, in the carpet. Big wide ones. Really big. And then I was actually sitting across some for ages - in a doorway, of all the wrong places.. and I might've broken a glass as well.. I'm not sure. And don't mention the lift, 'cause I was breaking lines all the way up. Well, I was maybe. Actually I'm not sure about that, either.."

Linda had a think, but couldn't quite place what she'd actually done wrong in the lift. Whatever it was, the extra couple of sixes made her feel like it didn't matter anyway.

"I suppose I just hate breaking lines.. and it's hard to say why. I feel like I'm interrupting continuity and kind of inviting bad things to happen, like it upsets nature's balance.. that sort of thing."

"Hmm-hmm.. annd?" Avalon's reply covered half a dozen notes and didn't seem too serious.

"And? I've got a million other rules that have to be followed, and I can't really explain any of them. I don't know most until something happens in the first place, so I couldn't tell you loads of them even if I wanted to. You'll think I'm some kind of loon, you really will."

"Uhuh," said Avalon, and nodded before quickly shaking her head. Linda sat down on the curved seat next to the dressing table, and leaned down to Avalon's level so that her chin was touching the table top. She watched Avalon dancing for a while, fascinated and captivated, letting her eyes follow the flurry of red pinpoints of light that trailed Avalon's hands. The song eventually faded to its end and the lights faded away with it, and Linda drifted back to what she was talking about.

"I have no idea why some things are so important to me, they just are. And I don't know why it makes sense to me that rolling some numbers or doing other things like that can make me feel better.. it just does. And different things work for different situations, depending on what I feel like I need to do. How come I do that?"

Linda was talking as much to herself as she was to Avalon, and wasn't hoping for an answer. That was fortunate, because Avalon didn't look as if she could give one anyway. She was too busy making dozens and dozens of different coloured stars appear in the air around her, in perfect time to the next track. Either certain words or certain notes determined the colours, and Linda couldn't quite decide which.

"And then even trivial things have to be right, like things have to match, or they have to be level or line up or whatever, or else I just go nuts. Or mits, as you'd probably say. It drives everybody round the twist, but I know they're all important things. Well, they are at the time, anyway. I expect you think I'm crazy? Everyone else does."

Avalon looked as if she was trying to answer, but seemed incapable of speech. The latest song appeared to have taken her over completely.

"Try turning the cd off before you speak, it might be easier like that?" suggested Linda.

Avalon gave the volume control a nudge with her foot and the music dropped away a little.

"Ooh that's better.. got my head back now. Stuff like the role of a dice is ever so important to you?" she said.

"Really important. The roll can mean a huge lot, because it's.."

"No, the role, not the roll. I think that.. maybe that's your Special. My friend Fhienelle reads pollen, and she's really good at it. And Auroria interprets clouds ever so well. But you sense harmonies around you. I can tell. So that's your Special, your Essence."

Avalon took on a very serious expression, as if she was explaining the meaning of life. She even turned the music down a little more, and very nearly stopped dancing.

"I think everyone has a Special, which is a something that nobody else can do. Or if someone else can do it, they do it a bit differently, because no-one's quite the same. And your Special is quite a lot of things. You've always nearly seen my kind, haven't you? And you could even talk to Mörrah, and get her annoyed!" she giggled, and stepped back up onto the cd player. Linda shivered at Mörrah's name, but Avalon carried on talking before it could bother her.

"And all that stuff about natural harmony and balance? That's part of what makes you special. Maybe some would say you've got less control of yourself than a leaf in a tornado, or maybe you're crazier than Crazy Gubbly, the craziest Gnome in all of Mudbump - and believe me, that is really saying something because Mudbump's where ALL the crazy Gnomes go. And maybe some would see you and say, 'Look there's Linda and she's so crazy mad crazy crazy crazy crazycrazycrazy.. "

"I get the idea, Avie.."

"..but not me. I don't say that at all, not even for a moment. I say you're Linda, you're special, and that's you," she concluded, and pointed up to her.

"At least I know," said Linda, shocked that Avalon hadn't decided to fly away somewhere far off.

"Yup. And at least you're harmless, unlike Fhienelle, but I'm not supposed talk about that.."

"I see. And what's your Special? If we've all got a something, what's yours?" Linda said with a grin.

Avalon turned the music back up, and flew a few feet into the air.

"Back Circles. It's not much, but hardly anyone can do these.. you watch me now?"

Her wings became a blur as she moved backwards in a large and hard-fought arc, kicking her legs until she reached the highest point and then gliding back down to the table top, completing the circle. She breathed heavily and looked very pleased with herself. Linda applauded.

"..and even fewer can do two!" gasped Avalon between breaths, and took off again.

"It's okay, you don't have to.." began Linda, but it was too late. She had already started the arduous upward flight, and put everything she had into reaching the peak. And then she stopped to catch her breath, which was a very bad idea. She dropped like a stone, landing on one of the settee's stray cushions with a giggle.

"See, my Special's one, not two.."

One phone call and a few songs later, Room Service delivered two huge silver trays overloaded with sandwiches, salads, Coke, tea, coffee, cakes, a plate of hazelnut biscuits and four silver bowls of hazelnuts. Any more bowls would take a day or two to organise, according to the maid. Linda and Avalon made the most of it all on the balcony, picking and choosing the best bits according to Avalon's peculiar knowledge of healthy food. They watched the busy street-life far below them, until the afternoon sunshine became too intense. They went back inside and Linda was pleased to notice how good she felt for having told Avalon about her view of life.

She changed the cd in the wall hi-fi and sat on the floor by the bed so that she could be at the same height as Avalon, who was sitting on the edge and pulling out long cotton fibres from the bedspread. Incredibly, she was able to put them back in as easily as she'd drawn them out.

"You didn't really tell me what you do, Avalon. And that vanishing book of yours, as well - what is it?"

"That's my Faery Journal, and it's full of everything. It's got my name on the front, all shiny. And I do all kinds of things. Things things. I made a mess of a rainbow once.. so they got me to draw them instead, for reference. I draw them in my Journal, but I don't always know where they're going to appear so I miss them quite often, but no-one's ever minded. And I have a really important job which is checking the leaves on trees."

"Checking the.."

"Uhuh. I make sure they've got enough. That was my idea. A big tree can take a whole morning to check properly. So far, every single tree's been alright. Isn't that good? But they change all the time and that means I get so busy."

"Well, who wouldn't? That'd take me forever. Have you been doing that.. very long?" she said, draining her Coke and rattling the ice cubes left in her tall glass before standing it on the bed. Avalon sat close to it and seemed to like its coolness.

"No, not really. Umm.. nine Fourth Degree Eclipses. In my years, that makes me just over 4. But in your years, I'm 167. And a half, probably. See, you have leap years and we don't, and that makes it complicated."

"Wow, you must be so good at drawing by now.. and even better at counting leaves?"

"I am. And I look for The Stone when I'm not doing all that," she said, pulling a face at her reflections in the glass and the ice cubes.

"The stone?"

"You must know about The Stone? Everybody.. no, actually there's hardly anybody who knows about it. I'm not really supposed to tell that."

For a split second, Avalon looked as if she was in a quandary - but it didn't last long and she quickly carried on regardless.

"Many, many, many of your years ago, when I.. when the rainbow went wrong, Kupula stopped me being in too much trouble by promising the High Council Of Flavll.. Flegll.. umm.. important ones in big chairs.. that I wouldn't help with any more rainbows because I'd be much too busy with my Important New Quest And Other Important Responsibilities."

"That sounds very official," said Linda, emphasising the 'very'.

"Yes, and it meant I had to create Historical Rainbow Files, and search for The Stone Of Odessa. Everyone found that really funny, but there's nothing wrong with making Rainbow Files. It was a new thing, just for me. Kupula said I was more suited to that, because I'm important. And then I said I could count leaves as well, and that impressed them, I think. Then I wasn't in trouble anymore."

"Well of course not - you're far too important. And I don't find it funny for a minute. So what's the big deal about that stone then?"

"Well.." Avalon replied, distracted for a moment as she wiped a hand through the condensation on the side of the glass. She held her arm high above her head to let a big, cool drop roll down to her neck. That made her giggle, so she did it again with the other arm.

"Ahh, that is SO much better.." she said, before shaking herself dry. "Anyway, your kind all think that The Stone's a big myth, and also my kind think so too, actually, but it isn't a myth. It's real, and I thought I knew where it was, but it wasn't there. So I was waiting for night time so I could go home and tell Kupula, but that horrid Ved'ma saw me and pretended that she was Kupula and asked me all about it and then she Cursed me into the doll to be mean. They do that," she added, furrowing her brow.

"That is mean. And the stone?"

Avalon leaned into Linda's glass and picked up the top ice cube, and held it for just long enough to have a look at Linda through it. Then she squealed and dropped it back into the glass, shaking her hands until the feeling came back. She shivered, gave the ice a hard glare and then fluttered a few inches away.

"What about The Stone?" she asked, innocently.

"You were telling me about it,"

"Was I? Oh.. yes, I was. Rumours, stories, my bit.. that's right.." she nodded, and looked up at Linda as if there was no more to say.

"And the thing it does is.." said Linda, patiently.

"Ohh.. and you know what The Stone does? It allows the strongest desires of certain Ground Crawlers.."

"Maybe 'people's a nicer word?"

"Yes.. it allows the strongest desires of certain Peoples to become real, and they're called Gifted Ones, and how much The Stone will do depends on who's trying to use it. It won't do the little stuff like 'I want some Hazelymits' - it only does the really big stuff, like 'turn the world into a big Hazelymit'."

Avalon giggled at the thought of such awesome power.

"Kupula says if it's really real then it might get into the wrong hands and could cause big trouble for everyone, and then she said that maybe the reason no-one believes it's real is because there's hardly ever been anyone who can do anything with it? Centuries of nothing, but then one day everything might be awful. That would be bad, wouldn't it?"

"Well of course.." said Linda, in an understanding tone.

"And Kupula wanted me to find it in case it's not just a myth, and then take it home to her in Hesperides where it can be kept safely away from everyone. So I've been looking everywhere. 163 of your years and.. two months. But even if I found it, I can't really take it back now, can I?" she said, patting her knees and looking troubled. She noticed her reflection in the glass and flew closer to see just how troubled she was looking. She pointed at her reflected face for Linda to see as well.

"Maybe that would change when you find it, if it's so powerful? Do you know where it is?"

Avalon took a while to answer. She was half in the glass, upside down and trying reach in far enough to pick up another ice cube.

"No. But I do know where it isn't," she said in a muffled voice. The ice had melted too much so she wriggled back out and shook off the water droplets,

"You know where it.. isn't?" Linda repeated.

"Uhuh.. everywhere it isn't," Avalon replied, slightly hesitantly. Linda could see she was proud of her role in life, but there was more than a hint of vulnerability in her voice so some friendly reassurance was called for.

"Well," said Linda, "..that's a good way of doing it. If you find out enough places where the Stone isn't, then sooner or later.."

"..I'll be left with where it is! You're clever like me!" she exclaimed, and turned around to bring out her Faery Journal. She proudly opened it to the first page, which showed a strange but carefully rendered outline of a dog, or perhaps a cat. It might even have been a sick horse. There was an X in the corner.

"This was a dog I met who was sort of grey. He did not have The Stone," she said articulately, and turned the page. It showed a lop-sided square, with an X above it.

"This was a box. The Stone was not in there. Or under it, or by the sides. I checked all round."

She turned to the next page, and giggled. Linda had no idea what it was a picture of.

"This was a flower-holder thing on a shelf in a house. The Stone was not in this, but I was for a while. This next one is the house from a long distance away, so it's quite small.."

Linda wondered how long this would go on for.

"Errr, Avie, how many of these drawings do you have?"

"How many? Loads and.. I've never counted. I'll show you."

The book turned into a blur as Avalon removed sheet after sheet, her arms moving faster and faster as she created a snowstorm of white pages across the room. Within minutes an avalanche slid down from the side of the bed, covering Linda and revealing Avalon, who carefully placed the final picture next to its other half. She held a drawing of the cruiser for Linda to see, and looked very pleased with herself.

"849,729 places where it isn't, including the boat this morning. Where've you gone?"

"Mmmmf.. down here.. I'm under the.. can't move.."

"Oh, sorry.."

Avalon clicked her fingers a few times and the pages raced back into the Journal, clearing the room within seconds.

"You're very thorough aren't you? That's really good.." said Linda, relieved to be able to see daylight again.

"I listen to People too. They never mention The Stone at all, that's how I know these ones don't know anything.. I've put a tick by the ones who are still alive.. your kind don't last long, do they? Even the old ones don't get all that old."

Avalon made her Journal appear again, and Linda didn't fancy becoming buried once more.

"Hold on.. hold on.. before you do that blizzard-thing again, have you ever heard it actually mentioned by anyone?"

"Yes! That's how I know it's also not in the Ilinsky Cathedral. I couldn't draw that because it was too big to fit on the pages, even when I was a long way away. The stone in there isn't the real one!"

"There's a fake?"

"Yup, it's a pretendy one. I got tired drawing things after the big war because everything was all broken. So I spent ages being Not Me's and went eavesdropping everywhere instead. It's not easy you know.. and there's so many places to be and I only got around to listening in the Cathedral a few moons ago. Anyway, I went in there because it was raining outside. That's where I drew the puddle, remember that picture? And I went into the rooms hardly anyone goes to and heard Church People and Government People whispering about The Stone, and I got so excited.. I changed back to Me Me and couldn't write quick enough and it sounded really important, so I concentrated hard to remember everything and then write down what I could. You want to hear it?"

Before Linda could even think 'yes', Avalon had opened it at a golden cord, halfway through.

"The Church wants The Stone, the Government wants The Stone, and so do I want The Stone," she said, turning the pages after every third or fourth word.

"So the Church keeps it in a vault under the Cathedral, and the Government knows it's there but they don't say they know it. They both want to find someone who can use it, and then they'll have so much power they won't know what to do with it all. So the Church has had it for centuries and centuries but pretend they don't have it, and the Government watches them and pretends they're not watching them. And the Government also pretend they don't even know the Church has got it."

"That's amazing! So it is real!"

Avalon wagged her finger up at Linda.

"No. It's a pretendy one.. you have to try and keep up with me, you really do."

Linda nodded, rather than spoil Avalon's moment. But there was something she wasn't quite sure about.

"So.. does the Church think that the Government know they're bluffing, or do they think that the Government suspect that they don't know the fake one isn't, in fact, not the real one?"

Avalon stared blankly at Linda for a moment and then toppled over backwards. She shook her head a few times, fluttered her wings until she was standing up again, and ignored the question completely. She wiped some of the condensation from the side of Linda's glass, and dabbed her face with it until she could think straight again.

"When they finished their talking, I waited and changed to a fly, then looked around for ages to find the vault they were talking about, but it's not a vault - it's like a small Cathedral under the ground. A really small one. And I took a look, but that Stone is just glass with blueness painted on the back, and it's not special at all, and tastes like Beetles - yuk. And there's made up curses written all over the place, and hexes that mean nothing as well! The Church People know it's just glass, but the Government don't. Or maybe they do and they don't say. Aw, now my head's gone all hurty."

Linda was impressed.

"Avalon, you are so much better than you think! You've done so well, haven't you? Now, did the Church people ever say where the real one might be? You don't have to tell me, if your brain's overheating.. d'you fancy an icecube?"

Avalon touched her head, nervously.

"Noo.. m'okay, I think. Nobody mentioned where they keep the real one. Then when I was waiting for night to fall so that I could go back and tell Kupula that The Stone's real, I met Mörrha and she tricked me. And then everywhere was dark for ages and I felt ever so sick, and then there was you, and now I'm here. And there's you looking at me. Your left eye's a blue one, and your other one's.."

"..a brown one, I know. It's been pointed out for most of my life. I'm going to get a coloured contact lens one day and be normal."

"Very pretty. And lucky, very lucky. See mine? Boring old silvery ones."

Linda's favourite track on the cd started playing, and Avalon turned it up and took off for some serious dancing. Linda talked up to her while she glided around the small chandelier, playing crystal-clear notes as she touched each glass droplet.

"So we know it's real.. so where would we start looking.. where do we start? Hmm. If it's been here for ages then it might have been mentioned in the town's history and archive stuff. Is there a library here, Avie? A big place full of books? I can't think of anywhere better to start.. what do you reckon?"

Avalon's reply was heavily influenced by the chorus of Waterloo, but fortunately it didn't really matter. Linda had a plan in her mind, and that felt pretty good. She shuffled through her bedside drawer and held up a new cd.

"You haven't heard anything till you've heard this in Swedish, you know, Avie! Get ready.."

CHAPTER NINE
Underground

The sun was lost somewhere behind the white sky, which gave Linda another really good reason to leave her hat behind. Her main reason for not wearing it was that she didn't want to risk being recognised by anyone as being the crazy girl off the tv, but blaming the weather was far easier than admitting that to herself. They made their way through the busy streets and soon arrived in the picturesque grounds of the vast Odessa Library, and hurried past the oddly sinister bronze statues of people sitting on benches which lined either side of the gravel path.

Linda would have been tempted to take a good look at them all, had the building's facade not been so overpowering. Six huge white columns ran from one side to the other, shielding a series of tall windows and the commanding main entrance. Avalon wasn't too enthusiastic about going in, and gave Linda's ear a slight tug.

"This won't be much help, you know. I mean, the first one was good, but most of it burned down - which wasn't entirely my fault, if you think about it. Then I had to wait ages for them to build this one, and then when it opened there was hardly anything in it.. and everyone knew that so they all stayed away, too."

"Are you sure they'd finished building it?"

"Yes. No. Well, the doors were open.. actually they hadn't even put them in. Just big holes in the wall, that's all. And one or two of these walls weren't there.. and most of the roof wasn't on either.. no windows at all.. not much of a book place, really."

Linda decided against taking the conversation any further, and stopped by one of the end columns to make sure Avalon was safely on her shoulder and hidden by her hair. She followed the arrows leading past the security sensors, and stared in awe at the size of the interior. Trying to search for anything here could take at least a billion years. She drifted into the first aisle which didn't have anyone else in it, and tried hard to look like a student doing research. She picked the first book that came to hand and sat down over by the window to whisper her Significant Plan to Avalon, while studiously turning the book's pages.

"What we need is the history of Odessa, Avie, rather than looking for a book about the Stone."

"Why?" she asked, braiding a long and narrow length of hair from just in front of Linda's left ear, and sealing it with a small dot of silver light. Now she had something easy to hold onto, and gave it a good tug to check it was safe.

"Ow. Well, if the Stone's been kept by the Church for heaven knows how long, it's probably been hushed up for ages - and hushed up really well, and that's why nobody knows about it. But there might have been a time when people did know, and maybe wondered what it was. How's that sound?"

"Okay.."

"So I'll wander around, and you keep an eye out for the section on Ancient Tales or Oldie Aged History or that kind of thing, okay?"

"Me?"

"Uhuh. I can't speak this language, can I?"

Avalon liked the plan, but felt the time wasn't quite right to improve on it. She looked over at the man watching them.

Mr Bagritsky, a veteran teacher at the School Of Music, leaned on his stick and paused for a moment. He glanced over at the strange girl seated in the Under 5's Learning section. At first he thought she was talking to herself, but then he noticed the songthrush on her shoulder, tangled up in her hair. The girl looked as if she was genuinely trying to teach it to read.. or maybe she was telling it a story? He sighed and wondered how the youth of today could ever have gone so wayward and astray, and began seriously pondering retirement before the start of the next term.

Linda put the book back, moved her cool shades up to the top of her head and smiled as she passed the elderly gentleman. For the next half an hour she walked up and down dozens and dozens of aisles stacked full of meaningless books. Her feet were beginning to ache, everybody knew her trainers squeaked on the varnished floor, and even worse, she'd lost track of whether she was on the left side of the aisle to balance the previous right side, or the other way around. Or maybe she was in a second consecutive left-aisle, which meant that she'd missed a right one, which meant she ought to roll a two and then a..

"Avie, have you seen anything useful yet?" she breathed, instead.

"Maybe. What were we looking for, again?"

"Regional History, or something like that. Old stuff," she said, hiding her despair.

"Oh, that's way back. We passed it ages ago. Back by the pretend plant and the wobbly table."

Linda sighed, and made her way back to the third aisle that they had passed. The end section didn't hold many books, just two narrow shelves with the books lying flat. They weren't in a good enough condition to stand up, which was due to a lack of use rather than too much use. She chose the large one that looked particularly old and opened it up. A drawing of a fat person with a big smile and an X above his head took up most of the first page, in a style which was unmistakeable.

"Avie.." she hummed, tapping the picture.

"This book's from the Old Library! See here? I've checked it already.. oh, I see what you mean. He's supposed to be in my Journal. Naughty round Person. I must have been so tired when I was there.."

Avalon opened her Journal to a blank page and pointed it at the drawing. The lines seemed to un-draw themselves and instantly re-appear in her book. She gave it an extra X, and then pointed down to the next row of worn books.

"Seen them, too. That was ages ago."

"Have you already been through all of this lot?"

"Yup. And The Stone isn't in any of them."

"Not one?"

"Nope. Everyone would know about it if it was here, wouldn't they? They'd all be coming for a look."

"Hold on.. did you actually read the pages of all these books, or did you just see if the actual Stone was wedged inside?"

"I was tired.." she shrugged, and took on an embarrassed pink glow.

"Aha, I think we have a lot to get through.. or we would if I had a clue about Russian or whatever. Can you make many of these out?"

Linda stood close to hide her while Avalon moved from one title to the next, running her hands over the words on the spines and covers, humming to herself.

"Hmm.. these only tell stories from years beginning with 17 and 18 and 19. That's not good is it? We need the older ones, the really old ones. They don't keep those ones out here."

Avalon dropped down to just above Linda's ankle, becoming a bird even to her eyes. She hopped along the shiny wooden tiles and stopped with her wings slightly raised. Linda hurried over, intending to block anyone's view, but Avalon had already flown back up into her hair. She tugged Linda's braid with excitement.

"That smell.. oldness.. in the air, on the currents. The Old Library had it, and this one does too. They look after the old books, in a place where People can't damage them. Don't know where, though."

"Maybe if we had a really old book to return, and I mean a reeeally old book published by Not You, they might take us through to them? We'd get into wherever the room is, and you could see if there's something important there, and find out.."

Linda jumped as a hard-faced woman shushed and tutted loudly, pointing to a sign which was undoubtedly the Russian for 'This Is A Library, Linda - Shut Up!'

It was time for a tactical retreat, and a new plan.

Outside, Linda sat behind a wide oak tree in the park beside the Library. She leaned forwards to let her hair form a curtain around Avalon, who tried out a few Literary Not Me's. Trying to become a living creature had always been a bit too demanding for her because there was so much that she had to get right, but a large book wasn't difficult at all, and Avalon seemed to be enjoying herself. As long as she didn't giggle too much, this might work. Linda suggested a few final artistic touches.

"Hmm.. a little more scuffed.. that's good.. dustier.. much more dust.. how about a gold clasp? And more gold trim.. some weird text in big letters.. and curled up corners.. bumpy beige pages. Perfect!"

Linda held the book, expecting to feel its hard sides and back, but instead she felt the feathery warmth of Avalon lost somewhere within it, and all around it. She felt as if she had taken the book from a dream, and was only allowed to hold onto it for as long as.. as long as.. as long as she didn't think too much about what she was doing.

She walked back up the Library steps with her heart in her mouth, holding a book almost twice the size of a telephone directory. To those who could see it, it was in a very sorry state and desperately needed renovating. The librarian behind the desk stopped typing at her computer, pushed her angular glasses back up her nose and eyed the strange girl suspiciously. Linda winced as if the huge volume in her arms weighed a ton, rather than being as light as a feather.

"Hello? Ooh dear, so heavy.. I'm Linda M Beaufort, here in Odessa with the British Government on Official Government

Business, overseas. I bring you an old Ukrainian book, from the vaults of The Royal Family themselves - yes, it's for you! Where can I put it?" she said, smiling and holding eye contact just like her father would do whenever he was trying to be sincerely convincing.

The librarian looked stern and puzzled, and gestured in a way that suggested she didn't quite understand what on earth Linda was doing there. The woman's hand hovered over the phone, and her finger was poised next to a white button on its touch-pad. She looked at Linda, and pointed back towards the entrance. This was going to be hard work, and looked as if it was about to become even harder. Another tactical retreat was called for, and an even better plan.

Back at the oak tree, Linda thought hard for an improved way to get in. She watched Avalon glide just above the tips of the grass, making small crop circles with her feet, and discretely applauded her every now and then for the particularly intricate ones. Once Avalon had brushed the grass back to its normal haphazard state for the tenth time, Linda had decided upon a plan of fool-proof simplicity which carried no risks at all, and definitely didn't involve potentially life-threatening situations with evil librarians.

"Avie, I have a plan.. it's time for a different approach. We follow your nose. I'll carry you around out here and you try to get a whiff of that old smell."

"Okay. Why?" she said, distracted by a ladybird on Linda's knee.

"Because if we find out roughly where the room is, we might be able to get in ourselves. It could be really easy, but even if it isn't, you could change back to Birdy You and fly there. How about that? Or we might even find someone who speaks English and lets us in!"

Avalon was happy with that and, for a while at least, so was Linda. They wandered around the side of the building, pausing when the wind was going the wrong way, all the time hoping that not too many people would notice them. The building's high-sides looked as if they could carry on forever, but midway along, the trees and grass came to a halt and a set of imposing tall steel gates took over. This had to be a staff-only section, and wasn't intended for just anyone. The only people who could get through here were people who had special keys or special permission - or had climbed up and down the side of St Catherine's Dorm on many occasions.

The fence proved to be no trouble at all, and Linda dropped down into a wide yard with a few cars parked in it. It only lead around to the rear of the Library, via a few more padlocked security gates, but that was okay. There were metal staircases here, and the smell had become a lot stronger. Avalon transformed herself into the ancient book again, and Linda carried on innocently ambling past the building, convinced she looked exactly like a Visiting Dignitary with a Royal Book to return.

"Eyh!"

A security guard armed with a mug of tea called out to them, and marched briskly over from a small room. Linda froze, and wished that she knew a few words of Russian. He peered down at her and fired off a whole series of questions, all of which sounded terribly important. Avalon offered a translation for her.

"He says you appear to have a very old book which is probably very expensive, and those sort aren't for borrowing. Oh, and you're in a Restricted Area. He's good, isn't he?"

Linda nodded, and smiled up at him. She tried to gesture with her chin towards her official-yet-almost-meaningless Identity Tag hanging around her neck. It was bunched up with part of her jacket and a stray length of troublesome hair.

"British Government.. Parleee-ahment," she said a few times, while nodding towards the Library.

The guard scrutinised her tag, and decided that the girl in mid-sneeze in the picture was very likely the same one who was holding the book. He said nothing, but seemed satisfied that she wasn't a terrorist and lead her back inside.

The librarian didn't look too surprised to see her again. She pushed her glasses back up her nose, switched the computer off and waved her biro in Linda's general direction.

"This.. eh.. your book? How?" she said, with a disapproving look.

"British Governn-ment, we-are-guests-of-your-town! See? That's me," Linda replied, and waggled her chin again towards her Identity Card. The guard nodded his agreement to the woman, who raised her eyebrows and sighed. She exchanged a few words with the guard who grunted and wandered off, and then she gestured for Linda to follow her. Avalon whispered the edited highlights as they walked through the Library.

"Gorislava says I'm probably another useless book being returned from a forgotten old back-room.. a pathetic gesture of goodwill.. she says you're only here because I'm in too bad a condition to show off anymore.. she doesn't blame you.. just your country and everyone who's in it. And she says Britain probably shouldn't have had it in the first place.. and she doesn't get paid enough.. and her telly doesn't work. That old smell is getting much stronger here, you know."

"Well that's good!" Linda replied, without thinking.

Gorislava looked around, wondering why the foreign girl had spoken. She was an odd child, that was for sure. Linda, however, felt incredibly important and just knew that everyone else in the Library was looking at her being so incredibly important.

They went through some creaky double doors leading to a series of brightly lit corridors, and stopped at the grey door at the end. A few flakes of paintwork dropped off as she pushed it open. Inside lay a series of benches similar in style to the Chemistry labs back at school. Pages and pages were spread out under magnifying lenses and special purple lights, in between large measuring jars full of liquids which gave the room a sharp smell of antiseptic and strange chemicals. This wasn't quite what Linda had in mind and she anxiously wondered what to do next, while Gorislava filled in a form on the front desk.

"Eww, hurts my nose.. keep walking.." whined Avalon as Linda drifted towards the back of the laboratory. Gorislava wasn't too pleased about that, and called something out to her which Avalon refused to translate.

"That old smell's here again and it's getting really strong.."

"..just about here, by any chance?" finished Linda. She was standing before a huge rack of burnt and withered old books, in various states of disrepair.

Gorislava soon joined her, not cross and perhaps even a little pleased that Linda was so obviously interested in the restoration of old works. She pointed out a few yellowed volumes and mentioned some very long names which might have been authors or perhaps titles, and went to take Linda's book. That was a bad idea.

Avalon squealed and immediately turned into a songthrush, and flew up to the highest rack where she perched on the burnt end of something potentially famous. Gorislava turned to Linda with a look of horror on her face, and Linda raised her eyebrows as high as possible and dropped her jaw dramatically to try and give the impression of being equally shocked. Gorislava fainted before she could say anything, and fell with all the grace of a sack of potatoes.

"Aw.." Linda moaned, "..I wasted my all time best-ever Stunned Expression on her.. I bet she won't even remember it."

Avalon turned into a faery again and settled back on her shoulder, and they both looked down at the woman on the floor.

"Is she dead? Have you killed her - already?" whispered Avalon.

"No, she's just fainted. You know, this is a right old day for doing that.." sighed Linda, feeling a pang of sympathy.

Suddenly, Avalon caught a strong scent and began following its trail towards the door nearest the book rack. She held back a sneeze, and pointed.

"This one. This is the really old smell. Can't you smell it at all? It's really getting.. getting.. ahhh.. ahhh.."

She just about managed to hold that sneeze as well, but failed completely with the next and sent herself somersaulting backwards.

Gorislava was still as white as a sheet and looked as if she was going to be out for a very long count, so Linda dared herself to take the bunch of keys from the nail by the door. The third key did the trick, and she carefully hung them back up as the door swung open. Whatever lay beyond was lost in darkness. She couldn't see anything beyond the first few steps down, and the light switch didn't do anything - even after the twentieth flick. And then it didn't even make a clicking noise for the last six or seven attempts. She gave it an extra flick to make sure it ended on an even number.

Avalon wasn't at all nervous, and darted off ahead, following her nose. Her glow didn't make too much difference to the inky blackness, but there was no way Linda was going to take a single step in there without being right next to her. She called her back, and Avalon returned immediately to hold the shining end of Linda's braid, and lead the way by hovering a couple of feet ahead.

Linda closed the door, careful not to let it click in case it locked itself - she'd had trouble like that before in a broom cupboard once. The first step creaked as if they were walking into a horror movie, and the remaining thirty steps became increasingly worse before Linda reached the uneven brickwork of the floor. Avalon was glowing more brightly than ever, and dropped the braid. She dodged in every direction as she hunted around for more scent-trails to follow, and then she gave up for a moment, to check what she was supposed to be doing.

"Well.." whispered Linda, trying to think of something really clever, "..we could have a really good wander around here, right, and then.. find all the old books and take them somewhere better so you can have a proper look at them. But there is a tiny problem with that."

"Is there?"

"Yup. We might need Gorislava to be out cold for at least three months. So, I think we just have a quick look now, and keep coming back again with another Not You Book until we find something.."

She stopped in mid-sentence. Gorislava's voice pierced the darkness, and Linda's heart jumped a mile. This was going to be so difficult to explain. She looked up towards the dark figure at the top of the stairs and prayed that the shadows down at floor-level were at least ten shades blacker than black.

"Oops. What do we do Lindy? She wants to know if you're down here.. but she doesn't think you are.. because.. no-one would ever be that stupid."

"Uhh.. let me think.." she breathed.

Linda was in a dilemma. On the one hand, she knew there was a very good chance she wasn't supposed to be this far off the tourist track and could therefore be in more hot water than the world's largest teabag - and that didn't appeal at all. But on the other hand, the prospect of being locked in a place that was spooky, pitch black and a bit chilly also didn't appeal very much.

The door above closed with a firm slam, followed by harsh rattling sounds from the lock. It soon fell quiet, and Linda stared up at the small ray of light filtering through the keyhole.

"T'riffic.." she whispered into the darkness, and waited for a few seconds, motionless. Nobody jumped out and grabbed her, nothing made scuffling noises and there weren't any footsteps echoing from anywhere. Despite all of that, she still felt awful.

"Have you finished thinking yet?" asked Avalon, as if absolutely nothing was wrong.

"Finished? I wish I'd started.. I'm really hoping this leads out onto our floor at the hotel.. really, really hoping."

As they wandered along, Linda's eyes grew accustomed to the darkness and courtesy of the pure light from Avalon's glow she managed to see that they were in an underground corridor, which was probably a remnant from the Old Library - and maybe even the buildings before that. The walls were made of thousands and thousands of narrow bricks, layered in crooked rows which were almost ready to collapse. She looked up at the bowing wooden beams which ran across the ceiling every few feet, noticing that a disturbing number of them seemed to have decayed away completely. Linda stopped looking at them.

"I wonder what all these wonky doors are for?" she asked aloud, not really hoping for an answer. Avalon took a closer look at each one, running her hands over the wooden panels and steel plates. She morphed into a fly, plunging the corridor into darkness momentarily, and then re-appeared brightly again as herself and rubbing her head.

"What happened there, Avie? Are you okay?"

"Uhh.. wanted to look inside, and a Not Me fly would fit through the keyhole."

"And you were too big?"

"Don't know. Missed the keyhole 'cause everywhere went dark.."

Linda decided to hold back on any more questions, and simply followed Avalon. A door was missing from one of the rooms, and after a quick look around inside, Avalon came back with the news that it wasn't full of torture equipment, strange medical experiments or scary things that hate daylight. It was full of nothing, except for a few broken bottles, old metal pipes covered in rust, and a twisted old coat stand. And not The Stone. That was good to know, and Linda's stress levels dropped all the way down to merely ludicrously high. A few minutes later, Avalon spun herself into a blur of excitement.

"This is it! Really strong now, really clear. It's been so long since.. well, wherever it was before. Long time ago."

"You remember smells?"

"Not all of them, mainly this one, because.."

She closed her eyes and sneezed two huge sneezes, sending herself backwards and turning her light out. The corridor went completely black for a few seconds, until she started glowing again. She gave herself a good shake, and flew back to Linda.

"Ugh, I did that last time.." she remembered.

Linda was starting to sense the musty oldness in the air, and began wondering how long it might have been since anyone had last been down there. Hopefully it had been a very long time, which would mean there were almost certainly no freaky deviants ahead, skulking and lurking around, waiting to jump out at her.

The corridor grew narrower and lower, and the doors that had been lining either side grew further apart, and their style changed to match the aged, older brickwork. Soon the ceiling had become almost as uneven as the floor, and there seemed to be more bricks lying on the ground than actually in the walls. This wasn't very good, Linda thought, and it wasn't helped by Avalon sneezing herself into darkness every few steps.

"Here we are! Beyond this.. ahh.. ahh.. CHOOO!"

"Oh no," groaned Linda, once the light had returned.

The corridor ended with a series of long steps leading down into a colder and far more damp kind of darkness. Cracks and indentations had formed in their stonework over time, and Linda shivered with each unpredictable footstep. She carefully edged her way down them until the wall, ceiling, rocks and general mess had practically merged into one. Nothing but a bank of rubble lay ahead, steeply reaching up to the ceiling.

Avalon soon found a gap at the top, and Linda started crawling her way up towards it. She didn't want to, but Avalon had already disappeared into it, and the alternative was too awful to think about. The tunnel was only a few yards long, but Linda had visions of being stuck there for ever, starving and scared, and waiting for something hideous to come along and make life even worse. She picked and crawled her way over the piles of bricks and earth, and looked ahead to where Avalon was hovering.

"How much further.. WOAH!"

She answered her own question, and rolled down a debris-strewn slope to arrive with a bump at the foot of an arched wooden door. The clouds of dust gradually settled again, and Linda sat back to try and figure out if she'd damaged either herself or the door. Nothing hurt too much, which was a relief, and the door's broad wooden panels and heavy iron slats looked completely unaffected - which was hardly surprising. It was enormous. If the whole of the Ukrainian region was ever struck by the world's most violent earthquake, this mighty door would easily be the one thing left standing.

Avalon hovered around its bizarre medieval locking mechanism, poking the black metal and sending heavy clusters of rust tumbling to the ground. She scratched her head, and began chanting strange rhymes while making looped hand movements above the keyhole.

"Is that working?" whispered Linda, rather impressed.

"No.." she replied, drifting away briefly.

She put her entire arm inside the lock, grimaced and made small clattering noises inside for a while. Her arm came out black, and dripped a thick blob of toffee-like goo all the way down to the floor.

It took three of her biggest shakes to get rid of it all.

"Can I do anything?" asked Linda, brightly.

"Hmm.." she pondered, tapping her chin, "..try rolling a five."

"Really? That's brilliant because.."

Linda explained her theory about the number five while shuffling around for her Underground Dice. She rolled it against the door while Avalon flew alongside, waving her arms. A five showed up on the third attempt, and they both looked expectantly at the door. It didn't move. Linda waited for a very long minute.

"Should something have happened by now, Avie?"

"Nope. I just wanted you to feel like you were helping, that's all. I've got one idea left, though."

She hovered back up near the lock, carefully chose a spot near the battered head of a huge iron nail, gave it a pathetic kick and then quickly backed away a few inches. Two or three seconds later the door shook as if it had been hit by an express train, and an explosion of dust billowed out from under its base. Rivers of brickdust cascaded down from the ceiling as the lock gave a huge echoing thunk, and the door scraped partially open.

"Ta-daaa!" sang Avalon, clearly pointing at the gap just in case Linda hadn't noticed it.

No sooner had they stepped through than the door closed itself behind them, and judging by the expression on Avalon's face, she wasn't quite expecting it to do that. Something very heavy on the other side collapsed and made the ground shake, and a band of pale dust inched under the door and into the room.

"I need to practice that door thing a bit more.." she said, wiggling her foot.

"Uhuh, but that was still err.. very impressive.." Linda replied, distracted. The door had been disguised to blend imperceptibly against the brickwork of the wall, and if it hadn't been for a short arc of cracks and missing bricks, there would have been no sign it existed. This was weird. Very weird.

CHAPTER TEN
The Book Of Dalovich

Avalon did a steady circuit of the walls, allowing her light to reveal what was possibly a very, very old study no more than ten or twelve feet long, and half that in width. It was lined on one side with a wooden cage, and on the other side by a dilapidated work bench covered in fragmented scrolls and papers. The stone wall at the end was cracked and might have had crude shelves once, but it was now bare except for a small rectangular door which, Linda was pleased to see, was a long way from being Avalon-proof.

The wooden bars looked more like the front of a jail cell from the days of the old Wild West than an actual cage. Behind them lay the decaying books that Avalon had sensed all the way back in the Library, and she darted from side to side in front of them, humming to herself and sneezing continually. She sprinkled a small handful of Dust from her pouch into her hair and finally managed to stop.

"These are incredible.." said Linda as she realised that there were just two rows of books occupying the entire height of the room. Each huge volume along the top row was almost three feet tall and at least nine or ten inches thick, separated by ramshackle wooden slats. They towered high above her, resting ominously on the creaking ledge. The lower row were all different sizes, and in a particularly dire condition. They either leaned or curved against each other, swollen from having spent the last few centuries soaking in puddles that had been constantly replenished from the small drips coming down from the ceiling.

Fortunately the locks along the front of the bars were just tangles of frail ropes which had started decaying a long time ago, and even with chewed fingernails Linda could open them without too much trouble. The strands fell apart in her hands, letting a few of the wooden poles clatter to the ground. Avalon gave a tremendous sneeze causing the entire top row to rock and then lurch a few degrees forwards, so Linda backed away and decided to leave the other knots for the time being.

Avalon floated by the works with her eyes closed, brushing her fingers along each spine as she went, and leaving a thin trail from one to the other through the grime. Her colour seemed to change a little, according to each volume. Linda crossed her fingers and hoped that if there was a right one, it wouldn't be from the bottom row. Foul spidery-bug-type-things were crawling all over one of those, and they didn't look at all friendly.

"Most of these are just Church songs.. written big so everyone can see the words.. Church stories.. big, big pictures.." called Avalon from the far end. Linda cringed as she dropped down and began hovering around the vile ones on the Row Of Doom.

"Hmm.. old stories.. history.. 17th Century.. 16th.. few more Church songs.. 16th again.."

Suddenly she darted into a gap left by a few books which had completely disintegrated. It was the kind of space which allowed just enough room for someone brave and daring to crawl in and join her. Linda crouched down and stayed where she was, nervously peering in past a volume that reeked of lethally-old cheese. She hoped that Avalon wouldn't have found anything useful and wouldn't stay there for much longer, and would therefore come away from the back wall and also come away from the large dark book she was prodding and pointing at.

"Look Linda!" she squealed, patting its drenched cover, "This one tells of.. of.. the days of the First Legion in the 9th Century.. the ninth one's old, isn't it?"

Linda nodded and hid a whimper as she noticed a milli-milli-millipede wiggle across the wall past Avalon's light. Luckily the book itself didn't appear to be too revolting, and Avalon didn't seem to mind it at all - she even moved her hands all over the moon-surfaced cover.

"..and it goes through to the 14th Century.. and that's when it was written. I like what's in here. Does that sound good to you?"

She turned back to her usual silvery-white glow and clapped her hands with excitement, only stopping to momentarily point back at the book. Linda bit her lip and just knew she was going to have to ignore all the crawly unlikeables, all the creaking wooden panels and all the horrendous smells of mouldy parchment as well. She tucked her hair under her jacket (except for the braid) and shuffled over the soggy mush, trying hard not to breath and trying even harder to pretend that her arms and legs weren't really becoming wet.

Fortunately, the book had spent much of its life well away from the floor, safely on top of two bloated volumes each the size of doorsteps, which seemed to have suffered most of the serious damage. It was far too thick to hold, so Linda gripped it by the damp sides and attempted to drag it out instead.

"Ooops, bad idea.." she muttered, as a handful of torn manuscript and most of the cover came away in her hands. Lifting from underneath was a better idea, and she managed to struggle with it all the way over to the work bench, only dropping it once.. or maybe twice, depending on whether the second one really counted because the book was already in a few parts by that stage. Surprisingly, the bench didn't collapse or even wobble very much while she piled the four sections of the book back on top of each other.

The leather binding was cracked, gashed and very wet, but looked almost new compared to the rest of the volume. Its thick paper was fire damaged, riddled with furry moulds and had been a reliable dining establishment for countless generations of weevils. Linda ripped through an inch of damp sheets as she tried to open the first page, which then fell apart completely when she tried to put it back. This was getting worse by the minute.

She lifted the first section off, and was surprised to see that a few elaborate illustrations had survived quite well and were even fairly clear, but the pages beyond were all bonded together into a dense, cold, maché slab. In certain places everything showed through the layers of parchment in a wild jumble of bled colours and squiggles, making it impossible to read. The other sections weren't any help either, although the final section had a few lines of huge black writing with the occasional red letter still visible.

"Avie, how can we make any sense out of this? It's all a big mess and those words look like Latin or Greek and whatever language those curvy ones are in. And the pages are all gunked.. yuk!"

Avalon didn't seem at all concerned and went twice around the piles, admiring Linda's attempt at not damaging the book.

"We don't read the language, that's never ever any good, ever. We read the heart of the person who wrote the words. A bit like how you understand me right now. And me you. It's easy."

"Really? I've been thinking that you could speak English.. is that how we've been talking like this? Heart to heart, almost?"

"Uhuh. It's so easy isn't it? Takes practice, but what doesn't? Even Not Me's take a bit of work. See, you can hear me like you hear anything, but you understand me inside your mind and heart without even trying - that's because you're special, so you can do it for this, too. You have to come up here, now."

Instead of being a huge revelation, Linda found the most obvious sense in what Avalon was saying. She climbed up onto the bench and sat beside the book, to where Avalon was pointing. She gathered the pieces back into one pile again, and held her hand out without being entirely sure that Avalon had asked her to do so.

"Don't even look at the pages, you promise? Or the pictures, because that's cheating.. now you have to be calm, like the air's carrying you everywhere in the whole world, all at the same time."

Linda closed her eyes after checking yet again that nothing bug-like was going to crawl out from the book. Avalon held Linda's little finger and lowered her hand down to the book's cover.

"..touch the pages.. now take your hand off a tiny, tiny way."

"I don't see anything.. I'm no good at.."

"Nice and calm, drifting on the air, calm, calm.. imagine you're a bit like a Secondary Sylph, carrying through.."

"A silf? But I've no idea what.."

"That's okay, be like Not Me, a bird instead.. flying high and letting the warmth of the wind hold you.. nothing to fear, nothing to keep you from soaring and soaring for ever.. and you're carrying the book somewhere in your heart, always with you, always touching it.."

Linda could feel Avalon's soft glow slightly above her hand, and imagined herself flying through it, letting its purity guide her to wherever she needed to be. Time slowly meant nothing to her, and she had no idea how long she was following Avalon's light before images began drifting through the clouds of darkness, showing brief glimpses of another time and place, somehow allowing her to know far more than words could ever show.

"..I can see.. it's like someone's reading to me without speaking at all.. oh that's weird.. wonderful.. I can sense the room he's in.. mmm, burning logs.. it's cold but he can't go any nearer to the fireplace because the ink dries too quickly and cracks.. he's got indigestion.. it's like I can see into his mind, everything he ever knew or felt when he was writing this.. he's a monk, isn't he?"

"Uhuh. Keep talking to me and don't think hard, you can only let it happen," Avalon replied. Her voice felt softer than usual, no longer confined to Linda's mind but all around her, in every breath and in every thought.

"Okayy.. he's Brother Dalovich, the one who writes of the Old Spoken Tales.. the stories handed down.. but there's so many.. how do we find the ones we need, Avie?" whispered Linda.

She kept her eyes closed and felt as if she was dreaming her way through a world that made no sense at all, and yet at the same time it made all the sense in the world. It was almost funny. Hysterically, insanely funny. Avalon gently lead her further.

"Fly through the air, through the stories, think about me being there, think about The Stone.. kind of midway through.. let the right place come to you as you come to it.."

Linda wasn't hearing Avalon. She felt as if she was lost within her voice instead. As she spoke, the clouds began to clear and images more real than anything she had ever experienced began to form around her, as if she was drifting into a whole new world that lay somewhere between dreams and reality.

"He writes about the court of King Metriev.. the Boriso Glebov Castle.. near the end of the 12th Century Anno Domini.. and the day the Traveller came.. or maybe there was more than one, he's unsure. Uhh.. the King was a man wealthy on the field of battle, yet bereft of riches when in.. enlightened gatherings."

"What's that mean, Lindy?"

"He was good at holding an axe but not much good at holding a conversation, I suppose."

"Ohh.."

"His second wife, the Queen Ephra, Queen of the land known as.. I can't get it.. Ovabro.. no, Obrovechen, maybe.. she was a devious and dishonourable woman capable of untold cruelty, feared and loathed in equal measure by her subjects. The first Queen was said to have abandoned her lands for foreign shores, but where and why was never.. uhh.. detrastuh.. common knowledge. Her disappearance added to the second Queen Ephra's reputation.. who was soon banished.. a second Queen Ephra? That doesn't make sense to me.. and I've gone blank now Avalon, the warmth's gone.. I think showtime's over.."

Linda opened her eyes and looked down at the book. It was such a disgusting mess, and her hand came away from it with a sticky smacking sound. Dark brown slime had steadily been rising up from the leather binding and had left a high-tide mark around her fingers and palm.

"Eww, gross.. look at this!" she said, holding her hand open in front of Avalon, who stared at it for a puzzled moment before giving it a lick. That proved to be a bad idea.

"Aaagh! Oh nohhh tha' ish sho baaad! Feeyul sho shick, shick, shick, SHICK!"

She shook herself into a complete blur and bounced around the room squealing each time she went anywhere near Linda.

"Here, have a.." Linda shuffled her clean hand through her pockets to find something sweet. She found part of a hazelnut biscuit, which she didn't remember putting there.

"Try a hazelymit?" she suggested.

Avalon devoured all the small broken pieces and munched them for a few long minutes until the taste of the slime had abated. Her cheeks bulged like a hamster's until she spat it all across the room with enough force to knock a deep hole into one of the other books. She settled down on the ledge of the bench with her Journal and calmly opened at a green cord near the front, and started writing in large symbols. She tapped her chin, and looked up at Linda.

"How would you spell that flavour?" she asked, quite seriously.

"I'm so glad I don't know.. maybe you could just say it's pretty bad? At a guess, beetles times ten? Or maybe cubed. Definitely not one to try again."

That seemed to be a good enough description, and she drew two large diagonals next to a strange outline that could have been Linda's hand. Once the Journal had been returned to wherever it came from, Avalon pulled Linda's hand back down onto the book.

"Mouth's all fine now!" she said, opening wide to prove the point, "And we need to See further. Doing this is good for you, isn't it? Follow now.." she said, happily.

Linda wasn't sure what to say, so she closed her eyes and tried not to think of the revolting goo underneath her skin, but the coldness and squelching noises didn't help at all. She imagined Avalon taking her hand away from it and leading her high up into a warm, golden sunset above the clouds, back through to their new world. She soon felt herself drifting, guided no longer by touch but by complete trust as they returned to that wonderful place, and she sensed Brother Dalovich once more. Again she understood his words and his thoughts as if she'd never left, and effortlessly followed Avalon through them.

"See what I See, Linda.. tell me what we See.."

Linda began speaking without even hearing her own voice.

"No-one saw the Traveller.. or maybe Travellers.. arrive, so the people assumed he came from the air.. from nowhere? The Traveller was not of this time.. and was said to be gifted with power far beyond the mightiest of Kings, although his ability was greatly limited.. something about a Gift.. a Gifted One. He brought The Stone, but did fail to possess it, for death surrounded him as surrounds all who dare.. something. What's that word? What's he mean?"

"Hmm.. don't know.. carry on.."

"The Stone was taken by.. oh it's all a becoming such a mess.. I can't keep my mind on just one section, it's like everything's racing at me all at once from everywhere.. I'm not good enough, Avie.. can you do this for me?"

"Only bits. You have to learn 'cause it's so easy for you, and now's such a good time.. come onnn.."

Linda felt Avalon leading her again, back to a place which was so very, very near.

"Let's see.. umm.. an order of monks who never speak of their trophy.. their Arcana Aeris.. huh? Arcana.. oh, Secret Of The Air. The Stone was to be kept unknown, hidden by the trusted ones, guarded by them.. the Silent Keepers. They were trusted to protect all who live.. and shall live.. on God's Earth, never to allow the power of The Stone to be realised.. show me where it is.. take me there.. is hidden in the place where the shadows meet and the stars dare not shine. Can you see this, Avie, what I'm seeing?"

"Uhuh.."

Linda felt as if she was looking down from a tremendous height at a building that was somehow all around her.

"Is that.. like a God-less Chapel.. the unblessed protectorate for Those Who Know, and a Vita.. Vita.. uhh.. it has a way for vanishing the Stone in case bad people try to.. not vanishing, maybe hiding.. no, escaping. He means escaping. If bad people come there's an aqua.. something.. a fool's column.. of water?"

"A pretend well?"

"And there, lies far beneath the highest.. point, maybe.. of the Scorpion's Third Rising.. huh? Whew!"

"Good, but also scary bad!"

Linda could feel a monstrous headache coming on. Either that or someone had put a bowling ball in her head while her eyes were closed. She rested her forehead against her clean hand and thought of nothing at all. Avalon drifted around her, singing a special Healing Song that sounded very similar to I Do, I Do, I Do, which worked its magic after a few minutes and Linda swung her legs off the bench.

"Avie, what d'you think the last bit meant? The stuff about the scorpion's.. whatever?"

"Star positions. And I know where they show up."

"You do? Where would.. yecch.. oh this goo's just so disgustingly bad, isn't it?"

Avalon shivered and flew closer to Linda, who was more concerned with finding something to wipe her hand on than finding out where the constellation was. She finally made do with the bench, while Avalon tugged her braid for some attention.

"The place where the stars don't shine and the shadows meet is really horrid. Full of tall trees, very tall ones, so it's dark in there all day and night. And they're all Black Roots, every one of them."

"They've got black roots?"

"Uhuh. Cursed. They attract the evil Spirits and shelter them and strengthen them, and in return the Spirits have to bring People in to wander until they die, and then the Bad Earth takes them and then feeds their Souls to the Black R.."

"Ugh! And you've been there?"

Avalon nodded, looping the braid around herself until she was a lot closer to Linda.

"Kind of. It was quite a while ago. It's the first place I ever got lost, because of the Wind Spirits. Not the good ones, I mean the bad sort who follow Evil Ones who are so evil that I've never even heard of them. They kept teasing me for almost a whole day and kept blowing me everywhere that I wasn't supposed to be.. it got so bad and scary, and then they got bored and let me go. Kupula was livid! Not with me, with them."

"Good for her! So you've seen the Chapel, then?"

"No, but it must be near there, I suppose."

"That's good.. but what's that got to do with scorpions?"

"The Scorpion's Third Rising is when the Four Somethings line up in the sky and make a big Scorpion which you can see really well in an open bit by the jumbley hills, and Auroria says she's seen it twice, but I think she was all mixed up. Anyway, the stars aren't what's important. The important bit.."

"..is that the secret way out of the Chapel was built where you can see the stars?"

"Yup. And the book showed where, more or less. Easy, wasn't it?"

Linda nodded, and wasn't sure what to say. The past few minutes had practically turned her entire world upside down. She put the book back near to where it came from, piece by piece, while Avalon opened the smaller door in her own special way. It stayed where it was instead of swinging open, but had gained a large splintered hole where the lock used to be. Linda pushed it open, hurried through and did her best to fit the lock back in place - but only managed to make it fall back through into the study.

"If anyone asks, Avie, we were never here, okay? And if no-one asks, we don't tell them anyway."

Avalon would have agreed, but wasn't entirely sure what Linda was talking about. The winding stairs went on forever, sometimes levelling off for a while, but mostly going on and on, steadily upwards. Much to Linda's relief they soon found themselves at an old fashioned door, a bit similar to the ones that had just been repainted back at her school. Those ones always had troublesome handles, but before she could even try this one, Avalon had already demolished its entire left side. Her white glow turned a shade of pink as she blushed amidst a shower of sawdust.

They emerged into a dimly lit store room, crammed full of old paintings, ornaments of gold and silver, and a vast collection of huge books that had been almost hidden underneath some blankets. Avalon dived under the nearest sheet and gave the volumes a quick check, and emerged from behind some curtains on the other side of the room, shaking her head and wondering how she'd managed to get there. The few beams of daylight that penetrated the white-washed windows didn't reveal very much, but from what Linda could see, the antiques and relics were in pristine condition.

"Either someone's really loaded and we're in their spare room, or someone's been collecting for their retirement. Just look at all this stuff.." said Linda as she edged around a Gatling gun, and then a stuffed polar bear with a large gold dish balanced on its back.

They wandered through more random artefacts and into two more rooms which were both much larger but full of less impressive bounty - and fortunately connected by unlocked doors. All the expensive paraphernalia had been replaced by filing cabinets, masses of junk and mountains of boring old documents. The final door was well and truly locked, and Avalon took up her door-opening position.

"Hold on, Avie," Linda whispered, "..this one might lead to

somewhere with people, and they might not like us wrecking more of the place.. besides, look up there.."

She pointed up at a narrow frosted window above the door, and Avalon flew up to fiddle with its latch while Linda tried dragging a filing cabinet underneath it. The metal cabinet was almost as tall as the door, which would make it ideal for standing on, but it refused to budge an inch. Judging by its weight, she figured it was used for filing stupendously heavy blocks of granite. Surprisingly though, it wasn't. Linda took a few minutes to remove all the densely-packed files from each drawer, and made a series of skewed piles on the floor. Then she slid the cabinet right up against the door, and put everything back inside. The drawers made a strange but effective staircase, and she soon found herself back with Avalon who was sitting against the window looking glum.

"What's up?"Linda whispered.

Avalon tapped the base of the latch.

"I've been trying ages and there's no way to get through this. It's like we're stuck here now, and now there's that big cabinet thing in front of the door as well!"

Linda lifted the latch and eased it open a little, much to Avalon's amazement.

"That is so.. how did you ever.. show me again, puhleeaze?"

After a few demonstrations and an explanation of the intricacies of window latches, Linda was allowed to open the window for long enough to see that the corridor on the other side looked clinical and well lit, rather like one in a hospital. Avalon's mood had switched from glum to extremely happy, and she flew out into the corridor. She perched over on a security light jutting out of the wall opposite, and gave a second-by-second safety report.

"Nobody here.. still nobody here.. still nobody here.. still.."

Linda squeezed her way through and dropped down onto the tiled floor, feeling rather triumphant. Once again, the training ground also known as St Catherine's Dorm was proving useful after all. And then just ten squeaky-steps into her hard-won freedom, she stopped. A large guard in a grey uniform had turned into the corridor, and he stared straight at her. His hand was poised near his gunbelt as he marched over, and Linda felt every one of his thundering footsteps.

There was something about the dust-covered girl that didn't strike him as being particularly dangerous. Well, at least not in a way that would threaten Odessa's main Regional Government Building. He stopped in front of her, blocking the corridor like a brick wall, folded his arms and said something in the kind of gruff voice that suggested he didn't try to be nice very often

Linda looked all the way up to his stubbled face, trying not to stare at his bent nose and the teeth marks on his chin, and knew she was supposed to say something because he appeared to have stopped speaking. A scared expression obviously wasn't the answer he was looking for, so he planted a hand on her shoulder and lead her along two smart corridors lined with small international flags, and then into an office.

He released his grip only after giving a brief report to the secretary, which she duly tapped into her computer. She gestured towards an unoccupied desk on the other side of the room, which resembled an administrative land-fill site. An elderly man who should have retired fifty or sixty years earlier sat at the one opposite, working his way through reams of numbers in columns, underlining some and highlighting others. Linda felt bored just looking at him and was pleased he was ignoring her.

The clock in the room loudly ticked away her last few moments of life, and she sighed as another long minute passed. Any moment now she would probably be taken outside and shot, with no questions asked. The British Government would be informed eventually, and maybe there would be a trade embargo for a while or perhaps the Ukrainian Ambassador in London would be shot in response. The guard blew his nose as if he didn't care. He probably shot people all the time.

"What would make a good last request?" she wondered, and decided that asking not to be shot would be a pretty good one. Or even better than that would be asking for Dee to be shot in her place instead. That would be a brilliant one. She pondered the points for and against choosing her sunglasses instead of a blindfold, and the likelihood of the tough denim of her jacket stopping any bullets. Neither prospect seemed very likely, so she cast an eye around to see if she could improve the situation by watching the minute hand clunk just once, but it was somewhere behind her, high above the security guard. Clock Watching was difficult enough to explain in English, so trying in a foreign language was likely to take for ever. Besides, none of the people around her looked like they'd be interested anyway.

A pointy-faced bald man in an over-sized suit hurried in, loaded down with yet more files and documents. His mobile phone was ringing while his pager flashed and buzzed, and he briefly glanced at her as he began trying to answer both - while removing his jacket and attempting to re-organise his desk into an even bigger mess at the same time. He eventually sat down, raising his eyebrows to her. His jacket slipped off the side of his chair and lay in a crumpled pile on the floor. He put it back and it promptly fell off again. And again. And again. And then he left it alone. Linda hoped that Avalon was somehow responsible, but couldn't see her anywhere. She tried to let her eyes wander around the room to look for her, while giving nothing away.

"Ahem-hmm?" said the man, clearing his throat and giving a long sigh through his nose.

Even though Linda's legs had turned to jelly and she was convinced that the next few years were going to be spent either being dead or being in a horrible prison somewhere vile and cold, she was suddenly struck with a moment of inspiration - and even a little confidence. She stepped closer to the desk, tried not to stare too obviously at his name plate, and put on her best diplomatic smile.

"Hello, Mr Duh-rats-oh-viv-feet-itch? I'm Linda M Beaufort, that's Miss Beaufort.. I don't mean the M stands for Miss, that's just my midd.. anyway, I'm here with the British Government Entourage from England.. see?" she announced, wiping the worst of the dirt off her identity tag.

"That's me. Just there, see me?" she said, and held it out to him, "And I'm sure the others were all supposed to meet me here, for a look around. We were going to have a tour - unless I've got the wrong building.. oh no, that would be SO embarrassing, it really would, because I'm representing.."

"Where is it.. that you are.. frhom?" he said, nonchalantly lighting a cigarette.

"England, I already said.."

"No, where Odessa?"

"Oh, you mean the hotel? It's The Pecherskij, but I can't pronounce the street. It took me long enough to remember the hotel's name and I had to write it down a load of times and I didn't think for a moment that I'd need to remember it, and phewee, aren't I glad I tried now, but that's hardly the point.."

The man stared at her, and she knew that a huge gulf had opened up between her mouth and her brain. He eyed her with more than a hint of suspicion and so did his elderly assistant. And then the secretary did, followed by the guard and also the person sitting in the corner wearing handcuffs, who gave a small double-handed wave.

The secretary announced something very Russian and clapped her hands while nodding towards Linda, which made them all laugh. The important man looked at her again, and pretended to drink from an imaginary glass.

"You, girl on tv? Today? Fall over with drink?"

Linda nodded, and remembered that she was holding a large cocktail glass when her moment of fame had arrived. She tried to work out if it was better to be thought of as drunk rather than just being too hot. She faked a hiccup and laughed, turning an embarrassed shade of red.

"We send you to Pecherskij home - sleep like baby!"

He made a phonecall, laughed at the end of the conversation, and then repeated it to the room. They all laughed as well, and Linda joined in for absolutely no good reason.

"Drunk and barmy, made a good impression here haven't I? Personal best.." she mumbled to herself as the atmosphere lifted and the assistant switched some classical music on.

A female security guard knocked at the door and marched in before anyone had realised she was there. Her name sounded something like Adelichka, and she lead Linda through a different doorway and into an ornate foyer which was filled with the echoing footsteps and conversations from dozens of important people. There wasn't time to admire all the marble and decorative sculptures, which was a shame but Linda figured she might like to come back sometime and have a better look.

"What is this place, Adech.. Adulel.. Adehlelhilka?" she asked, using a trick of her father's for trying to get a stranger 'on-side' by saying their name. Just in case the guard was one of those people who couldn't speak English, Linda waved a hand in a small circle between her head and the central staircase, and adopted a puzzled expression. The reply was rapid and completely unintelligible, but ended with the young woman pointing at Linda's tag and then at the rest of the building.

"Aah, it's some kind of Government-place then, for Odessa?" Linda replied, and immediately wondered why she'd bothered - there was very little chance Adelichka had learned to speak English since the first question. The woman simply smiled and shrugged, then showed her triple-layered Pass at the Security Gate near the entrance, and made Linda do the same before ushering her out into the day's sunshine.

They stood at the roadside to wait for the car to arrive. After a few minutes Linda's eyes had adjusted to the summer brightness, and she looked around for Avalon. A bird, possibly of the songthrush variety, was flying from branch to branch in a beech tree, no doubt counting the leaves in the way that some birds do.

Now that she could see the building from the front, she had no idea what part of the town she'd wound up in and was glad she was going to have a free lift back to the hotel. She tried hard to think of something to say, just to be polite. Not speaking the language was becoming a real problem, and she made herself promise to learn a few words. Well, one day, perhaps.

A shining black limousine complete with a small Ukrainian flag soon pulled up, and the driver held the door open for her. Linda watched through the back window as Avalon flew down from the tree, and looped around twice before soaring high into the sky. She kept up with the car, soaring and swooping through the streets of Odessa, and made the journey back to the hotel feel very, very good.

A crowd of her father's party were gathered outside the Pecherskij Hotel, no doubt waiting for something important (such as having their pictures taken). And unless Linda was very much mistaken, the one looking directly at the car was none other than Her Royal Dee-ness. With a few careful prods and gestures, Linda managed to get the driver to park next to the group. This was a time for feeling rather important, and she waited for him to open her door before even considering getting out. Everyone's attention fell on her as she left the car.

"Thank you, very good driving umm.. Hercule. This is for you and your little ones. Excellent work. We and our Government salute you!" she said, reaching deep into her inside pocket and handing over a couple of small notes, which judging by the driver's bewildered expression were of an even lower value than she'd thought. Dee hurried over, clutching a large bag from one of the town's more exclusive stores.

"Ooh, look at you! What's with the fancy car? Wherever have you been, Bel?" she asked, looking thoroughly flustered.

"Me? I was over in that huge big Government building in the

middle of the town. The one with the flags and the tall whatevers outside. Aren't they all so friendly in there? They gave me such a good look around, we had a chat about things like you do, then Afternoon Tea and the most delightful Ukrainian biscuits.."

"And then you fell over and got all dusty-filthy like that? Honestly, you and gravity.." she said, flicking a spider from her hair.

"Oh, yeah.." mumbled Linda, as Dee padded a cloud of dust up from her shoulder, "..had a very slight accident, but nothing to hold the front page for."

"And what have you tied your hair with? Is that.."

Dee poked Linda's braid, staring at its end. To Linda it looked like a small circle of pure, shining silver light, just as it had done when Avalon had put it there.

"..it's a feather? How the.. how did you manage to tie a grotty feather like that? Was the bird dead when you pulled that off its bum? Bel, for heaven's sake, there must be a million things to hold the end of that braid - people are going to start talking about you, and that's only a good thing if you're someone important. Honestly, putting that in your own hair.. ugh!" she said, with a shiver.

"Well, birds seem to get by alright with feathers," said Linda, enjoying the fact that Dee wasn't capable of invading her new world with Avalon.

Dee lowered her voice to mutter something about washing it non-stop for a week, and went back to her group. Linda hurried inside, and without thinking chose to ignore both open lifts and steadily walked up the eighteen flights. She needed some time to wonder how much the Government knew, how much the Church knew, and how the Silent Keepers fitted into everything. And above all, how she'd done that weird book-reading thing with Avalon. By the time she reached her room, she'd established that the lines between dreams, myths, weirdy stuff and reality were becoming very blurred and very strange, and that was all she could be sure about.

The next hour disappeared. Avalon re-acquainted herself with the Greatest Hits cd while Linda waged war against all the dust and dirt which had bonded onto her. The filthy corridors, tunnels and rooms under the Library were probably spotless now, because all those centuries' worth of filthy grime were either in her hair or on her clothes. After much struggling and a barrel of shampoo, Linda felt able to face the world again and was just about to call Room Service for one of those nice Afternoon Feasts, but Constance beat her to the call and informed her it was time to go down to dinner.

The evening had come around far too quickly and Linda was soon sitting at a noisy table for six, watching her father eating. Her eyes were drawn to him in much the same way that a moth gets drawn to a lightbulb. Both activities are pointless, dangerous and for some bizarre reason, completely unavoidable. She watched each fork-full of food leave small remnants tangled behind in his moustache, and she followed their journeys as they worked their way lower and lower into the tangled mess of his beard. He remained happily oblivious to this, but Linda couldn't no matter how hard she tried. Dee was about to dab his face with her napkin again in a bid to prevent a small, glistening piece of carrot from disappearing completely into the lower reaches of his beard, but he brushed her hand away and started speaking to Linda as if she was five years old.

"So have you been a good girl for me and packed allll your things away then, Lindabunny?"

"Packed?" she said, as if she had been shot. That was the only word that could strike her harder than the loathsome 'Lindabunny'.

He rolled his eyes, and his daughter aged a few years.

"Oh do tune in, I told you this morning! Try and remember we're off at ten o'clock sharp tomorrow. And don't be late because we don't want to keep the limos waiting - that wouldn't look good at all. Very irresponsible and highly inappropriate."

"Unless you've fainted again, and then it's okay," added Dee, thoughtfully.

"I'll do my best not to, really I will," Linda replied, trying hard to avoid sounding too sarcastic and trying even harder to hide the dreadful feeling that had swept over her. She hadn't given a thought all day to moving anywhere else. Her mind ran in circles for the next few minutes as she poked her food around the plate, desperately trying to figure out what to do. Anything resembling a clever plan was a long way out of reach, so something shamelessly pathetic would have to do instead. She took a deep breath.

"Umm.. I forgot we were leaving, daddy. Couldn't I stay in Odessa? I'm not exactly the most important one here and I don't really like all the travelling around, I'm not used to it.. so perhaps.."

Her father wasn't impressed. He pushed Dee's hand away from his mouth again, and raised his over-loaded fork like a conductor's baton to emphasise his words.

"Don't be ridiculous, Linda. You're here for lots of good reasons. Good public relations and family-value photos are essential to this visit, and that makes you very important. Just because you're not in the meetings with us grown-ups doesn't mean that you're not equally as important as the rest of us. In many ways, you're even more important! How about that?" he said, and the final piece of potato threw itself from his fork.

Even Dee cringed as his last remark sank without trace. Linda hadn't a clue what to say, and figured she'd have to sort something out with Avalon. Anything.

"Don't you be too bothered, Bel, 'cause we're back at this place for the final two days and we're not going to be moving around all that much anyway.."

"Really? Oh that's brilliant, 'cause I really do like it here and there's so much.."

Linda started talking at a thousand words per minute and came to an abrupt halt when she noticed that her father wasn't paying the slightest bit of attention to her. He was having a quiet word with Dee about the pros and cons of giving away too much information, and Dee seemed to be getting rather annoyed. Linda left half of her dessert, excused herself and headed for the lifts, and realised when she got there that she was still holding a cup of coffee from the restaurant. She finished it off and handed it to a surprised receptionist just as the familiar 'ding' rang out from the far lift. The doors opened, revealing the ancient speech-writer, Mr Evil Oldperson, who looked very disgruntled at having to share his journey with someone who had an Honours Degree in Throwing Bread Rolls. Linda didn't fancy waiting a year or two for the other lift to arrive so she took a chance and stepped into the compartment, squeaking a 'hello' and pretending to be fascinated by the patterns on the carpet. She counted all the way to 427 before Floor 18 finally decided to show up.

"Good Evening and Good Night, Mr.. Sir," she said with controlled confidence, forgetting his name as politely as possible. She walked in the most dignified and lady-like manner she could manage until she heard the doors close, and then ran like a lunatic for her room.

Avalon was casually darting in and out of the open balcony window, humming to herself. She immediately flew over to Linda, pointing wildly at the cd player.

"Song's are all gone! All of them have gone away, all of them! What did I do wrong?"

"Nothing, nothing.. the batteries are worn out, that's all. I'll pick some up tomorrow, don't worry. Actually I might have some spares with me, I think.. somewhere around here. But more importantly, there's a big Major Issue Event now happening. I have to get packing because that lot downstairs won't let me stay here on my own. How about you come along with me to wherever we're going, and see somewhere different? It'll be great! And we'll be back here in a few days which is no time, and then we can get the Stone and sort everything out for you! Do you like the sound of that?"

Avalon stared at her, and reached tentatively for the braid.

"You need to say 'yes' here, Avie, because I really can't get out of this and there's no way I'm going to leave you behind all by yourself."

Avalon looked a little nervous, and then started to look very anxious as she looped the braid around her waist twice. And then a third time.

"Is it far away?" she asked.

"Uhh, it might not be. Why?"

She fluttered up close to Linda, and spoke very quietly while resting a hand on the end of her nose.

"I'm not supposed to be anywhere else. This is where I'm put. My kind aren't really supposed to be where we're not put, and I was put here, which is where Odessa is. When I see Kupula again she might get cross with me."

"Don't worry, Avie, no-one's going to be cross with you just for being somewhere else. After all, how pleased is everyone going to be when you get back to Hesperides? You'll have The Stone, and that'll make you a real hero especially with Kupula because you'll have proved to everyone that she was right - not just right about the Stone but also right to trust you as well. So if anyone gets even slightly annoyed, she'll sort them out. And besides - you've been here a long time so it would be nice to see a new place, wouldn't it?"

Avalon thought for a moment or two, then glowed brightly as her mood swung all the way back over to Very Happy. She took off for a few high-powered circuits of the room, and only stopped when the sight of Linda packing became too intriguing to resist. After a close inspection of the suitcases, she carefully drew each one in her Faery Journal and marked an X beside them. The Journal disappeared in its usual manner, and she returned to her expert demonstration of Getting In The Way.

"Oooh dear.. ooh.. that's not good.." she fussed, moving a sock back onto the bed. Avalon had spotted a few dozen contraventions of Natural Law, or at least her interpretation of what Natural Laws might be. They really weren't her strong point, not by a long way - they were more of Linda Thing. She hovered around the suitcase, occasionally moving from one side to the other, tutting to herself and trying very hard to look deep in thought.

"You're not putting that blue thing on top of the yellowey thing, are you? Oh no.. and they're both on the left side of the redley-pink things as well. Did you mean to do that? You'd better go and say bye to everyone you've ever met.. umm.. because darkness will be heading their way. So maybe you could roll a few fives and move things around and then.. carry on?"

Linda had only managed to pack two pairs of trousers, a jumper and one shoe in ten minutes.

"Avalon, are you making all this up to make me feel really good?"

"Maybe.." she replied, poking her head up from behind the suitcase lid.

Although Avalon's heart was in the right place, she definitely needed distracting and entertaining. Linda put a reliable cd into the wall hi-fi, and immediately transformed the entire room into a place for Avalon to dance and create her small-but-wonderful light displays.

And then everything changed.

CHAPTER ELEVEN
Ring, Ring

The walls shook and the floor juddered as an explosion roared into the night, triggering alarms throughout the building and the entire street. Somewhere in the brief chaos Linda was sure she heard gunshots, but it was all over so quickly she immediately wondered if she could have been wrong about them.

Avalon darted through the open window to see where the noise had come from, and Linda nervously fiddled with the lock on the balcony door before crouching down and scurrying out after her. She kneeled down with her head just above the stone balustrade, and looked over to where the roads crossed. In the darkness and smoke she could vaguely make out the scattered remains of a car barely a hundred yards away, next to the demolished front of a smaller hotel. The strange wailing sirens of police cars joined the commotion, and most of Odessa's emergency services began descending onto the area.

For a moment Linda wanted nothing more in the whole world than to be with her father, but realised that she had no idea what room he was in, which meant she couldn't even give him a call. She looked out at Avalon, who had tied the silvery end of the braid around her waist and was hovering just beyond the balcony. Suddenly Linda felt that not being with her father didn't matter so much anymore.

"Avie, come and stay close to me, now," she said as calmly as she could manage, settling down behind the small stone columns to watch the fire engines arrive. Avalon took refuge somewhere in her hair, shuffling herself around on Linda's shoulder, trembling against her neck.

"It's not the war again is it? That went away a long time ago - is it back? It's not is it?" she said in a shaky voice.

"No.. it might only be an accident Avie, it might be okay.."

Linda's eyes ran over the scene again and again. She hoped she was mistaken, but she had that undeniable feeling inside that a Half-There or maybe a certain silhouette had been standing on the other side of the wreckage-strewn road. It was probably nothing, she told herself. After all, the night was dark and the street was a long, long way down, and completely frantic and busy with randomly flashing lights, so there probably wasn't..

"Do you think Mörrah's there?" said Avalon, clambering across her face to stare straight into her blue eye.

"Umm.. I don't know. Maybe.."

"She's never been this bad, it's not what her kind do.. but if she's reaching the end of her life.. what if she can do anything? What if she's been storing up all her badness for years and years? Now I'm really scared!"

"No Avie, this wouldn't be just an old Ved'ma. She might have helped with the bad feelings though," said Linda, surprising herself, "This is more of a people thing.. ground crawlers at their worst."

The sound of the phone ringing back in the room carried through all the sirens and megaphones, and they hurried back inside.

"Linda M Beaufort? Code Red, Code Red, Code Red."

"Hi Constance. What's a Code Red? And why have you got three of them? How come no-one tells me anyth.."

"Didn't you read Chapter 114 of your Official Ukrainian Tour briefing sheets? The yellow section."

"My what?"

"The Official Ukrainian.. oh, here they are.. well I never. They should have been at your home on top of your new suitcases.."

Constance trailed off into a rare silence, no doubt underlining or circling the guilty assistant's name. Linda watched with a combination of relief and amazement as Avalon steadily became less concerned with the noise and chaos outside, and more and more caught up in the music again. A drawer slammed shut somewhere at the Whitehall end of the phone line and brought Linda's attention back with a jump.

"Well anyway," Constance continued, "..if you had read them you'd have known there was a 38.2% chance that certain undesirables might create a scene, which they do indeed appear to have done. So you must now go down to reception and meet your father, Mr Beaufort, to establish matters further because he has already been thoroughly briefed.. uhh.. last Tuesday in fact. He'll be standing next to the tall cabinet beside the early 18th Century nautical clock."

"So it was a bomb then? And that really was gunfire?"

"Yes and also no, to neither question at this precise juncture."

Linda would have said something, if her brain hadn't fallen over. Fortunately Constance carried on talking and probably missed her saying 'Huh?' twice.

"Everyone at your location undoubtedly believes that to be the case, but until it's confirmed by an Official Ukrainian Government Representative and then formally acknowledged by our Foreign Office, all I can say is that what you heard was a loud noise or a series of loud noises, perhaps linked to the damage caused to a nearby hotel at the same time. I trust that's clear?"

"Yeah, clear as.. something unbelievably clear, after a really good rinse. I'm genuinely glad you called."

"Excellent. I must inform you that your allocated 90 seconds of Awareness Information are almost over, and therefore I.."

Constance put the phone down on the ninetieth second. Linda sighed and put her phone down as well. She went and closed the balcony door properly, wondering if she really had seen another glimpse of Mörrah. However, that really didn't seem quite so important now that everything else was moving along at such a pace, and a lifetime's practice at dismissing Half-There's allowed her to push it out of her mind without realising that she had done so. She turned the music up a little more, as it appeared to be having such a good effect on Avalon.

"Avie? I'm off downstairs to see my dad for a few minutes, okay? I promise I'll be back up before you know it."

Avalon nodded and waved, completely lost in her own world. Linda stepped into an almost deserted corridor and eventually followed a few important people down the stairs. Her father was exactly where he was supposed to be, although Constance had neglected to mention that Dee would be there as well. Constance was very good at not mentioning Dee at all, Linda mumbled indignantly as she crossed the busy floor.

"Ah, Linda! Expect you noticed the bother out there? Seems there's people who view the nuclear sites as undesirable, and this is how they make their point - so I don't want you to be around here any longer. It's Code Yellow for you."

"What does that mean?"

"Home. You're going back tonight. It's for the best."

"I don't want to go back there! I want to stay.." said Linda, feeling as if her world was about to end.

"No arguing!" he snapped, raising his voice and his finger, attracting the attention of a group of people near by. Linda knew it wasn't a good idea to even begin trying to argue with him. The only good aspect of living at St Teresa's was that she was far away from his flashes of temper, and at that particular moment her deep-rooted wariness and fear of him spread all over her, just as it always had done. She hadn't seen his 'other side' for almost two years, and hadn't missed it one little bit. Trying to argue would be such a waste of time. Besides, even if he stayed totally calm, his entire career revolved around tying people up in verbal knots or rendering them incapable of thinking straight, and she was nowhere near being a match for that, yet. His moment passed, and he carried on talking as nicely as he could manage.

"Thing is, it might look bad if you were seen to be umm.. running away from our hosts at this moment, wouldn't it? That could easily give the impression that I didn't trust your safety with them."

"But you don't!"

"I know that, and you know that - but we can't show that, can we? Maybe when we're back in England I could make a serious point regarding the danger my only daughter was in, if I were to be on a chat show perha.."

Dee jumped in, flipping open her Personal Organiser with a bleep.

"But you are on a chat show, remember? We were just sorting it this afternoon.. look, it's on.. August the 8th, BBC1 at seven thirt.."

"Yes Dee, thank you so much. But my point is, Linda, I want you to leave here rather furtively, okay? That way we're all happy, aren't we? You won't have offended the Ukrainian Government plus you'll be nice and safe back home, far away from this desperately grave situation. Hmm, that's a good one isn't it? Desperately grave situation.. do remember that line, Dee - no, write it down. Where was I? Oh yes.. we will organise some Executive Personal Transport to the airport for you.."

Dee looked bewildered, and gestured towards the entrance.

"Will what? It's already outside, we just spoke to the taxi dri.."

"Thank you again, Dee. Maybe you should only talk if I point at you? And I'm not pointing at you now, am I? Here, this can be a practice one."

He raised his finger once more, this time to point just in front of Dee's forehead, causing her to look embarrassed and livid at the same time. She said nothing, and glared at him instead. The bearded one was in for a hard time later on, and Linda figured he deserved it.

"So Linda, go back up to your room and finish packing your bags."

Dee rolled her eyes with despair.

"What is it with you tonight? Her bags will be outside her door by now, and the staff are probably making up her room alread.."

"Dee! Would you mind trying to help? Mouth closed, mind open - like we discussed, remember?"

Dee scowled, and her cheeks flushed scarlet. Mr Beaufort turned his attention back to Linda.

"Your very own Personal Limousine will take you to the airport and you'll be back home in good old Blighty before you know it. It's for your own good, Linda, especially if people outside this party don't know that you're not here.. you understand?"

"No I don't. What d'you mean?"

"Well, once you're back home, it would be very helpful for the perceived success of this entire visit if you kept a low-profile, until the rest of us arrive back when the trip's officially completed. You see, you're supposed to be here with us, aren't you? The marketing whizzos can always add you into the photos later with all their clever computer jiggery-pokery! And I'll see that you get mentioned in Hansard again, but for a good reason this time - how about that?"

"So I stay at home all by myself and do nothing?" said Linda, dismayed to see her father nodding. Dee jumped in again.

"You could brush up on those bad exam results, couldn't you? Constance says they're so awf.."

"Dee, for the last time, can you let me handle this?" he said, harsher. "Linda, maybe you could go to Andie's? And then the day after the rest of us get back.. that's the 24th, I think.. you could drop round to the school and emphasise how good the entire trip was. You see, word spreads and Constance informs me that one of your friends has a father who's brother-in-law writes for The Times! Your young-person angle could land some important publicity for us all."

Dee perked up, and tapped something into her Organiser.

"And I could fax you a list of quotes and things you could tell her!" she said, waiting for Linda to nod. She didn't.

"Well done Dee, that's a good idea! See, you can do it, Honey Snuggles, can't you?" he cooed, and followed his top-rate patronising with a small kiss on Dee's cheek. Linda very nearly surprised herself by not feeling the slightest trace of annoyance. A day or two ago she would have been irritated beyond words, but not now. Now she felt that she didn't know the couple in front of her. They belonged with all the other people she didn't know in the reception and the bar.

"Now, what do you say, Linda?" he said, grinning down to her while slipping an arm tightly around Dee's waist.

"Umm.. what can I say?"

"Excellent! Hurry up then, and we'll see you back down here in.. ten minutes. That taxi's charging by the second!"

Her father pressed the button for the lift, while Dee grabbed a final word.

"And Bel? Dress a bit different, like in a disguise just to be sure absolutely no-one from the press spots you leaving! Tuck all that hair out the way, and put on those kitschy sunglasses!"

Dee was awarded another kiss for that one, and Linda watched the two of them drift away into a passing group.

Eighteen floors later Linda stumbled out of the lift, gasping for fresh air. Two very large men had entered on Floor 2, smoking cigars which resembled tree trunks. They absolutely reeked and must have been more Amazonian than Cuban, and for a moment near Floor 10 she could easily have keeled over again. She survived by discretely wrapping her arms across her face and breathing in small gulps while kneeling down and pressing herself face-first into a corner.

Her feet stopped wobbling midway along the corridor, and she soon found herself outside Room 18/86, staring at her bags. She wondered who had finished the packing for her, and then wondered if it was really worth wondering about that. Even if she allowed herself to get annoyed, there was nothing she could do about it. Constance probably knew the inventory for each suitcase anyway.

She checked through her cases for her mother's picture, and could have cried with relief when she found it. Nobody, even the worst of the rotten bunch back at school, ever touched, ever knocked or ever picked up her one and only picture. She wrapped two protective jumpers around it, but couldn't find the elder branch anywhere. Then it was time for Avalon.

She swiped her key-card through the door's techno-lock, but the small green light didn't come on, and the red one didn't even flicker. She tried again, then turned the card around, upside down and then over once more. The door stayed shut. This was one bad thing too many. She didn't even try to hold back her tears of frustration and made her way down the eighteen flights, wanting to race and slide on the rails to get down quicker, but couldn't allow herself to miss out a single, solitary step. And that only added to her mixture of frustration, anger and irritation, making her more annoyed with herself than she was with her father, the bombers, Dee, and just about everyone else in the entire world put together.

Her father and Dee were over in the bar, and appeared to have forgotten their earlier bicker. Linda stood as near as she could manage, not wanting to get too close to their exclusive world.

"I can't get in my room because this stupid key thing doesn't work anymore and.. I need to find mum's picture 'cause I hadn't finished packing and it's not in my bags and now.. I can't.. get.. back in.."

Linda wiped her eyes and put a slight wobble into her voice, knowing full well that a touch of emotion could work wonders. And it did. Her father stood up straight away.

"Ahh, they're quick around here aren't they? See, that keycard's bound not to work because your room's already been cancelled. Tell you what, let's go and get you a new one! God almighty, I dread to think what the taxi's going to charge.. check he's still waiting, would you Dee? Smile at him and do some of that fluttery eyelash stuff."

A few minutes later Linda and her father stepped into an immaculate Room 18/86, which looked as if she'd never been in it.

"It's got to have fallen down here somewhere.." she bluffed, looking under the bed and then behind the settee. Her father went into the bathroom, and Linda headed for the balcony. She looked around, but couldn't see Avalon anywhere.

"Avie? Are you here?"

A songthrush flew onto the stone rail, immediately becoming Avalon as she landed.

"You have to listen to me because.." Linda began, before her heart jumped twice as her father arrived in the doorway. She glanced at Avalon, who seemed unruffled. Fortunately, her father was equally unruffled.

"Linda? Are you talking to birds now? Because if you are.. tell you what, I'll book you in to see Dee's therapist when I get back, okay? She's very good.. and unbelievably patient. God, how she's patient. Did you find that picture yet?"

"Oh.. err.. yeah, it's all packed now, thanks."

The bird hopped to the far end of the balcony where the room's lights didn't reach, and Linda pointed down at the street below.

"So is that the taxi down there, dad? That dark one down there with the orange strip on the top? That's the one that's going to go to the airport with me in it? In a few minutes?" she said, ignoring the countless police cars hurrying to and fro, and all the flashes from eager photographers which were creating a chaotic melée.

"Yes.. for heaven's sake how difficult is this? It's for your own good, so don't start getting all tetchy. Now then, you'll have to buy your own ticket at the airport, and this should cover it.."

He handed her enough English and Ukrainian money to drive a Ved'ma into a really foul mood, and Linda's eyes almost popped out.

"..and it'll get you through any diversions or delays in every airport between here and Heathrow. I know what you're like, young lady, and I'm half expecting the plane to end up on Mars."

"It's bound to happen one day," she said, sure he wasn't listening.

"Anyway," he continued, "I've no idea when the next flight is, but just make sure you're on it and then call me when you get back home - but call the hotel, not my mobile. Now do you have this number?"

"Yeah, it's on all the biros and free stuff. So the car down there.."

The songthrush flew down towards it, and Linda didn't need to finish speaking.

"Oh for heaven's sake.. just go to it, Linda or all of this cash won't even cover the taxi fare."

A slender, dark haired woman stood hidden in the shadows across the street and smiled a cold, calculating smile to herself as she watched the Gifted One and the man leave the balcony. People continued to hurry past without even noticing the elegant woman, but that was something she had grown used to. For the first time in many long years, she felt that the insufferable ignorance of these peasants was perfectly acceptable - they simply no longer mattered. She looked over at the madness outside the wrecked hotel, and her smile grew wider. Gambling on this scale and causing so much violence was so very draining, and that was almost too dangerous for someone of her age, but if it paid off.. the reward would more than justify the risk.. it would be worth more than life itself. She watched the activity in the Pecherskij foyer, and waited. Patience, patience, a little more patience..

The porter loaded the suitcases into the boot while Linda brushed the peanuts and crisps off the back seat of the taxi. She waved to her father and Dee as the driver closed her door, happily giving the impression that she was about to do exactly what she was supposed to do. However, a plan of supreme brilliance and unmatchable genius had appeared in her mind on the way down to the lobby. Linda smiled to herself. She was in charge now.

The car gave a wobble and grumbled into life, soon leaving the flashing lights and blaring sirens behind as it picked up speed. She wound her window down, hoping that Avalon might fly in before getting left behind or lost.

"Close it close it closeitcloseitcloseitcloseclose.."

Linda looked around to see where the voice had come from and saw Avalon behind a rear headrest, where she was clinging onto the metal support and desperately trying not to get blown into the view of the driver.

"Can't do Not Me's and hang onto stuff! He thinks I'm someone's glove.. birds are never very welcome inside anywhere! People don't like them indoors.."

The driver looked around as Linda laughed, and assumed the girl was a little unhinged. That would explain why she was being bundled off to the airport at such an hour. And who would wear sunglasses at this time of night? The kind of person who would laugh at nothing, that's who. Linda had the vaguest sense of what he was thinking, and that made her laugh again, which made the urge even worse and she laughed some more. It didn't occur to her for a moment that understanding his feelings was new and perhaps just a little out of the ordinary.

They joined one long road, and then turned into another. Now it was time for The Big Plan.

"Umm.. here! Here please!" she said, while pointing at the first good-looking hotel which had a name that she could actually read. The driver turned around, looking puzzled. He didn't slow down at all, and repeated the word 'Airaport?' a few times, so Linda waved a handful of notes and held up her identity tag.

"No, no, not now thank you. This one, the Hotel.. uh.. Kras-nayy-ahh. Krasnaya for me, and look, money for you!"

He shrugged, drove around the block and pulled up outside the smoked-glass entry doors, while Linda felt a huge knot forming in her stomach. She had never even daydreamed about doing anything deliberately defiant in her entire life, and now that she had actually done something that was definitely off the script.. it was suddenly too late to change anything. Her heart pounded as she dropped the money onto the passenger seat, and then pounded even harder as she went around to the back of the car.

Avalon settled on the head of one of the two ornate white statues which stood either side of the doorway, while the driver gave a hand with the suitcases. And then he was gone, and Linda found herself alone in the hotel's quiet and sumptuous reception hall. She stepped back out to watch the car's lights disappearing into the night, amazed at what she'd just done. She felt as if the entire world knew that she'd committed a major sin, and her father and a load of reporters would jump out at any second. And maybe Constance as well.

A snooty receptionist looked over to her, and Linda felt about an inch tall. She took a step towards the desk, but then she stopped for a moment to wonder if a genuine jet-setter would be leaving her bags at the door. Did Princess Diana ever lug her own suitcases into hotels? No. Did Abba ever carry all their instruments and costumes all over the place? No again, probably. So Linda decided she wouldn't either. She beckoned a bored porter to run over with his chrome trolley so that he could do it for her, and then she strode to the desk, feeling much better about being there.

But then, for a reason which made sense for no more than two seconds, she felt the urge to throw absolutely everyone off her trail by completely re-inventing herself. That way, nobody would know the old Linda was here because the all-new one wasn't English, wasn't called Linda, had absolutely nothing to do with the British Government whatsoever, and had actually just arrived from an exceptionally trendy part of Paris.

"Bonsoirez-vous!" Linda announced to the receptionist, while removing her shades with Gallic panache (or something very similar).

"Je m'appelle.. Amélie uh.. Bardot et je voudrais une bonne chambre pour un personne pour.. uhh.. trois jours, s'il vous plait. Avec uhn télévision. Oh, et uhhn hi-fi dans la.. wall.. pour les cd's d'Abba. Et aussi oon kettle pour la thé, si vous plait."

The receptionist raised her eyebrows and spoke in fast and fluent French, ending with a smile and the kind of expression that suggested she didn't really expect Linda to know what on earth she was talking about. And she was right.

"Pardonnez moi?" Linda responded, nervously.

"Would you like a room here, Mademoiselle Bardot? One with ah balcony, per'aps?" she replied, very slowly and clearly, laced with a slight Russian accent.

"Umm.. oui."

"Well then Amélie, please fill in this form, ici, ici and ici. Merci."

"Uhh.. oui."

"Très bien. Ring the bell when that is accompli."

The woman handed over a form and Linda filled it in as Frenchly as she could. Three days here was going to more expensive than she'd hoped, so a less pricey hotel would do for afterwards - after all, there was a week or so ahead of her and she still had to fly back to England at some stage. She wasn't too worried though, because this was one of those rare Win-Win situations. Even if everything went wrong and she had to explain to her father why she'd spent everything and stranded herself in Odessa, the worst that could happen would be a few sessions with Dee's special Head Doctor, which might not be such a bad thing anyway.

But in the meantime, this was now officially her holiday and despite the prospect of occasional bombs or unwelcome appearances from a weird Ved'ma, Linda was sensing a real freedom - and feeling a bit like a criminal as well, but that didn't matter too much. If she wanted to spend her holiday looking for a mind-blowingly strange Stone-thing with Avalon then that's exactly what she'd do. Besides, if they didn't find it soon, she could just go back to St Teresa's and take Avalon with her, and come back to Odessa every now and then to have another look for it. Simple.

Her room on the very top floor was almost half the size of her bedroom at The Pecherskij, but she was happy with it. It was elegant and had a huge tv, the balcony was small but met with Avalon's approval, and the view was stunning. She leaned against the central window and stared out at the sea of flickering lights which seemed to reach out for ever. For a while she felt as if the whole of Odessa belonged to her, every warm breeze, every star's light, every..

"Are the Battuh-reez here? I can't find any at all.. what do they look like?"

Avalon had noticed that the walls didn't have any hi-fi's, concealed or otherwise, and tugged at Linda's braid while waving an arm at the entire room. For a moment, Linda wonder if it really was intended to be just a faery's seatbelt. Still, keeping Avalon happy was pretty much top of her list of Important Things In Life, so she loaded up the cd player and shuffled a chair outside onto the balcony. She hung the headphones on an empty pot-stand, turned the volume up, and settled down.

Her cares soon drifted away as she watched Avalon fly in long swooping arcs against the backdrop of the night sky, painting the most wonderful clusters of tiny sparkling stars that nobody else in the world would ever see. She didn't want the music or Avalon's dancing to ever end, but after a while a light breeze brought with it the distant rumbling of trains, and drew her attention down to the cars passing by in the street below. And that reminded her about something important.

She left the balcony door wide open, allowing the night air to gently sway the net curtains while she settled down on the bed with a Krasnaya pen and plenty of Krasnaya paper. Avalon followed her in, looking tired.

"What're you doing?" she said, settling on Linda's knee.

"I need to work out when to phone dad to let him know that I've arrived back in England, you know - just like a good girl should do."

Avalon looked blank, and appeared to have missed Linda's briefing session earlier.

"Right.. it's 11.25pm now, and we left the other hotel at 10.05pm so assuming the taxi took X number of minutes to reach the airport like it did on the way over, and we waited Y minutes at the terminal for the plane flight, which took Z hours to get back to Heathrow, we would need to phone at.. at least X plus Y plus Z from precisely now in order to be convincing.. allowing for baggage claiming.. not forgetting the time difference.. call those W.. hmm.."

The first logical step would have been to ask reception for the phone number of the airport in order to find out when the next flight had been due to leave, but there was a good chance that Ms Oh-So-Fluent-In-French might answer the phone. Linda didn't really want to speak to her again for a while.

Instead, she figured that a call to the Pecherskij at precisely 4.20am would do the trick. Granted, that might possibly play havoc with her father's blood pressure and might also disturb Dee's beauty sleep (assuming she was there) but all things considered, the safe arrival of his only daughter back in England was an important event and he needed to know about it. Linda set her Mamma Mia alarm clock for 4.00am precisely.

A familiar bleeped melody heralded the early start for her, and she switched on the bedside lamp. Avalon yawned and emerged from a blanket of Linda's hair.

"First things first, Avie.." she mumbled, trying to wake up quickly.

She phoned the night porter for some tea, and began thinking of Good Answers To Difficult Questions, just in case her father had been up for the entire night unable to sleep, sick with worry about his daughter's first journey all on her own. After filling up three more pages of Krasnaya paper, she felt both prepared and awake enough to call him. She slid a couple of socks over the mouthpiece to take away a little clarity from her voice, because judging by how long the plane flight the other evening had taken, there were at least twenty thousand miles between Heathrow and Odessa.

Avalon hovered close to the phone, adding to the effect by scrunching up a piece of the Krasnaya's finest stationery, while trying desperately hard not to giggle. Less than half a mile away, the Pecherskij's sleepy receptionist put the call through to Mr Beaufort's room, and after a few hundred rings he picked it up, dropped it, and picked it up again.

"Woozthis, hmm.." he dozed.

"Hello? Dad? Is that the right room this time? I want to speak to Mr Beaufort," said Linda, up and down the scale.

"Whuhh.. L'nduhh? Zzat eww-thuhr?"

"Hello? It's me, Linda! Is that you? Can you hear me? Hello? I'm calling from an airport phone back haffumm'num.. it's a bad line.. just letting you.. phlfflmph with it landed safely and didn't lose any luggage or.. mauhmtfluphmm and sorted, I'm pleased to say. Um noffnofffnah anymore, so that'll be yes except now! Isn't that good?"

"Whuh.. whuh time's it? Four somethin'? God almigh.. this line's really bad, I can hardly hear you. Why didn't you choose a phone that sounds better? Uhh.. glad you had a safe trip and all that. Stop it, Dee, I'm on the phone to Linda.. yes, stop it now you little.. now then Linda.. you still there? Us over here're moving for most of tomorrow, no tomorrow's today now.. ugh. Got a meeting later on and then moving after that.. give a week for other visits, yahda yahda yahda.. then we're seeing.. Dee behave, this is kind of important.. so Linda, give me a call when the rest of us get back to this Perch-whatever hotel next week. Don't try my mobile 'cause I hate that damn tune it plays and I might be in a meeting. How's that sound?"

"Really bad to me - you're right, this is an awful line. I'll be.."

The maid began opening the door, struggling with a large tray of tea and a huge plate covered in the creatively-arranged contents of two packets of hazelnut biscuits. Avalon instantly dropped the crumpled paper and darted behind Aggy's new chair and then finally disappeared under the bed. Linda took over scrumpling the paper while the maid looked for somewhere to leave the tray.

"..I'll be at Andie's or maybe nurfpm round at someone else's so Constance might have a hard time getting hold of me, but.. uh oh, uh fnnumran else wants to use dith phone after me.. ishumimm.. think the line's break ufhnupnow.."

She moved the phone further away from herself as she spoke, and rubbed the ball of paper against the mouthpiece. She brought it closer again, and raised her voice.

"Well bye dad and Dee, byeee.. hello? Hello? I can't hear you?"

"Yes, bye Linda, be good! No, not you Dee, you can be.."

Linda put the phone down and pointed to the end of the bed. The maid carefully put the tray on the duvet and looked at the strange girl who had been talking to a phone-sock through some paper, and decided against waiting for a tip. She muttered to herself and looked back with a very puzzled expression before closing the door.

Linda basked in the glory of her Oscar-winning performance, feeling amazed with herself - and also a little scared at suddenly having such complete freedom. A few hours ago she was merely in the wrong hotel, but now she was in the wrong hotel and also in the wrong country - officially.

She poured herself a celebratory cup of tea, and dunked a biscuit in the way that Andie's hopeless now-her-boyfriend had once shown her. It broke off just like it usually did for him, and landed with a wet thud on the sheets. Meanwhile, Avalon had emerged from under the bed and performed two excited circuits of the room before settling down on the pillow with a few carefully-chosen biscuits. She managed to spread crumbs everywhere while carefully devouring only the hazelnuts.

"Biscnits are a lot trickier to handle than chocliate, but they're much less messy, aren't they?" she declared, surrounded by a carpet of crumbs and feeling pleased that she didn't need to shake herself at all.

Linda didn't entirely agree, but she nodded anyway.

CHAPTER TWELVE

The Scorpion's Third Rising

Linda slowly woke to a nearly-sunny morning and the sounds of the maid apologising for waking her. The woman stacked a pile of fresh towels onto the dressing table, and closed the door quietly behind her as she left. Linda blearily saw the green numbers on the bedside clock flick over to 10.00AM. Avalon emerged from under the bed and settled on the pillow, delicately grooming her wings. Her fragrance made Linda feel as if she was waking up in a meadow.

"Ooh, thought she saw Not Me for a second. Who's a sleepy head then?" she sang, full of life and overflowing with energy. She hopped forwards and carefully moved Linda's long fringe to one side well away from her eyes, and then moved it over to the other side. And then back again.

"You know, Aluvonn, I must remember not to phone people up at four in the morning, 'specially after a late night. It's such a.. umm.. Not Good thing."

Avalon nodded in agreement, noticing how an interrupted night's sleep seemed to stop Linda's brain from working. She gave a small squeal of triumph as she found a slightly nibbled hazelnut in one of the folds of the duvet, and proudly showed it to Linda before finishing it off.

"Now you have to eat something too, Lindy, because today's a good day for looking for The Stone, and that means you have to start today properly."

Avalon took her Journal out, opening it to show a rectangle drawn on one page and a narrower rectangle on the other page. They both appeared to have small squares drawn inside them, and very little else apart from a cross beside each one, indicating that the Stone wasn't to be found in either.

"These are nice places which lots of People eat in, right from early in the morning 'till quite late at night and we're near them both! You might like them too. Shall we try the tall one? How about now?" she said, while pointing at the door.

Linda took the hint, and was soon dressed and ready for the day ahead. Her shades still looked cool but the hat would have to stay in the room, planted firmly on Aggy's head. There was a fair breeze blowing in through the windows which could only be bad for a shady hat, so Avalon could always take refuge in her hair if she needed to.

They made their way onto a vibrant and busy street, overlooked by an austere Opera House standing far away at its end. Midway along, Avalon suddenly took off from Linda's shoulder and flew around a corner. Linda hurried after her, and saw a songthrush perched a few yards away in the shade of a parasol, on a cluttered table outside a café. Even though it was in a very attractive setting and lined with trees, this was a definite No Go area for her. The road had been pedestrianised with a billion or more small bricks in a lethal herring-bone pattern, creating a minefield of misfortune. There was no way she could ever get to Avalon without breaking the most incredible amount of lines. The songthrush sang loudly to the world, and people on neighbouring tables laughed and threw small pieces of pastry and bread to it.

"There's a time and a place for getting messed up about this kind of thing, and it really doesn't have to be now.." Linda said to herself, nervously gauging the size of the first brick with the tip of her trainer. Meanwhile, Avalon showed no sign of moving anywhere else and was happily picking at a large segment of a croissant.

"I can do this without going nuts.. I can do this.. no I can't, no I can't, no.."

She felt in her pocket for her dice. Her thumb went on the six, which was just perfect. Blocking the most broken up side of the dice was a truly awesome stroke of luck, and ought to offer protection against the line-breaking ahead of her. She took a step, then another, and then another. The world hadn't ended yet, but then again, that was no guarantee that it wouldn't end soon. Even though she was pressing the six as hard as possible, Linda felt as if she might as well have been walking on hot coals. She took a final few leaping strides, sat down with a big shiver at the table and lifted her feet completely off the ground. Three fours later, she felt much better and rested her feet on the safety of the chair next to her. Avalon looked like Avalon again, playing with her food and apparently oblivious to the traumatic crossing.

"This is so nice! Sweetberry goodies!" she exclaimed, and began trying to pick up a discarded blob of jam which was almost as big as her head. Linda scooped it up for her.

"What's.. up.. Lindy?" she asked, in between small bites. An elderly couple walked past, and left a plate of their Danish pastry scraps on the table, gesturing towards the songthrush and laughing to Linda. She smiled back at them and waited until they were out of hearing range.

"It's not what's 'up' it's what's 'across'. All those lines! Millions of them out there, and I walked all over them.. every single step!" whispered Linda, trying to keep her voice steady and also trying to look as if she wasn't talking to herself - or a bird.

"Yup.." said Avalon, dropping a lump of mushy strawberry onto her foot, "Oops.. still, you managed it and that's what's important. I knew you would."

"Huh? You chose here on purpose?"

"Uhuh. You see, it's good for y.."

The waiter finally decided to see if the strange girl wanted to order anything, or preferably if she'd be leaving very soon. He wandered over and ran through Russian, German, Polish and French before trying out his best broken English, while Linda politely put her feet on the ground. Well, nearly.

"Zomathink for you? And for tho bordy, porraps?"

Linda realised that feeding an old croissant and a blob of strawberry jam to a songthrush might not be an everyday occurrence in these parts, so she smiled up at the man and tried to sound as normal as possible.

"Ah, yes thank you, garçon. Can I have a big cappuccino please, a few more croissants and some scrambled egg too, but on toast though. I mean the egg needs to be on toast, not the croissants on the toast, and then maybe some bacon with the egg, and plenty more of this lovely jam off your table," she said, holding up a sample on her fingers, "..but by itself, not with the bacon and eggs, because that'd be mad wouldn't it? It needs to be separate, maybe in a jar if you've got one, like we do in England. Oh, and some hazelnuts as well please - you might find them in biscuits or cakes, but just on their own would be divine if you could manage that, thanks ever such."

The waiter wrote down as much as he understood, and wandered off to the kitchens. Avalon tried the crumbly grey stuff in the ashtray, and decided she didn't like it very much. She kicked it onto the next table, spreading ash and cigarette-ends everywhere. The unfortunate people at the neighbouring table got up and left.

"Ew, tongue'sh gone.. funny.. akk.. akk.." Avalon spluttered, and

149

tried to push as much jam into her mouth as possible. Most of it seemed to go around her head, so Linda scooped up another blob for her, to help out.

"So what should we do then, Avie? How do we get to the spooky trees and the black roots place?"

Avalon lifted her face out of the jam.

"Oh, that is so-wuh much better, you wouldn't believe. We get one of those Tackacees like last night."

"A taxi? It's that easy to get there?"

"Yes. No. Sort of. It'd be easier if we fly there but you don't do that, so we Tackacee the first bit to the park, the one with the man from space. Then we walk the rest of the way! Well you walk, I don't. We get there like that. Easy!"

"The park with the man from space?"

"Gagarin Park," said the waiter, as he arrived carrying a tray loaded with food. Leonid was sure she'd asked for all this, but her words had been rather fast and somewhat peculiar.

"Uhri Gagarin! Two, three kilometair from here. First of men in space! America so jealous, ha ha! Soviet first! And we name park thih Park Gagarin."

He laughed a gruff smoker's laugh until he realised that the girl had obviously been in the middle of a deep conversation with nobody at all. He warily unloaded the coffee and all the plates of food onto her table, surprised at how calm and unafraid the bird was. If anything, it seemed impatient for him to hurry up.. and it had jam on its head?

He wrote down the odd assortment of items on a small bill, but couldn't help but be distracted by the girl as she sneaked all the cakes and biscuits into her pockets, while discretely whispering down to the songthrush. Then she pointed at each of the three croissants as if she was asking the bird to choose one of them, and then established how much jam it would like spreading on. And then.. Leonid stopped writing and simply watched as she dabbed at the bird's head with a napkin. He'd seen many strange things over his years of dealing with tourists, but this was something else altogether.

"Haff good day, be good, yes? I say bye, enjoy foods, bye bye."

He scrumpled the bill up and dropped it into a replacement ashtray, and then went back inside. He looked out from near the coffee machine, hoping she might leave soon and be a crazy-mad-person somewhere else, preferably without scaring off too many of his customers first. Linda, however, was amazed. She jiggled the ashtray, rocking the ball of paper.

"They're always doing that here. It must be like a custom or something. Beats me, really does.."

The taxi ride only took a few minutes, and Linda soon found herself standing at the foot of a large bronzed statue of a serious-looking man who was holding a space helmet and a hammer. It probably made complete sense to the people who put it there, but Linda was mystified by it. Avalon soon arrived from somewhere high above, and settled on her shoulder.

"It's much nicer here than where we're going, but we can't stay. See the big pointy hills all the way over there?" she said, already starting to feel nervous about the journey ahead.

"Those ones? They're miles away, Avalon. We'd need another taxi and a plane as well.. and then another taxi after that, and maybe another plane as well."

"That's okay, because we're not going to them. We're aiming for the bit off to the left.. the patch of trees that look like green with too much green. It's the longer way round.. but we don't go through the widest part of the forest that way, see? Around, not through. Well, not through much, anyway."

The park and all its noises were soon left far behind them as the neatly mown areas gave way to heavy undergrowth and very narrow footpaths, which in turn gave way to dense forest. After two or three hours, or maybe even more, Linda was convinced they were in the middle of nowhere.

"Are we.. umm.. nearly there yet?" she asked, trying not to whine. Avalon turned around twice, and shrugged with a twitch.

"Ever so probably, or maybe even closer. Why? Did you hear something scream?"

"No, I was just wonder.. scream?" said Linda, as her voice fell to a whimper.

"I.. err.. didn't say scream, I said 'When the shadows are a bit longer, and start joining up.' Because that's when we're getting in it."

They kept going, with Avalon leading the way by hovering two or three feet in front of Linda and only occasionally pausing in order to fly up into the sky for a quick look around. Two long hours later she started to become very quiet and stopped going for her flights, and Linda sensed the atmosphere had changed. The trees seemed quieter, the undergrowth was quickly becoming heavier, and the air had taken on a very definite edge. Even the colours of nature were missing, steadily replaced by morbid, dark shades of brown. Avalon shivered and flew close, wrapping the braid around herself a few times. When she spoke, Linda could feel the quietness around them.

"This is the Outer Reaches and it goes on for a bit.. but not all that long.. we just keep going, one step then another.. not scared, not scared," she said, cautiously looking around herself.

A long and very deep moan rolled through the densely packed masses of trees and vines, carried from somewhere far away. Linda looked at Avalon, who looked straight back at her, terrified. A breeze as cold as ice snaked around Linda's ankles, rustling the leaves at her feet before withdrawing to wherever it had come from.

"What.. was.." she quivered, staring at the wide rut of disturbed leaves leading into the trees.

"The Dead Wind! It's the Dead.. lie down, close eyes! Now now nownownownowNOW!"

Linda lay with her face pressed against the damp ground while Avalon scattered a layer of rotting leaves over her before shuffling the alexandrite necklace around so that it lay on full show between her shoulders. She settled herself underneath it and trembled against Linda's back, clutching the chain as tightly as the gem, and repeated the Rhyme Of Protection that Kupula had tried teaching her so long ago.

And then the moaning came again, but this time it was so much nearer and so much louder. Its raw, burgeoning power shook the ground as it tore through the trees, hunting misery as it passed. Linda couldn't breathe. The moan no longer held a solitary resonance. Now she could tell it was filled with millions of voices that made it what it was - the wretched, captive souls of the Black Roots Forest, those spirits who hadn't yet been taken by the trees and could do nothing but stay within their confines, helpless, lost, and waiting for their time to come.

The Wind soon reached them. It passed by not as wind does, but as a powerful, violent force, pounding earth and trees, feeding on life and dragging all but misery from anything that hadn't already surrendered to it. Linda shook as if an earthquake was devastating the forest, not knowing if she was ever going to open her eyes again.

And then it was gone. The Dead Wind had passed by and its voice fell to nothing, leaving an overpowering silence in its wake. Linda kept herself under the safe blanket of leaves, much like she used to hide beneath her sheets for entire nights cowering from vile entities who might have escaped from her dreams. The ground was so lifeless, its stench of death so utterly revolting.. but she couldn't make herself move for a long while.

Eventually she felt a pair of small hands flicking the leaves from her, and then they started moving her necklace back around to where it belonged. She lifted her head a little from the damp earth, and Avalon raised her hair enough so that she could see.

"What.. what was all that? It was awful, that was worse than bad.." she whispered, sitting up and trying to see if her back would ever move again. She felt as if a steam roller had been over it at least twice, and then parked there for a while. Avalon gestured for her to keep her voice very low.

"Gone now. And so would we without the Alexandryite.. not nice. It knew we were here, but couldn't see where. How's that for close?"

Avalon settled on Linda's shoulder and took refuge wrapped in waves of hair, and made sure the braid was tied tightly around herself. She clutched the small gem, and rainbow colours ran across its surfaces as she pointed it in different directions to ward off the countless evil spirits which Linda hadn't a hope of seeing. She decided not to mention any of them and tried humming Knowing Me Dancing Waterloo instead, to show Linda that there was absolutely no need to be scared anymore.

Every tired step now broke the silence. The sharp cracks and rustles sounded as if they were gunshots that could carry for miles, announcing to the entire forest that outsiders had arrived.

"Wow, look!" whispered Linda almost an hour later, lifting the oppressive atmosphere for a brief moment. She pointed at a short, lone blade of grass standing prominently from the muddiness around it. Avalon clapped wildly, and almost launched herself high into the air with excitement. She managed the entire length of the braid before quickly coming back.

"We're getting there! That means we're nearing the other side of all this, and then things won't be nearly so bad, I think. What do you think? They won't be bad, will they?"

Linda could see that Avalon needed reassuring, even though she was the only one who knew this place.

"Yeah, I can't wait. Fresh air, sunshine, blue sky.."

Half an hour later the sun was casting long and bright shafts of light through the branches, illuminating small insects and burning away stubborn mists. Avalon felt it was safe enough to leave Linda and take her untethered lead-position a few feet ahead again, and shortly afterwards they raced triumphantly into a sunny clearing, not stopping until wide-open fields rolled ahead of them. Avalon had to give her wings some proper exercise and soared high up into the sky. She dived back down so quickly and for so long that Linda was convinced she couldn't possibly stop in time, but somehow she merely brushed the grass at break-neck speed before racing back upwards. As if that wasn't crazy enough, Linda noticed that Avalon was singing loudly while she did it.

"Abba in Swedish," thought Linda, and wondered what Dee's psychiatrist would make of this. Maybe he wouldn't be too bothered because of the insane things that Dee probably talked about? Maybe the world in Dee's head was even barmier than any of this? That thought made her laugh until her sides ached, while Avalon plummeted earthwards for another heart-stopping close call, before looping back up into the blue sky high above. It was all too crazy by at least a mile and four hat stands, and Linda laughed until she couldn't stand up any more.

Linda regained enough composure to realise that a third crazy dive might be one dive too many for Avalon, so she rummaged through her pockets to see if many biscuits were left. Most of the supplies had managed to fall out during the clambering and trudging through the forest, but she managed to find one that was packed with hazelnuts, so she brushed off a few stubborn leaves and held it up towards the small dot in the sky. For reasons that could only be known to Avalon, it worked. She came back to Linda in three or four lazy circles, softly arriving on the grass in front of her, giggling and absolutely worn out.

"Fun, fun, fun, funfunfunfunFUN. Whew.. and now this too! Today just gets better and better!" she said breathlessly, looking at her well-earned Prize For Being Mad. Linda lay in the grass and broke small pieces off to make it more manageable, happy to stay there until Avalon felt like moving on.

A short while later the forest was well behind them, and the grass and clusters of trees were becoming interrupted by large outcrops of rocks, jutting up like huge grey teeth. Eventually the ground became split by small fissures and crevices, and Linda had to start being careful about where she stepped or took footholds. Avalon darted a few yards ahead, and settled over on the side of a broad rock. She called back, very excited, and Linda hurried to her. She was looking down a gentle slope which lead into a shallow valley perhaps a hundred feet below, which ran for miles like a green river between two steep banks of rocks.

"Let me guess.. you've found a comfy rock?"

"Nope.. well yes I have, but also look over there!"

Avalon pointed far away to the left, where the sun was sinking. Linda's eyes widened as she saw a collection of buildings about a mile away. Some had tall pointed roofs, most were pale grey, and one in particular was very dark. Linda shivered. Other larger and more modern buildings were dotted nearby, along with half a dozen cars parked beside them. Another two vans arrived from somewhere, and disappeared behind a high wall.

"D'you think that's it, Avie?"

"Uhuh.."

"So Brother Duvahlavlich was right then.. but where's our way in? You know, that Scorpion's Third Thing? I couldn't see it clearly enough when we read his book. I mean, the fake-well can't be too far off, can it?"

"Nope. See, there's the jumbley hills over there.. so Brother Dalovich must have been thinking about somewhere way over that way in his book.. or maybe the people who told him the story were thinking of it. Anyway, I've got a pretty good idea where it ought to be. Or.. we could find it by waiting for the stars to line up again, then just go to the place where we can look up and see the big Scorpion lighting up in the sky?"

"That sounds like a good idea to me. When's it due to happen?"

Avalon counted out all her fingers, and raised both feet.

"In your years, or mine?" she asked, scratching her head with her wrist.

"So we go for a wander instead?"

"No. I think it'll be a lot quicker if I go and take a look first, but.. it's all getting scary again. Bad things are around," said Avalon, ending in a whisper.

"Well you can take my mum's necklace if you want.. I don't mind, really I don't. I trust you," said Linda, fiddling with the clasp.

"No.. okay then.. yes, no. No. You might need it here without even knowing that you need it.. but I won't say why 'cause you'll just get scared that way. I know I'd be scared, if I was you. Really scared."

"Thanks, I think. Just be as safe and quick as you can, okay?"

Avalon took to the air and flew high above the valley, trying to lose herself in Brother Dalovich's book again. She closed her eyes and let the winds carry her, swooping here and there, guiding her away from evil spirits. She held onto that weak link that might lead her to where she needed to be. That hardly ever worked usually, but with someone as Gifted as Linda in her life, she had found that confidence was easier to come by. Trusting her heart had worked through the Black Roots Forest, and it could work again now - because it had to. She flew through fleeting images of his writings, and soon found the world around her matching the world within her. She was right where she needed to be, and managed two small back-loops with excitement. Linda would be so pleased, and not just about the back-loops. She hurried back, flying faster than she'd ever tried to fly in her whole life.

Trying to stop or even slow down with such tired wings proved far too difficult, and she arrived in Linda's hair with an undignified whumpf, and completely tangled herself up. That nearly spoiled the moment, but once Linda had found that she wasn't being attacked by Evil Flying Thingies, she seemed as happy to see Avalon as Avalon was to see her.

"What's it like then?" Linda said, while waiting for her heart to start working properly again. Avalon shuffled in a pocket to try and find a few biscuit pieces, and soon crossed to one of the others.

"It's like a big door," she replied, and moved to another.

"A big door? That's brilliant, and you weren't gone for long at all. Is it far off?"

Avalon stayed quiet for a moment while she concentrated on rooting around inside one of Linda's larger side-pockets. Only her legs and the lower half of her wings poked out, until she emerged with her arms full of broken biscuits, torn tissues, and some small Ukrainian coins. She dropped them all on the ground, so that Linda could join in and pick out whatever bits she might like.

"Was it far from here?" Linda repeated, picking out the tissues.

"Yes. Actually no. Imagine where we are now, but over on the other side of the Chapel, just off the valley. So that means.." she looked thoughtful while she figured out the exact distance, while at the same time testing to see if the smallest coin tasted good, "..eww! It should take a year or maybe more, I think," she said, and threw the coin like a frisbee into the bushes.

"Huh? Let's hope it's more like an hour. Do you think it looks like rain? I hope it doesn't.. you wouldn't believe what my hair's like when it's wet. Believe me, you wouldn't want to hitch a lift then. Your braid would be totally off-limits because.."

They moved back to the edges of the wooded areas while Linda explained the down-side to having left her hat with Aggy, and Avalon pretended to understand while keeping an eye out for unwelcome spirits. They made their way along the undulating side of the valley, staying low and hopefully out of sight.

The Chapel lay less than a hundred yards away, and Linda dared take a look. She clambered onto a table-sized rock in between a mass of dense bushes, and peered through the greenery. In a way, it was quite disappointing. The drab stone walls looked so old and ordinary, and it was less than half the size of St Teresa's Chapel. It had been added to over the years until the walls extended far out into an overpowering complex of taste-defying structures. A few grand old houses lifted the Style Factor, but not enough to save it from being an ugly mess. She watched a few people milling around, and wondered if they were carrying guns or maybe had clever Bond-esque weapons tucked up their sleeves.

"Hmm.. I could do with a troop of lethal SAS soldier-types, and then enough helicopters and tanks to wipe.." she said to herself.

"You've got me, so that's a start," whispered Avalon, and spun around until she went dizzy.

"Yep.. and that'll do fine.." said Linda, while Avalon became tangled in her hair again.

They kept going until they were almost a mile beyond the Chapel, and safely out of sight behind more banks of rocks and towering pine trees. Avalon raced ahead and stopped at the verge of a place which didn't look either special or door-like at all. Linda caught up with her and gazed down a short incline to a collection of broad, grass-covered rocks in the ground, surrounding a gap barely wide enough to notice. She slid most of the way down towards it across the wet and muddy ground, stopped for a few seconds.. and then slipped down a bit more. She stayed on all fours and crawled across the last bumpy section to the opening.

"Is this it, then?" she said, surprised and apprehensive.

"Uhuh. Definitely sure about that. Pretty much."

Linda picked her way to the side of the small gap, and noticed that the cracked rocks were a little too similar and well-organised to be there by accident. She edged sideways to try and rest each hand on the least damaged rocks, well away from any serious cracks.

"Umm.. Avie, isn't there another way we can do this, like maybe wait until tonight and then sneak into those buildings back there? Everything around here's.."

"..got cracks and all that stuff?" she said, standing on one and pointing at it.

"Yeah, and that can't be good, so something really bad's just bound to happ.."

Avalon hovered up to her Clear Thinking Level, which was about three feet off the ground.

"But this way you're not stepping on cracks, you're going through them which makes a BIG difference, unless you happen to be stuck in one, in which case.. you'd.. already be there.." she managed, before digging herself into silence.

That wouldn't have made the slightest bit of sense coming from anyone else, but from Avalon.. that was perfectly believable. Linda sat next to the gap and dangled her feet down into the darkness, feeling the back of her trainers knocking against stone and mud, and sighed to herself. There was practically no space to spare, and she couldn't see anything at all beyond her feet. Avalon settled on Linda's knee, and gazed down into the darkness.

"Don't you think you ought to go head first? I did when I took a look earlier on," she suggested.

"Head first? Avie, feet first's going to be bad enough. It must be crawling with hairy-legged uglies and hideously vile Mutant Thingies down there."

"Yup, it is. And going head-first means you'll see every single one, and then you can avoid them."

"See them? But it's all pitch black in there! I don't want to do.." she whimpered.

"Don't worry, I thought about that. I'll go first and point them all out - easy! Besides, there's loads more Creeplies out here than down there," she said, adding 'probably' onto the end so quietly that she didn't even hear it herself. She dived down between Linda's feet and immediately came back out again, nestling up on her shoulder, and piling layers of hair over herself.

"Not scared, not scared at all.. really I'm not," she jabbered into he ear. Linda sighed and began lifting her feet out of the gap.

"Okay, we'll both go down there at the same time. Now get ready.."

She tucked as much hair out of the way as possible, held her breath for no real reason, and began wriggling into the darkness. Once they were well into the crawl-space, Avalon ventured a few inches ahead of her, illuminating a very strange place indeed. Even though the well was almost vertical, the walls had collapsed and subsided over the centuries and it had steadily filled with earth and rocks, and maybe a stray cow or two. Or rather, Linda hoped the bones were from cows, and not from any huge not-so-prehistoric dinobeasts that only liked living near Odessa. But being positive, she did notice that the solid stonework was still looking pretty good, and that's what she told herself over and over again as she inched her way downwards from one narrow cavity and crawl-space to the next. Avalon tried to help with morale, in her own way.

"See these grooves around the wall? These ones here.." she sang, patting one.

"These ones which my face has been pushing and dragging against for the last twenty minutes?"

"Uhuh. I bet they were used like a ladder. That'll be good for you on the way out, won't it? What do you think?"

"I think.. I think I'm not toooo bothered right n.."

The earth and rocks began moving and Linda was carried helplessly down by a seismic shift that felt like it must have turned the entire world around. The ground stopped moving as suddenly as it had started, and Linda lay squashed in the darkness, looking for Avalon's glow.

"Avie? Where are you? Are you okay? I'm stuck.. uh oh.. no I'm.."

Linda slowly slid headfirst for a few seconds in the darkness before stopping against a big flat rock. Avalon appeared from a small cavern in the wall where a boulder had been, and flew down to her. They both squealed as the eye sockets of a skull rose up from the muddy earth.

"Avie, I thought you said this place was just like a big door?"

"Well it is."

"HOW IS.. how is this death-trap anything remotely like a door?"

"Well, I wondered just that to start with. Then I worked out that if you go through a door you get somewhere else, don't you? And once you've gone through here, you'll be somewhere else. So it's just like a door. A really thick door, a big dark one that's ever so difficult to get through.."

"And you're totally sure we're in the right place?"

"Yes.. sort of."

"Sort of?"

"Well I didn't go down anywhere near this far - I just looked in the top because you weren't with me and it looked too dark and scary. Besides.. we'll never get all the way back up to the top now, so it has to be the right place doesn't it?"

Linda was in no mood to start questioning Avalon's logic - or lack of it. Instead she crawled down a little further and felt herself being moved sideways, stopping only when she became wedged hard against the wall. Fortunately, she was almost getting used to being upside down and wasn't feeling nearly as bad as when she had started. Bugs and creepy things were the last thing on her mind.

"Oh, I am so stuck.." she moaned, finding that she couldn't move at all, other than waggling her foot, "..now my stupid shoe's coming off.. Avie? Where are you?"

A few seconds later Avalon Not Me'd herself through a small gap to appear in front of Linda's eyes.

"Uhuh?"

"Avie, I'm unbelievably really stuck this time.."

"Don't worry.. there's just a huge big stony thing in the way, that's all.. but there's an even more hugely big gap under it. Really big! And there's water way down below as well so you won't get hurt when you land.. won't be a minute.." she said cheerfully, and disappeared back through the gap.

"When I land? Avie! Avie!"

Darkness and eerie silence engulfed Linda as soon as Avalon disappeared. And then a very faint tapping sound came from somewhere down below, sending intense shockwaves through the rock - and also through Linda. It was the kind of sound that she had heard somewhere before.

"What's that noise? Avie, are you making that knocking sound? Uh oh.. are you doing your Door-Thing on this.. oh no.."

A van-sized boulder that had spent the last 600 years supporting nearly seven tons of rubble finally gave way, and shuddered down forty feet with Linda being pushed around its side by a deluge of gravel and earth. It came to a deafening halt as it ploughed into the wide base of the well, closely followed by Linda who was immediately submerged in two feet of icy cold water. The boulder was too long to land flat, and tipped sideways to form a protective shield between her and most of the rocks above. She kneeled up to her waist in the water, and waited for her brain to catch up with wherever she was.

"I'm.. I'm not dead? I can't be, I'm too cold and drenched to be dead. Avie? Where are you? Are you okay?" she called through the sound of cascading gravel, which was splashing into the water like hard rain. Avalon appeared from behind a jagged striation,

"Me? I'm fine, I am," she replied, and performed a small twirl to show how fine she was. "Why?"

"Oh, no reason, no reason.." sighed Linda, wondering if Avalon was watching the same channel that she was.

She flew off to take a look around the small cavern, and soon found a gap in the wall just above the water level. It was almost completely blocked by the side of the rock, leaving a triangular entrance slightly smaller than the entry-one high up above. Linda splashed her way over, and gladly wriggled after Avalon inside. The rough stonework soon lead into a cramped but well-preserved tunnel, made up of small bricks across the flooring and lots of small slabs for walls. The arched ceiling looked so insecure that Linda kept her eyes well away from it, firmly fixed on the almost-even floor.

She crawled along following Avalon, trying hard to ignore the stale air and trying even harder to ignore the distressing sounds of stones pushing against stones, which seemed to be coming from all around her. They reached a crescendo with a thunderous crash a little way back in the well, and Linda crawled as fast as she could through sprinklings of brickwork and earth until she had to stop and catch her breath. She lay in the dark for a moment, unable to even sit up in the narrow archway. Avalon hovered next to her head, rather than get any of the damp slime of the floor on her feet.

"Well, in certain ways this is much better, Avie."

"It is?"

"Uhuh, I'm not upside down any.."

A pair of eyes like two yellow slits raced out of the darkness and went straight past her, then briefly re-appeared barely inches away, staring intensely at them both before disappearing. A stench of decay filled the tunnel.

"Akkh, what is that? And what were those, Avie? Where did those eyes come from? Tell me they're just fire flies?"

Two more pairs of dull yellow eyes passed by, this time even narrower and even closer.

"Yes! That's all they are, fireflies, Lindy, that's all. And maybe just a few little spirits raised from the dead by lots of curses and things, and maybe they're cross that we're here disturbing them. You should be glad you can only see their eyes.. can we go any faster?"

Avalon held Linda's braid, and made sure that she kept moving. Linda crawled as fast as she could, ignoring all the dark side tunnels and only stopping to squeeze past small piles of fallen bricks. The eyes stopped following after a while, but the fear they left behind didn't leave Linda for a moment. She only stopped moving when her entire body went on strike, and she took a moment to look at the new style of brickwork. There was some carving on one of the rust-red bricks near Avalon.

"Oh wow, it says M-D-C-C-L-.." she whispered, rubbing the grime from the last few numerals, "..we must be in the wrong place entirely? Look - it says 1782. That's probably the date this tunnel was built. Brother Davul wouldn't have known about this, would he? He must have been writing about a different tunnel altogether.. we could be anywhere," she said, ready to cry with despair.

"Hmm.." pondered Avalon, "..we could find out if it's the right one, like we did with the book?"

Linda wiped her eyes.

"I don't think I could even if I tried. I'm shattered, and if I close my eyes for a second I'm sure I'll open them and see those yellow ones staring back. You do it Avie, and I'll stay here on Freakwatch."

Linda waved her alexandrite to reassure her, and Avalon reached in between a gap in the brickwork. She pulled her arm out very quickly, and shook it twice.

"Yep! First tunnel built in 1187, collapsed in 1188, rebuilt then rebuilt then rebuilt then rebuilt lots of times ever since, especially in 1782 when it all caved.. umm.. these bricks look really solid, don't they? And that's good," she said, giving the nearest one a good pat. A chunk of it fell onto the floor, followed by a dozen smaller pieces.

"Umm.. we ought to be moving again.. those Bad Spirits might be following right now.. ooh scary bad spirits.." she said, waving her arms to emphasise the scariness. Her glow took on a slight hint of pink, and she started to head further into the darkness of the tunnel, giving the braid a good tug. Linda started crawling again, wondering if there was ever going to be an end to this miserable place. Her elbow pressed against something which gave a sickening crunch, and then went very slippery.

"Yeech.. Avie, I feel worse than a tramp's pants. Can you try some magic on me? You must have got something left that works on people.. like a Hot Bath Spell, or even a Quick Shower one?"

"Nope. Just do this, like I do," she replied, and gave herself a good shake, casting off all traces of dirt in less than a second. She glowed brighter than ever, the tunnel lit up a little more, and she looked a lot happier with herself.

"All clean!" she announced, "Could you blow on my wings, puhhlease? Especially the right one.. still a bit dusty.."

Linda sighed and gave a gentle breath which seemed to do the trick, and then started crawling again.

Half an hour later Avalon brought the longest ever rendition of Take A Chance On Me to an end, and stopped at a rusty metal panel which blocked the entire end of the tunnel. There was nowhere left to go, and she nervously looked around to Linda.

"Hmm," pondered Linda, watching closely as Avalon repeatedly moved across it from one side to the other.

"There's no handles or anything. This might be tricky," whispered Linda, pressing against one side, "..actually this is way beyond Not Good.. it won't budge or anything."

"It's okay, I've got an idea," said Avalon, lining her foot up with its centre.

"No, no.. we don't know what or who's on the other side so we need to be really quiet.. shhh.."

Linda pushed against each corner, hoping one of them would give way, even just a little. Nothing happened, so she tried each one again, and then again.

"Oh no.. what do we do now?" she moaned under her breath.

"You could try pulling that handle at the bottom. That might do it?" said Avalon, pointing.

Linda gave it a go, feeling embarrassed. The plate jerkily swung inwards on its rough hinges allowing a dull light into the tunnel - and then it came off completely. She tried holding on with her finger tips, but too much of it was hanging over the edge and it gradually slipped away. It landed with a tremendous clatter a few feet below and she buried her head into her arms, praying no-one was down there.

CHAPTER THIRTEEN
The Stone Of Odessa

Linda watched nervously as Avalon fluttered down into the murky darkness of the chimney. She settled about six feet below, safely hidden amongst a broad spread of unlit logs and coal. She opened her Journal and drew the hearth across two new pages, marked it with an X and took off for a very quick look around.

"Nobody's there!" she chirped barely three seconds later, as she came back up. Linda lowered herself down, hanging from the ledge while Avalon told her where to aim for. She landed in an undignified heap, and as soon as her foot had stopped hurting she picked up the metal plate and tried to jump up and gently lob it back into the tunnel - but missed completely. It clattered back onto the floor again and she froze for a few seconds, convinced that someone was going to come in and be incredibly annoyed with her. One long minute later nothing had happened, and she ducked under the top of the fireplace and stepped into the large Victorian-style meeting room, setting a Personal Best for feeling scared and vulnerable.

"Do you think this is the Chapel then, Avie? It looks more like someone's house, doesn't it?"

The lights gave out a dull, orange radiance which was barely strong enough to reach into the shadows of the room's bizarre decor. On the far wall beyond the long oval table, strange luminescent patterns linked huge seven-pointed silver stars, which in turn were linked to dozens of portraits around the other two walls.

Linda forced herself to leave the hearthplace and follow Avalon over to them. Most showed the heavy cracks of age and the subjects were lost within their own sombre darkness, but a few revealed the shady features of some very intimidating men. Their eyes burned into the room, as if they were challenging anyone who dared meet their gaze. Avalon began drifting past them, shying well away from certain ones before finding a row full of surprises.

"He's Mr Paustovskiy! He had the small vegetable shop on the wide street before the Old War.. that's Mr Korolev from the Government, that one's his brother.. that's Father Sarmeniov.. this is all kinds of People! What are they here for?"

Avalon flew right up to Linda's nose, breaking the hypnotic hold one of the men held over her.

"Lindy? Look-at-me! Me! LOOKATME!" she shouted, and gave the braid a tug.

"Uhh.. Avie? I was.. I nearly read one of them, or he read me.. I couldn't think right for a moment there. It was awful.."

"That's because there's something bad here.. and I can feel it too.." Avalon said, shaking. Linda looked back at the portrait, keeping her eyes well away from his face, and a few feelings fell into place.

"Secrets.." she said, "..it's full of secrets. This might have started out with good intentions, but these people don't feel righteous or protective at all.. to me. And I bet the Church and the Government don't know anything about it. It's like a cult.. totally secret, and these scaries must have been its leaders over the years. We're so far out of our depth, Avie.. Avie?"

Linda hurried across to Avalon, who had flown over to the other wall. She was staring in silent awe at a collection of portraits which were slightly more colourful than the others. They were of children and adults who wore strange blue robes and had the kind of halos that Linda had seen in paintings of Saints. All of the figures posed the same way - one hand was lost in a ball of white light and the other hand was raised in a gesture of piety. And they all had the same haunted, lifeless expression in their eyes.

Avalon touched a gold-leaf symbol embedded in the background of one of them, and immediately dropped down into a collection of silver goblets. She shook herself into one of her blurs and darted back onto Linda's shoulder.

"There's.. there's bad things written around them! They were all cursed and.. then something about The Stone. They could all do things with it, these are the Gifted Ones. I don't like it here, Linda! I don't want The Stone anymore! And look!"

She held her head as if bells were ringing all around her and flew up into the darkness, next to a painting of the most forlorn and scared girl Linda had ever seen. One hand was lost in the usual ball of light but her other was long and disfigured, and painted a sickening red and black. Even with Avalon's glow it was impossible to see clearly, much to Linda's relief.

"This one's holding Hecatia! Hecatia!" she squealed.

"Listen to me, Avie, calm down and come and tell me wh.." whispered Linda, trying to hide her anxiety. Avalon moved faster than

Linda could blink, and wrapped herself tightly in her hair.

"Heca.. Hec.. it's the Demon Root," she cried, "..with all kinds of Life Blood on it and it's used to bring Spirits of Darkness back so they can walk with the Living! She must have been here during the worst times ever! This is where she would have summoned the Bad Ones to come back to.. I want to go, I want to.."

Linda held back a wave of emotions as she first sensed and then understood that the girl had willed herself to die rather than live in this building. Suddenly, everything in her mind screamed for her to turn around and get out straight away, to get back into the tunnel and just keep crawling until she was safely in the outside world - and heading for the airport with Avalon like a good girl should have been doing last night. But a feeling in her heart that defied words simply wouldn't let her. It was that certain something that she couldn't argue with or ever understand, the part of her that could contradict every ounce of common sense.. the part that saw Half-There's. She stood frozen to the spot, completely unable to work out what the right thing to do might be. Avalon tugged her ear, and shouted something about the ceiling.. and eventually Linda looked upwards.

The sounds of muffled voices drifted through the deep-carved plaster, and footsteps thudded above her head. The shock sent a huge burst of adrenaline racing through her, and she would have passed out if she hadn't been holding back a yelp due to Avalon attempting to leave her shoulder without untangling herself first. Avalon flew to the huge door across the room, briefly morphing into a small fly to disappear through its keyhole. She re-emerged and waved Linda to hurry up, and darted to her shoulder where she wrapped herself tightly in the braid. Linda prayed the door would be good to her. As expected, it wouldn't move at first, and its handle wouldn't even twist a little. But then at the precise moment that she stopped trying, it gave way completely and swung silently open, allowing her just enough space to step through.

The air was heavy with the smoke from dozens of incense cords and dishes which hung from the ceiling's black wooden beams. Linda's eyes raced around the heavy stone-work of the room. It was less than half the size of the meeting room, and dimly lit by three candles on a thick-set table opposite her. Their flickering light was reflected by a five-armed gold cross, making the room feel alive with shadows. Linda put her ear to the door, listening for the slightest trace of sound. She couldn't hear anything, but the light coming through the keyhole and the small gap under the door had grown stronger. Somebody was in there.

"Now what?" wavered Avalon, rocking anxiously from side to side, nudging Linda's neck. Linda looked around through the gloom.

"One of those two?" she whispered, pointing to the gaping arched doorways either side of the table, and took out her dice.

"Here we go. Odd means left and Even means right, just like always," she half-said and half-thought, which pleased Avalon. The dice rolled perfectly along a grooved floorstone, and came to rest near a discarded handful of hair and coarse grey powder.

"It's Left! No, no, that's Right, isn't it?" announced Avalon. She hurried to retrieve it, and shivered as she blew all the ingredients of an unmentionable curse off its sides before daring to touch it.

The left passage was cold and impenetrably dark. Even Avalon's light offered no help, and she soon stopped pretending to lead and instead settled behind Linda's necklace, clutching the long braid as well. The stone stairway lead down and down into a tightening spiral, coming out into the middle of a room entirely covered in black and white tiles. Avalon squealed.

"They're.. they're only gargoyles, Avie.. they're not real.." Linda whispered, trying to convince Avalon (as much as herself) that the evil stone-carvings glaring from the wall's pillars definitely weren't going to lunge down at her. The light from a dozen candles shone brightly in their jewelled eyes, making her feel unsure about that.

She crept around the base of the staircase, noticing that each of the four walls had an elongated doorway at its centre, fronted by shallow dishes filled with magenta flames. She flinched as shadows flitted across the perfect white tiles and disappeared into the black ones, as if they were being drawn towards the dull lights dancing on the dishes. The acrid smoke of one thinned enough to reveal lines of heavy symbols and markings that had been carved deep into the stonework beside each doorway, which Avalon could only avoid looking at by shuffling behind Linda's neck.

Linda silently stepped back to the foot of the staircase, and reached into her pocket to choose which of the doors to go through. She touched the six on her dice. Being an Even number, she counted clockwise around from the doorway that she was facing when they first arrived, and found herself staring at a dark entrance with a black sun painted above it.

"That one, then," she thought, not even trying to find her voice. Avalon nodded, nervously.

They were soon lost in darkness again, on another long march downwards through biting cold air. Linda kept one hand on the wall as she picked out each step of the way on the treacherously wet steps and quickly lost track of whether they had turned left more times than right, or if the circular sections had turned her back on herself or not. In the silent darkness it didn't seem to matter that much. Suddenly Avalon gasped, and held up the necklace. The gem was filled with its rainbow colours just as it had been since they were in the Black Roots Forest, but now it was changing. They were no longer drifting from one colour to the next, but were strong and separate as if they could fall apart at any moment.

"Tell me that's a good sign, Avie?" breathed Linda.

Avalon looked around herself, confused and very scared.

"There's more Evil Ones and Bad Spirits than ever.. there's curses all around us on the walls.. hexes everywhere too.. nobody should be here except Protected Ones.. I'm really.. really.. I'm ever so scared now.. ever.." she trembled, and finished with a sniff.

Linda had no idea what to say. She'd felt too scared for far too long, so she did the only thing she could think of. She cupped her hands protectively around Avalon and gave her a small kiss, or as near as she could manage on a faery, then moved all her hair onto her left shoulder to give her plenty to hide under. And then she carried on walking through the darkness.

A few minutes later, Linda began feeling small hollows and shapes carved into the wall, and gave a mini-cheer as she reached the end of a long, curved corner. A line of candles offered light for the entire passageway ahead, and there didn't appear to be any monsters, weirdos, bad guys or Ved'mas for at least the next fifty yards.

She ran light-footed and silent past even more gargoyles, rushing from candlelight to candlelight, glad to be able to see properly but painfully aware of the need to be in and out of it as soon as possible. A rectangular doorway, wide enough to drive a State Limousine and half a taxi through, lead her back into the inky blackness. The steps quickly narrowed and she stumbled down the last few to arrive in a short meeting-point where a series of passageways converged. Each one had a small candle above it, flickering wildly as if caught in breezes strong enough to blow out far larger flames.

"Are we still looking for the Stone, or a way out?" Linda slowly whispered, looking at each one.

"Why?" asked Avalon.

"I don't know.. it's just important that you tell me.. so that I choose right.." she said, unable to put into words the strange feelings running around inside her, which were all being held in place by a sensation of pure calmness.

"Umm.. I don't mind, really I don't.. maybe Stone first, then we go far away? But I don't mind.." Avalon whispered back in a trembling voice, from somewhere behind Linda's neck.

That was good enough. Linda looked at the candles and counted across all seven, first up to six from the left, then back from the right, and then from the left again. She felt as if she had given the candles their appropriate number-names and could discard what would have been the seventh one. She rolled her dice to find the safest doorway.. unless the first number happened to be a three in which case she'd roll again because a three could be deceptive, and always needed confirmation by a second throw, unless it bounced off a wall in which case it..

"You choose it, not the dice thing. Find the right one in your heart, just once, for me?" Avalon whispered in her ear.

That made sense. Linda stared at the ceiling, not thinking about anything or focussing on anything, and kept her eyes still until the small lights of the candles drifted in and out of the darkness and each other. The third one from the left felt a little brighter than the rest, and for a few seconds even looked brighter, maybe. She touched the dice in her pocket just to double-check, and felt a three.

"How about that.. three it is then."

The third entrance held a faint light, a sickly orange glow coming from around a corner at its far the end. The candle above its entrance disappeared as soon as she walked underneath, which Avalon noticed but decided not to mention.

Linda peered around the corner, across a passageway and into a place more sinister than any nightmare she'd ever been through.

"I think we're here, Avie.."

Linda stood in the ancient entry to the Ceremonial Sanctum, transfixed by the sight before her. The entire end wall of the long, narrow room was occupied by an altar lined with row upon row of flickering candles each held in red glass, giving the room an atmosphere of malevolence and foreboding. A mosaic covered the entire floor, depicting spirits and demons that made Avalon want to be anywhere else in all of Odessa but there. Another five-armed gold cross, over twice the size of the other, stood on the altar crowned with a ruby-eyed silver skull which glared imperiously down at anyone who dared enter. Linda dared.

She stepped tentatively forward, feeling every footstep give way a little on the strange tiles, and walked painfully slowly until her eyes had grown used to the subdued light. She stood before the candles, and stared at the jet-black wall behind the altar, which began revealing its ghostly designs to her.

A sparsely-jewelled image of a huge dark sun occupied the entire wall, and its shining black beams reached around the room, spread deep across each of the other walls. Her eyes followed the dark, painted beams past screaming images of horned and satanic faces and hundreds of angular figures being drawn back into the sun's centre - where more dire portraits of the most powerful Gifted Ones gazed forlornly out. Each frameless painting was encircled by countless gold symbols, white-lined star signs and sweeping Latin words, all of which drifted back into the darkness as her eyes moved from one to the other.. to the other.. to the other..

Avalon broke her dreamy state with a slight tug on the braid. She flew from Linda to hover before the very centre of the altar, where the midnight-blue velvet was raised off the floor, gathered up into a pinnacle. The heavy material had been parted in the middle to reveal an elaborate arch of gold beneath the altar, and Avalon floundered around in front of it, just inches away from hundreds of sparkling gemstones.

"Linda.." she whimpered, and finally dropped to the ground, stunned. Linda crept across to her, trying to make out exactly what she was pointing at.

She had never seen anything so beautiful. For a long time her mind was almost a complete blank, and she was aware of nothing else in the whole world except for the magnificent Stone. If a comparison could be drawn, it resembled a large teardrop-centrepiece from a grandiose chandelier, the kind that hung in the impressive stately homes her school was so fond of visiting. Only the weak candlelight shimmering across its countless facets gave it any form at all. It lay resplendent in the darkness, surrounded by diamonds and sapphires, each clasped in gold and each large enough to be centre stage. But the Stone overpowered them all, held from beneath in the vice-like grip of a claw of gold - four powerful talons intricately detailed, thick and encrusted with diamonds. Everything about it was so unimaginably beautiful, so..

"Linda?" whispered Avalon, sensing that she was lost and far away somewhere, "..Linda?"

"Hmmm..?"

"Can you come back to me? Talk to me sweety.. put your eyes on me.." she sang, trying her best not to sound too scared. She gave the braid a small tug, because that always seemed to work. Linda blinked slowly, and felt as if she was yawning without actually yawning. She looked at Avalon, and smiled to reassure her.

"Sorry, Avie, I was.. uhh.. something. I'm not sure what. It doesn't look much like a stone does it? It's more of a big crystal.. maybe Brother Dubblitch wasn't so good at listening to people?"

"Maybe.. but just look at the hexes around this, Linda! It's got s-so many really powerful things puh-protecting it.." she said, so excited and frightened that she kept forgetting to flap her wings..

"What do all these mean? Are they curses and stuff?"

"Uhuh.. all of them. And look at that one!" she squealed, and pointed at a series of dark and thick brush strokes running along the top of the altar's cover. The words looked as if they had been written by a madman, and seemed to have captured all of his hatred and torment. Avalon sniffed the air above it before racing back into Linda's hair. She took out her Journal, opening it near the front.

"That bit on the left represents.. control over the Evil which surrounds the Stone and.. oh no.. it has to have been written in generations of Eagles' blood, layered over and over again!"

"Why pick on eagles?"

Avalon shuffled close to her ear and whispered.

"They're not scared of anything so they're supposed to carry the Souls of the really Evil Ones to the lowest part of The Underworld, and leave them there. I'm sure it's true but I've never, ever asked one."

"So there must be all kinds of people and spirits after this?"

"Uhuh. How scary. I bet I can't go near it at all - you watch."

Avalon went as close as she could, changing to a sickly colour as she neared it. And then she wobbled through an extra few inches, and actually tried to touch it. A dozen small flashes appeared from nowhere, with her at their very centre. Linda scooped her up off the floor and blew most of the soot off her.

"Are you alright? Don't do.."

Avalon shook herself into a dizzy blur and disappeared for a few seconds in the clouds of black dust from her hair.

"I'm fine.. fine me now.. fine.. akk!" she choked as her glow returned to normal.

"Shhh.. listen.."

Avalon sat perfectly still on Linda's lap as they strained to hear anything. She took off and flew in a giddy line over to the doorway, and perched on its rough stonework. She felt the vibrations of voices through the air, and of footsteps marching in heavy unison. Low monastic chants drifted from a corridor that could have been near, far.. anywhere at all, and she darted back inside.

"It's Peoples! What now what now what now whatnowwhatnow WHATNOW-UH?"

"We stop getting freaky! We don't get freaked yet! We have to hide somewhere, very quick.. maybe there!" she whispered.

Linda pointed to the low table of ceremonial crosses and knives, which ran along one side of the room. It had a heavy cloth reaching to the floor and would be ideal to hide under, or as close to ideal as they could manage. Avalon shivered. There was something she didn't like about it.. something very bad. She pointed by the doorway.

"Let's be there instead! Ov'theretheretheretherthehtheh.."

She flew over to some tall black curtains which reached from the entrance over to the side of the room, covering the far wall. Linda hurried into the narrow gap behind the thick material and pushed herself as far into the corner as she could, while Avalon tried hard to stay on her shoulder.

"Me not.. it's the.. they've put things here.. to even keep my kind away.. so sleepy here.. must be right under a bad curse.. sleepy.."

Linda couldn't see anything at all in the darkness behind the curtain, but she managed to edge sideways to find a better place for Avalon, shaking as the morbid singing came nearer and nearer. The first monk trudged into the room and Linda froze, not daring to move or make a sound. Something sharp and metallic pressed into the back of her head, and she quickly realised there was a series of metal spikes embedded in the wall, fractionally away from her back. Avalon became more awake and alert again, and hovered all the way along to the very last fold in the curtain, almost next to the entrance. She beckoned Linda to keep moving, inch by inch, to come and join her. That had to be the craziest idea ever, but Linda made herself trust Avalon's judgement and kept shuffling along, not even daring to breathe just in case someone heard her. The small gap at the end of the curtains revealed a procession of heavily-shrouded monks walking in, and she tried to ignore them and keep her eyes on Avalon, who was still waving her arms wildly for her to hurry over. A dozen silent and terrified steps later, she was there, leaning back into a slight recess in the stonework.

The room began filling with sombre chants and stinging smoke, quickly joined by saccharin-sweet aromas of incense. Avalon held her nose and her mouth, until her glow turned a dull blue and she tumbled down into Linda's hands. More footsteps lumbered through the corridor, and she watched as a man wearing white robes entered the room, just inches away from her. He was followed by two others, both clad in dark cloaks, pushing a semi-conscious man in a wheeled chair. And then the curtains moved.

One of the monks stood in the corner where Linda had first chosen to hide, and began dragging the heavy curtain back across the wall. His steps matched the pace of the chanting, which grew louder as the people in the room joined in one by one, and her skin began crawling with icy perspiration as he slowly came nearer.

Avalon had clambered up and held tightly onto the side of Linda's neck as they both shook with the fear of being discovered. The chanting reached a crescendo and suddenly stopped, and for a second so did Linda's heart. Less than a foot of densely-folded curtain remained at her side to be moved, and she eventually breathed again - but only when she absolutely had to. She glanced sideways to see that the spikes that she'd felt were actually candle holders on a huge pentagram. The monk carefully lit each one, and went back to his position in the room, thankfully out of her sight. A man, presumably the leader, spoke in a strong and commanding voice. Avalon listened intently to his words, holding Linda even more tightly.

"They're summoning the Black Spirits.. through the Black Roots all around this place.. and he wants the Gifted One to say things.. bad things.. very bad.. to get The Stone to raise the levels of the seas.. in special places.. and for bad diseases to spread more quickly.."

The man grew louder and more aggressive as the Gifted One obviously failed to do his bidding.

"Now he's really cross. They all are.. and he says he wants to initiate a new Gifted One because this one's no use anymore.. he used to be good.. but he's got no mind left.. so he needs removing. The new one.. to begin on the next Fallow Moon.. two days from now."

After the longest thirty minutes of Linda's life, the ceremony was called to an end by the mournful tolling of a bell. The leader was the first to solemnly leave, followed by the two men with the Gifted One. Linda watched the emaciated wreck pass her by, and took a shred of comfort from his dreadful condition. At least he could no longer have any idea where he was or what he was supposed to be doing. The last of the monks blew out the candles on the wall, drew the curtain back across the pentagram, and took his place at the back of the procession. Soon they had all gone, and the room was left in miserable silence. Linda was ready to fall apart, and stayed behind the curtain until she felt able to step back out into this evil world. Now that she had seen so clearly what she had stumbled into, she was terrified. Avalon returned from a quick safety check.

"Gone now. All of them gone. Now what?" she said, tying the end of the braid securely around her waist.

"Huh?" breathed Linda, still too stunned to think straight.

"What do we do now, before anyone comes back?"

Linda stepped out from the curtain.

"We get that Stone-thing, that's what we do," and pointed a shaking finger at it.

They hurried over to the altar, which was now only lit by five small candles. One of the portraits had been taken from the wall and lay face-down before the golden cross, which had been draped with bloodied fur from each of its five arms. Avalon hovered as near to the Stone as she dared, pointing alternately to it and to Linda.

"Look at The Stone, Lindy!"

Linda stared. It was no longer perfectly clear. Dark clouds of red and black raged within it, moving faster and faster until the Stone seemed completely solid. Linda watched, confused and scared. Something within her was trying to make her very calm, but she wasn't sure how to allow it to happen.

"Okay.. okay.. stay normal.. feet on the ground.. stay normal.. find how it's attached. This claw must be part of something.." she said, and lifted the dark blue material around its base to show a block of granite. Like everything else, it was covered in symbols and strange words. She let the cloth fall back down and gave the claw a push, but its thick gold arm was set deep into the stone, and felt as if it reached all the way down into the very heart of the world.

"This is awful.." Avalon said, despairing, "Now we're here and The Stone's right there, I can't even do anything to help."

"Nor me.. it's set in all that gold and I can't even imagine what else is holding it in place, I really can't."

"But you're a Person. Another Person must have put it there, so you can take it back again, can't you?"

"Things don't really work like that.. I'm not sure what to do."

Avalon paused for a moment, and had her all-time best idea.

"We could try the book thing? Switch your mind off, and hold nothing but what's in your heart.. see if that works? You can follow me again, if that helps? Then I'll be being useful."

Linda knew she had to do something, and so far.. that was the only plan they'd got. She kneeled down on the floor in front of the altar to be closer to the Stone, and closed her eyes, ready to follow wherever Avalon might lead her. At last, the calmness drifted over her and her breathing become deep and slow, and she only heard the first few words that Avalon spoke. She was ready to fly, to soar high through beautiful white clouds and up into the other world with Avalon, to that place where dreams merged with reality, where her own rules were the only ones that mattered and nothing could ever, ever be beyond her.

She imagined being an eagle, as strong and as powerful as the one who dealt with evil spirits, and she was flying effortlessly with her mighty wings, and it was a wonderful feeling. She saw golden clouds beneath her and raced past them and down through them, and then joined Avalon miles and miles above them. The exhilaration was overpowering so she slowed for a while to gather her thoughts and her feelings. The Stone. She was supposed to be doing something about the Stone. But where was it? She couldn't see it, and anyway, it wasn't supposed to be up above the clouds, it was down in that evil place.. and then she stopped soaring, and began falling. Far away, she could feel Avalon's voice telling her to simply fly and to stop thinking, to just let everything come to her, because that was how it worked. She could be everywhere, but only if she didn't keep trying.

And that made sense, so she stopped wondering. She began gliding again, nothing but gliding, racing higher and higher, swooping and turning far above the clouds, and loving her freedom. Avalon laughed and waved for her to go even higher, and she did, leaving the best friend she could ever have, leaving her so far behind once more.

It was so easy, and Avalon would still be right beside her because in this world, sense didn't matter in the slightest - acceptance brought understanding, and that made everything fine.

And now the Stone was easy as well. It was there, wherever she wanted it to be. All she had to do was ask for it and it would be hers, because there was nothing to keep it from her. She flew higher, into and through even more clouds, making the shape of the Stone with her hands and her heart, asking and yet commanding it to appear. It was safe and right to do that, and the Stone was before her, around her and within her, it held no secrets, it was beautiful, it was..

..the words instantly disappeared from her as the faces and voices of every Gifted One to ever hold the Stone screamed through her mind in a split-second of fear and pain..

..and then she was falling, faster and faster, as if she was carrying something that was far too heavy, something too heavy for anyone to carry. The world came nearer, the Chapel came nearer, and Avalon came nearer, taking her hand, singing and gently guiding her for the last few seconds, returning her gently to the centre of the bad place.

Meanwhile, Avalon had been hovering at the altar-front, watching intently at the moment when Linda reached for the Stone. She was pleased to know that she hadn't really been needed on Linda's first serious foray. She knew that the Gifted One had to be on her own this time, to find out for herself what she should or shouldn't do, and apart from one understandable mistake, she had done well. She was so tremendously Gifted. Fortunately most People weren't, but, as she'd known all along, this Person was really, really special. And then Avalon had started wondering if Mörrah might have known that as well? And perhaps that was why she had given the doll to Linda in the first place, in which case all this..

..but Avalon hadn't been able to finish the thought. Linda had leaned forwards and placed her hands around the Stone, and Avalon watched in amazement as it immediately became perfectly clear again. Linda still had her eyes closed, and was even laughing quietly to herself as she lightly touched each talon. One by one, they silently and willingly opened, surrendering the Stone to her. She lifted it away in her hands, barely touching it. And then she looked troubled by what she had done, as if something inside her was beginning to realise the scale of what had happened. The talons suddenly curled into a tight ball, which Avalon tried to ignore. She flew close enough to touch Linda's face, trying to feel what was happening in Linda's heart and mind, and spoke to her, calming her with a Summer Song, helping her back safely. She watched as Linda grew calm again, and felt unsure whether to be excited or terrified - because Linda had done something that was almost too powerful.. something that was so right.. and yet could easily be so dreadfully, dreadfully wrong.

..and Linda felt herself drifting away from a dream, and wasn't entirely sure what it had been about. It wasn't a proper one, it had been like reading that Brother's book again, except this time she had been up in the clouds with Avalon, without all those stories appearing around her. The room steadily came back into focus, and she sensed that she was still kneeling in front of the altar, surrounded by bitter smells and darkness, and looking to Avalon for comfort.

And then she looked past Avalon and down into her trembling hands. The strength went away from her arms as she suddenly realised that not only was she in huge trouble, but she'd also broken countless laws of physics - and even rolling a million straight sixes and getting them all to land in the exact centre of a salt-circle wouldn't make up for that.

"Oh no.. how did that happen, Avie? I can hear the doctors warming up the brain-probes already, and those monks aren't going to be too happy either!" she whispered in one high-pitched breath.

Avalon touched the Stone quickly, and wasn't struck by lightning. She touched it again, just to make sure.

"Hex is gone! Curses all broken too.. you know what that means?"

"You can see if it tastes of beetles?"

"No.. well yes, but I won't try just now. It means that we're a bit vulnerable and in SO much trouble, and besides.."

Avalon was interrupted by the sounds of footsteps above. They were heavy and dulled as if the people were a few feet above the ceiling, and it was definitely time to leave quickly. The pocket which Linda chose for the Stone wasn't really big enough, and already contained a hair-band and a big mess of broken hazelnut biscuits. It dropped out as they reached the doorway, and rolled with echoing, sharp clacks back across the mosaic floor. The weak flickering of the remaining candles made it hard to see where it could have gone.

"Oh great.." she muttered as a headline appeared in her mind.

"Lindagate: Weirdy Schoolgirl Drops Odessa Stone - AAAGH, EVERYBODY RUN! AAAGH!"

She squinted into the darkness, hoping it was somewhere obvious.

"I am so embarrassing, aren't I?" she sighed to Avalon, "A thing like that spends centuries locked in a big claw, and then I come along and see if it bounces. Did you see where it went?"

Avalon shrugged, so Linda began crawling around for it, making her way along the veiled front of the long ceremonial table, wanting it to be lying somewhere nice and easy to find. She reached the end and made her way back to double-check, and moaned with the realisation that she was going to have to do the obvious. She sighed and lifted up the thick material, and stared into the darkness beyond. Avalon shivered, and flew to her.

"Avie, you stay out here and keep watch for anyone.. I don't plan on being two seconds, but if I'm not back in three.."

Linda slowly crawled under and began patting the ground, convinced she was going to touch something vile - or something vile was going to touch her. She tried to block everything out of her mind but that just seemed to make every fear at least a billion times worse.

"Oh, it smells so ughh under here.." she mumbled, trying to make herself feel braver by making a noise.

"Can you see it yet? You have to hurry, I can hear the footsteps again.." whispered Avalon, nervously hovering by the symbol of a three-eyed skull, which Linda had crawled under. Its eyes had narrowed and seemed to follow Avalon's every move, even if she edged backwards away from it.

"Lindy.. it's staring at me, the Bad Thing's staring!" she whimpered.

Linda suddenly threw the thick material up into the air, and shuffled a little into the room, grinning at Avalon. Her black eyes held more evil than Avalon had ever felt in her life.

"Come to me Ahvalona, come to your friend.." she croaked, reaching out towards her.

CHAPTER FOURTEEN
Sceleste

Avalon backed away, terrified of her instead of pleased to see her. This Linda had deathly white skin and wore a dirty old smock instead of a blue jacket. Her eyes narrowed, and she twisted her head slightly, smirking.

"Ahvalonaa.." she hissed.

"Who's you?" squeaked Avalon, "Linda's not got black eyes.. you're not.. you're not anyone! Go'way.. go'way please please please go'way.."

Another Linda, identical to the first, appeared from under the veil a few feet further along. The first one laughed, and crawled out a little further. The other Linda choked and tried to speak.

"I'm your friend, little one, aren't we? Come to me, come to your friend.. we're so alone in here," she whined through a wicked grin. Avalon squealed and found that she couldn't fly anymore - her wings felt as if someone invisible was pinching them together. She crawled backwards across the mosaic, onto the image of a demon feared even by spiritae far, far stronger than faeries. Her strength deserted her as she backed across its heart, and she lay helpless. The second Linda cackled to herself, and scratched her way even further onto the floor than the first one.

"Linda! Lindaaa.. there's Bad You's out here, Linda!" Avalon called, but her voice couldn't cross the hexes carved around her. Suddenly the two Lindas looked back at where they had crawled from, and scurried away, fading into its darkness. Silence fell over the room, and Avalon finally took to the safety of the air, darting as close as she dared to the table, desperate to know if her Linda was still alive, and shaking as she felt the dull footsteps and voices above becoming so much heavier.

"Linda! Real Linda! Where's you, pleease? Lin.." she cried.

The veil suddenly moved at the very far end, next to the altar. The real Linda crawled out waving the Stone towards Avalon, while trying to shake a museum's worth of dust from her hair.

"Found it! Right at the back, wouldn't you just know it. Lucky it was glowing or else I'd have been in there ages! Blimey, Avie, this is going to put me in therapy for the rest of my lfmphgerr.."

She found it hard to finish the sentence with Avalon hugging her face so much.

"It's you, it's you!" Avalon wailed, "And there's bad types closer and we have to leave here right now right nowNOW.."

The corridor was far lighter than when they had arrived, dimly illuminated by long lines of candles which had been lit for the ceremony. They hurried back into the room with seven doorways, where Avalon went to the right instead of back out to the left, and Linda soon found herself slipping her way up a short flight of heavily-worn steps.

"Is this the way we came in, Avie?" Linda whispered.

"Came in?" she replied, looking genuinely bemused.

"Huh? Doesn't matter.. look!"

The stairs had lead to a small landing, where they branched into three separate flights, all of which lead into complete blackness. Avalon steadily hovered before each one, listening intently.

"There's voices up this one.. and this one.. but not this one.. which could be good, or it could be really bad, because.."

"Okay, okay, we'll chance the quiet one. I'd rather meet something horrible that doesn't make much noise than one of those vile monks."

Avalon settled back onto Linda's shoulder and clutched the alexandrite. The stairs lead upwards for a short while, and then turned back on themselves to go down in a long, broad circle before joining another dimly lit corridor.

"I think we're under the Ceremony Room place," whispered Linda, and carefully lifted the Stone out of her inside pocket. It was pulsating with a faint yellow glow, just as it had been when she found it under the table. They both jumped at the sound of distant footsteps coming towards them from somewhere in the darkness, and they ducked into the nearest room. It was the same size as the Ceremony Room, illuminated by seven thick candles on the side-wall, each of which had been placed behind dark glass at the points of a black star. They crouched down behind the white altar at the far end, beneath lines of satanic verses and imagery flickering in the candlelight.

"We're getting to be good at all this hiding aren't we, Avie? Avie?" she said, noticing that Avalon was turning a dull grey, and had curled up in her hands.

"Too evil.. it's so bad.. bad place.. Lindy.. under a bad sign again.."

Linda shuffled for her necklace, and lowered it for Avalon to hold. It hardly made any difference to her colour, so she moved as far to the edge of the altar as she dared to go. Any further and someone would be bound to see her.

The footsteps came to a halt in the doorway, and were soon joined by others. Linda tried to understand what they were saying, but couldn't manage it. That was definitely an Avalon thing, she told herself. A lifetime later the voices faded away and Linda stepped out from the altar, and shivered with revulsion when she saw the frightening images that had been above her. It wasn't so much what they were of, because they were entirely unrecognisable, but it was the way they'd been created. The strokes and marks felt as if they burned with evil.

"It's okay, we're going now, Avie, we're going somewhere nice, I promise we are."

Avalon's glow became purer and stronger as they went further away from the altar and by the time they reached the door she was fluttering her wings again and seemed almost fine, although still very scared. And then she squealed, pointing to the corner of the room.

A solitary candle burned weakly at the front of a chalked quadrant between the door and the wall, which to Linda didn't look any stranger than anything they'd seen before. After all, there wasn't much in it apart from a few weird symbols and an open silver casket the size of a suitcase. She squinted into the poor light at the dark rags bunched in its centre.

"Oh no.. is that a cat? What have they done to her.."

Linda crossed over the lines, cracks and arcs, and for the first time in her life couldn't care less if she stood on any of them - and didn't even notice that she had scuffed and smudged some of them. She kneeled at the casket, and looked down to where a thin black cat lay restrained by thirteen narrow silver wires, each cutting deep into her fur. The ends were held in place by thick silver nails which stood like pillars out of the black silk, and her body was covered with a scattering of decayed thorns which Linda began gently removing. She stared at Avalon in disbelief.

"They even do sacrifices in here? This is so sick.. and she's in a such a state.."

"Lindy we have to go, puhleeease can we go? It feels so bad in here.." hurried Avalon, snatching glances around herself.

"Okay, but we can't leave her, can we? D'you think she's still alive?" whispered Linda, running her fingertips along the cat's back.

"Linda.. look at the symbols everywhere around her! This one means.." said Avalon, hovering in front of a perfect glass sphere which was partially buried in a fold of silk. She ran her hands all around it, and her glow turned dark red. Words inside the glass that had been invisible now trapped her light, radiating briefly before disappearing.

"She's the key.. the important part of a hex.." Avalon wobbled, and warily moved to the next sphere, brushing at her arm where she had accidentally touched the glass.

"..and she's.. she's on her Ninth Life! She's between life and death! They're so dangerous when they're like that AND she could be carrying all kinds of curses and spells and jinxes from.. all these other hexes around her! See?"

Avalon pointed to one of the many Latin words hacked into the blackened wood around the cat's head. Linda strained her eyes in the darkness.

"Hexes? I can't see the words properly.. Scelestus, Calig-something, Vectoris, it's too dark to make them out, Avie. What's a Scelestus then?" she whispered.

Avalon pointed frantically at the long, smeared word underneath all the others and immediately raced up to the ceiling.

"She's the Curse Bearer! She's the Curse Bearer! It doesn't get worse! If she dies while we're with her.."

Avalon breathed deeply to try and calm herself enough to speak, and flew down to hold onto Linda's fringe. She looked straight into her blue eye.

"Linda, we really have to go, pleease nowww Linda!"

"Avie, she's just a cat. That whole nine lives thing is just a load of waffle, I saw a programme about it once."

"Well exca-yoooose me Mrs Four-Sneezes-And-I'm-Dead-Can't-Step-On-Cracks-Rolly-Dice.."

Avalon had a point. Linda looked past her and tried raising the tightest wire, the one across the cat's face and ears, but it was under too much tension to bend or give at all.

"She must be in so much pain.." Linda breathed, feeling a storm of emotions run through her, ending in the same feeling of calm that she had experienced at the altar. She wrapped her fingers around one of the broad nails and felt it rise out from the ancient Witchwood beneath the silk. It came away as if it was drawn to her fingers, slipping effortlessly and smoothly despite its length and jagged sides. And so did the next one, and the next. Linda wasn't entirely sure whether she twisted them or pulled them, but it seemed to work just as long as she didn't really think about what she was doing. Avalon stopped hovering and moved onto Linda's shoulder, hiding in her hair.

The cat lay perfectly still. She was deathly cold and Linda sensed the weakest of weak heartbeats beneath her fingertips as she stroked her. The Stone echoed the heartbeat warmly in her pocket. Outside in the corridor a loose piece of the ceiling's brickwork fell onto the steps, making Linda jump and take her hand away. Avalon darted to the doorway for a nervous look, and came straight back into her hiding place.

"Couldn't see anything, but it's dark out there and the stairs go round a corner as well.."

Linda's hands were shaking. The room had suddenly become cold enough for her breath to appear in small clouds.

"Avie," she whispered, "Can your Faery Dust help her? I think she could do with it.."

Avalon frowned and had a look in the pouch on her belt.

"Mmm.. haven't got lots left, and it's her Ninth Life so it won't do much good anyway.."

"I know, but look at her.. we have to do something and we can't leave her, can we? Can we, Avie?" she coaxed.

"..no.." came a very shaky reply, somewhere near Linda's left ear.

"Exactly. It's worth a go because she's such a mess, and besides, all these symbols and things are just thought up by lousy people so it's not real.."

"Try telling her that," said Avalon as she sprinkled the sparkling Medicamentum powder a few inches above the wounds. For a few seconds it stayed in the air, briefly letting in a beam of pure sunlight before being engulfed by darkness. A powdery white cloud rolled over her worst marks, taking away the scars and replacing them with thin grey fur.

Avalon threw the last handful of Dust into the air above her patient's nose, making both of them sneeze. The cat slowly blinked her eyes open and Linda gently picked her up, holding her close.

"You're not jinxed are you? You're gorgeous.. and if you really are jinxed then we are as well.."

"Nowww can we go?" urged Avalon, tugging at the braid.

Linda followed Avalon through the dull light, treading as carefully as a scared person could, not wanting to risk stumbling over and hurting the cat even more than she'd already been hurt. The sparse candles guided them into a stairway which quickly divided into two. Linda rolled an even number so they took the right one, and they eventually arrived on the second floor of another part of the building, overlooking a small central forecourt.

"What's down there?" breathed Linda, staying in the safety of the dark stairway. Avalon turned herself into a butterfly and flew over to one of the banners hanging against the walls. She came back a few seconds later, and Linda was pleased to see that she didn't appear to be scared out of her mind. She was even humming to herself.

"People's down there! They look like Guards with guns and things but they're dressed in clothes I haven't seen for ages, just like the colours on the banners up here. And there's doors too, and loads of curses and all that stuff again.."

"Anything else?"

Avalon had a think.

"I could feel freshness in the air, so outside's nearby. But there's so many People someone's bound to notice you. And her, too."

Avalon pointed her leg towards the cat, who seemed happy to lie cradled in Linda's arms.

"And how about up here? Are there more doors or anything?"

"Nope, just this one, but you're already in it. See?"

Avalon waved her arms in a circle, pointing to the walls and the ceiling so that Linda would understand. Linda sighed and they went back down to rejoin the poor light of the passageway by the Feline Sacrificial Whatever Room. The cat hissed weakly and her fur bristled as they walked past. Strangely, Linda felt more comfortable now about finding her way back to the Fireplace Room. She had begun thinking of how good it would feel to be closing the metal plate in the chimney, and leaving behind the horrendous world that she'd found herself in. The lefts and rights began to feel obvious, and navigating in complete darkness was a breeze as long as she thought about where she wanted to get to, rather than how to get there. She even blew out any candles on the way.

A few minutes later they emerged in the room lined with black and white tiles, and Linda had to wonder how she'd managed to get there so easily. She also wondered why she hadn't waited to see if there was anyone around before marching in, and decided to be a lot more careful in future. The spiral staircase was incredibly tiring, but nowhere near as long as she remembered it being. The pervading smell of incense soon began creeping around her, and the smoky haze at the top of the stairs carried a familiar orange glow - but this time it was stronger, because this time there were more lights on in the room. Avalon transformed into a fly, and flew in for a speedy look around, and returned quickly.

"No-one there, but my eyes are all watery and everything now!"

"It's okay, we're nearly out of here.."

Linda cast a glance at the five-armed cross on her way across the room. How did people think that stuff up? She stopped, and stared at her reflection in the shimmering gold, wondering what made anyone create such..

..the huge door rattled. Avalon tugged her out of her thoughts and darted behind its large wooden frame, followed less than a braid's length behind by Linda. It creaked loudly and scraped against the floor as two heavy-set guards pushed it open. The door stopped just inches away from Linda and the cat, who raised her head disdainfully while Linda trembled like a leaf.

Avalon fluttered down to floor-level, buzzed as a fly around the door and into the room, and changed into a wolfhound over by one of the far doorways. The guards shouted at the intruder, and Linda dared to peer around the door to see both men racing into an archway, guns drawn, chasing after her.

Linda looked into the Fireplace Room through the crack in the door, to see if it was clear. Apart from a Half-There which was very likely Not There, the room was fine so she took her chance and ran over to the fireplace.

She looked up at the hatch and realised it was going to be a whole lot harder getting back up there than it had been coming down. She stood on the logs to try and start climbing out, using one hand to keep the cat on her shoulder, and placing each foot on either wall of the chimney, and began inching her way up - and stopped. This was hopeless. She needed both hands to manage this, and another pair of hands to keep hold of her cat, so she dropped back onto the logs and jumped up, carefully lobbing the cat through the gap into the tunnel. A troubled 'meow' came from somewhere in its depths. Avalon flew down, and watched her struggling up the chimney.

"Well, if she wasn't on her Ninth Life, then she is now," she said.

"Avalon? I thought they were chasing.."

"..a big dog, not a bird! But I think you ought to hurry, 'cause they might come back and light those logs down there."

Linda felt as if she'd climbed a skyscraper by the time she shuffled into the tunnel, and lay on her back for a moment to try and figure out if any part of her didn't ache. She held her breath as the men's panic-stricken voices soon drifted up from the room, and wondered for a dreadful moment if the metal plate was lying anywhere obvious.

"Avie? Did you get what they were saying?" she whispered.

"Yup. The Stone's gone, and they're too scared to tell anyone yet. Wouldn't they be cross if they knew you had it? And their Curse Bearer, too!" she giggled. Linda felt sick, and held her cat.

Carrying a cat and trying to crawl was more difficult than Linda had imagined, and they moved far more slowly going back. After a few minutes Avalon flew ahead and came back quickly.

"It's blocked up there, remember? We ought to take one of the other ways.."

Linda wasn't feeling confident enough to trust her own judgement, so after a quick roll of the dice they took the fourth dank and gloomy side-tunnel that they came across. Fortunately it seemed to go upwards on a steady incline, which was at least the right direction in principle. An hour of uneven shuffling later, Avalon sensed the night air drifting into the stale atmosphere. The brickwork began merging into rock, and after a few very narrow squeezes they emerged into the most wonderful night time ever - or at least, it was the most wonderful in Linda's opinion. She wriggled free of the rocky entrance and jumped around on the grass, much to the surprise of her cat.

"Oh fresh air, big spaces, sky, sky SKY! Trees and grass and proper soft earth! Ohhhh.."

Avalon left her alone to have a mad moment, and even joined in for a short while, but there was something around them that wasn't quite right, and she didn't like it at all. Linda stopped to get her breath back, and calm down.

"Where d'you reckon we are then, Avie?"

"Hmm.." pondered Avalon, looking up at a perfectly black night sky, "..definitely Black Roots, it's horrid in the air.. but listen."

Apart from the gentle hum of Avalon's wings, there was absolutely no sound at all.

"I can't hear anything," Linda whispered.

"Nor me, and that can't be good, can it? There's nothing here, which means the Evil Ones are keeping quiet," she said, turning in a wide circle before returning to Linda, who was looking puzzled.

"And no Evil Ones is bad, is it?" she asked.

"Maybe. They should be all around us, but they're not. They're staying back and I'm more scared of that than I am of them."

"Maybe it's our new friend here?" Linda suggested.

"Yup. Now do you see how scary a Curse Bearer is?" she said, discretely pointing at the cat.

"Well.. okay, so they find her scary.. good. We can get back to the hotel easier, can't we? D'you think we're right in the middle?"

"Uhh.. we might not be right in the middle. Not the exact middle, anyway. Off quite a bit, maybe.."

"So that tunnel wasn't really another way out, it was a route back into big trouble - or no trouble, for us!"

Avalon nodded, and then shook her head, which soon spread across her whole body.

"Yes, but don't say that, because something's bound to happen."

"Avie, nothing's going to happen. We've left that all behind and besides, now that we've got the Stone.."

A low groaning and grinding noise came from the darkness behind them, and the rocks and earth closed together, sealing over the tunnel's exit and leaving the hillside looking as if the gap had never been there. And then the earth spread across the rocks, hiding them completely.

"Do.. do you know your way out of here?" whimpered Linda.

Avalon shook her head.

"No, but I might be able to find the way to go. Watch me do this!"

Avalon yelped as she plucked a tiny silver hair from her head, and gently stretched it out little by little until it reached the length of her arm. She licked one end and folded it over to form a small loop, and looked up at Linda.

"Have you got any Elixir of.. something.. it ends in -eeghurrm?"

"No, is that a hugely big problem?"

"Yes. No. I hope not," she said, then hovered a few feet in the air and spun herself into a blur before releasing the hair. She dizzily settled on Linda's arm, singing a Lost Song and watching intently as the strand twisted and turned, gently drifting to the ground.

"See? Now we know where to go."

"We do?"

"Uhuh. We go in the direction of the looped end. Or the pointy end.. one of them, anyway. No, the looped end is where we are now, and the other end is where we go. Usually. That's good!"

She picked the hair up, straightened out the loop and put it back in the exact place on her head where it had come from. The rest of her hair immediately grew to match its length.

"That is so cool, Avie. I wish mine did that! Long hair looks good on you, you know."

"Uhuh.. but it really gets in the way when I fly, you watch me try.."

"It's okay, I can imagine. Shall we start moving out instead?"

Avalon shook her head while agreeing, which struck Linda as being odd until she noticed Avalon's hair going back to its usual length with every shake. Nothing could be odd after that. They walked for well over an hour (Linda wasn't entirely sure) in what was hopefully the right direction, and the forest started to gradually improve. Even a few stars appeared in the sky, but Linda was getting tired and didn't even have the energy to feel pleased. She was feeling the effects of having had nothing to eat since breakfast, and needed to stop for a while.

"I'm getting really dizzy.. I had no idea it was getting so late. How about a bisc-nit break?"

Avalon clapped her agreement and lead the way through the trees and perched herself on a rock, clearing away moss and leaves with her foot to leave a small, luminescent picnic area. Linda piled two handfuls of cake-crumbs, broken biscuits and hazelnuts onto it.

"I've got to get a some supplies sorted out, I really have," she said absently to herself while failing to get the cat to show any interest at all in a section of Odessa's finest caramel wafers.

"You need a name first, don't you sweety?" she said, dropping the biscuit and stroking her head instead.

"A name for her? She's got loads already, on the Witchwood," said Avalon, flying close to whisper them. "There was.. Scelesta, The Curse Bearing Companion Of Evil, She Who Walks With.."

"Far too dramatic. I like Sceleste, though."

Avalon shook her head and wagged both hands towards Linda.

"A Scelesta's a jinx, and a bad one, too. So having a Curse Bearer with no lives left called Scelesta isn't the best.."

"Sceleste, not Scelesta. With a soft 'c'."

"Oh, that's different. That's nice. Like that. Like this, too," she replied, and held up a hazelnut which she quickly devoured. She licked her fingers, and looked around herself.

"It's dark here, isn't it Lindy? Really, really, reeeally dark.. no moon up there at all. Scary."

"Well, this Stone was glowing a bit, earlier on - it'd be good if it'd start up again. I wonder why it did that? Bizarre."

Linda gave it a shake, and nothing happened. Avalon had an idea.

"Remember that thing you did with the claw? That was pretty good Magic for a Person. Or anyone, really. Even Spiritae."

"Oh yeah, I'd forgotten about that. That was really weird, too. I wonder how that happened?"

"Hmm.. maybe getting The Stone to glow would be a bit like reading that big old book? Relax your mind, and let your heart carry you to where you need to be? Somewhere nice and safe, and maybe The Stone would be all proh-tecative for us?"

For a few seconds the moon came out from behind the clouds, which Linda put down to coincidence. She could see that they were near the edge of the trees, just a mile or two from the sea, which meant that hopefully Odessa wouldn't be too far away. There was a long road just a mile or so to their left, and that had to lead somewhere that might have taxis. But as for where the hotel might be..

"It's okay, I can see civilisation now, so we don't have to bother with any scary Stone stuff. We just head back to the hotel and figure out what to do there, and we don't have to do any weird whatevers with this thing."

"We do, we dooo.." pined Avalon, wrapping the braid around her waist, "..the darkness isn't just darkness around here, and the bad spirits keep getting closer even with the.. Sceleste. That's how bad it is. Puhleease make it glow? Show them you're in control of it.."

"Well.. I suppose the worst that could happen is nothing."

Avalon almost said something, and immediately forgot what it was. Sceleste purred quietly to herself.

"Okay, Avie, but you have to help me.. and you Sceleste, if you're awake.." she said nervously, giving her a hug, "..let's have a go."

CHAPTER FIFTEEN
Rome

Linda sat on the ground, put the Stone a little way in front of herself, and made sure Sceleste looked comfortable on her lap. She forced herself to close her eyes, and imagined the Stone at the top of the most enormous lighthouse, illuminating the entire world brightly enough to scare away the demons of the night. After a few seconds, Avalon started patting her on the nose.

"Umm.. open eyes, Lindy.. open them now, puhleeeze?"

Linda tried to, but could only squint and hold a hand across them. A hundred beams of white light reached out in all directions from horizon to horizon, announcing to those-who-know that someone very gifted now possessed the Stone, and announcing to everyone else that something very weird was happening. Avalon looked up, peeking between her fingers.

"Too much, too much - only a little glow would be fine, really it would! Hardly anyth.."

"I can't help it! It just keeps going! I can feel it reaching further and further.." Linda screamed, and crawled forwards to hide the Stone under her jacket - but Sceleste seemed to be trying to get in the way. Her heart pounded even faster, and she felt a huge wave of panic engulfing her.

"What's happening, Avie? Everyone'll know where we are! What do I do? What do.."

"Don't know! Don't know! Umm.. you could.. close eyes, don't think of anything! Nice and calm, nice and calm, like an eagle on the wind, gliding, gliding, gliding.. up into the night sky where the sun's setting and dusk is everywhere, nice and calm, nice and calm."

Linda closed her eyes, but the light followed her as if she was still staring into the very heart of the Stone. She tried to imagine herself casting a huge blanket across everything, one that wouldn't hide the light for ever, but just until she knew what she was doing. Unknown to her, the night began reclaiming the sky, shade by darkening shade, until an area only a few feet wide around Linda was left flooded with pure white light. She opened her eyes, and imagined a smaller blanket drifting down, gently falling through the brightness and onto the Stone. And then the light was gone, leaving the Stone lying in the grass and glowing slightly. Sceleste licked at Linda's hand, and almost meowed. Avalon fluttered down for a close look.

"Annnd.." she said, watching waves of colour disappearing inside it, "..now it's all clear! You're so clever, really you are!"

Linda was too stunned to say anything. If Avalon hadn't given it a lick to see what it tasted like, Linda would have been too scared to ever touch it again.

"Hmm.. sunshine. It tastes how sunshine ought to! And also that feeling I get when something's really funny. Now you try?"

Linda picked it up, trying to keep her hands steady.

"Maybe later, Avie.. later.." she said, pushing it deep into her inside pocket. A beam of light flashed out for a fraction of a second, surprising her but also giving her a chance to try blocking it again. She picked up Sceleste, who gave her another weak lick.

They wandered towards the road, and Avalon quickly worked out that they needed to go right. An hour later, the lights of Odessa were drawing closer and Linda still hadn't managed to prevent stray beams of light exploding from inside her jacket. She limited them to one every ten minutes or so by keeping her mind as clear as possible, and occasionally imagining an impenetrable fortress all around herself. That was pretty good thinking, according to Avalon.

The road eventually wound into the residential part of the city, and soon lead into areas that were nearly familiar to Linda. A distant churchbell chimed midnight, and was then corrected by another distant churchbell in the opposite direction. Neither agreed with Linda's watch, which was understandable considering all that her consolation fairground prize had been through.

The streets of the main shopping centre weren't too busy, but there were enough people around to look at her as if she was an alien, and make her feel very self-conscious. She crossed over the junction near the Opera House, and began the mile or so trek back to the Krasnaya. Avalon was getting anxious.

"Sceleste keeps staring at People - can you stop her doing that? People keep getting scared and they don't know why, and your kind always hate that."

Linda stroked Sceleste and made some noises that were meant to sound comforting.

"You know, I'd be really surprised if people didn't feel a bit scared, Avie. I'm muddier than a hippo's wellies, Sceleste looks like she died a hundred years ago and I'm talking to a bird who's standing on a cat's head."

Avalon had a think and then took up her usual place safely within Linda's hair, convinced that would make all the difference. Normality prevailed for a while, but then midway across a main road..

"You know what you haven't done for ages?" asked Avalon.

"Nope.." Linda replied, hoping Avalon wasn't going to mention great big light beams.

"You haven't done any great big light beams."

"Oh don't say things like.." she said as a narrow beam of light shot up into the sky. It lasted for two of the longest seconds Linda had ever felt. She hurried past the startled tourists and club-goers, and raced to the corner of a shop door where she waited until she felt sure the display had stopped.

She began the long walk down Rishelyevskaya Street, keeping an imaginary blanket wrapped tightly around herself and the Stone. Occasionally she noticed cars swerve for no reason, as if the drivers had their eyes on her instead of the road. That was odd, but maybe they were tired or they'd had a drink too many? Her father was always terrible at driving whenever he'd had a little too much, so she ignored them and kept on walking, trying to fend-off tiredness and just keep going. They soon reached the point where Avalon had flown away from her that morning, when they had been going for breakfast. She stopped for a moment and looked over to the darkened café, and felt as if a complete lifetime had passed since they had been there. So much had changed, so much had happ..

..she stopped in mid-thought. Somebody near the trees stared at her and immediately started talking on a mobile phone. Then someone else did exactly the same. Probably. Mistakes were easy enough for her to make in the daytime, and were unbelievably easy to make in the middle of the night.. but she was too tired and it was getting too late to be bothered. Even Avalon had been quiet for an unprecedented ten minutes.

Wonderful aromas of cooking drew Linda into a small 24-hour delicatessen-café to get some supplies. Avalon stayed outside to avoid landing Linda in any trouble, and flew up to a lamp post for a look around. She had been watching people intently for a while and was growing very wary, but didn't want to say anything until she was sure - and from this vantage point, she was more than sure.

Inside the store, Linda picked up two shopping baskets. One to carry Sceleste, and one for life's essentials. The sounds and smells of sizzling food pulled her to the far end, and she became wide awake for long enough to buy a steaming baguette of squelchy-stuff. It must have been a strange local speciality, and tasted a little odd but at that particular moment, it was better than anything she had ever eaten. She soon wandered away from the diner-end and over to the aisles to load up with biscuits, drinks, dried fruit-things, and a large carton of milk - semi-skimmed like the Home Economics teacher always said. And then without thinking why, she put it down and picked up a full cream one instead. The shop assistant kindly let her keep both baskets, didn't charge for the half-eaten bitochki baguette, and even held the door open for her to leave. Avalon flew down to her as soon as she stepped back onto the pavement.

"There's People watching here! Or there were. They went away when you got near the door just now. One's up in that building, with a little black box that clicks a lot. He pointed it at me when I went up there."

Linda looked up to where Avalon was pointing, and smiled for the camera. She'd seen too much today to be scared by these people, and besides, she knew a thing or two about being spied on. She'd heard so many tales of cunning escapades from her father over the years that deciding what to do next wasn't very difficult at all.

"Can we hurry to the hotel, Lindy? It's not far anymore, just 'round the corner.."

"Not just yet.. I think it's taxi time, Avie. I have a plan."

Linda combined her baskets into one, apologised to Sceleste and waved for a cab. One soon turned up, and she asked the driver to take her on a sight-seeing route to a hotel with a name she vaguely remembered from the previous day. A quarter of an hour later they arrived outside the Chernechesk Hotel, and much to Avalon's surprise, they actually got out of the taxi. Linda paid the driver and gave the kind of tip that would make sure he remembered her, and even waved him off. Avalon landed back on Sceleste's head.

"This isn't our hotel, is it? Look, our one's different. See?"

She flicked through her Journal and held up a rectangle with a small square near its top. The page next to it had a drawing of Linda's jacket, but instead of the usual X next to it, there was a tick.

"Don't worry, Avie, I know where our hotel is - but we might have been followed if we'd gone straight there. That's why we get dropped off at this one. Whoever follows us might think we're staying here instead! Now we just walk back to our actual hotel by staying safely in the side roads and shadows, where nobody should see us. It's a bit like what dad calls the Primary Evasion Ploy. Pretty clever isn't it?"

Avalon stared blankly at Linda.

"Thuh.."

"The Primary Evasion Ploy.. it's pretty clever stuff, isn't it?"

"Thuh.. the.. one of your eyes is blue, and the other one's.."

"And that's always good to know. Now then, you need to fly up high and get your bearings, cause we're not taking the short route!"

By the time Linda reached the entrance to the Krasnaya Hotel she felt almost sure that no-one had seen them. Of course, the world's scruffiest girl with a homing-songthrush, a cat in a shopping basket and a mountain of food was probably easy to spot, but as far as she or Avalon could tell, they were in the clear. She strolled inside and gave a friendly wave to the multi-lingual receptionist, who gave her a very strange look in return.

A few minutes later, Linda had achieved what she had begun to think was impossible - she was actually clean again. She was still tired, bruised, scratched and paranoid, but at least she'd managed to scribble one horrible thing off her list.

Avalon stayed out on the small balcony, happily flying around where there weren't any Dark Spirits, and keeping an eye out for any unwanted visitors who might arrive somewhere far below. Meanwhile, Linda quickly packed everything into her suitcases. All she really wanted to do was go to bed and worry about the Stone and all the weirdos tomorrow, but she knew that couldn't happen. Anyone could be part of that cult, and someone was bound to know where she was by now. The time had come to move on.. but where and how? She sat on the bed for a moment, stroking Sceleste and looking out at the starry sky beyond Avalon, and ran through some of her father's Journalist Olympics. There was a time, around two years ago, when he was unofficially seeing a hideous regional tv presenter called Veronica Someone-Or-Another, shortly before she got divorced. There had been lots of fun and games involved there, and more than enough embarrassment at St Teresa's for Linda.

"Hey, Avie? You coming in now? It's major brainwave time. I have another plan, and I can't believe dad's barmy world is actually coming in useful for once! Or twice, now. This plan's even better than the last one!"

Avalon only just managed to stop in front of her face.

"What last one?"

"Yep. My dad did this once when he was.. having troubles. Top Notch Diversionary Tactics."

She pressed the phone's reception button and put on her most convincing French accent.

"Allo? Je voudrais.. pardonnez moi? Ahh, oui c'est moi, Amélie, encore une fois! Ah wuhd lahk to boook a taxi-eee si vous playy, pour l'airoporrr. Uhh.. 'ow you say.. can you book for me teeckettes pour la Roma, la grande ville dans la centre de l'Italie - or est-ce-que c'est pour moi to do? Uhuh.. uhuh.. le nom? Bardot, Amélie, M. Et merci! Oui, je suis trés Francais! Bon nuit, Madame la Réception!"

Linda put the phone down, feeling pleased with herself. She gave Sceleste a good scratch, which made Sceleste look pleased as well. Avalon settled on the pillow and looked worried.

"What was all that for? Tickets and things.."

"If people are watching us, they'll see a taxi arrive won't they? So when it turns up they'll waste time waiting for me to go down to the car, and then after ages they'll get bored and ask the receptionist about it, or maybe even the driver. That'll make them think I'm off to the airport and going to Rome with their Stone, so they'll be convinced the Pope or the Mafia or maybe a Government are going to get hold of it."

Avalon looked as if she had been following, so Linda slowed down for the big finale.

"They'll send lots of their own people to the airport, all booked on the next few flights to Rome! And here's the clever bit - we leave here through a different exit, and sneak off somewhere safe instead."

Avalon nodded thoughtfully.

"See, my dad did the Sleeping Taxi Routine with a bunch of journalists once and it worked like a dream. Loads of them ended up in Prague, while him and Veronica Tart-Off-The-Telly went for a dirty week.. they went to Margate. How about that, then?"

Avalon stared blankly back at Linda.

"I've finished talking now, Avie."

Avalon kept staring.

"The plan.. I've finished.. what do you think?"

"One of your eyes is blue, and the other one's.."

Linda didn't have time to explain it all again, so she asked Avalon for one of her Very Late At Night songs instead, and finished cramming everything into her two suitcases. Five minutes later she was packed and fiddling with the door handle.

"You forgot Sceleste!" said Avalon, tugging the braid and pointing back to the bed. Sceleste lay on the pillow looking pitiful, and Linda realised she didn't have enough arms for two cases and a cat.

"Maybe she'll fit in the bigger case?" suggested Avalon, tapping her chin and looking serious.

"Y'know, I give up with me, I really do.." sighed Linda.

She unpacked the suitcases, and combined the contents as much as she could. For a moment there was no space for Aggy, but three cardigans and a jumper were evicted to make just enough room. The locks strained and it weighed a ton, but at least she now had an arm free to carry Sceleste. She carefully picked her up, and when Avalon gave the all-clear she ran for the Fire Exit at the end of the corridor.

Rather than risk her luck down at ground level again, she hurried up the wire-frame steps instead. The roof of The Krasnaya was vast, uneven and full of peaks, store rooms and chimney stacks. It formed an uninterrupted link across the tops of other buildings for a long, long way, and she soon had to stop for a moment to try and get the feeling back in her suitcase-hand. She edged over to the front of whatever building she was on and looked down fourteen floors to the street below to see if anything was happening. A stomach-turning feeling of vertigo swept every way around her, making her feel like the whole of Odessa was in an earthquake of cartoon proportions. She stumbled backwards, and sat down quickly.

"Should I do that?" said Avalon, helpfully.

"Good idea.. very good idea.. have a look-see what's going on down there."

Avalon darted back towards the hotel and dived down to the trees opposite. She soon returned, laughing.

"Black cars, and a white one and your taxi too! Nasty People are everywhere and some of them saw you going to the hotel, and they think you're inside, but you're not are you? They'll never think of looking all the way up here!"

"I hope not, but we can't stay here for long - we'll have to do some wandering unless you know anywhere that's easy to get to and really out of the way?"

"Not that we'd all fit into," Avalon shrugged, and they carried on along the differing roof tops until a side-road separated them from the next old building. Linda crawled over to the edge for a look, and realised she hadn't a hope of doing a Hollywood Hero jump across. Even if she had one of the bikes from the ET movie with her leviathan suitcase properly balanced in the front basket, it would still be way too far. Instead of trying anything too dramatic, she took one shaky step after another down the zig-zagging Maintenance Ladders, and dropped the final ten feet back onto terra firma.

Her suitcase had long since buried itself into a rubbish skip, and was thoroughly revolting to retrieve. However, that didn't matter too much because the important thing was that it looked completely undamaged, which meant that despite the long drop from the rooftop, her mother's picture should still be perfectly fine. Sceleste managed a small stretch followed by an attempt at walking which didn't last very long, and she soon meowed until Linda went over and picked her up again.

The new street was empty except for two old cars, but it was well lit and Linda felt as if the entire world was not only watching her every move, but could hear her every footstep as well. The buildings were fronted with metal shutters and locked doors, so she hurried from one to the next into a twisting series of narrow side-streets. There were no abandoned buildings, practically nowhere to hide, and.. plenty of places for other people to hide, perhaps. The streets finally lead her to a vast multi-laned junction. A million lights and not quite so many cars lay before her, and Avalon darted off for a quick look around to try and find the next place to go. The only real option was the one Linda was hoping to avoid.

"In there?" she moaned, while Avalon hovered at the wide entrance to the subway, nodding. "Oh great.." she sighed to herself, and ventured down the slope into the dim light.

"Eew! This smells like dogs and.. umm.. dog sick! Linda, why does it smell of.."

"Shhhh.. I can hear something.. like a shuffle.." whispered Linda as she strained to hear anything, and wondered if her imagination was turning a fraught situation into a full-blown scary one. She kept walking through the wide passageways underneath the rumbling cars, and followed whichever dark path felt right, all the time struggling to avoid the suitcase's wheels rattling loudly on the bumpy tiles. And then the shuffling grew louder. She stopped under one of the few subway lights that still worked, and peered into the inky blackness. A dishevelled and very drunken man staggered to within a few feet of her, and slurred something while waving a fist at her.

"What's he saying, Avie?"

"Ooh! This could be good Reading Practice for you! Imagine you're flying like an eagle again, let your heart and your mind drift towards him.."

"This-is-not-the-time," breathed Linda as the man lurched two steps sideways. He waved a broken bottle as if he was intending to inflict some damage, and she backed away until she felt the wall behind her. Avalon did a quick flight around him, and came back.

"Hmm.. he's all dizzy in the head, and he's a little cross because he's had an accident in his trousers.. again. Eew!" she said with a shiver of disgust, "And he thinks it's all your fault, because.. uh.. well, you're the only other Person here. So it must be."

"Terrific.. but what are we going to do about him?"

Avalon consulted her Journal for an entire second.

"Ahaa.. here we go! Try looking at me and thinking of scary things, and see them in your mind when you say them."

She hovered close to the floor, just inside the range of the small ceiling-light. Linda tried to ignore the smells and noises coming from the drunk, but couldn't clear her mind enough to think of anything. He took a big step forwards and shouted something at her, which seemed to help.

"Okay, uhh.. a huge big Russian bear, Sister Mariephred, dad's beard, Brenda's dodgy front tooth, Dee doing that laugh, and that horrid receptionist's horrid glasses.. is that okay?"

Avalon became a frightening hybrid of them all, but could only hold it for a few seconds. However, that was more than long enough and the man collapsed, clutching at his chest and mouthing silently to himself. Avalon flew back to Linda's shoulder.

"Oops. D'you think he'll be alright, Lindy?"

He lay on the floor, face down and motionless. Linda poked him with her foot, hoping he might move or groan a little, or at least blink. He didn't.

"Well.. I'm no doctor, but I'd say he'll be fine in the morning after a good night's sleep. Now let's get very far away.. pretty quick, too."

They hurried on for an eternity, and emerged in the perfect area to lie low for a while. The seedy, cramped terraced street ahead was lined with tall houses, most of which had either been burned down or needed to be burned down. Even the more presentable ones looked as if only rats had been near them for decades.

Linda paused below the filthy street sign to roll her dice and find which house ahead would offer the safest refuge.. and soon arrived at the fifth of the houses which met the correct criteria (- an easy way in through a broken front door). She stared at the 1313 written above the doorway, and found herself in one of her most advanced Triskaidekaphobia Dilemmas ever. Should she defy the dice, or defy the excessively bad pair of numbers? The remnants of the front door were more or less already open, and once Avalon had made sure it was completely open and done an extremely quick check for scary things, Linda dared to enter. They went up all three flights of stairs to the moonlit landing on the top floor, and finally found an empty room with no huge gaps in the floor. It wasn't quite The Ritz and the boarded windows didn't help its appeal, but it was somewhere to stay for the night and it met with Avalon's approval.

"Look where we are!" she exclaimed, flying around in excited circles, "This'll be perfect won't it, Lindy?"

"Perfectly imperfect, and I'm too done in. Let's settle down, shall we? My brain keeps switching off 'cause today's been way too long and way too weird."

She made a bed from a few towels and blankets taken from the Krasnaya, and padded them with all her clothes from the suitcase. Aggy made a very good pillow, and Linda lay down and watched Sceleste lapping slowly at a saucer of cream. Avalon's glow gave a very cosy feel to their small part of the world.

"How come she was treated so bad, Avie?" she asked, sleepily.

Avalon consulted her Faery Journal, while Sceleste tried standing by the saucer. She wobbled and lay down again.

"Here we go.." she said, pausing for a yawn, "..dum dah dum.. The Ninth Life. It's a very scary path to get there, and it takes lots of horrid Dark Spirit Rituals, and I'm not telling any of them to you, especially at this time of night."

"Really, it's okay, you can tell me. I ought to know what she's been through," she said, quietly.

"No, I mean the Journal won't tell me. It says so here - 'I am not telling any of them to you, especially at this time of night'. All it says is that if she dies, she takes the Spirits of those around her down into.. a really bad place. The kind of place even the most evil Demons daren't go. Ooh, I really hope she likes that cream.."

She fluttered over and tried a handful of it, and rolled around squealing until the taste had gone. It was even worse than Old-Book Goo. Sceleste watched her for a while, interested and intrigued, and went back to lapping at the bowl until her front legs gave way again. Linda crawled over and picked her up, taking her back to the make-shift bed where she bunched the sheets underneath her cat until she looked comfortable. She gave her a long hug and and smiled to herself as she noticed that the small heartbeat felt a little stronger beneath her hands, and then stroked her black coat to gently try and smooth away the deep furrows left by the silver cords. It would probably take a long time to make them go completely, but that was fine by Linda. Sceleste could have all the time in the world.

Avalon gave Linda a very sleepy face-hug, and quickly prepared a blanket for herself and Sceleste from Linda's hair. For a moment the curse-bearing cat looked confused and a little distressed by all the attention, but soon purred softly as Avalon snuggled down against her.

"Do you think she'd like some Abba, Linda? I unpacked us the Headuh-phonez and everything."

"Well, I don't know about her, but I certainly would. Put it on quietly, though.. 'night-night, Abbalon."

CHAPTER SIXTEEN
April In The Park

The first light of the day filtered through the narrow cracks in the boarded windows, casting thin strips of sunshine across the bed.

Avalon was dreaming.

She was in Hesperides, laughing while all her friends said 'Hello' to Linda, as they made their way to see Kupula. Linda flew alongside her, and they kept stopping to look at all kinds of important and colourful things. Sceleste was there as well, jumping up through the tall grass, flying with them and loving her world. The three of them flew high over the meadows, throwing the Stone to each other over and over again, watching it move slowly through the air. They laughed as it began shining brighter than the sun and all the stars put together. And then Rhaedlin joined in, and that was perfectly okay, because she was a friend and friends were allowed to join in. She passed The Stone to all her Sylph friends who swept around the entire Earth with it, bringing it back to Avalon in the blink of an eye. Audlyn beckoned them down to her, down to the waters of the world, and she took it away for a while. She was allowed to do that, as well. She carried it from wave to wave, through every ocean and river of the whole world, and launched it high up into the sky for Avalon to catch. And Kupula was waiting patiently where the sunshine played upon the spray of the waterfall just like she always was, and she was so pleased with her New Favourite One who had been so very, very good..

.. but there was something bad. How could that be? Nothing bad came near Kupula, ever. But this was bad, and it made hard noises, noises like the footsteps of a Ground Crawler. Hard, sharp footsteps that had found their way into Hesperides. But that couldn't be right, could it? There was nothing in Hesperides that could make those kind of sounds. And then everyone was scared because It wanted Avalon, and Avalon was more scared than anyone, because she knew It didn't just want her, It wanted Linda as well, and that was so very, very bad. Avalon looked for Linda to warn her to fly as high as she could, away from the ground and the footsteps, high into the

sunshine where Kupula would be and she'd have the Stone and..
and.. Avalon flew to Sceleste, and held her. And the footsteps faded,
and the badness went away..

The first light of the day filtered through the narrow cracks in the
boarded windows, casting thin strips of sunshine across the bed.

Linda was dreaming.
She was running towards St Teresa's again, and running really fast.
As always, she was late for a History lesson - and sometimes History
could be so important. Everybody was in the playground, pointing
her out to their parents as she ran this way and that, and they all
laughed at her as she tried to remember what room she was
supposed to be in. They knew she would never, ever remember it,
and then they all left to go back to their homes, their perfect homes
that were all next door to each other. But then they didn't matter any
more. None of them did. Avalon had flown down from nowhere,
smiling and singing something pleasantly familiar, holding the
picture of Linda's mother. And then Linda remembered she didn't
have to worry about the History lesson. Avalon was there, and she
was far more important than anything else. She wanted to have a
look around the whole school, and make all Linda's bad memories
disappear and be replaced by good ones.

So Linda began doing just that. But where was her beautiful black
cat? If only Sceleste was there, being loved and kept safe with her
and Avalon, everything would be wonderful. And then Sceleste was
there - she was everywhere. By her feet, in her arms, up on window
sills, on desks, on chairs, wherever Linda wanted to look. That was
so funny, and Avalon laughed with her.

They went along the main corridor, and heard voices coming from
one room. It was her old Form Room, the one where she had spent
her worst and loneliest year, the one with the most teasing and the
worst teachers and the worst friends. She peered around the door to
see who was in Detention. It was Dee. How hysterically funny.
Avalon kept singing Dee-tention, and Sceleste walked up and down
in front of the door as if she owned the place. Linda looked in again.
Her father was there as well now, writing out lines about all the
things he should not do with Dee. And Dee had to write an essay
about all the things she should not do with him. Oh that was brilliant.

Agnetha sat at the teacher's desk and gave a small wave, and when Linda looked again, she had changed into Frida. That was a little odd, but still really good, so Linda quickly shuffled through her suitcase to find all those Abba cd's for her to sign..

..but then there was something bad. Somewhere at the end of the corridor where the darkness took over and nothing could possibly exist, there was a noise. Sharp, hard and very deliberate footsteps. High heels with diamond points, echoing, echoing, every step louder and sharper than the last, bringing jealousy and hatred nearer. Linda knew what it wanted.. it desired and craved the Stone. The Stone? Where was.. where.. it wasn't in any of her pockets, and that made her feel sick, and proved that she was useless. Maybe Avalon had it? If only there was time to think where it might be. But the footsteps came nearer, and she couldn't do anything to stop them. She was in such trouble now.. and reached for Sceleste without looking, trusting her to be there.. and she was, and Linda held her close.. and the footsteps faded, and the evil went away..

The first light of the day filtered through the narrow cracks in the boarded windows, casting thin strips of sunshine across the bed.

Sceleste was already awake.

Unblinking, she watched the shadow arrive in the room. She watched its every move.

The previous few hours had been the first in her entire life where she had felt safe and loved. And that was good, good enough to let her sleep under the Gifted One's arm, and good enough to sleep beside the harmless faery. Sunrise had been a long way off when she first awoke, sensing the evil in the air. She had stared into the darkness, every part of her tortured soul straining to find the intruder's presence, to sense its form. But there was nothing. It had passed, taking the danger away, and once again sleep had swept over her. She couldn't fight sleep, not any longer. The girl and the faery were safe, and so was she. She could sleep, for a while.

But the moments before sunrise had brought her abruptly back, wrenching her from dreamless realms. The hunter had returned and found its quarry. Sceleste woke instantly as it drew near again, and she watched the shadow. It arrived through the door and the floor, and moved to the corner of the room, into the darkness where it belonged. She could smell its age and feel its desperation and loathing. It had been patient for many centuries, but its patience was now gone. It was dying. She watched as the evil took to its human form, standing tall in the shadows.

The figure began approaching. Her shoes made hard, clacking steps against the floorboards as she crossed the room to the Gifted One, stopping only when she sensed that two yellow eyes were glaring into her. Sceleste hissed the lowest, strongest hiss she could manage and the Ved'ma had no choice but to walk away. The evil spirit uttered a curse, but dared not place it upon the Bearer Of All Curses. She faded back into shadow and spirit as she neared the door, and her footsteps faded away with her..

..and Linda woke up with a yawn, almost convinced she'd heard footsteps somewhere. But the room was just as she'd left it last night, though, and that was a relief. The chair was wedged against the door handle, her suitcase was on the chair, her picture and a near-empty bowl of cream were beside the bed.. nothing was wrong.

"Dreams can be such a pain in the neck at times, they really can," she mumbled to herself. Sceleste purred and for a moment seemed agitated, but a hug soon took that away. Avalon woke up slowly, looking as if she was trying to remember where she was for a moment before stretching her wings and giving a rendition of her Morning Song. To the untrained ear it sounded a lot like her Midday Song, her Afternoon Song and also her Evening Song, but Linda was starting to recognise the one or two notes which made all the difference.

"What are you going to do with that now?" Avalon asked, prodding Linda's inside pocket. Linda reached inside and held the Stone up into the sunlight, and watched as it trapped the rays before releasing them.

"Well.. I was hoping you'd know?" she said, while Avalon circled it twice.

"Nope. Not unless we really can get to Hesperides using it? Then everything would be really good again."

"How could we do that?"

Avalon hovered about four feet off the ground, at her Serious Thinking Level, and minutely adjusted herself up and down until she was at exactly the right point for her very, very clearest thinking.

"Weird stuff. Same as last night when you made everywhere look like there was too much daylight, maybe? Or the same as when you took The Stone or even Sceleste, or when you lead us back to the tunnel from all the dark corridors. But except this time.. umm.. I tell you about my home, like you read me. Then we'd just be there, and give Kupula The Stone, and.. and.. everything's how it should be?"

"Hmm.." Linda thought for a moment, on the brink of complete confusion. How would that work? She could almost remember walking through the dark corridors underground, how she had been lead to where she wanted to be.. but she had lead herself there by wanting to be there.. as if the Stone allowed her to follow her own deepest feelings and needs.. so who was leading who - and how would that lead to Hesperides? And then a larger thought hit her, and all the other questions suddenly meant nothing.

If there was even the tiniest chance that she really could go to Hesperides, regardless of 'if' and 'how' that might happen, there was one place where she had to try and go first. That would be the one place which in many ways she'd never, ever left. She held the chance, assuming she could manage it, to change the most important event in her entire world.

"Can we try something first?" she said, and Sceleste's ears pricked up, "All my life I've wanted to change one thing, and put it right. It would only take a second, and then we could go to Hesperides straight afterwards.."

Sceleste stared harshly at her, and Avalon looked as if she knew what was coming.

"I just want my mum," said Linda, trying to keep her voice steady, "..that's all. I can't tell you how many times I've dreamed of seeing her stepping into the road, and I'm always too late to stop her and she always has the accident, and if I could really stop her, she'd never.. I'd.. I can't explain how it feels.."

As Linda spoke she realised that her words weren't just the usual wishing, these were ones that could actually happen.

"You remember the traveller who brought the Stone to the castle in Brother Whatever's book? Well he just appeared from nowhere, didn't he? So maybe he managed to go from one place to another - but through time, like he was just visiting the past.. so maybe I could try doing that. Do you think we can?" she said, sensing that her hands were going cold.

"Yes, no.. yes," said Avalon, shaking and nodding her head at the same time. There was something about Linda's idea which felt very wrong, but she had no idea what it might be. She looked over at Sceleste, who appeared to have lost interest and was licking a paw.

"Changing history might be a good idea Lindy, especially for your Mum, but it might be a bad one as well. One or the other, but not both. Unless they really are both good? Or bad. Umm.. maybe you could try rolling first?"

"Okay.. and then we'll go to Hesperides once I'm back in a real, proper home, and everything'll be great for you and me, and we can stay friends all the time! Wouldn't that be the best thing ever? And as for you.." she held Sceleste, "..you can live with me and Avie, can't you? Nice and safe.."

Linda stroked Sceleste's head, and then took out the official Overseas Visitation Dice, and held it between the palms of her hands. She whispered a few words to it.

"Four means 'Yes'. I know I never really ask questions as simple as Yes or No ones, unless I'm really stuck - and I'm really stuck now, so if we get a Four we can try and.. make things better."

The dice bounced and rolled through the light and shade as if it would never stop. It hit the far wall and came all the way back to where Avalon was standing.

"Four!" she squealed, and looked up at Linda.

"Four? Oh wow.." she replied, and a nervous silence fell over the room for a few seconds. Suddenly Avalon looked very excited.

"Actually, if we're going to go back to change Past Things there's a couple of little ones I'd like sorting out, too."

She spun around and a narrow scroll of paper appeared in her hands. It rolled out across the length of the floor and stopped just before the door.

"Okay then.. starting in your 1863, March, on the really sunny day, near Mr Govorun's Paper Storage place - the day of the big fire. I'm sure that wasn't really my fault, but it'd be nice to make sure it wasn't. Then afterwards in the April.. on the second quarter moon, near the Distill-ery.. that one definitely was.. and we can stay for the next day because of the Ammunition Depot problem when I.."

Linda was feeling nervous.

"We'll see how we get on with my mum first? You can't imagine how much this means to me."

"Yes I can, and I bet Sceleste can too," she said as the scroll wound itself up into nothing. Linda sat cross-legged in the centre of the bed, held the Stone in front of her and thought for a while. It remained clearer than glass, and steadily took on a gentle blue. Rays of faint white light began drifting deep inside it, like sunlight reaching down into the ocean.

"Stone of Odessa,
Grant unto me,
Umm.. the wish in my heart,
Uhh.. and.. umm.."

"What are you doing, Lindy?" said Avalon, hovering just in front of her nose.

"I'm.. I'm making a wish, aren't I? Asking for one.. I thought it would sound more official like this?"

Sceleste lay down and covered her head with a paw. How could someone so Gifted have so little idea? Avalon despaired and settled on Linda's shoulder.

"Are there instructions written on the back that say it has to rhyme? Let's see.." she said, and did a quick check, "Ooh, no. No instructions at all. There's just you, The Stone, and what's in your heart. That's all you could ever need. Think about everything you know, and think of your Mum, and.. maybe just say where and when? There can't be much more to it than that?"

That made sense. Linda tried to keep her hands still, but they were shaking too much. She placed the Stone on the floor a little way in front of herself, shuffled back to the bed and closed her eyes. She imagined flying high above the clouds for a while, soaring and gliding until she felt calm and distant, and then spoke of everything she knew about that day. She imagined flying through the images as she thought they would have been, and repeated everything that she'd ever been told by the people who were there, even the trivial things and all the contradictions. The truth would be in there somewhere. She talked and talked, feeling the image building up around her as if she really was there, back when her entire world changed, longing to be there just a few minutes early and..

..suddenly the air became cool around her, and Linda opened her eyes. The room was still there, but the Stone lay in the centre of a neon blue arc, perhaps twelve feet wide. Trees in a blue and white park faded into nothing at its vague edges, and the grass met the floorboards in a blur just a few inches in front of her knees. She stared into a very real world that seemed to stretch out before her, as if she could just step straight into it.

"Look.. Avie.." her voice trembled, "..what have I done?"

Avalon flew backwards, nearer to the bed before darting up to Linda's shoulder.

"Wh.. where's all that p..place?" she stuttered, peeking from behind Linda's hair.

"It's the park.. the park by the town where my home is.. that's England.. here.." Linda replied, too stunned to make sense of what she was actually saying.

Sceleste tried to venture closer to the scene. Of all the strange things the Curse Bearer had seen the Stone do, she had never seen anything even close to this. Her weak legs gave way beneath her as she reached the Past World's edge. Linda went to pick her up, cautiously trying to stay away from the bright neon light, but as Avalon shuffled to a new and safer position behind her neck, a stray length of hair fell forwards from Linda's shoulder, and its very tip broke into the tiniest part of the glow, and suddenly..

..April colours spread through the park, pushing the arc's edges out to engulf the room, taking away everything in it, around it and beyond it. Linda was still kneeling down, but instead of being on hard floorboards near a shambolic bed, she was on soft, cool grass amongst the trees, on a cloudy April day. The leaves and branches rustled and swayed, birds sang - and Sceleste lay in her arms looking rather unimpressed. Avalon flew high up into the sky for a look around, and returned a few seconds later.

"This isn't Odessa, Linda! Where's this? What tree's that? Who's.. what's the.." she babbled, disorientated and scared. In a daze, Linda picked the Stone up from a collection of small weeds and put it back in her inside pocket. She looked up to Avalon, and held the braid out for her to take hold of.

"I.. I think we're actually here.. all that time ago.. this is it, this is where it all happened.."

They walked through the front gates of the park, and along the main road up towards the town. People stared at the scruffy girl who had a bird on her shoulder and a cat in her arms, as she wandered along. Their thoughts drifted into Linda's mind as she passed by, but she didn't notice or even care.

"..she must be a runaway.. why isn't she in school.. useless kids.. blame the parents.. she ought to be anywhere but here.."

The last one almost registered, but she was in no state to try and work out how she was in a place and a time that had passed twelve years before. She kept on walking, and her heart kept on pounding. The town was so different and yet so similar, and people were dressed in the naffest of clothes. Some shops were missing, reclaimed by ones long-forgotten to Linda. Even the familiar stores had their names presented in different ways on their panels. She stopped for a moment outside Dr Poppenchart's Music Lab, struck by the posters in the windows and the list of New Releases.

"Stop thinking, stop thinking.. just look normal and try singing instead of thinking, people sing to themselves all the time.. okay.. Friday night and the lights are low-wuh.. looking out for a.."

Avalon joined in quietly, and that helped her stay on track. She walked past three people, one after the other, who looked like younger versions of people she vaguely knew. Maybe they were, or maybe they weren't. She managed to fend off the urge to speak to them by telling herself over and over that she had a job to do and she had to keep on walking. And singing, quietly.

She leaned against the traffic lights at the top end of the main street, feeling a cold sweat break out as the lights turned to green. It was going to happen about forty yards away, and it was probably going to happen very, very soon. She looked across the road, and down towards Eve's Feast, the grocery shop. There was no sign of her mother. Maybe she was still inside? Or maybe the stories were wrong and she wasn't in there at all? Or what if it was the wrong day? What if stupid old Linda had got it wrong? Why should she be any less stupid just because she had the Stone?

And then she was there. The woman from Linda's picture was there, wearing a beige raincoat and standing in the doorway, edging her baby daughter's pram over the small step while finishing off a conversation with Mrs Jackson.

"Avalon.. look! Look in the.. outside the grocer's! That's my mum, and her new pram.. that's m.. that's me with mum! She's really.."

"Linda, you stay calm, you have to stay.." whispered Avalon reassuringly, and gently tugging at Linda's ear.

"..there.. there's Mrs Jackson.. she picked me up off the road and wouldn't let go of me, even at the hospital.. she's with mum.. my mmuh.." Linda said, and felt numb. Her mind and her entire body felt as if they belonged to someone else.

"You have to hurry up Lindy! It's her bad time soon, isn't it?"

Linda stood on the wrong side of the road, and didn't know if she was going to pass out or explode. The traffic lights seemed to be stuck on green for ever. She put Sceleste down beside the letterbox at the corner, and Avalon went up into a tree. Linda's legs felt like jelly as she stepped out onto the crossing, and she prayed they wouldn't let her down.

No-one beeped as she ran across the road. Or maybe they did? They could have launched missiles at her and she wouldn't have noticed. She wanted to run and run, not just to stop the accident ever happening, but to actually be with her mother, to throw her arms around her and tell her how much she loved her over and over again.. so she ran. She ran faster than she'd ever done in her life, knocking into people on her way, blind to them even being there.

In slow motion she looked over to Billings Butchers and saw Mrs Daniels begin to raise her arm, to make that simple wave which would cause it all to happen. Linda felt her throat tighten as she tried to shout anything that would distract her mother by just a second, maybe two. That would be more than enough. But she couldn't do it. Her heart was pounding too hard and her voice wasn't working and there was so much to shout.. and her mother was actually there, just a few yards away and..

..and then Linda fell. Three or four yards short of her mother, her foot caught the raised corner of a cracked paving stone and she fell. She hit the pavement with a hard and unforgiving smack, leaving herself stunned and helpless, breathless under the entire weight of the world and her own stupidity. She had to get up, but she couldn't. She lay on the cold ground, knowing that everything hurt all the way from her face down to her feet. She was too shaken to even cry. Any second now there would be the sound of brakes and tyres and screaming, the sound of a young mother being hit, the cries of a child lying in the road and the sound of feet hurrying past.. first Mr Collins, then Mrs Gillsburgh, then the girl from the card shop who later became a nurse, then..

"Hello? Are you alright? That was such a nasty tumble.. here you go, hold still.."

Someone helped Linda to sit up, and carefully stroked her hair back for her from her face. And then she even started to softly wipe the pavement's grime away from Linda's cheek with a handkerchief. It smelled very, very nice. It held the faintest aroma of a certain perfume, a smell that roused a memory from somewhere deep inside her.. but for the time being she couldn't think straight or even breath properly, and the fragrance was nothing more than something pretty.

A few moments later the numbing pain had started to ebb away, and Linda raised her head up a little more - and looked straight into the face of her mother.

"Are you feeling better now, sweetheart? Anything broken? You must be careful love - you're so fragile, aren't you? And in such a hurry too, my word you were in such a hurry."

Linda stared straight back. Her face was beautiful, and her voice.. that was really her voice, all those wonderful words.. and her arm was around her, loving and caring just like in the picture. Tears welled up and took her mother away in a blur and Linda wiped at her eyes, desperate not to lose a single moment. She tried to speak, but hadn't a hope of saying anything at all. Mrs Jackson bent down, and took over.

"It's alright Louise, I'll take her inside. I'm not surprised she looks shaken - that was a horrible fall, wasn't it? A cup of tea'll sort her out and she'll be fine. See you tomorrow then, and you can tell me how the decorators get on with.."

Linda watched helplessly as her mother gave a smile and stood up to leave her. She clung onto her hand for a second longer, and then it was gone, and she held nothing but air. Her mother adjusted the pram and didn't go near the road, because Mrs Daniels had crossed over instead. They laughed together and started walking away, and life carried on as if nothing of any importance had happened at all. Mrs Beaufort paused and turned around and caught Linda's eyes for a final time, and perhaps there was a moment of something that passed between them.. but Mrs Jackson put an end to it by dabbing her apple-polishing cloth at her eyes. In her friendly way, she insisted that Linda ought to try and get up - and noticed something odd.

"Ah, you're another one with different colours! There must be something in the water 'round here, there must be.." she said, and then pushed some tissues into Linda's hand and took her inside the grocery store.

A few minutes later, Linda was back on the street, still rubbing her knee, but at least able to move everything else properly. She looked around, desperate to see her mother again, not sure what to think anymore. Deep down, she knew the time had come to leave but something in her heart wouldn't let her. Maybe she could find her again just to thank her for helping, and share a few more precious moments? That would only take a minute, and..

"Lindy?"

Avalon was sitting on the roof of a car parked outside the card shop, next door. She fluttered over and settled on Linda's shoulder, and whispered to her.

"You did it, and that's good and that's all you wanted to do. But we can't stay here.. you know we have to go back. This isn't where we belong, is it? See, we might cause problems if we stay too long.."

Linda knew she was right, and although she wanted to try and change Avalon's mind, she knew that she really had to go. She made her way back along the street and crossed at the traffic lights, not thinking about anything and not putting too much pressure on her right knee. It really did hurt a lot, not that it mattered.

Sceleste had wandered a little from the postbox, and was happily sitting in the middle of the pavement looking quite content, eyeing a small beetle scurrying past. The people walking around her looked less happy, but that didn't seem to bother her at all. Linda picked her up and they wandered back to the secluded area of the park where they had arrived earlier.

She sat against one of the trees, and closed her eyes for a long, long time to try and gather her thoughts together. A light rain began to fall, and with a little prompting from Avalon she took the Stone from her inside pocket, and held it tightly. Eventually she described the room in Odessa, seeing it in her mind and in her heart, and saying as much about it as she could manage. The freshness of the park in spring and the sound of the trees moving in the breezes gently faded away to nothing, replaced by the smell of old wood, cigarettes and plaster, the stillness of the old room.. and she opened her eyes again. The Stone felt warm in her hands, and a million thin strands of soft colours drifted and twisted inside, gradually merging to leave it clear once again.

The room was full of warm mid-morning sunshine, and Linda figured they must have been gone for about an hour. Avalon flew to the boarded window and took a look outside.

"It's still there!" she called back, sounding very happy.

"What's still there?" said Linda, steadily regaining her composure.

"Odessa. All of it's out there!" she sang.

"That's good. Anything suspicious? Big cars, sneaky people, weirdos.. that kind of thing?"

"Nope. Unless they're already here, but around the other side where we can't see them.. or maybe they're coming up the stairs?"

"Thanks, that's very comforting. But it might not matter anymore, because if we go to England now, I should be able to just go home! Mum and dad might even be wondering where I am!"

Linda enjoyed saying that. It felt so very good, so right. A lifetime of dreaming and longing was almost at an end, and all she wanted to do was go to her family - and there was nothing that could possibly get in the way.

"What.. no, what if.. where.. the.." muttered Avalon, turning a different way with each word. She still didn't quite know how to say what was troubling her, and Linda's effervescent joy and delight wasn't helping.

"Then as soon as I'm home we'll conjure up Hesperides, and you can step through and I'll carry the Stone for you - or maybe Kupula will do that, and you'll be a hugely big hero! Won't that be something brilliant? Then we'll summon up my home again, I step through and leave the Stone with you, and you can come and see me whenever you want and we can stay friends all the time, like Pooh and Piglet - friends forever!"

Avalon replied with an optimistic two-note 'hmm' but didn't sound at all convinced. She tried hard to think what might be wrong with Linda's Big Plan, but couldn't work it out at all. She needed some serious Figuring-Out Time, and nearly had a good idea how to find some.

"Don't you need to be packing the suitcase first? There's all your things here and all over the place.. and back at the hotel as well."

"I won't need them anymore, will I? I'll have a home that'll be absolutely full of everything I could want! And if anything's missing, I'll just go shopping with my mum. You could come too!"

Seeing Linda so happy made Avalon decide that she didn't want to work out what was wrong anymore. Maybe everything was perfectly okay, really.

CHAPTER SEVENTEEN
Lindagate

Linda carefully placed the Stone down in the centre of the room, and sat on the bed with her eyes closed, trying to be as calm as possible. She described the park again, and gave a very specific date - Friday, June 13th, which not only happened to be the day of the trip to Odessa, but was now her last ever day at St Teresa's House Of Pain. But then she quickly changed it to June 14th, because arriving anywhere on a Friday which happened to be the 13th would have to be a really bad move. Besides, if today was the 17th, the 14th was barely three days ago which Linda felt was probably a whole lot easier for the Stone to manage. She didn't want to take any risks.

She soon found herself back in the shaded secrecy of the trees, more or less in the same place that she had just been in, and the park looked pretty much the same. A few trees and maybe a few bushes had either gone, been moved or been planted, but now that she could compare it in a way that no-one had ever done before, twelve years hadn't left too much of a mark. Being June, the day was filled with far more sunshine of course, the air was pleasantly warmer and there were far more people around. She sat and watched the world going by until it all made a bit more sense.

Linda picked up Sceleste and they crossed over the main area where the huge annual July Fair was normally held. They hurried past the swings and the Kiddie Splashpool, then through the screeching gates at the side. Families seemed to be everywhere, and for the first time ever, Linda didn't feel even a twinge of longing or of being left out. She felt wonderful.

"Where are we going? This isn't the way we went before, is it?" asked Avalon, making herself a new braid out of Linda's hair. And then another. And another.

"Nope. We're not going to the town, we're going to the place where I used to live. After mum's accident, dad moved us a mile or two away which is fair enough if you think about it, but that doesn't matter one bit 'cause I'm going home! I feel so good saying that! And then we go to your home - isn't that just the best?"

They waited at the bus stop on Cavendish Street for ten long minutes before she realised that it was a Saturday service, and therefore the buses wouldn't be running the usual timetable. So five tedious minutes later she caught the 122 a few streets away, and fifteen excruciating minutes later it arrived at the top end of Eldridge Close. Linda ran off the bus and hurried along the quiet street, only slowing down when Sceleste complained about the ride.

She knew the number of the house, but wasn't entirely sure what it looked like. There had only been two occasions in her life when she'd gone past the building that should have been her home, and both of those times had been when her father was in a nostalgic mood - combined with a hangover. He had only ever grunted and gestured with his thumb towards it, and for Linda aged 4 and then aged 7, that wasn't much help.

Sceleste purred nervously, and Avalon fluttered from tree to tree along the road. She came back to Linda's shoulder, still feeling uneasy, and immediately tied and untied five new braids. Only the usual one remained as they reached the entrance to a narrow Edwardian terraced house.

"Number 45! We're here.. we're actually here. I am so nervous, I am so nervous, I am SO nervous," whispered Linda as she wandered into the driveway. A front door key hadn't magically appeared in her pocket, which was a little annoying but that wasn't really anything to be worried about. Time-travel probably had lots of rules and quirks that she couldn't possibly imagine, so she didn't waste any time trying to figure out what should or should not be anywhere. Instead, she pressed the doorbell and a very faint 'ba-dingh' came from somewhere inside. Her heart pounded as a figure on the other side of the frosted glass made its way towards her. The door opened as far as it would go on the safety chain, and a short woman with grey curls peered between the narrow gap.

"H'llo yes?" she said, in a light Scottish accent.

"Oh, hello. Uhh.. I thought the Beaufort's lived here?"

The woman took the security chain off the door, and opened it further. She seemed friendly enough.

"The Beaufirts? No, they moved to th'new Princess Estate about two, mebbe three years ago. This place was getting too small for them all! Are you a friend of.. I forget her name.. d'you want their address? It's not far.."

Twenty minutes later, Linda stood at the driveway to 52 Janred Avenue, trying to get her breath back. The house was almost twice the size of the one on Eldridge Close, and she ran her eyes over every glorious detail, not wanting to miss anything. Sceleste meowed and wriggled until Linda put her on the top of the low, decorative front wall, but even then she didn't look any less wary. She turned her head away from the house, raised her tail in a tall curve, and fixed her gaze firmly down the road.

The walk there hadn't done Linda any good at all. Now she felt nervous, as if it wasn't just a dream or an adventure anymore. This was all so real, almost too real. She crossed over the front garden, admired the huge conifer and four crescent flower-beds, and pressed the doorbell. She tied her hair back, to feel a little more presentable.

"Hi mum, I forgot my key.. Hi mum, it's me.. Hi.." she practiced, while waiting for a reply. She rang it again. And then once more.

Avalon arrived, hovering between her and the door.

"No-one's inside. I took a look in all the windows while you were talking to yourself, and no-one's there. Maybe nobody lives here really? Some houses are like that."

Linda checked the number on the wood-cut panel.

"Uhh.. well.. this is 52 and we got the right road.. they must be out somewhere. See, I should probably have a key of my own so I could just let myself in, but maybe I don't.. so watch this.."

Linda removed one of her spare hairgrips from her jacket cuff and bent it slightly in the middle, and again at the end. She slid her id tag into the door frame next to the main lock, and poked the hairgrip into the one above it.

"Back at St Teresa's I only need the hairgrip to do any of the doors, even the one for the Staff Store Room and you wouldn't believe what they have in there, honestly there's mountains of crazy stuff but I never really keep anything, I always put it back usually. They hadn't a clue, except one time when.."

The door obligingly clicked open, and Linda's excited rambling came to a halt as the hallway opened up before her. All the ordinary and simple things that she had never experienced lay in front of her. Light summer jackets hung from the coat-hooks, shoes of all sizes stood in a wooden shoe-rack underneath, and there were even some plants in a huge, rounded glass bottle at the foot of the stairs. She hardly dared step into such a perfect world.

She slowly closed the door behind her, briefly glancing for Avalon to make sure she was still there with her, and breathed in the aromas of a family home. Somewhere in the air was the trace of the meal from last night, lingering defiantly alongside some bacon from the morning's breakfasts, plus a welcoming hint of coffee. And there was that special perfume, holding everything together. Perfect.

Avalon took off for a quick tour of the house, hoping that she was getting closer to figuring out what exactly was bothering her. She was nearly getting cross with herself, because if only she knew what it was, she could look it up in her Journal and maybe find out what to do. Or not to do, perhaps.

A Labrador came bounding out of the kitchen and jumped up to greet Linda, slobbering and wanting some attention. She gave him an equally friendly greeting, once she'd realised he wasn't going to rip her to shreds, but once the initial friendliness had passed he backed off as if he was unsure about something. Avalon returned, and took a close look behind the coats and around a calendar in her own peculiar way. She opened her Journal and was about to draw a few things in it, and then remembered that she didn't have to do that anymore. Instead, she flew over to Linda.

"There's definitely no-one else here, anywhere. The rooms are very nice though!" she said, and pointed upwards. Linda nodded, and clapped her hands for the dog to come back to her.

"He seems a bit strange.. he recognises me, but look at him."

The hefty golden Labrador looked from Linda to Avalon, and began grumbling and whining up at her. She fluttered down, lifted his ear and whispered something to him, and he trotted back to his basket in the kitchen, with his tail between his legs.

"What did you say?"

"I said he needn't be scared of me, and that if the scent on you is just like you, then you are you and he didn't have to worry. I think he's okay now."

"It must be these different clothes?"

"Hmm.. or maybe he can smell Sceleste?"

"Ahh.. I bet that's it. I ought to change, I think. Now then, where's my room?"

Linda took her time going up the stairs, enjoying the difference between the ones here and those at St Teresa's. No echoes, no worn-out rubber slip-strips, no marked walls and best of all, only one flight of steps. The third room she came to had a nameplate with "Linda's

Boudoir" written on it, in very twirly letters. That was a bit too cute, but all things considered, there was nothing really wrong with something being cute. She held the door's handle with no strength at all, and gave it a weak push. It swung open very slowly, and she stood motionless in the doorway, terrified that she might suddenly wake up and find herself in her room back at school.

The first thing she noticed were all the posters, especially Princess Diana and Abba smiling out from the near wall, greeting her like life-long friends. And then as she went in, everything seemed to jump out at her from the room's pastel shades. There were teddies all over the place, some alongside Aggy on the bed, but most of them were on shelves and the floor, in no kind of height, size or colour order at all. That would definitely need changing, but not for a while yet. Not until she was no longer being thrown around by a million emotions all at the same time. She edged a little further in, and took a slow look around herself. A gleaming tv sat in the corner with a trendy see-through pink cd player next to it, a pair of discarded trainers with badly knotted laces lay tangled together on the chair beside the dressing table, a tie from the nearby King Henry's school lay coiled snake-like on the floor underneath, books were standing up or lying flat which was something else that would need changing.. and there was something odd about one of the posters.

"Oh wow, Danny O of DaHapnin'Squad is missing! Da Squad without D-O. I wonder when he left.. and who's that in his place? Weird.. weird.. I mean, this is only Saturday, isn't it? I ought to know something like that."

Avalon had a think, and tried to look behind the poster.

"Maybe it's because your Mum's okay? Maybe it's because she did something tiny which one way or another changed how things worked out for Danneeoh and he wasn't ever in Daskwod?"

"Hmm.. yeah, how bizarre. I liked Danny. He wasn't my favourite one, but it's not like I ruined things for them.. at least there's no chance of changing anything for Abba," she added, pointing at a familiar poster.

As Linda waffled she arrived at a large maroon-coloured message board covered with postcards and photographs. A girl grinned widely in all of them. She wasn't just fake-smiling either, these smiles looked like big genuine ones. Her eyes were blue and brown, and she had fluffed hair which didn't even reach her shoulders, and she looked remarkably similar to Linda.

"Look at the all-new me.. that's me.. with pierced ears as well! I wonder when these were taken? Yikes, who's this?" she said, pointing at a photo-booth picture. Avalon took a close look.

"Eww! Spots.. messy hair.. looks a bit shifty.. he's a Boy. There's lots of them everywhere. I bet he smells funny too, 'cause they do, you know.."

"Thanks Avie. Wow, I've got a boyfriend who I don't even know.. is that worse than knowing one who I haven't got? I'll have to write to Dr Beryl about that.. and look! Here's one of Andie! And another - isn't that great? We're still friends and she's still got that hopeless boyfriend! This is too brilliant.."

Linda traced her finger from one to the next, going along in ordered lines from left to right, and then right to left without losing contact with the board once. Even at times like this, ensuring continuity and respecting fate was too important to risk.

She gazed over holiday photos taken in sunny places, where her father looked normal and harmless, and her mother looked simply wonderful. In the biggest picture, a couple of rows below those, Linda was holding twin baby girls no older than a few months, and in the one just below that one she was holding them again only this time they were a little bigger, and were very awake. Her mother was seated next to her holding a small baby in a blue shawl.

"Look at these Avalon.. look at them.. two sisters.. and a brother.. that's a huge whole family. This is all because we stopped the bad thing happening, isn't it just.. so.. this is all my family and, and.. there's.. look Avie, that one there! There's that one of me and mm.."

Linda touched the beloved photograph of her and her mother that had been beside her every day since it was taken, and couldn't finish her sentence. A tidal wave of emotion swept over her, and she sat on the bed as the first of countless tears started pouring down her face, and she completely lost herself. The Labrador trotted into the room, and with a small whimper rested against her, propping his head on the crumpled blue duvet.

Avalon was finally starting to understand why this Linda was different in so many ways to the Linda in the photographs. It wasn't just the hair or the earrings or any of the obvious things like that. The difference was the girl behind the eyes. The Linda who was in the pictures had lead a completely different life to the Linda who was crying on the bed. It was all very nearly beginning to make sense.

She shuffled the white Strand-Band down from Linda's hair and groomed it all back into its usual uncontrolled style, while the sniffing and nose-blowing gradually came to an end. She pushed the hair band into Linda's biscuit-pocket and went to hover by the mirrors on the dressing table, where she settled down on top of the tallest one.

"Have a looky here! This is WOW just so oh fantastic and interesting, ooh it's amazing what's over here.. I'm so glad I'm over here looking at this! Ooooh!" she called, waving her arms and kicking her legs. Linda wiped her eyes and wandered over to the dressing table. Avalon pointed down to a picture stuck on the big oval mirror and looked away.

"Ohh, yes - that's Andie, Avie.. looking like she does anyway, and there's me.. with my even shorter hair - and it's got summer-streaks, too! Why point this one out, Av.. huh?"

Linda finally noticed her reflection, and touched her hair. It was still an unruly sea of long waves, and wasn't short at all, and definitely had no highlights.

"Why's my hair.. how can all those pictures.. why's this stupid mess still here? When does the magic happen that turns This Me into New Me, Avie? I live here now, I've got a home and everything!"

The clasp on her necklace finally decided to give up, but she didn't even notice it falling. It steadily made its way down from her shoulders, hindered slightly by all the long hair, and came to rest on the table. She was too upset and confused to notice. All she could see was the same old Linda with the same old hair, un-pierced ears and scrawny big-eyed face staring straight back at her.

"How come I'm still like me, Avie? How can I explain suddenly growing all this hair to them all? What's gone wrong?"

Avalon almost mentioned the necklace, but Linda's question and the weight of the impending answer had thrown her completely. She didn't even know how to explain what she was thinking, and tried finding her Very Best Thinking Level, but that proved to be impossible. A car outside sounded loud and important, so she flew over to the window instead, leaving Linda staring in the mirror. A large dark blue Nissan rolled onto the driveway, and she began nervously darting around the room. The dog ran downstairs, throwing a big friendly woof back up to Linda, and Avalon flew back to the mirror.

"Lindy, I think we really have to go.. I knew this wasn't a good idea, and now I know why I knew that.. you have to look out there, now, very very veryveryveryveryquick - nowww-uh..." she said, and gently tugged the narrow braid to make sure she followed over to the window. Linda kneeled on the bed, accidentally nudging one of the small bears off the windowsill, and looked down through the net curtains. She watched her clean-shaven father closing his car door. He seemed so high spirited, so.. happy? Mr Beaufort opened one of the large estate's rear doors and picked up one of the girls, who was no older than the twins in the photos. Linda's eyes widened as her mother stepped out of the car. Twelve years had transformed her in ways she had never imagined. Her hair was different, she may even have been a little heavier, but she was real and she was there and she was so beautiful. She began shuffling in the back seat with the baby chairs, before emerging with the other toddler.

"That's my mum! Look at everyone! And who's.. who's.. me?"

Linda watched as a very trendy and fitter version of herself stepped out of the car, holding a sleeping baby. She was laughing and said something to her father, who pulled a face back at her.

"Yup. And she's standing on that long crack in the driveway like she doesn't care too much.. and I think that maybe the you down there is a bit taller than the you up here, but I wouldn't like to be around and see you standing next to each other.." Avalon said, ending with a shiver.

The front door opened and the dog ran out to greet everyone. He jumped around and wagged his tail, and then barked up at the bedroom, looking confused. He ran over to have a look at the cat on the front wall, but Sceleste glared down at him and he bounded back to the safety of the family.

"There's another you down there and that's what was bothering me all along, since before we came here.."

At last, Avalon knew what question she needed to ask, and that meant she could finally consult her Journal. It immediately opened to the short section about Linear Time Travel, and the pages turned themselves to the chapter on Cross-Dimensional Hypotheses & Arguments, stopping at the blue corded page about Theoretical Self-Duplication. She immediately scratched her head, and sneezed.

"Oh I don't understand this at all, it's too difficult for me - it's taken me all this time just to think of why this was bad. Maybe we could go now and we'll sort out why later 'cause I don't think we're supposed to be here anymore. Linda? I said.."

Linda didn't answer. She was captivated by the people in the driveway. Avalon fluttered around her head and took a very large deep breath.

"Hey Lindaaaah! We have to go now! Bad things! Bad things! We go now, now, nownowNOW-WUH.. puh-leeeeze?" she added, with a final tug.

In a daze Linda opened one of the bedroom's back windows and climbed out onto the kitchen's new extension. She did her best to close the window again, and then she crouched down tight against the wall, waiting for the noises and laughter in the driveway to go away. The front door shut loudly and might have opened again, so Linda waited a little longer until she felt sure no-one was left outside. Her heart jumped as someone opened the window just inches above her, and the smaller one above it soon followed. People started talking inside, so she made her way across to the side of the house, feeling like an intruder as she left the muffled voices and laughter behind.

She held onto the drainpipe and edged down into the laurel trees that separated Number 52 from Number 50, and crawled her way as quietly as possible towards the drive. The car's engine started up just as she was about to emerge and she froze against the side wall, praying that she hadn't been seen.

"Avie? Where are you?" she whispered to the air. Avalon flew down from the top of the house.

"Don't go out yet, they're not gone. Well, your Dad almost is, and Other You is waving him off, so wait a bit longer. See, he forgot to get Newspapers this morning, and Other You said.."

The front door shut soon after the car sped away, and Linda hurried across the drive to pick up Sceleste. She couldn't think of anything to say or even how to feel, so she just started walking, simply taking one step after another.. after another.. after another.

Eventually she arrived back at the park and wandered over to her favourite secluded tree, the one near the pond which she'd spent many lonely days sitting under during previous summer holidays. Sceleste almost went for a walk but changed her mind and clambered back onto her lap where she promptly fell asleep, while Linda watched the normal people wandering through their normal lives. Occasionally she recognised someone, and one or two people even looked twice at her. Reverend Williams offered a wave before thinking he'd made a mistake, so she let her hair fall forwards to cover most of her face. And that felt good. She always, always felt better like that.

She stroked Sceleste for a long time, knowing that there was simply far too much to think about, so she tried not to think about anything. Meanwhile, Avalon established that Linda's Tree had the correct number of leaves, and moved on to examine other equally important things nearby. The grass showed all the correct shades of green and matched perfectly with the Acceptable Green-ness Charts in her Journal, and she carefully noted that some of the uncut areas were taller than herself, and that practically all the flowers nearby were looking at the sun exactly like they were supposed to. She came back when she sensed that Linda would feel like talking again.

"I don't get it Avie.. my dad isn't in Odessa because he's here in England, which means he never actually left England because he never worked for the Ministry Of Defence because he only worked there after mum's accident.. and that's how there's another me here.. so where does that leave Me Me? And what about everyone who knew either of me?"

Avalon settled on Linda's knee and opened the Journal to the tassled purple bookmark.

"It says here you've created an Alterneyate Reality. That makes sense."

"You understand that?"

She flicked the page over, and turned it upside down. And then back the right way.

"Uhuh, really. This is your world on Saturday, June the 40th.."

"14th.."

"..yes, that too.. June the 14th.. because your Mum never had her accident twelve years ago, okay? The events that lead to you going to Odessa never happened, blah blah blah big words and then some filler bits for a couple of pages.. aha! In a nutshell you can't just step into your Alterneyate Life because Other You never left here in the first place. So now You You, who I'm talking to right now, is a Duplicate and you've broken so many rules about Existence And Time. Fancy that. Or maybe Other You's the Duplicate? Hmm.."

Avalon pressed her hand lightly against Linda's cheek as if she was making sure that she was talking to the right one. She was, apparently, and carried on reading.

"Uhh.. can't make any sense of the next bit."

"So if there's two Me's, does that mean you're a duplicate too?

And Sceleste as well?" wondered Linda. Avalon flicked ahead a few pages, and pointed at some bizarre squiggles.

"Nope.." she said, nodding.

"How does that work then?" Linda asked, ending in a sniff.

"Umm.. it says you have the Real Stone, and Real Me and Real Sceleste.. because you've only changed things here.. so nothing's changed in Odessa from the moment you arrived there - that's the Key Moment. So People in Odessa who only ever knew Long Hair You plus The Stone still know Long Hair You.. and The Stone. So nothing's changed there, except your Dad's not there. Isn't this good? It's a shame there's no pictures in here.. there usually are."

Avalon gave the Journal a shake, but it made no difference. She turned a few pages until she found a section she could manage.

"So you've got a choice, Lindy. If we go back twelve years again and allow the accident to happen.. that means we stop Hero You from saving your Mum.. and then we go straight back to Odessa, everything will be just like it was. Your Dad'll be there, and all his friends too, even the one you don't like.. but if we don't let the accident happen.. then this is how the world is now. And another thing," Avalon trailed off and stared up to Linda, as if she was about to say something incredibly profound.

"Hmm?" said Linda.

"My thinky bits have gone all hurty."

"Have they?"

"Uhuh.. you ought to have written all that down, 'cause there's no way I'll ever be able to repeat that lot again.."

Linda sighed, and thought for a while about what the right thing to do might be, and couldn't make sense of anything. Instead, she followed her heart and went with what felt right.

"No, I won't change this.. I can't do that. That's my family and they've got everything I've ever wanted in my whole life, so even if I can't be a part of that, at least I know it exists for them.. and this really hurts," she said, holding back the tears and trying to ignore the horrible, tight feeling in her throat.

"I know, Lindy, but it says here you've messed up the Natural Order of things, so maybe other things have changed in the world since you tripped over?"

"Maybe, maybe.. I don't know what's right anymore.. but I'm not changing their world for the one I used to know. You saw what they've got.. and I'd rather have.. rather have nothing than take that away from them," she said, and wiped her hand across her eyes.

"How do I manage it, Avie? I just get worse and worse.. I try to do the right things and just make it all so much worse."

She didn't want to start crying again, but knew she was going to, sooner or later. Avalon hovered close, and picked up the braid. She tied it around her waist.

"Well.. we could all go to our room in Odessa and then to Hesperides and we'll take your Mum's picture, too. You'd still have that, and Kupula would love to see it, I know she would. And Aggybear. She'd even like Sceleste, as well."

Linda absently wound a long piece of grass around her fingers and watched as Sceleste left her lap and tried going for a short walk in the sunshine. She seemed to be moving much better now, and made it all the way to the pond without wobbling. A dozen ducks took noisily to the air as if something had frightened them, and Sceleste began slowly walking back, fascinated for once by everything around her.

"Yeah.. you're right, Avie, I know you are. We'll go back and get This Me's stuff. It's not much, but it's mine," she whispered.

Avalon thought of something else and flicked through the Journal before she could forget what it was. She was almost keeping up with herself, and getting very excited.

"And here's the most important thing," she said, turning to a new page at the back. But she suddenly looked very puzzled, and then cross with herself.

"Oh, there's clever drawings here but they're so liney.. oh my head. I've done too much now, stupid Avalon.. haven't a clue what's going on anymore. Go away, rotten book.. you teasing me 'gain."

The Journal disappeared, and Avalon looked upset. The last drawing had been confusing, but had reminded her of something else that was very important.

"I'm ever so sorry Linda, really sorry.. I knew there was something wrong before we came here and I didn't think of it until it was too late and now everything's a big mess and you're all sad.. and.. and.."

Avalon wiped away a large tear, and sniffed.

"It's alright Avie, it's not your fault.." whispered Linda.

"Yes it is! And you hate me now.."

"No I don't, I couldn't h.."

"You do, you do because I saw your necklace fall on the Mirror Table but I forgot to tell you about it.. and I'm so sorry.."

"My.."

Linda felt around her neck. The gem was gone, and the chain was gone as well. For the first time in as long as she could remember, she wasn't wearing her mother's necklace. One bad thing too many pushed her even closer to falling apart, but seeing Avalon so upset changed her feelings. She leaned forwards and cupped her hands behind her, barely touching her wings.

"Avie, don't be sorry, not even for a minute. There's nothing to be sorry about, is there? Up until today I'd never heard my mum's voice, and I'd never even seen her move. But now I even know what it felt like to be held by her. And I know what perfume she liked as well, and I'm sure she sensed something when she looked at me. It was like she looked right into me, and I just can't tell you how that felt. And it's all because of you, isn't it? I might not have got much now, but you've given me more than I could ever have dreamed of in my whole life.. and I've still got you and Sceleste too.."

Linda wiped away her tears on her sleeve, and choked her last few words, "..and I wish you had some idea how much all of that means, I really do.."

She rested her head against her knees and let the tears flow, and only opened her eyes when she felt Avalon nudging her cheek, nestling up against her. Sceleste poked her way under Linda's arm, and purred warmly. It all made sense, in a way, and a few minutes later Linda was feeling almost ready for the world. But then she realised something awful.

"Well, I've finally, genuinely earned one.." she moaned as a technicolour headline sprang into her mind.

"Lindagate: Doughbrain Schoolgirl Duplicates Self & Rewrites Past 12 Years - God Very Angry."

Linda absently picked a few small grass cuttings out of Sceleste's fur, and Avalon soon joined in and took over. She was much better at it, and a whole lot faster. Sceleste seemed to be enjoying the attention, so Linda left them to it and watched a few children throwing bread out onto the pond. The scared ducks returned very quickly. A few mothers looked on, chatting about whatever mattered to them, completely oblivious to the wonderful, ordinary things they had in their lives - just like the rest of the world's families were, probably. Linda wished that she had a Thinking Level. One of those would be incredibly useful to help sort out all the crazy things that were rushing around in her mind. She sat back against the tree and settled for talking out loud.

"Okay.. okay then, Avie.. I changed the past, and that's really screwed things up for us hasn't it? And I'm the same old Linda that now never was, who doesn't belong anywhere anymore, and I've not got too much money and I need to be heading back to a foreign country where a freaky cult and maybe the Government, the Church, and that weird Death Spirit Ved'ma friend of yours are all after me. How good does it get?"

She felt a laugh coming on, but knew that if she started there would be a very good chance she would never, ever stop. Sceleste seemed to purr in agreement, and nuzzled her head against her again. Avalon looked thoughtful for a moment.

"Yup, but at least you did it for all the right reasons. Kupula will sort out what to do and she's bound to let you stay with us. But you can see why The Stone has to go to Hesperides now, can't you? In a bad Person's hands it could be awful, couldn't it?"

"Oh yeah, and then some," Linda nodded.

Avalon finished Sceleste's beauty treatment and hovered up to her Serious Thinking Level, tapping her chin as if pondering something very important. She flew from side to side, appearing to become increasingly serious. The turn of events had lead her to think of a Very Good Plan which Linda needed to know about.

"Can we get some Haze.. more cream and things for Sceleste and you before we go back? And maybe find the Hazelymits shop first, puhleeeeze?"

Linda managed a safe, normal laugh, which felt so very good. It really was time for some Extra Supplies shopping, and her pockets were soon heavy with an array of essentials and useful things from Johal's. Most things in this New Now hadn't changed, and the packed shelves at Mr Johal's Delicatessen were just as they should be. He even picked out a few cat toys which Sceleste demurely showed no interest in at all, but Linda bought them for her anyway.

A short while later they returned to a quiet and hidden area in the park, well away from everyone. They soon emerged back in the room in Odessa, some time in the afternoon.

Linda sat on the floor preparing an odd sort of lunch for them, with a lot on her mind. For a while she wondered what the Other Linda was doing at that precise moment, and then wondered what her mother might be doing on a summery Tuesday afternoon with the family - and then she had to stop herself wondering and tried to think of anything else instead, and that wasn't easy. She looked over at Sceleste, who was staring up at the door. Her fur bristled as she crawled towards it, and her eyes had narrowed into yellow slits. But then whatever was bothering her suddenly wasn't bothering her anymore, and she came back to Linda. She lay stretched out on the floor with her eyes closed, looking as if she'd just disproved the theory that cats always land on their feet, and let Avalon give her some more serious grooming. She soon returned the favour by planting a paw across Avalon's legs and licking her face and arms.

"Aghh! What's your tongue made of? That's so.. aagh.. stopstop oohLindaaaaAAAGGH!"

"Ahh, she's being nice to you, that's all."

"No she isn't, no she isn.. aaaghh!"

"See? She thinks you look lovely now! Good Sceleste! Try and encourage her, Avie, she's not used to being loved. Or even cared for, come to think of it."

Avalon wriggled free, and hovered over to Linda.

"I want us to go home, ever so now, please," she pined, trying to remove some cat hair from her wings. Her own hair remained a lop-sided spiky mess even after three big shakes.

"Okay, Avie," said Linda, tapping out the remnants of a crisp packet for Sceleste to try, "..let's aim for Hesperides then."

Sceleste stood upright, her head moving in small nervous jerks as her eyes scrutinised every tiny part of the smaller of the two boarded windows. Every muscle in her body seemed tense, and her fur bristled again. She limped quickly over to it, meowing and hissing.

"Sceleste? What's wrong?"

Linda kept low and hurried over to peek through the slats to see if anyone was outside. Maybe there was an old lady across the road, but on the second look she was a middle-aged woman, very tall and elegant, looking straight back up. A lorry rumbled past and she was gone, and Linda dismissed her latest Half-There moment, even though it felt more like a rare Three-Quarters There moment. Sceleste went back to where she'd been lying down. She needed time to sense what was wrong.

Linda sat down by the Stone, and looked at it. It had suddenly taken on a dull grey colour, which formed small bursting clouds of black every few seconds. That was odd, but then again, what wasn't? After all, weird things did weird things, and that Stone was obviously a weird thing. She was far more bothered about how to conjure up Hesperides, which was likely to be difficult. She rested her hand on the Stone and the clouds soon disappeared, leaving it perfectly clear again. Then she nudged its pointed end and watched it spinning around, finding that it would slow down or speed up depending on whether or not she wanted it to do so. Avalon applauded, and tried having a go herself for a while. Nothing happened, so Linda cheated a little for her.

Sceleste sat bolt upright, with her nose as high in the air as she could manage. She sensed the evil spirit had just returned to spy on them, but it had ventured a little too close and revealed itself. It was a dangerous spirit, one that held its secrets well, but it was also desperate and needed to force something to happen. Sceleste's nose traced the air, recognising the scent of malice as the same one that had visited in the early hours of the morning, and again at sunrise. She followed the trail until it became an irrelevance, and she knew that trouble had already been visited upon the room. She opened her eyes to find herself staring at a worn old telephone directory, propped harmlessly against the wall. But she recognised what it was being used for, and knew it had to be destroyed. She lashed her long claws across its cover, and prepared to rip each one diagonally into the next..

"She's jumpy isn't she, Avie? Maybe she wants some more cream?" said Linda, as she crawled over and unknowingly picked up the directory instead of Sceleste. The cat jumped at it as much as her legs would allow, digging her claws through the front cover and ripping a montage image of Odessa's landmarks from one side to the other. Linda screamed.

"No! Bad Sceleste! How could you be so.. so wicked! That's my.."

CHAPTER EIGHTEEN

Fourways

A few minutes earlier.

The woman listened outside the door, her slender black dress pulsing with dark blues and even darker reds wherever the light dared to catch it. She smiled to herself as she heard their return from a place that she didn't care to imagine. She ran a fingernail slowly and gently down the door's rough wooden panels, cast her long black hair around her neck as if it were an elegant wrap, and drifted backwards a little. The loathsome cat had sensed her presence immediately, just as it had done earlier at daybreak. And now, after centuries of seeing her Stone held so tantalisingly close yet rendered beyond her reach by every protection known to the worlds of The Living and The Dead, it was finally free and lay just a few feet away from her. She laughed to herself at how the fates conspired to deal such amusing and unexpected twists in her life.

Mörrah had spent the day contemplating the countless ways to retrieve the Stone from the Gifted One, but had failed to find even one that would allow her to cross the girl's Beast, that wretched Curse Bearer. The hours had slowly gone by, and as her hope was being destroyed by her frustrations, she finally thought of a trap that had made her laugh with its simplicity. Her spell was prepared and discretely laid a matter of seconds before the capable fool-child had chosen to return.

And now she drifted further away from the door until she stood in the empty doorway of a room across the landing, but that still wasn't far enough from the repugnant feline one. Now she had to go, she had to leave the dismal building and settle beyond the Beast's alert senses. She merely had to wait, that was all. A little more patience was required, and that would be so easy. She faded from the hallway and re-appeared in a shaded alley across the road, still listening intently to their ridiculous conversations, waiting for the great moment to arrive.

She had sensed the presence of the Gifted One at the very moment the child called Linda had set foot in her territory of Odessa. At best, the girl's tormented nature could have provided her with enough energy for a few more weeks of living, perhaps even months. At worst, the girl would merely be made to touch a trapped low-faery and take away some of its pathetic Magics. The faery, the vile low-faery.. that a spiritae of such contemptible unworthiness could ever have discovered the Stone's true existence was infuriating, and Mörrah knew it could never be allowed back to its homelands, not with such knowledge. And the girl could easily take care of that. So Mörrah had willingly surrendered the creature to a Gifted One, relieved that it would undoubtedly be condemned to the worst possible life for its kind - one of loneliness.

But now the world was a different place. The Gifted One had not only gained the trust of the faery, but had actually understood its empty-headed prattlings. That achievement alone justified a degree of respect, but the devious thinking required to find the Stone, release it from the Silent Keepers and then to avoid so many Brethren and Government fools.. well, that commanded far more respect. However, the Gifted One had now served her purpose and had become no more than an irritation, a minor obstacle to be dealt with, and one that would be so easy to crush. She had already been tested in the hotel lift and proved herself to be nothing more than a scared and broken creature, almost pitiful, if she was worth pitying..

..and now Mörrah stayed across the road in the shadows of the alleyway, as much a part of them as covered by them, and rubbed her hands with impatience. The time was drawing closer for her to reclaim the Stone, that key to immortality and greatness which had been revealed to her so long ago. The Gifted One would soon give her a greater power than she'd ever craved or dared to dream of. She listened ever-closer to the inane chatter in the room, frustrated as it carried on in ever-widening circles of confusion. But that was fine. Extremely irritating, but fine. If only the idiot child would stray into..

Her patience began slipping, and for the briefest of moments she left the alley and entered the room, drifting in a little through the boarded window, invisible to all but the wretched cat. And then she returned, back to the secrecy and the safety of the shadows. The child had peered through the boards and had briefly seen her, but that didn't matter. The girl had no reason to be suspicious, for she had no idea of what deceit lay ahead of her. The child would be hers, and this time she would be sure not to lose the Stone again. But the Beast, the foul Beast, had sensed her trap and almost ruined it..

..and then the Gifted One screamed, and Mörrah's eyes flashed up to the boarded window. She stared into the room and laughed more than she had managed through all her centuries. She gladly succumbed to the wildest hysterics that had ever taken control of her, and relished every glorious moment.

"No! Bad Sceleste! How could you be so.. so wicked! That's my family!" screamed Linda, and held the Beaufort Family Album protectively in her arms, shocked beyond words that Sceleste could be so vicious and cruel. The thick volume was filled with every picture she could ever need to see, and she had to take it away somewhere safe. She clambered onto the rickety pile of drawers, ready to kick for all she was worth if the cat came near her again. She cried with relief to see that the cover wasn't really harmed at all, and ran her fingers across the smooth front photograph which showed her mother being hugged by her father while they both hugged her. And there were sisters, brothers, and so many grandparents, and then all the aunts and uncles, and even more friends. It was the best picture in the entire world, which is why it was on the front. This album was so special. It didn't just hold images, it carried feelings and it carried memories, and it made sense of everything. Linda shielded it with her arms and her hair as much as she could.

Avalon flew near to see what was so wrong, but backed away as Linda swung her hand out at her.

"Lindy? What's the matter?"

Linda stared up at her, wild-eyed and full of aggression.

"You're not taking it! Beast tried to spoil it and I hate her! Don't you try too! You'll be sorry!" she shouted.

Avalon flew to the window, and heard the faint laughter coming from somewhere very close. Sceleste paced the floor beside the drawers not sure what to do anymore, while Avalon flew to Linda again, who was smiling widely and had started to turn the pages.

"Listen to me, Lindy - that's not whatever you think it is! It's been spelled or jinxed or something by Mörrah! She's playing with your mind like she did with me!"

Linda didn't hear anything. She was in a world of her own, a happy place full of stability and security, where everyone loved her - and she had the pictures to prove it.

"Look Avalon! This is me and mum in those gardens we went to and had such a good time.. and this one! My big sister took this.."

"It's not real! She's tricking you! Look at me now, take your eyes off it and look at me!" screamed Avalon as Linda turned to another ripped and faded page.

"Oh wow! Mum wrote down what we all did! Listen to this, it's so funny. This is what happened when we went to Shevchenko Park last year! Now there's me and all my friends when.. ah, listen to this!"

"Don't read anything out! It's not memories it's incantations! You're not saying what you think you're saying!"

Linda began speaking words which sent a chill through Sceleste. She knew those lines from a thousand grievous ceremonies, and desperately tried to climb the drawers and do anything to stop her Gifted One reciting them all. The Incantation Of Zalozhnye was a vile sacrificial procedure which left the body useless but unharmed, but took the chanter's soul to another place, at the mercy of the one who cast the spell. But Sceleste was too weak to reach her so she settled down beside the Stone, curling her tail around it. She knew of a different approach, and needed to prepare herself for what lay ahead. It would work, but only if the girl was very, very Special.

Avalon was becoming frantic as Linda started the next series of verses, and took a huge risk. She slid onto the pages of telephone numbers and began tearing them in front of Linda's face, wildly ripping them to shreds until nothing but a blanket of scattered pieces remained. But it made no difference. Linda was still turning the pages of a book that only she could see. The Ved'ma had her, but Avalon knew that as long as she hadn't finished the verses, there was still a chance. She wasn't going to let Mörrah keep her.

She held Linda's braid, and closed her eyes to try and see what Linda could see, to be going with her wherever her soul was going. Her voice had fallen to a whisper, but that was nothing to worry about, as Avalon was already aware of a sunny day full of people who had never existed. She could see Linda running around from one person to the next, being told everything she could possibly want to hear, crying with happiness at how wonderful her life had become. Avalon stayed back amongst the high branches of the trees and waited for the inevitable change to happen.

The sky clouded over as the Linda back in their room in Odessa uttered the final line of the incantation. The heavy clouds became darker and lower, and Linda stopped running around as she started to notice that the people were laughing at her instead of welcoming her. And then they all began fading, leaving her alone and bewildered, staring helplessly as the bright colours drained away. Greyness swamped everything, and the heavy stench of decay filled the air. Avalon shivered in the sudden coldness, and flew to her.

"Avie! Wh.. what's happened? They were all.. where's everyone gone? Where are we?"

Avalon hugged Linda's cheek.

"It's Mörrah. She must have hexed that big old book with something clever while we were gone. She's horrid, isn't she?"

They both jumped as a magpie seemed to mock them before taking flight from a wizened tree, which stood apart from all the rest.

"A book?" she said, completely bemused.

"Uhuh. You thought you were looking at the best picture-book ever, and you started to read out words you thought your Mum had written about the pictures, but it wasn't a good thing at all. It was a way to a bad place, right here. I've heard about these kind of things."

Linda coughed in the foul air.

"I'm so sorry, Avie.. it was all so real, it was like being carried along on a rollercoaster ride, and I couldn't stop. And I dragged you in? I am so.."

Avalon shook her head, closely followed by the rest of her body.

"Nope. I came with you so you wouldn't be alone. Like when we read the Dalovich book together, under the Library - remember?"

Linda couldn't think of what to say, so she gently placed her hand around Avalon and held her softly against her face. Hugging a faery wasn't easy. Avalon sneezed twice.

"Bless you, twice. I don't see what good all this can do Mörrha?"

"She wants The Stone, doesn't she? Well, the Real Us are back where you read the Incantation, in a kind of sleep which has a special name. And Sceleste's back there and so's The Stone. And Sceleste. And us. And The Stone is as well. You know, this is a bit like how Mörrah trapped me, only loads worse. Really loads worse. Loads and loads and loads and.."

"Ouch. So we're in a dream?"

"No.. yes.. yesno. It's like a real kind of dream that's happening in the bad Spirit World. Our Souls are here, where Mörrah's kind keep Souls that they've won, but she hasn't won ours yet."

"Hasn't she?"

"Nuhuh. It's all just a game for a Ved'ma. They play games all the time. If we lose, then we're stuck here and we won't ever be going back to Real Us unless she says so, which I really don't think she ever would do.."

"..and she'll have the Stone?"

"Yup. She'll wait for Sceleste to get weaker and then just take it, and all your abilities will be here with her. But if we get out of here then maybe we just wake up back in the room - and she gets even more annoyed?"

"Charming. I wonder how we lose?"

They both flinched as thunder rolled across the entire sky, shaking the ground as it went.

"Don't know. Maybe we wander until we can't go on anymore - wouldn't that be the worst thing ever? She'll get stronger as we get weaker, and then we're trapped here until she finally dies.. and then our Souls die too."

"Oh great.."

"Yup. But if she gets The Stone and all your ability to use it, she could go on a long time, couldn't she?"

Linda looked around, hoping for either a flash of inspiration or a large door marked 'Exit'. All she could see was a puddle-strewn grey pathway, leading far away.

"So what do we do to get out of here?"

"Don't know that either. I've never been in one of these before. Heard about them, but that's all. And look.." she said, and turned around once and then once again, but more slowly. Her Journal didn't appear either time.

"But at least I can still fly!" she said, and spun around a few more times to give a better demonstration.

"Well, that's something. Which way do you reckon then - left or right?" Linda said, trying to sound optimistic. Avalon looked around as the trees began gradually disappearing under a rolling mist.

"I think there's a something up there.." she said, pointing away to the right, where the path ran along an incline. There was little to see within the patches of mist except for the dark blur Avalon had pointed at. That was better than nothing, so they began nervously making their way through the greyness of the park. The gravel scrunched and grated with every step, and the gaps in the pathway soon grew larger and broader until it was little more than a series of odd shapes in the dark grass. But then Linda felt as if her teeth could curl as the brittle blades scraped and cracked under her feet.

The signpost stood where four wide paths met, a little off centre. It was tall and battered, with four crooked panels pointing out at the top which Avalon flew around.

"Four ways!" she announced.

"Fourways? Is that what this place is called?"

"Huh? There's four ways here.. Doom.. Disease.. Death.. and.. this one hasn't got anything on it. Maybe it's Threeways?" she said, carefully trying to avoid the last panel's long splinters.

"I say we go for Death."

"Death?" she called down, tapping at the rotten wood of the blank one. It wobbled and then fell onto the ground without making a sound. Avalon quickly flew closer to Linda and hovered closely in front of her eyes, hoping that she was joking.

"The Death one? But that one there doesn't say anything bad at all, doesn't it?" she said, pointing down to the panel.

"And that's why we don't follow it, 'cause I think it's too obvious. It could lead anywhere, and's probably the worst of the lot. Besides, I feel safer with all the 'D' words," she said, and pointed to the fragments on the ground, "That one down there breaks the continuity."

"Unless Mörrah knows you'd think that? So that would really make it the best of the lot, unless she knew that you'd know.. that.. thuh.. knew.. me.." Avalon bit her lip and pointed at Linda, "..one eye is blue and neither's that one," and then went completely blank. She scratched her head and made her way onto Linda's shoulder.

"You could always roll for it?" she whispered, a headshake or two later. Linda crouched down and nervously rolled her dice against the post, and it danced a strange route until coming to rest on the empty sign. The white dots stared up at her.

"Six! Okay then here goes, nearest first.. One's Despair, Two's Death, Three's Disease, Four's the Missing Bit, Five's Despair, and.. hello again, Death. So it's Death."

Avalon groaned, and wrapped Linda's braid of hair around her waist. The path lead in a broad curve through the mist, which lifted a little after a few more minutes of anxious, loud walking. Something caught Linda's eye for the tiniest of moments, but it was too quick for her to recognise what it might be. She looked around, but let it go as they passed through the branches of a long line of willows.

"Look!" breathed Avalon, not wanting to break the silence. She pointed to a small village made up of shacks, all in varying shades of grey and all merging into a dark haze. Linda stood perfectly still, not daring to go any further.

"Oh no.. I saw one just like this in a film once. It was ages ago, and so scary! One of my dad's friends thought it'd be really funny for me to see an 18 movie - he's the Minister for Education now. Well, he was before we changed things. Maybe he still is?"

"Still's what?" asked Avalon, but Linda let it pass.

The shacks began creaking as if they could collapse at any second, sending a chill through Linda. There certainly wasn't any creaking in the film, because the creatures that dwelled inside were..

"Maybe everything'll go away if I stop thinking about this?" she said, surprising herself with the strength of her voice. She tried clearing her mind, but nothing happened. If anything, the village had gained even more lean-to wrecks.

"I don't think it's that easy.. let's just try not to think of scary stuff, and maybe nothing else will appear?"

The mist thinned enough to reveal a huge skull forming in the clouds across a third of the sky. Flashes of lightning spread out from the dark eyes, illuminating its face.

"That's Baba Yaga's Fire Bringer! He razes everything, even in Hesperides! We're all afraid of that because he's so hard to stop! Baba Yaga sends it to.."

"Avie! Thinking about scary things is what brings them in here, so.."

Linda trailed off. She vaguely noticed an old man in the middle of a nearby field, partially covered in a low band of creeping fog. Something in her mind pushed her to go towards him. She didn't like the feeling, but couldn't think of anything else to do instead, so she left the path and immediately felt her feet sink a little into the damp earth. As she drew nearer, she could see that he was chipping and carving into a long horizontal slab of stone, which was raised slightly on a platform. She stopped a few feet away.

"Hello?" she said, nervously, "Are you here to help us? We're really lost and need someone to.. umm.. be on our side?"

The old man ignored her, and ran his hands along the smooth top of the block of stone, admiring his craftsmanship. Linda took another step and tried again, intending to sound friendly but her voice came out even weaker and higher.

"W..wuh.. we're lost here," she stammered.

He turned just enough to look at her.

"Lost?" he smirked, and went back to his carving.

Linda was close enough to see that he had been chiselling letters into a lid which was partially covering a long, dark stone box. He blew a cloud of dust from the lid's surface, revealing a name which was just at the wrong angle for her to read.

"Are you real?" called Avalon, and immediately buried herself under Linda's hair. He glanced at her, and then to Linda.

"Touch the stone," he said, slowly.

Linda touched the top of the stonework, and shivered at its icy coldness. She drew her hand back as she realised he was finishing a coffin.

"Does it feel real to you?" he said, pausing above the final letter.

"Yes.." she gasped, and stepped backwards.

"You're not lost," he whispered, "you've arrived," he said, looking at her with dead eyes and nodding as if agreeing with himself. Suddenly a shower of soil landed over Linda's shoulders and caught in her hair. Avalon squealed, and brushed and kicked it all off her as quickly as she could.

"It's earth from a grave! Don't get three casts on you!"

Linda turned around and saw that the mist had lifted enough to reveal hundreds of gravestones running in long and perfectly straight lines. A man in white robes stood next to a solitary open grave, and threw more of its earth over her. He struck the ground on each of side of the rectangular hole with a tall serpent-like staff, and turned to face her, revealing vicious scars where his eyes once were. He pointed towards her, and Linda felt the staff reaching far across the graves and pressing against her heart.

"Commit this Sacrifice to the Heart of the Blessed Servant Mörrha, bring the Gifted Soul unto those who wander in Her legion, to offer the burial and rebirth, forever to honour and revere the name of Mörrah, she who.."

"It's Vilevsk The Seer! Run run RUN!" screamed Avalon, pulling her braid.

Linda turned and ran, and the third handful of earth missed her by inches. The old man made a half-hearted attempt to grab at her, and laughed as she ran just beyond his tired hands. He had seen so many before her do the same.

"She turns to run, she turns to run, I curse the hope of a foolish one.." he murmured to himself, and began chipping her After Name into the coffin lid, the one by which she would be known in Mörrah's lands. The blind man raised his staff once more, and the spirits of those who had fallen prey to Mörrah began forming in the mist.

She followed her footprints back across the field, trying not to wonder why some were missing, hoping to reach the path again. But instead she arrived amongst the shacks, at one which stood out from all the others. It was dirtier, a little larger, and much, much darker. The nailed door and each boarded window seemed to be holding all of her own fears inside, straining and waiting to free them from her and unleash them upon the whole world. And she had to go to it, to open the door and embrace that side of herself which needed to seek revenge on everyone who had the good things in life that had always been denied to her.. and she knew they deserved it, everyone deserved it, and all she had to do was stand at the door a little longer and command it to open, and..

..Avalon pulled her braid as hard as she could, again and again until Linda stumbled sideways. She fell to the ground, numb with fear at what she had just been feeling, and started stumbling and running away from the evil place, and onwards through the labyrinth of muddy passageways.

Gifts for the dead lay scattered outside every door, each looking like the ones Mörrah had been trying to pass on to unwary victims back in Odessa. A small girl stood outside the entrance to one creaking and swaying hut, and cried out as Linda ran closer.

"You took my flowers! You took them from me! You took.."

Linda froze and stared at the emaciated girl. Her rags hung loosely from her small, thin arms as she pointed an accusing finger, screaming the same lines at Linda over and over. The girl's voice grew louder with anger and pain, forcing Linda to remember the flowers that she'd taken from Mörrah, and left in the churchyard. She felt sick with grief, and rooted to the spot with her guilt. The girl stepped further forwards, and screamed at Linda. Avalon flew in front of Linda, to do anything to break the hold the girl had over her.

"Linda! We have to go!" Avalon wailed, and pulled again at the braid, "Look at me! Look behind us! Look anywhere! Me me me me memeMEEE!"

Avalon grabbed at handfuls of hair until she finally blinked, and the girl drifted silently back into the shadows of the hut. Linda slowly looked over to where Avalon was staring, and whimpered when she saw countless short trails of fire snaking along the ground, emerging and disappearing back into the earth. Crowds of shadowed figures stood partially lost in the depths of the mist, and dozens more began appearing between the shacks. They didn't move, they all stood and looked at her. Linda closed her eyes until she was barely squinting, turned away and ran for all she was worth.

The girl and the shack reappeared every few seconds before finally fading into the gloom with the rest of the village. Avalon looked back to convince herself that they had all gone, and stared up at the skull in the sky. The Fire Bringer had become clearer and more threatening, now as much a part of the clouds as it was a part of the mist. It was a little smaller, but felt so much closer and intense than before. She buried herself under Linda's hair.

Vilevsk The Seer stood in front of the village, ignoring the lost spirits behind him. He struck the wet ground with the staff, sending straight lines of fire racing out in all directions, and waited for each trail to die away before slowly walking after Linda. The massed Legion followed.

Linda ran along the path, shielded by the tall hedgerows on either side, until she had to stop and try to catch her breath. She leaned against a decrepit wooden fence and looked out at a pure white horse in the field beyond. It was a beautiful sight, like an oasis in the most hostile and barren desert. A single beam of sunlight fell onto its back, spreading into a circle on the ground around it, bringing a powerful wash of colours into the drabness.

"Look Lindy! That has to be good, doesn't it?" exclaimed Avalon.

"Yeah.. uhuh.." Linda panted, "..it's not got any graves or coffins near.. an' that's a big improvement."

The horse lazily swished its tail, leaving a blurred trail of white for a few seconds. And then the sun grew a little stronger, casting a path of colour through the grass to the fence. That looked good to Linda, and she began trying to climb over its slats, struggling to keep her footing on the damp wood. She tried to ignore her aching legs, but didn't have the strength to stop her trainers slipping at the top. Her bruised knee gave way and she felt herself falling backwards..

..but time seemed to stand still, and in that small moment she looked through all the mist and sensed something that changed everything. She hit the ground with a harsh thud, and lay motionless on the gravel trying to make sense of what she had just experienced. The horse turned its head upwards and glared straight over to her, showing its jet-black eyes.

"Lindy? Please be okay please please please.." begged Avalon as she brushed Linda's hair from her face, too scared to remember any

Healing Songs.

"I'm fine, Avie, and I think we both are, now. It was Sceleste, I'm sure she was.."

"Really? Are you sure it wasn't Mörrah teasing us again, to take us away from the sunshine?"

"No.. no.. it wasn't Mörrah, it was Sceleste. I didn't see her.. but I felt her. She was a long way over there.."

Linda pointed further along the path, and into the murky depths. She looked back at the horse. Suddenly the field didn't look quite right, and the horse seemed eerily unnatural, as if it was too perfect on the outside, but far from that on the inside.

"Perfectly imperfect.. perfectly imperf.." Linda breathed. The horse shook its head wildly, then turned away from them and bolted into the distance. Linda watched the colours fading away behind it. She was getting close to sensing something important about the entire world around her, as if the spell was about to be shattered and the nightmare around her would fall apart. For a moment she felt a surge of confidence, as if she was throwing off all the fear and confusion.. but then someone called her name. It was a taunting voice, as much a feeling as a sound, and so much like her mother's - but with a frightening and chilling edge, and it distracted her for just long enough to take her away from the answers. The voice laughed, carried away by footsteps that crunched loudly through the gravel.

The thunderstorm rumbled in the distance, relentlessly coming closer and carrying the Fire Bringer nearer. Linda looked over to the hill where she knew Sceleste had been, and pushed her way through a weak part of the hedge and hurried into the knee-high grass of a huge field.

"Why aren't we on the path?" asked Avalon, shuddering against Linda's ear as a barrage of small biting noises chattered through the grass, and more thunder rolled across the sky.

"I saw Sceleste through here.. wherever the clear side of that hill is. On its east side, maybe, maybe east feels right.. and she knows the way out, I'm sure she does."

Linda closed her eyes and imagined holding her, and tried to feel where she had gone to, but absolutely nothing came into her mind. A sick feeling started in her stomach as she realised that she couldn't keep her mind on anything at all, as if her one chance to see this world for what it really was had come and gone.

She bit her lip and hurried defiantly across the field, and began the steady journey up the heavily wooded hillside. It seemed to rise higher and higher, reaching up through the mist. She stopped midway up at one of its jagged outcrops, and almost collapsed against a group of large rocks. Her legs had brought her entire body out on strike.

Avalon flew as high as she dared in order to have a good look at where they were, but didn't get beyond the braid before deciding to quickly come back. Linda peered over the rocks and saw the mist rolling away, back to the horizon like a huge wave retreating from the shore, and they both looked a long way down the southern side of the hill to a procession of hundreds of people, all clad in black. They stepped slowly in time to a monotonous, rhythmic clanging sound, walking a route marked by burning torches. Linda's heart jumped as she recognised the small figure leading them on their way, tapping the ground in front of himself as he went. Vilevsk raised the serpent-headed staff in Linda's direction, and struck the ground loudly. The babble and moaning suddenly stopped, and every head turned to look up towards her. She faintly heard him shouting back to them, and a black banner rose in the centre of the throng. The people separated either side of it, revealing the stone coffin on the back of a cart. Two followers climbed up and removed its lid, laying it at the side.

"Who are they?" whispered Linda. Avalon tried to stop shaking, but couldn't.

"Muh.. Muh.. Mourners. Spirits that she's won. They're doing what we'll be doing. They don't know where to go, so they just keep walking the path The Seer allows them to walk."

"So.. if they get to us.. that's how we lose?"

"Uhuh, and if we don't get.."

Linda missed whatever Avalon was saying. Sceleste had been with her again, so close and strong for barely a fraction of a second, but enough for Linda to know beyond any doubt that she had gone from the clear side of the hill and all the way across to the dark woods beyond. The clanging and chanting began again, and Linda made herself move. She passed down the east side, staggering and running from one thicket to another before arriving breathless at the start of a mile or more of muddy wasteland that bordered the woods. The blackened, skeletal trees were as free of mist as they were of colours, and held the most unnatural darkness Linda had ever seen or felt.

"She was in there.. somewhere.." Linda wavered.

"The.. the .. those woods? But look at them!"

Avalon had a good point, and Linda hesitated, trying to tell herself to trust in her heart that she was right and that Sceleste had really been there. Or was she there? Avalon sensed that she was scared, and hovered in front of her, tugging the braid.

"I.. I believe you if you say so.. that's good enough for me, really it isn't. Is. And the Mourners are getting nearer.."

Linda realised how much louder the clanging and low chanting was becoming, and pulled her feet up out of the mud with nauseating squelches. More footsteps ran past, pounding over matted layers of dead vegetation, again with no-one in sight. Teasing voices carried in the air beckoning her on towards the woods, and she paused for a moment, bewildered by them.

"Ignore them Lindy - listen to me, no, listen to YOU!" said Avalon, waving her arms and pointing over to the woods, which were still at least half a mile away. Burning torches suddenly appeared either side of them as they made their way along, dotting and marking the route behind. No matter how much Linda wandered to the left or over to the right, she was always perfectly in the middle of the next two. Avalon ran a hand across the rusted emblems on the front of one, and flew straight back to the safety of Linda's hair.

"Do you know what the symbols mean, Avie? And if it's bad, you don't have to.. y'know, tell me, if you don't want."

"Umm.. nothing to worry about.. nothing at all.. nothing no. Can we go now? Lots quicker than before?"

"Maybe they're not real.." wondered Linda aloud, hoping to calm Avalon down a little. She pushed one over to prove the point, easily toppling the wooden stake, and watched its flame die out in the mud. A wild scream tore through the air, and in the time it took for Linda to spin around and see where it came from, the torch had righted itself and was burning strongly again, as if nothing had happened. Linda's heart was in her mouth for a few seconds, until she realised the sound of the Mourners had drawn even closer - and then she ran.

A few minutes later she stood at the peak of a vast, sodden bank which seemed to be made up entirely of dead foliage, and looked out at the masses of blackened trees immediately ahead. They seemed to merge together, forming an impenetrable darkness and shrouding themselves in constant night.

Linda stumbled down to the woods' edge, staring into black

nothingness and begging in her heart for a sight of Sceleste, not only to see where to go, but also for reassurance that this was definitely the right place. She stared and stared, but there was no glimpse, no feeling, and absolutely no guidance for her. She moved some more hair over to Avalon, and took a moment for some deep breaths to try and make herself think clearly.

She had to be strong. She had to trust herself more than she'd ever done before, she had to trust her own judgement, and above all, she had to trust completely in Sceleste. She closed her eyes, desperately trying to concentrate, and began counting to ten in her mind. She only made it to seven, but that was good enough. She imagined being surrounded by seven huge protective pillars, and tried reaching far out from in between them, searching for Sceleste, silently calling for her in the darkness, knowing that she would be there.. somewhere.. anywhere. And then it happened.

She sensed her, leaping left and right with small effortless bounds, past the countless hidden razor-sharp thorns, over the twisting roots and vines, past the ruts and ditches, and far beyond the clutches of Dark Ones. Linda kept her eyes closed and followed the pattern, stumbling from one point to the next, and ignoring whatever writhed beneath her feet and against her legs. Voices shrieked around her and icy winds blew harsh against her skin, but she stayed focussed on Sceleste and kept walking to her, not caring if the branches which dug into her arms and legs really were branches or were perhaps something far worse. All that mattered was that each one was another left behind, another that wouldn't stop her. She kept a hand protectively over Avalon, covering her safely against her neck, ensuring a thick layer of hair covered her. Soon the voices stopped being meaningless sounds, and became like Brother Dalovich's words - the language may have meant nothing, but the feelings behind the words meant everything. She closed her mind as tightly as her eyes, and blocked out their loathing, abuse and bitterness, and.. and.. and then Sceleste was gone.

"Sceleste?" whispered Linda into the darkness. A chorus of wild, baying laughter taunted her from everywhere, each one urging her to follow. She summoned all her courage to choose the next step, and strode forwards.. and felt herself falling, rolling down into darkness, on and on..

Linda lay against the hard stones of a pathway and opened her eyes. Her head was still spinning, but she felt pleased to be able to see again, even if there was only large gravel and strangely warm mist to see around her.

"Avie? Speak to me Avie, are you okay? Where are you?"

Avalon wriggled out from underneath Linda's head, and flew in a dizzy figure of eight barely an inch or two above the ground.

"Ugh.. I wasn't expecting that, but I'm glad you did it. What did you do?"

"I don't know.. I fell over or something.."

The skull glared down at them, now just a few hundred feet above the ground. Its cloudiness was giving way to areas that started to look like great plains of charred bone, and the temperature of the wind had begun to rise. Avalon dived back under a mass of hair, while Linda struggled to her feet and winced from the pain in her right foot. It felt as if it had been twisted around at least twice, and had triggered her right knee to join in from earlier, as if the two were conspiring to slow her down as much as possible. The monotonous clanging and chanting drew even nearer, far less than a hundred yards away, and seemed to be closing in from every direction.

"Where to, wheyuh toooo?" squealed Avalon, muffled by hair.

Linda saw the weirdest, blurred flicker of a Half-There and started to run along the path towards it, hoping and trusting that it had been Sceleste. The path rapidly broadened until the sides were too far apart to be seen, and she stumbled to a halt.

"Why have we stopped, Linda? Why-would-we-stop-nowww?" Avalon wailed, deciding not to tell her how close the Mourners were. Linda was stunned and confused, and was staring ahead to where she had just seen Sceleste - but four of her, each as clear as if they had actually been there.

"There were four Scelestes and a huge gap between all of them.. but they all felt the same.. which one should I follow?"

"Try doing the rolling-thing again, but ooh really quick!"

Linda threw the dice high in the air, giving it an extra spin.

"Two!" she announced, before it had even hit the ground. It bounced for what felt like an eternity before two white dots duly stared upwards

"Yes, but which way? Two from the left or the right?" asked Avalon, retrieving it slowly in the dry heat. Linda hadn't thought of that, and rolled again.

"Uhh.. Odd's from the left, right's Even.."

She didn't even look at the result or care where the dice had gone. Her mind had cleared enough since her fall to know which one felt like Sceleste and she hurried as much as her foot would allow through the thinning mist and onto the small brow of the hill. The pathway emerged from the roughened ground, and lead them downwards. Avalon felt something frightening pull her attention, and she looked behind Linda to see three black cats appear and merge together in a single bound. She turned away and buried her face in Linda's hair, trying not to look at Mörrah glaring back at her, who stood where the cats had joined.

Mörrah waited less than a minute for her Mourners to arrive. The game would soon be over, and she allowed herself to laugh. She summoned the Fire Bringer lower, and the skull hovered like a dense cloud of hatred above the legion of her dead. Her laughter became a scream as the procession of damned souls trudged before her, and she faded away, ready for the Gifted One's final trap.

Linda ran for all she was worth, slipping and stumbling as the path turned to rubble and then into steep banks of broken stones. She reached the edge of the final bank and tried to look for Sceleste, but the ground shook with a thunderous roar and her legs buckled beneath her. The stones gave way and she fell, rolling and sliding to the end of the long slope where she lay in a dazed and bruised mess, her head spinning and spinning until Avalon tugged at her braid.

"How much did that hurt? It wasn't much was it? Say it wasn't.." she squealed, struggling to fly in the heat.

"Ugh, you couldn't imagine.."

"You have to get up, pleeease ever so - they're catching up and we have to keep going away!" she cried, waving her arms further down the path.

The procession clapped in time with their own steps and couldn't have been more than fifty yards away, just beyond the top of the shingle banks. Linda kneeled up and looked around. The slope narrowed a few yards further on, forming a path which curved between two steep, sandy inclines. A woman lay sprawled against one of the embankments, and Linda's heart almost turned to ice. Facing the Mourners would be nothing compared to facing her. Avalon pulled the braid as hard as she could, but there was no force on earth that could make Linda walk past her mother.

"Linda?" moaned the woman, "You've come to me.. to help me, I need you to help.. I've waited so long for you.. I knew you'd come.."

Linda stared at her. She wore the clothes she had worn on that dreadful day all those years ago. Her legs were mangled, her hair was dark and matted in places, and her coat was torn and bloodied. She kept her face turned away.

"Oh Linda, you do love me, after all.. please don't look at me.. don't see my disfigurement.. I beg you not to remember me like this! Oh the pain you caused me, all because of your selfish crying.. your endless crying.. you made me hurry, I left the shop early because of you and your wretched impatience.. you caused this to happen to me.. but now you can help.."

Avalon screamed at Linda.

"It's not her, it's not her! You stopped this, we stopped it! It's a trick, it's a.."

The chanting grew closer. Avalon tugged Linda's braid with all her strength, which made no difference. She let go of it and looked back in horror up the slope. Vilevsk stood at the top and raised his hand, bringing an end to the dirge.

"She is here!" he exclaimed, "Our Legion grows with new Spirit!"

The skull sank through the crowd and into the ground, sending flames high into the air. Avalon began to feel the heat rising even higher, but Linda felt nothing. The woman before her was so real that she couldn't take her eyes away from her pitiful wrecked body. She took a step forwards. The woman turned towards her a little more, and began to speak, but was interrupted by Avalon.

"Linda puhleeeaze listen! It's a trick again! We changed it! Your Mum's safe back at her home with her family! A big family! And a dog too and babies.. everywhere!"

The woman glared up at the foul creature, spitting at her. She screamed at Linda with a ferocity that made her shudder.

"You changed nothing! Don't you understand? The Stone deceived you! You destroyed my life, but you can change it now! Come to me, you must come to your mother, I still love you despite what you did!"

Avalon held Linda's ear, and shouted for all she was worth.

"Your Mother wouldn't know about The Stone! She wouldn't know.. Linda puhleeaze listen!"

Somewhere very deep inside Linda's mind, she heard Avalon and knew she was right. She didn't know why she was right, but she trusted her and accepted the fact, and took a step backwards, feeling close to understanding where she was again. She looked from her mother to the approaching crowd. None of this made any sense at all, and that meant everything was wrong - which meant that the woman might not be her mother, perhaps? Avalon saw Linda coming out of Mörrah's hypnotic grip and tried to say more to her, but by now she was too scared and her voice had deserted her in the searing heat. Linda jumped as if she had been electrocuted.

"Sceleste?" she shouted, jolting herself around from the Mourners, and looking down the path. That was where she had to go, because.. because.. she knew her cat would be there. This was right, and was the only thing in her entire world that was right. Sceleste would be there, Avalon would be safe, and that was all that mattered. She didn't need to understand why. She ran along the curve of the pathway, past the steep embankments and onto the viciously jagged stones and burning rocks of the beach. Her trainers were quickly torn apart, leaving her to run barefoot across the last agonising mounds.

Sceleste sat at the water's edge. The small black waves lapped silently against the shore, forming a semi-circle around her as if they daren't touch such a creature. She was staring a few feet above herself, out to an indistinct point over the water, impassive and unmoved by Linda screaming her name. Avalon trembled and cried, covering her eyes and trying to keep hold of Linda's braid. She recognised this place from countless tales. The sea stretched out like an endless black sheet, rising and falling as if it was breathing, while a long and empty boat drifted silently towards them, dragging a wall of darkness behind it.

The Mourners broke their ranks, and their pounding footsteps and shouts grew louder as they clambered over each other to get onto the beach. Avalon couldn't fly for shaking. She held onto Linda's neck, wrapped tighter than ever in her hair.

"Look where Sceleste's lead us! It's the Sea of Lost Spirits.. there's nowhere left to go.. we're trapped!" she cried.

"She won't.. won't have let us down.. I trust her.." Linda gasped in painful short breaths, staggering the last few yards to Sceleste.

"But.. but look at all.." Avalon cried, pointing wildly around at Vilevsk, the Mourners, the Sea, and finally to the woman gliding effortlessly through it all, Mörrah.

"Do you see, Lindy? We're trapped.. all four ways are.."

Linda fell to her knees and threw her arms around Sceleste, who continued to stare upwards, while Linda strained her parched eyes to see what held her so spellbound. A bright star appeared in the sky, lengthening like a rip of light through the darkness, allowing powerfully intense rainbows of colour and brightness onto the misery of the beach. It defied perspective, reaching down past the horizon, through the shore, and stopping just above Sceleste.

"Jump through! Tha.. mus'be th'way out of here!" screamed Avalon, hoarse and struggling to breathe. She tied the narrow braid of hair around herself and prepared to fly harder than she'd ever done, before the heat could take her wings.

"Lhinnda, pleee.." she begged, weakly tugging at the braid as her wings became useless.

Linda bent down to pick up Sceleste, but she was suddenly so heavy, so completely immovable. She tried again and again, feeling the pounding vibrations shaking through the scorching rocks beneath her, and saw the hundreds of Mourners forming like a wall of misery and hate around her. She clutched Sceleste tightly, and cried helplessly. Avalon tugged the braid as much as she could, and Linda stared up at the now-gaping bright rip. Her frantic mother crawled close to her, shouting and screaming at her to jump into the light. Linda wanted to, she wanted to jump more than anything in the world, but not without Sceleste. She couldn't abandon her in a place like this, and she screamed through her pain at the woman.

"N-no I.. I'm not leaving S'leste.. I'm not leaving her.. and you won't hurt Avalon.. I won't.. I won't let you.." she sobbed over and over, oblivious to the shouting, the stamping and the fires all around her. She held Sceleste closer than ever, and covered Avalon with her hair, unaware of the chaos drifting away.

Sceleste purred softly and calmly, and the hard stones faded into the hard floorboards of the room in Odessa. The stench of decay had gone, and the aged aroma of wood and long-departed smokers took over. The rip of light turned to a faint darkness, and stayed in the room like a shadow floating in midair. For a moment it formed into a human shape, as if it was a shadow cast by a tall and elegant woman, and then disappeared immediately. But Linda saw it before it had gone, and so did Sceleste. They both knew who it was.

A few moments later, Avalon hopped down onto Sceleste's head to anxiously check her wings a dozen times before remembering that her body hadn't actually been anywhere. She flew around the room twice just to make absolutely sure they still worked, and finished with a cried Welcome Song.

Linda wiped her eyes and eventually felt able to let go of Sceleste. She gave her an extra-special hug, and watched her wander over to the bed where she settled down as if nothing much had happened. Avalon flew down to the floor just in front of Linda and sat on top of the Stone, still shaking. Linda lay down so that her head was at Avalon's level and hummed a few bars of an Abba chorus to her, until she seemed better.

"You were so good, Avie, you really were. I'd have been lost there forever without you.. wherever that was.."

Avalon fluttered nearer for a long hug, before drifting next to where Linda had grouped a small pile of hazelnuts for her. She arranged them into a single column, slightly shorter than herself.

"There were four ways to get trapped, weren't there?" she said, picking one from near the base.

"Maybe a fifth if you count that weird light-thing," said Linda, "..or maybe Vilevsk counts as part of the Mourners, so that's really just one way not two, and that means there was only.."

Avalon interrupted in her own way by hugging Linda's face again.

"Stop thinking so much," she said with a sniff, "Maybe there were millions of ways to be trapped, but there was only one way out and you made that."

"I did?"

"Uhuh. At the most horrible time you wouldn't leave Sceleste or me, which is selfless and Ved'mas can't deal with that. That would have hurt her so badly. It'd be like you getting hit by a huge building, then another one, and another. Only worse. Much worse!" she added, nodding to herself.

A few minutes later Avalon let go of her and devoured some of the hazelnuts, saving the the very middle bits for Linda. Apparently, they were the nicest part. Sceleste lapped at an over-filled saucer, Avalon found out how to make a cd play softly to the room without the headphones, and normality had returned - or as near as Linda was likely to get to normality, anyway.

She lay on the bed and watched Sceleste finishing off the cream, jumping when her cat suddenly stopped to glare over at one of the windows, baring her teeth and giving a frightening hiss. Whatever was there didn't bother her for long and she soon went back to her saucer with a definite air of triumph about her. Linda wasn't quite so dismissive, and waited an eternity for her heart to stop pounding. She stroked Sceleste and watched Avalon fly into every nook and cranny of the room. When Avalon was happy that nothing had just been cursed or spelled, she fluttered down and settled on Sceleste's back to sing one of her special Serenity Songs for Linda. A wave of calm drifted over her, making everything in the entire world feel just about fine, more or less. Something inside told her there was nothing to be scared of anymore.

Moments earlier, shortly after Linda and Sceleste had watched the rip of evil darkness fading from the room, Mörrah reappeared back in the shadows of the windswept alley. She threw her arms in the air and screamed her frustration in silence to the sky. It had all started so well. The child had easily surrendered her soul to the Higher Power, exactly as she was meant to. But that repugnant, odious, intrusive low-faery had damaged the spell, presenting a sliver of weakness to be exploited - and oh, how the cat-beast had been able to exploit that.

She clenched her fists until the joints of her fingers snapped and the bones split, and she collapsed exhausted and despairing, destroyed by the effort and the energy wasted on such a futile venture. She looked up at the window. Perhaps scare tactics might work? The cat was weak, its body was as worn as its life.. perhaps she could roar into the room, appearing in a heart-stopping blaze of hatred for long enough to bring about the final death of the cat? And she could leave quickly enough to avoid being dragged into the lowest grave in Hell by the loathsome creature.. that had to work, it had to. And then she could return and take The Stone, her prized Stone, and serve her long awaited revenge on the world and every Spiritae and Ground Crawler in it.

She glared up at the window, summoning the last of her strength to venture close once more, and felt the tired Curse Bearer barring her way. Mörrah had no choice. She backed away, deep into the shadows of the street once more. She had never, ever felt so weak. The final gamble to cling onto her life and prevent it from ending had failed, and she had nothing left.. and her long, long existence faded into the wind, carried through every part of Odessa, back to the Black Sea.

CHAPTER NINETEEN
The New Plan

"Hesperides, Avie. We have to go to Hesperides," whispered Linda, noticing that Sceleste had fallen asleep.

"Uhuh," nodded Avalon, who moved onto the cd player.

"I think your home's the only place for this Stone thing."

"Yup," she said, "nice and safe."

"But how can we get there? It's not like I know what to think of," Linda said, tapping the Stone against her head. She put it back on the floor and waited for Avalon to get comfortable on it, and then coaxed it with her mind into a gentle spin.

"Not too quick, not tooo.. ahheeheeheee.." she giggled, "..you could try reading me? I'll think of Hesperides, you empty your head more empty than it's ever been, and then maybe maybe.." she said, and flew up to Linda's shoulder, still spinning.

Linda placed the Stone a little further in front of herself, and gently moved Sceleste onto her lap without waking her. She gave her a kiss and wondered how any cat could sleep so much, then closed her eyes and tried to imagine taking flight again. It wasn't easy to relax enough at first, but Avalon whispered to her about the golden sunlight on the clouds far below, the wonderful feeling of warm wind blowing through her hair, and how easy soaring high and low could be. And once she was there, she felt as if she'd never been away. Avalon was with her, talking in words that Linda didn't recognise yet somehow she completely understood. The clouds gradually took on the shape of vast rolling hills, and soon became covered in trees and colourful scatterings of flowers. Glorious sunlight flooded in from all different directions and a feeling of complete safety overpowered her as she watched Avalon's glow becoming wider until it blended completely with the world around her. She flew lower, closer to the ground until she could almost touch the thick grass beneath her, every soft, warm blade..

..Linda opened her eyes, and saw Avalon fly silently into the blue and white landscape in the centre of the room. She turned and waved eagerly for Linda to follow, so she stood up and stepped towards the brightness. The room disappeared, and she found herself in the gentle warmth of Hesperides. It was welcoming and tranquil, quite the opposite of Odessa and the world which they'd left behind. The drifting breezes were more refreshing than mountain streams and lazily brushed Linda's hair this way and that, and she loved it. Birds sang hidden in the rich foliage of mile upon mile of forests, and the soft padding footsteps of animals seemed to be coming from all around - but Linda couldn't see any of them. She stood at the highest crest of a seemingly endless field, and looked out over its gentle undulations towards the soft blue haze on the horizon.

"There's two suns here.. and there's another one, a small blue one just behind the larger one! What's all that about, Avie?"

Avalon looked confused and on the brink of crying, and flew close to Linda's face.

"This is home, but there's no-one anywhere.. maybe I still can't come back? The Sylphs know we're here.. can you feel them around us? But I can't.. see anyone.."

"Those breezes are Sylphs? Would it help if I waved the Stone around for everyone to see?"

"Maybe.. but nobody would know what it is, though. Even Kupula won't until we get there bec.. look at Sceleste!"

Sceleste's thin fur moved under invisible hands, making the rough grooves and scars from the silver wires finally disappear, and her weak, grey fur became thick, healthier and jet black. Sceleste calmly looked around to see who was doing it, and went back to sleep.

"See, Linda? They know we're here, and I know they're here, but I still can't see them!"

"Maybe Kupula would know why? She's a really important spirit, so she might be able to appear to us. Where abouts does she live?"

Avalon looked surprised.

"Don't you know? I thought everyone knew that. She lives through the Falls Of Enchantment, and I love it there. She'll be so pleased to see us, she really will! And she'll be so happy with me, and you as well, and Sceleste despite all the curses and stuff, and.."

Avalon went through one of her extreme mood swings, and was almost ready to explode with excitement. She fluttered two or three feet ahead of Linda, chattering endlessly about different parts of Hesperides and pointing out places of apparent significance that Linda ought to know about.

"And this is where I ate four acorns all in one go by myself and couldn't fly for ages because there was too much me.. never do that it's really badawful.. and over here's where I saw three Flutterbyes who made me laugh.. and this is where.."

Linda made all the right noises to keep Avalon in a good mood, while trying to fend off her own nagging fears that they weren't going to find Kupula. Suspicions began turning into common sense as the journey progressed, and she soon worked out that the Stone offered no back-door into this magical place. She began thinking of what to say if things really did turn out how she dreaded.

"Not far now!" sang Avalon as Linda walked effortlessly through waist-high grass, brushing her free hand through the feather-soft shoots and blades. The field began sloping a little and they soon arrived amongst a band of enormous pine trees lining a sparkling, broad stream. The steep banks were going to be a real problem for Linda to walk along, but that was fine by her - the water looked so pure and so inviting that she took a moment to weigh up the pros and cons of just wading through. She couldn't quite tell whether the water might be a few inches deep or a few miles deep, but something about it felt safe and she sensed that any fears of drowning simply weren't necessary around here.

Avalon lead the way, hovering in short swinging motions to the left and to the right, humming as she made each turn and guiding Linda by her braid from one bank to the other, depending on where the breezes were most encouraging. Linda happily walked in the crystal-clear water, sometimes up to her knees and sometimes even deeper, and paused to scoop up a handful - initially for Sceleste to drink, but really to give her a much-needed wash. Sceleste didn't like that second part at all, but could tell that the Gifted One's heart was in the right place so she didn't complain too much.

The small pale blue sun gradually became hidden behind the larger white one, and the middle-sized sun steadily drifted far over to the other side of the sky. This meant no shadows could fall anywhere, and made Linda feel as if she was walking through a surreal and beautiful dream. Avalon lead her from the water and onto a flat sandy bank, where she dried in the warmth as they wandered around an almost-endless curve. The stream broadened into a river, then a few minutes later narrowed to a trickle, and then spread far out again. Linda tried not to think how weird it all was, but gave up. It was weird, and she couldn't deny it.

They eventually passed through an area which Avalon called The

Whispering Trees, but she became too excited and impatient to explain what they whispered about. Instead, she darted ahead and called back to Linda to catch up, and waited by the side of her all-time favourite larch - the one that never, ever had the right number of leaves. They had arrived at the heart of the river, a vast, languid pool of perfect blue water with a mountainous rockface looming majestically on the distant far side. Linda guessed it must be at least twice the height of St Teresa's Bell Tower, which she had been too scared to ever forget was 168 feet tall, plus seven eighths of an inch.

"So in metres, that would be.. umm.. totally not important right now.." she mumbled to herself, becoming captivated by the stunning beauty ahead of her. A single waterfall cascaded gracefully from its top, feeding into the first of countless hidden reservoirs in the rock, which in turn spread out across the face. The result was a curtain of impenetrable white water, wider than anything Linda had ever seen, which roared into the lake below. It was truly breathtaking, and the fact that she had only been able to hear it after she had seen it simply didn't register. The noise was wild and overpowering, and should have been terrifying - yet to Linda it was strangely alluring. This world was full of the most bizarre contradictions, and she was a long way past the point of wondering about any of them. She followed Avalon around the shore of the lake, to a narrow ledge between the rockface and the torrenting water. The noise suddenly fell to the level of a light shower, and then stopped as if it had suddenly been switched off. Complete silence surrounded them as they made their way further behind the crashing waterfall.

"Through here.." said Avalon, who was falling into an emotional quandary. She looked excited, scared and nervous all at the same time.

The cave was brighter than the day outside, as if the three suns were somehow shining directly into it. It was dry, easily as large as St Teresa's school hall, and one part reached all the way through the rock, narrowing as it neared the sunshine on the other side. Avalon flew ahead into the passageway, constantly racing back to make sure Linda hadn't forgotten to keep following, and then racing off again.

The way out was blocked by another waterfall, but this one was much weaker and thinner, more like a film of water running over a clean window, than a proper waterfall. It came from somewhere just inside the passageway, pouring down from the cool-grey rocks above them and shimmering in the golden sunlight of the world beyond.

Linda's eyes were drawn to the floor, where the water was making a placid whooshing sound as it hit the dark stones - and disappeared. No puddles, no pools, no splashes, nothing. Linda tried not to think about it, and looked out at the sunny world beyond.

"Another waterfall? Avie, I thought we just went through the Enchanted.."

"No, no, those were the White Veils. Not everyone's allowed through those. The Charmed Sister makes sure of that, and if she lets us through here, we can get to the Falls Of Enchantment and then Kupula comes to us - but only if she wants to. But she's my Matriaere and she always does because she loves me!"

"She's got a charmed sister?"

"Uhuh. Wouldn't this be so much easier if you had a Journal like mine? The Charmed Sister is Iugula, and she's Kupula's younger sister and she's very careful about who sees Kupula because she doesn't like everyone.. I don't know why. It's not the kind of thing to ask, is it? She likes me though. Anyway, she lives in these rocks and knows everything about anyone who comes near. So if the Gate Of Iugula," Avalon pointed to the waterfall in front of them, "..stops flowing when you go near it, you're allowed through, but if it doesn't.. then you'd better not."

"Why's that?" Linda asked, nervously stroking Sceleste. Avalon either shrugged, or shivered.

"Don't you worry, because I'm allowed!"

Linda started to feel dreadful. The fear of Avalon being heart-broken was now matched by the fear of meeting the all-powerful guardian-spirit-thing 'Yug-yewwla' in a world where ground crawlers didn't belong, especially a ground crawler who was carrying a curse-riddled death-cat. And maybe Kupula wouldn't be too pleased, either.

Avalon flew to the waterfall, sang a strange verse, and waited. And waited. And then waited a little more. She looked around to Linda, and her bottom lip gave a definite wobble.

"Maybe it's because I'm here, and Sceleste as well?" said Linda, in her most re-assuring voice. Avalon took a deep breath and sang to the sunlit water again. Nothing happened, so Linda took evasive action. She thought of the Stone in her pocket, imagined the waterfall stopping and all the reasons why it needed to stop, and how happy Avalon would be once they could walk through.

Avalon squealed, clapping her hands and waving for Linda to hurry over.

"It's stopped for me! It stopped! We can go through now! Thank you, Iugula, thank you!" she called, and flew to the sunny world outside. Linda had surprised herself, but not Sceleste.

The three suns now shone with a subdued brightness, and cast an orange glow across the landscape, adorned here and there with a hint of deep blue. They wandered along a broad, winding route lined by lush firs and cypress trees, all linked by a blanket of countless flowers which seemed to change colour and height with the winds.

"Look look looooook!" Avalon called, tugging Linda's braid in a huge loop before letting go.

Linda wasn't entirely sure if she'd turned a corner to arrive at the Lake Of Enchantment's shore, or if the lake had simply appeared ahead of her. It didn't really matter much. She looked across to the Falls Of Enchantment, a beguiling, idyllic sight that stopped her noticing the warm water that had begun lapping around her ankles. Avalon spun herself into a blur, and returned dizzily to Linda.

"Over there.. over there!" she sang, and clung onto Linda's hair until she could fly properly again.

Linda stepped further into the lake without hesitating, while Avalon happily swung the braid as she guided her across, never causing her to wade deeper than her knees even at its very centre. After a few minutes Linda felt the ground change from soft river-bed to broad, rounded stones which lead up to the foot of the stunning waterfalls. They were almost silent, far shorter than the White Veils, and barely ten feet wide - and yet the power within them seemed infinitely greater.

The water crashed against the smooth stones on the raised bank, and seemed to leap high into the air like great white horses charging into the lake, each one dancing and brushing past Linda. She stood in the spray surrounded by a million rainbows, and watched Avalon hovering ahead of her in the mist, singing as she approached the harshest and most powerful wall of water.

The faint image of a woman with golden hair flowing down to her feet appeared somewhere within the torrent. Linda stepped a little closer to try and make her features out, but the more she looked, the more vague the figure became and Kupula's colours and shape were gradually carried away, back to wherever they came from - and only returned when Linda stopped trying to see her. Avalon started her song again, this time with an upset wobble in her voice, and Linda began to understand her words.

"It's me Kupula! We've got The Stone and it's here for you and it's safe and where is everyone and I couldn't come back but I am now and please come to me pleeease and Linda's my friend and she's here for you as well and you were right about The Stone and.."

Kupula held her arms out to Avalon, almost becoming solid and real within the white water. Avalon tried flying into the waterfall to reach her, but it pounded hard against her, throwing her downwards. She flapped vainly to try and fly upwards and reach Kupula again, but the relentless barrage pinned her hard against the stones where she lay exhausted, crying and almost lost in the heavy spray. Linda kneeled down and crawled over to her, and gently picked her up. She carefully eased her onto Sceleste's back, where she lay weak and sobbing. Linda tried to think of what to say while Sceleste purred softly, but nothing came to mind so she did the only thing that seemed right. She kissed her, and hummed one of Avalon's songs for a while. It soon drifted into an Abba one, but that didn't matter.

Kupula grew much clearer again, and Linda could see and even feel the pure blue essence of her eyes. The spirit mouthed silent words to Avalon, pointing and smiling at Sceleste and Linda, before slowly fading away. Avalon reached out again as she faded, but hadn't the strength to even call her name. She looked up at Linda and managed to squeak between sobs.

"She's gone.. now? I still don't.. belong here.. that's why.. I can't.. see anyone.. you know what's worse?"

She lost her voice for a moment, and wiped her eyes a few times before trying to speak again.

"I couldn't understand what Kuplia said or anything.." she whispered, and covered her face with her hands. Linda looked into the countless white horses leaping around her, hoping for another glimpse of Kupula.

"Well, I don't know what she was saying either, but I do know what she was feeling.." Linda said, and began walking back into the lake, thinking hard to find the right words that Avalon needed to hear.

"She was really happy to see you again, and she wouldn't have minded even if you hadn't got the Stone, and.. uhh.. she'd been really worried about you, and.. and how could I forget? She thinks of you every time the wind rustles through the leaves on the trees, and.. and loves you more than ever, too!"

"Really? All that? How.. how do you know she said all that?"

"Because I do. That's why."

Avalon gave a huge sniff and shook her wings until the last droplets had fallen into the lake, and settled onto Linda's shoulder. She rested against her neck, quietly tying and untying the braid and adding more dots of colour before leaving it as it was, and only stirred to give the occasional prompt as they made their way back past the streams and White Veils.

The sky had become a smooth palette of warm blues and purples, and the night seemed to be falling quickly. By the time they reached The Whispering Trees, Linda was almost fit to drop. The day had been one long emotional rollercoaster, interrupted by a few physical assault courses along the way. She couldn't work out how long they'd been in front of the Falls, and that soon lead her to wonder how long they'd been anywhere - and she hadn't a clue. But she did know that if she didn't have a break pretty soon, her legs were probably going to go on holiday by themselves, and maybe take everything except her head with them. She settled down in a bay of thick grass in front of the trees, and watched the light from the moons shining on the water. Sceleste appeared to enjoy having the occasional piece of biscuit thrown to her and even tried pouncing on one, but it obviously wasn't worth the effort and she didn't bother again. Linda reached over and fed them to her instead, while Avalon gathered up the other pieces.

"This is such a weird place.." Linda thought to herself as a small moon re-appeared from behind the larger one for the fourth time in rapid succession. It stopped, briefly, and then went the other way.

"Now what do we do?" munched Avalon, covered in biscuit crumbs and still looking a little out of sorts.

"Well.. I think we just go back to Odessa and figure out the next step, and.."

"Eek!" Avalon shrieked, looking past Linda's shoulder and somewhere into The Whispering Trees.

"What's up?"

"Uh oh.. forgot to tell you.. there's Trusted Dark Spirits here!"

"Dark Spirits even here?"

"Uhuh, but only at night though - they help to protect all my kind when the Moon's have gone! They never have too much to do, but when they do, they don't hold anything back!"

Linda looked up to see that the sky was growing darker, and the moons had begun to fade.

"Is that bad?"

"Yes, because I can still see them - and they're getting together in the Trees.. and they'll think we're Intruders, especially you.. so you might want to get us back to our room, ever so quick!"

Linda placed the Stone on a raised mound, stood up with Sceleste and described the room back in Odessa, while Avalon fluttered around her head holding onto the braid. She tapped Linda's ear as the blue and white image of the room began to form.

"I mean really now.. a now kind of now.. nownownownow five, two, threefourwonne runrunRUNNNN!"

Linda felt something brush against her back as they returned to their room, and she turned around in time to see the dark blue landscape fading away - and unless she was very much mistaken, a very hairy and thick hand which was the width of at least three shovels disappearing with it. But she could easily have been wrong about that. She sat down next to Aggy, and gave her a hug.

"Blimey Aggs, this is all getting to be so mad.. you don't know what you're missing."

Avalon flew to the window to check that Odessa was definitely still out there. It was, and she looked out at the sunset, feeling pleased to have caught its colours before they had all gone.

"Isn't Kupula nice?" she said, drifting down to the small pile of cd's near Sceleste. She seemed to have left most of her upset behind her - but not all of it, Linda felt.

"Yes, she's very nice. You're lucky to have a Maytuhe.. Marh.. uhh.. such a nice lady. And you'll get back to her, don't worry," Linda said reassuringly, and sat down near the cd player.

"You promise?" Avalon asked, picking one from its case and looking at her reflection in it. She watched herself flutter her wings, and giggled.

"Uhuh, I promise," Linda said, trying to sound confident enough to make Avalon feel much better. Avalon seemed convinced, and accidentally found her elusive Good Question Level. It had been right by the floor all the time.

"What do we do now, then?" she asked, narrowly side-stepping another grooming-session from Sceleste.

"Well.." Linda sighed, and thought hard for a moment before having a minor brainwave.

"How about if we try and go back to when it first went missing in the 12th Century? We've seen and felt where it came from, so we might be able to conjure it up and go back there?" she said. Avalon nodded, but still looked as if she wanted to hear why.

"If we stop it being stolen," Linda continued, "the people who brought it to old Odessa in the first place can have it back.. so.. they can carry on doing their research or whatever they were doing, can't they? They must be really clever if they could make something like this, and clever types aren't war-mongerers because they're too clever for all that! I mean, they must have got a lot going for them?"

Avalon liked the sound of that, and even stopped trying to find out how much of her leg could fit through the hole in the middle of the Voulez-Vous cd.

"But then what? We'll be stuck back in the past. They might not have Battuh-ries for your Headuh-Phonez in the past."

"Well," Linda pondered, "maybe they'll figure out where we belong? Or they might even want us to stay with them! That could be so amazingly cool, couldn't it? I mean, it's obvious they haven't been able to make another Stone or else they would have used it to go and get this one back ages ago, in which case nobody would ever have heard about the Odessa Stone. So we'll tell them everything, and.. make it all loads better? We're dealing with clever people."

Avalon scratched her head, and slowly nodded.

"Well, I prefer that to being chased by Bad Types.." she said. Sceleste meowed at her, and she nodded back.

"Ooh, yes.. Lindy, what if we went forwards to when it was made?"

"Forwards in.. can you understand Sceleste?"

"Yup, but only in bits. Cats are difficult, especially.. you know.. ones like.. you knowwwuh.." she said, trying to discretely gesture towards Sceleste - while being watched closely by her.

"Oh, right.." said Linda, moving rapidly along, "So we try going forwards then? Umm.. forwards, forwards.."

Linda hadn't thought of going into the future - and that might just be a brilliant idea. She placed her hand on the Stone and took a few quiet minutes to try and sense where it had come from. Nothing came into her mind, so she imagined flying higher, holding it in front of herself, letting the clouds drift further away beneath her and looking into.. into.. no, nothing. There was nothing to guide her, nothing to be read, and she knew a huge headache would be starting if she tried any harder. She carefully opened her eyes, pleased that the room was in such mild, dusky light.

"Nope, I don't know what to think of in order to get us there - there's no destination for me to talk about or anything, is there? But even if we could, why would they believe that we're returning something that they might not even know has been stolen yet? Or they might even think that we're the ones who took it! Oh my brain.. then we'd get stuck wherever and whenever that is, not knowing anyone and having no money or anything - maybe even in prison, and that would be worse than here.. pretty much. So maybe we stick to the past instead, then?"

Avalon hadn't understood a word Linda had said, but if it all made sense to such a Gifted One, then it must be okay. She pressed the triangle button on the cd player and took to the air, while Sceleste continued grooming her new-improved fur. A few songs later, Linda felt that the threat of a headache had completely gone so she finished off a self-heating coffee, temporarily gathered Sceleste onto her lap, and waited for Avalon to finish having another dance.

"Here's what we do," she said, gathering Sceleste again, "We both think about Bav.. Duvl.. oh, that monk's book, and the bit about that castle, so that world appears here and then we can go there before the Stone was lost or anything."

"But we've already got it.. it's just there," said Avalon, pointing.

"Yes, but.." Linda knew that no explanation would be adequate. "Oh yes, so it is, isn't it? Silly me.." she said instead, and held it up.

Sceleste tried wandering off again so Linda picked her up, then stood up to make sure she wouldn't go again. She closed her eyes, and without trying too hard she soon imagined herself drifting far above the clouds, and then through the Book of Dalovich. She started with the room that Brother Dalovich had used for writing in, and dream-talked her way through all the images and sensations of the stories people had told to him, until she felt herself nearing the place where she wanted to be.

"So it's 1186.. the day the Stone arrived.. the Boriso Glebov Castle.. 1186.. I remember the feelings from the book.. the people who told the stories.. all around me, the land is Obro.. Obrovechen.. I can feel summer.. I can feel.. feel June.. I can feel the early morning.. I can.. I can sense the Castle.. every texture, every smell.."

"So can I," wavered Avalon, prodding Linda to open her eyes, "..it's over there!"

CHAPTER TWENTY

1186AD
The Queen Of Obrovechen

1186AD, Sunday 24th June, 7.10am

Mörrah lay in bed, very bored. There was all but nothing in her life these days except for tedious, yawnsome, monotonous boredom. Everywhere she looked, she saw something else that was boring. Being Queen wasn't nearly as interesting or entertaining as she'd hoped. Well, that would have to change one way or another, she decided, because she deserved some kind of respect and authority simply for putting up with her two-legged ox of a husband. In fact, a real ox would make far better company and perhaps be more concerned with personal hygiene. She glared at her Lady In Waiting who was laying the dire Morning Robes across her Reading Chair. The woman approached the foot of the four-poster bed, timidly standing by the furthest pillar as if it was a shield.

"Queen Ephra? If it pleases Your Majesty, it is time to prepare for the Saint's Mass, a special Sanctum Sanctoris, and Father Czaslas has expressed his dearest wish that this week you might grace his congregation with your pres.."

Mörrah threw back her covers and stormed from her bed to the chair, brushing past Ennafa as if she didn't exist. She snatched the bright red garments and held them up into the sunlight, examining each and every join before casting them out of the window. The unwritten Rules Of Court demanded that a Queen's wardrobe be appropriately colourful - but Mörrah demanded it did not, and watched with a degree of satisfaction as the robes floated a long way down to the ground, causing a fight to break out between a group of commoners who weren't really built for such clothing. She turned back to the woman, who had retreated to safety near the door.

"How many times? BLACK! Every single day, I wear black! BLACK! If I ever have to tell you again.." she screamed, pointing an accusing finger, "..if you dare bring me loathsome attire like THAT I'll have you fed to the most mange-ridden mongrel packs in this Kingdom, and so help me I'll make sure they finish every one of your bones! And if they don't - then I will! Get out! Get out NOW!"

She hurled a hairbrush as the woman scurried away, and laughed loudly when it broke against the back of the door. She stood on her bed and threw back her mane of black hair, still laughing for all the world to hear. The day had started well, and that made a welcome change, especially for a Sunday.

For the first twenty years of her life, Mörrah had been an ordinary peasant, a mere Ground Crawler in a small village near the Black Sea, in a land which would be known, many centuries later, as Odessa. She lead a futile existence which she hated as much as the world around her. Everyone had seen her grow from a nasty child into a far nastier woman, and her venomous mean streak and volatile temperament had always made her worth avoiding - and everyone always had avoided her. But worst of all, they all knew that she was plagued by visions of Dubrava, an old woman, a feared spirit-woman only ever whispered of by the elders in the village. They knew of Dubrava because they had grown up with the stories of her evil ways, and they knew she had left them in peace for many years not through choice, but because of her age. And when she did choose to appear in the village, there was just one person able to see her, just one girl she could call upon.

Although her daytime visitations were rare, she had appeared to Mörrah in dreams almost every night of her life, never speaking to her and never engaging her in any way. And that in itself was infuriating for the girl, and her anger showed in many ways. People accused her of being unbalanced, the progeny of a Witch and a fallen Priest, or perhaps she was simply an attention-seeking fool - but if that was true, she was a fool who had always seen the knowing look in the eyes of the elders. They never explained her torments to her and merely chose to keep their distance, which made her seething resentment of them grow day after day after day..

But after twenty long years, the old woman chose a clear, bitter winter's night to finally break her silence, calling Mörrah to the banks of the Black Sea. She claimed to be a Ved'ma, an elderly Spiritae, a servant to the Lady Morganna, the High Priestess of all Ved'mas. Mörrah had laughed and ridiculed her, which the old woman seemed to enjoy, much to Mörrah's irritation. But in the course of that one night, the aged Ved'ma finally reached the end of her millennium of life and a young and worthy woman was initiated into the world of the Dark Spirits. Mörrah's weak human body was given to the waters of the Black Sea, and her spirit was given to Lady Morganna. The High Priestess was pleased with the weary Dubrava, and allowed her to pass into the Sea, untroubled and peaceful. She could see that the chosen successor had magnificent potential.

Her first hundred years as a Ved'ma had given her a small taste of power, but also decades of dismay as she had grown to understand her own limitations, and also the limitations offered by the region which she had been granted by Lady Morganna. She could easily exert cunning and guile over weak-minded peasants and inferior spiritae, but they offered very little challenge and as such were never going to strengthen her as much as she wanted. Regardless of how many she tormented and cursed, their misery could never provide her with enough energy to reach the heights of power that she desired. And so her longing for a grander existence grew over the passing decades into an unbearable frustration.

And then fate had provided a way to quench her desires. In the year 1182, King Metriev had moved the capital of his kingdom to Obrovechen, a small trading thoroughfare close to the Black Sea which happened to lie at the very heart of Mörrah's territory. Over the course of two years, she patiently watched in silence as the sparse collections of towns and villages steadily merged into a vast and sprawling city with a population that reached dizzying levels. She preyed upon on the greedy masses of new victims, soon finding herself able to exploit all of a Ved'ma's tricks and deceptions at will. She was young and strong, and so spiritually well-nourished that everyone could see her - and if she chose, fear her. And for a while, life was just as she wanted it to be. And then she began sensing the frustrations, the feelings that once again she had reached the very height of her powers. Even with new arrivals in the city and the ports, she wasn't growing any stronger because no Ved'ma could ever rise above the Natural Limit granted and imposed on her by the High Priestess. And Mörrah's feelings of frustration and futility with her life quickly returned with an unforgiving vengeance, far worse than ever before.

But the castle had been completed around that time, and filled with Ground Crawlers whose minds and spirits were stronger than those of peasants. These people were exactly the kind she had been looking for - they were more of a challenge, their sufferings were far more amusing, and perhaps these fools were even worth controlling?

For several nights she would visit the castle, passing as a shadow through its corridors and rooms, finding her way around, easily becoming familiar with who resided there and the purposes they served. She quickly knew a great deal about everyone, and soon presented herself to Queen Ephra's inner circle. Nobody knew where the slender, enigmatic woman came from, and they never felt able to ask her questions in the same direct way that she could. However, her charm was irresistible, and she soon gained the trust and friendship of the royal entourage. She became an invaluable source of knowledge and amusement for the Knights, savouring their ambition and relishing their disregard for human life. Even the Ladies at Court enjoyed her company, despite her barely-contained resentment for their passive ways. But she loved their jealousy, and thrived on their insecurity. The academics respected her command of languages and were easily humiliated by her turns of phrase, while others admired her incredible knowledge of the region's history. Above all, everyone at all levels throughout the castle drew upon her endless wisdom and advice.. and most felt as if she knew and understood everything about them.

Mörrah loved the opulence, the wealth and the splendour of Queen Ephra's life, and soon found herself regarded as Her Majesty's most essential confidant - the closest of all friends, and the one who just happened to feed on her distrust and loneliness. Many people commented on the marked similarity she bore to the Queen, and a few dared to wonder if that similarity had been quite so strong when Mörrah had first arrived - but no-one ever spoke of such ludicrous concerns. And when she wasn't with the Queen, she was behaving either coy or flirtatious with the King, preying on his weakness and desires in the face of the slightest temptation.

However, there was one section of her perfect community who suspected her for what she really was, and toyed with her on occasion, always edging her to reveal her true self with their clever wordplay and writings. The Religious Ones knew of the existence of Ved'ma, although they could never have reason to recognise one. Occasionally she would burn herself on the crude protective hexes placed here and there, but avoiding them was usually simple. And over the course of a month or two, she saw to it that the hexes were gradually and unwittingly removed, one by one. But the Church was no great concern of hers, it was just a minor inconvenience and she simply tended to keep well away.

And after one long year of playing games with her new inferiors, she made her move. The Queen, always so hopelessly naive, was easily disposed of, along with one of the King's most trusted Knights. It was presumed the couple had eloped together, and Mörrah had been more than happy to sustain that rumour, adding more scandalous details every time she raised it. Of course, she had never said where they really were. After all, why would anyone need to ask her such a question? The Black Sea was loyal to all Ved'ma and had kept many secrets for a long, long time, and it would keep the bodies of her two 'secrets' safely hidden as well.

The King had needed comforting, and Mörrah was more than capable of overlooking his countless bad points to keep her eyes fixed on the solitary good one - the Queen's vacant throne. It had stood next to his in the Great Hall, permanently sparkling with 4,958 minute diamonds and 2,682 sapphires, which she had obsessively counted on her very first nocturnal visit. But it was now locked away in a distant storage room, waiting to be dismantled and destroyed. So one autumn night, not even four days after the Queen's presumed adultery, Mörrah took a gamble. She visited King Metriev shortly after midnight, gently assuring him that her love was so deep that she would even change her name to Ephra just for him. After all, outside his Kingdom, a name would simply be a name and no-one need ever know that the first Queen Ephra had deserted him in favour of a mere soldier. She asked for no ceremony, just the title and her rightful place alongside him. And he liked that. As the night wore on, she promised to be better in every way than the last Ephra, and a worthy Queen to his million subjects. He liked that even more, and in the middle of the harsh October of 1185, Mörrah quietly signed the Marriage Charter and became the second Queen Ephra.

But in the eight months since taking the throne, she had been frustrated at every turn, and taken to spending as much time in her own Quarters as possible. Such a senior royal position should have brought the desired changes into her life, but it had offered far less than she'd even had before. She had wanted the power to create a little chaos in the land of Ground Crawlers and perhaps start more than just the occasional battle or two. Small conflicts were entertaining and occasionally rewarding, but ultimately boring and usually worthless. Sometimes the wretched people didn't even fight - they just signed agreements and went back to whatever pitiful lands they came from.

From the day she took her throne, she wanted blood to be shed in her own name, she wanted a few kingdoms in far off places, the kind of places that didn't freeze over for months on end. She could have a mighty empire that fought nation after nation, growing to sizes unheard of and all overflowing with subjects ready to die for her. And she wanted to be the Queen of all those regions where other Ved'mas lived - how hysterically amusing would that be? The thought of such an achievement had made her laugh at the precise moment that the golden crown was placed upon her head, much to the consternation of her husband.

She knew her goals would have to be achieved quickly, before she would undoubtedly have to face the wrath of the Veidate Senate (the High Council of Ved'mas) for interfering too much in the world of Ground Crawlers. She knew the others would be jealous though. They might Damn her for a while, perhaps even bring Lady Morganna herself to pass judgement, but away from the Council, they'd all admire her and that respect would belittle whatever punishment they might pass.

But since her coronation, she had begun to wonder if any of that would ever happen, and she was beginning to feel that it simply couldn't. And ever since December, the wretched Father Czaslas had made public his hopes for her to enter his church every Sunday, the very place where her defences could be stripped away, where she could so easily be cast back to where she came from. This wasn't how it should be. And now another Sunday had crawled around - and even worse, it was another Saint's day.

Mörrah picked up the broken pieces of her hairbrush, and willed them back together. She stared down from the window of her turret, and pursed her lips at the exodus of odious filth making their way across the Trading Courtyard. Sunday had arrived, again. The day that peasants and nobility alike all bowed down before their God and begged His divine forgiveness for having done precisely what they had begged His divine forgiveness for last time around. They may well have been an almost inexhaustible source of strength to her, but they were so very dull. She loudly screamed in time with the bells as they rang out from the church, scaring the maid who had come to make her bed. Mörrah laughed again.

She settled on the ugly chair at her window, glaring far over at the church and began carving her nails against the stone wall while waiting for its service to end. The countless grooves were worn deeper as the bells rang out again half an hour later, and Mörrah finally had to dress for breakfast. She chose her darkest green gown, which held a symphony of colour compared to her other garments.

"It will do.. will do.. WILL NOT DO.." she thought to herself, unsure if she said it as well.

"You look like a trollop! Now away and put something good on, woman - you're a Queen, not a serving wench! Do it or I'll have you paraded like a cheap God-less harl.."

Most of the 200 people attending the St Alekseev Day Morning Banquet joined the King in laughter, and so did the second Queen Ephra, briefly. She made her way back through the hordes of rabble as they continued to arrive, and she hurried up the main stairs and across to the narrow winding staircase that lead all the way up to her private Majesterial Quarters, feeling more humiliated and angry with every step. She was ready to explode.

She picked the silver vase from her flower table and hurled it across the room, watching with glee as the lead window panels shattered. She ran to see if someone would be getting cut to ribbons, and tutted with disappointment as the shards all landed harmlessly. Dozens of magpies took flight from her roof, raising a cacophony of squawks and cries around the turret. Their noise was laughter to Mörrah, and she leaned a long way out of her window in order to see them high above.

"See? The dark ones dare not cross me!" she shouted to the courtyard below, breaking off the remaining triangles of glass from the window frame. She ripped the sleeves from her dark green dress and threw the torn material and final shards as far out as she could. The peasants would undoubtedly feel rich with such gifts. She shouted for the least stupid of her maids to come and assist with an appropriate choice of Celebratory Morningwear.

Shortly afterwards, Mörrah's latest Lady In Waiting knocked lightly on the door, and she was soon ready to be escorted back down to the Great Hall. They walked in silence down the spiralling stairs and out onto the main landing, where Mörrah froze for a moment. Something was wrong, something around her was definitely wrong, but what? She leaned on the stone rail and looked down into the huge Entrance Hall, scrutinising its every detail for anything (or anyone) that shouldn't be there. One of the banners on the stairway had been ripped but that could only be an improvement, the one next to it was crooked but acceptable, the next was fine, and next..

"My Lady, the music you hear is from a troupe of entertainers, if you please. They arrived mere moments ago, and are want to amuse the Court. His Highness kindly granted permission - and I believe they have a bear!"

Mörrah accepted that. Entertainers, or wandering misfits as she considered them, had odd ways and some knew far more than they ought to. She grudgingly crossed to the wide steps and made a deliberately slow descent - and then froze again, a short way from their end. An icy chill ran through her heart, far stronger than before.

"Are you not well, my Lady?"

She steadied herself against the balustrade, and stared at the long banner hanging from the wall. Had those wretched monks hexed it? Were they toying with her again, trying to unsettle her and reveal her as a Spiritae in human form? She waved her hand to dismiss Ennafa's concerns, and marched down the final steps - but stumbled slightly on a filthy brown rag at the foot of the stairs. It made her feet ache as if she had walked barefoot over a thousand cobblestones, and under her breath she insulted the troublesome monks for leaving a pathetic trick lying around for her.

"Remove that vile cloth from here immediately," she growled, "or I'll remove you from here - in pieces."

The Lady In Waiting nodded and waved for a guard to come and take it away. She carefully took Mörrah's arm again and lead her to the Great Hall where she was met by polite applause, and a loud belch from her husband - which was also met with a round of applause. She took her place by his side, and feigned interest in the antics of the performing imbeciles who were striving to entertain them. They weren't awful, and certainly weren't the worst she'd seen by a long way, but they were still thoroughly unbearable. She groaned as the King enthusiastically insisted they start again from the beginning, so that his beloved wife wouldn't miss any of the marvellous show.

Thankfully, they were interrupted shortly after re-starting by shouting, cries and scuffling noises coming from outside one of the windows. That was the kind of entertainment she preferred, and even smiled as she turned to what might be happening. Moments later a silence fell over the Great Hall, and the crowd parted to allow an armour-clad Ensign Guard to enter, followed by around a dozen of the Prime Guards. He bowed before King Metriev, and stood to one side.

"Your Majesties, this intruder was found approaching the castle gates. His cohorts have slain many of our finest, but our numbers overpowered them. Their weapons.."

"Where are his associates?" snapped the King.

"They lie where slain.. but their weaponry, it was of the likes I have never seen, Your Majesty."

"Excellent," King Metriev said, and turned his attention to the oddly-dressed prisoner.

"Who are you, foreigner? From where does such a man hail?"

The man remained silent as the King walked around him, inspecting his strange clothing. Mörrah was transfixed. He was handsome, almost a foot taller than her fool husband, and dressed in a way she could never imagine. But there was something else, something that was much more attractive. He had a strong air of ruthless confidence, and he simply exuded power and authority. Perhaps that was it? She stepped closer, sensing the devious connivance behind his pale grey eyes. He looked straight at her, and as he held her gaze she understood that the loss of his companions hadn't troubled him at all. He was wonderfully unconcerned, as if their lives had been inconsequential, even less than trivial. She made herself look away, breaking his gaze and taking a small step backwards. King Metriev was losing his temper.

"Do you not understand? Am I to have answers dragged from you? I asked who you are, traveller!"

A silence hung in the air until a solitary church bell signalled the start of St Alekseev's day of celebration.

CHAPTER TWENTY ONE

1186AD
Castle Boriso Glebov
that same morning

1186AD, Sunday 24th June, 7.10am

Linda felt herself drifting through the images within Brother Dalovich's book, nearing the place she wanted to be.

"So it's 1186.. the day the Stone arrived.. the Boriso Glebov Castle.. 1186.. I remember the feelings from the book.. the people who told the stories.. all around me, the land is Obro.. Obrovechen.. I can feel summer.. I can feel.. feel June.. I can feel the early morning.. I can.. I can sense the Castle.. every texture, every smell.."

"So can I," wavered Avalon, prodding Linda to open her eyes, "..it's over there!"

Linda stood on the side of a long rolling hill, blinking in the bright sunlight of a summer morning. She hurried into the shade and safety of the tall pine trees making up a dense forest, and looked out to the imposing castle just a few hundred yards away.

"That's how they should look!" she whispered, "Whitey-grey with turrets and flags and no tumble-down bits all over the place.. that's a proper one, that is," she declared. The one on her last school trip hadn't been too impressive at all.

"Well it's new, isn't it, and.. where's The Stone?" shrieked Avalon, looking from Linda's hand back to where they had run from, and back to Linda's hand again. She flew around it twice before checking behind each finger, and then checked the hand that was somewhere underneath Sceleste.

"Hmm.. it's here, somewhere - over by the castle. I can almost feel it.. almost touch it.. I just know the Stone's already here, somewhere. That kind of makes sense, doesn't it?" said Linda, wondering why she hadn't noticed it was gone.

"Yes. No. Yes. Why?" Avalon replied, flying in a stressed circle until Sceleste meowed at her.

"Because maybe there can't be two in the same place.. unlike duplicates of me. It must be really powerful.."

"So now we've got to find it all over again?" said Avalon, with her hands on her hips. She sighed, took out her Journal and opened it to the page where she had drawn Linda's jacket. She replaced the tick with an X.

They stayed under cover of the trees and heavy undergrowth, gradually making their way around to the outer grounds of the huge castle, and then even further along to within fifty yards of the tall entry gates. Linda crouched behind a large bush, dismayed to see hundreds of people milling around inside the courtyard.

She closed her eyes and tried to come up with a plan of such devious cunning that James Bond would have been proud of it.. but that was proving to be very tricky. Avalon was pre-occupied with the ladybirds crawling on the bush's leaves and wasn't being much help at all, and Sceleste had wandered off for one of her longest walks yet. So Linda stayed still for a while, hidden under the hedge, keeping the gates under surveillance and hoping that nothing bugly was crawling anywhere near her.

The church bells rang out loudly and she watched as the crowds all moved away, no doubt making their way to wherever the castle's church was. She scurried over to where Sceleste had decided to lie down and picked her up, then crawled on all fours to a less-filthy vantage point to see if maybe the guards were supposed to attend church as well. If Sister Mariephred was here, they'd have to go to the service even if there was a major battle raging - but she wasn't here, so they just stood there, half a dozen of them either side of the huge gates, all looking bored and highly unlikely to be going anywhere, ever.

The ringing eventually staggered to its faltering end, and silence fell for a few minutes while the crowds all disappeared. Faint music drifted from the forest, steadily growing louder until a large troupe of entertainers made their way to the gates, where they were given an intense checking by the guards. Linda thought for a moment about discretely joining them and sneaking into the courtyard as part of their group, but then she acknowledged that wasn't her best idea ever because no-one could get away with that, even in a cartoon. She watched as the guards allowed them through, and then returned to their posts. Linda was feeling stuck, and time was dragging by.

She kept low against the ground, and crawled all the way around to see if there were any more entrances on one of the other sides of the castle walls. Avalon went for a closer look, and came back shaking her head. This was turning into a very tough situation, and Linda crawled back towards the entrance with absolutely no brilliant schemes at all for how to find the Stone. Maybe this was game over, no more routes to take, no more anythings anymore and she was stuck there in a land where tv's didn't even exist and..

Suddenly the air was filled with shouting, and very small, sharp gunshots. The guards ran from the gates and past the front wall, disappearing around the far side. One remained, but he was anxiously looking around himself. More shots followed, and then even more shouting, and at last he left his post.

"Oh God this is it, we're going in, we're going.." she whimpered as she crawled from the bushes, and started running for all she was worth.

The Trading Courtyard reeked of animals and countless other things which she didn't want to think about, and her eyes darted everywhere all at once to try and find somewhere to hide. The bells rang out again, and hordes of people began leaving the church, heading her way. Despite her heart pounding like a pneumatic drill against a bass drum, her mind stayed calm and some common sense guided her. She grabbed a heavy blanket from someone who was hopefully only sleeping-off a hangover, and wrapped it around her shoulders to hide her modern clothes. The first of the commoners walked past, and ignored her completely. Avalon tugged at her ear.

"Good thing your hair's like it is 'cause you blend right in! Imagine if it was.."

"If you stop there, I can still take that as a compliment.." she whispered, trying not to move her lips as she wandered past more people. She passed mounds of hay and grain, crude tents and very skewed tables, and into a relatively quiet part of the courtyard, near a long dividing wall with a huge archway at its centre. A busier courtyard not too dissimilar to the Trading one lay on the other side, along with the church in a clearer area.

If the traveller would be anywhere, she figured he'd be in the most important part of the castle grounds, so she strolled as casually and medievally as she could towards a huge building with turrets and two large flags on its flat top. A stream of better-dressed people were making their way into it, and a nervous guard stood at its entrance admiring a bear which the entertainers had brought along. Linda crouched on the opposite side of the courtyard behind a barrel of something putrid, and tried not to breathe in. She slipped her shoes off and pushed them into her jacket pockets - white trainers probably weren't very trendy in the 12th Century, even ones covered in grime.

"Avie, have a fly around and see if there's another way in th.."

Suddenly a window shattered, and a dozen or more magpies took noisily to the air from a turret over at the far end of the building's front wall. Glass fell to the ground, shortly followed by a torn dress. A woman shouted something, but it was lost in the general noises of the townsfolk who seemed to be making up for having spent the last half an hour being silent in the church.

"That's a big bunch of magpies," shivered Avalon, making a sign in front of herself which Linda tried to copy.

"I think a bunch of them's called a murder. Or is that crows? Maybe it's a tiding, I can never remember. I got it wrong in an English lesson once and Brenda.." Linda paused for a moment, "..you know, I really don't care what she said. They're called a Murderous Tiding as of now, and that's that."

"Well that Murderous Tiding didn't go far - look!" said Avalon, pointing at the turret. The magpies had already returned, and there seemed to be even more of them.

The bear was frightened by the noise of the glass as it rained down onto the flagstones, and began dragging his master back towards the main gates. The guard laughed, and wandered back to his post, and Linda decided his mood was probably right for her to take a chance. It was time for Operation Sir Grinalot. Her father had often faced down the most awkward of questions and situations on tv by continually smiling and pretending there was absolutely nothing to hide. Generally, it tended to work so Linda tried her own version.

Lady Grinalot adjusted the blanket to ensure that everything was covered, and nonchalantly walked over to the Entrance Hall as if she was part of the tail-end of the people going inside. She even smiled at the guard, as if there was no reason at all for him to think she was in the wrong place and time. And it worked - he even smiled back.

Linda stood inside the entrance, wondering what to do next, and noticing immediately how cold the castle felt. The crowd were steadily making their way ahead into the Banqueting Hall, and some were already looking at her as if she didn't quite fit in. Four guards ran down the broad main staircase, and would have looked extremely well-trained and intimidating - if one of them hadn't missed the top step and accidentally torn the first of the huge banners hanging on the wall. He used the next banner to help himself stand up again, and then he chased after the other three guards. They all stormed past Linda, probably to help sort out the noisy trouble somewhere outside the castle.

"Now what do we do?" whispered Avalon, peering through Linda's hair.

"Umm.. we.. hide somewhere until everywhere's quiet again," she said, struggling to keep hold of Sceleste. The last of the St Alekseev Day Morning Banquet guests looked back at her, so Linda did her best to act like a normal person who was in full control of herself, but she couldn't quite manage it. Sceleste was wriggling and twisting, intent on getting out from underneath the horrendous goat-hair blanket, and quickly succeeded. She gave it a meow of disapproval, shook herself and then wandered over to the main staircase, which lead up to the first floor. She struggled up the first four steps before stopping for a well-earned lie down near the last of the banners which lined the staircase. Linda played to the audience by tutting loudly and hurrying to pick her up. The last of the guests weren't very interested in a barmy urchin and her equally barmy cat, and finally drifted inside the Banqueting Hall.

Linda looked around. She was alone at last, but now what? She bent down to pick up Sceleste who trotted away, disappearing behind the nearest of the enormous banners. Linda groaned.

"Sceleste? We haven't got time for.." she whispered, warily lifting the material away from one of the castle's huge supporting pillars, revealing the wall behind. She crouched behind the material, scooped Sceleste up and nervously stepped back onto the staircase.

"Remember how you were looking for a hidey place?" said Avalon, pointing back at the banner. Linda went red, and sneaked behind it again. There was just enough space for her to stand with her back to the wall without causing the looping folds to look unnatural. Sceleste started wriggling again, so Linda quickly stepped our from the banner, and tossed the blanket to the foot of the stairs. Avalon took off for a quick check further up the staircase, and returned even faster than usual.

"No-one's anywhere except for two People coming down some stairs! Not these stairs, there's other ones from even higher up."

"That's good then. Did you see where they are?"

"Nope, but their footsteps were coming this way. And now they're.."

Two women's voices carried in the emptiness, one cold and harsh, the other very nervous. They were still beyond the top of the stairs, talking in a near-forgotten dialect which Linda tried to tune into. And she very nearly managed it, if Sceleste hadn't distracted her by bristling uncontrollably. The women began walking down the main flight of stairs, talking and muttering, and to Linda's horror the sound of their steps came to a halt a few inches in front of her. She held her breath, convinced that the slightest movement of air or perhaps even her heartbeat would give her away. The friendlier woman spoke, concerned about something, but there was no reply and the two of them carried on their way. Linda had almost understood what she had said, and if they had managed a few more sentences she might have grasped it.. but they were gone. The one in a bad mood spat some words at the foot of the stairs, but her aggressive manner made Linda too nervous to try and concentrate.

Avalon waited on the floor until their footsteps sent no more vibrations through the stonework, and flew up to the very top of the banner for a safety check. She patiently watched a guard taking Linda's horrible blanket away, and watched him making a circuit of the hall. And then she came back so fast that she needed to use Sceleste in order to stop.

"Sorry Sceleste, really sorry!" she said, giving her a hug, "Look out there now Linda look now, look looklooklooooook.."

Linda shuffled sideways and moved the edge of the blue material as much as she dared, and looked out from the staircase. A tall man was being lead by a troupe of guards across the hall, towards the Banqueting Room. He wore a smart suit and carried a silver briefcase, as if he hadn't even attempted to try and blend in.

"That's the traveller?" whispered Linda, a little disappointed that her imagination had been completely wrong. He wasn't a white-haired old man, he didn't have any good-looking assistants with him and he didn't even have a Light Sabre, a Space Podule or even a Hover Board. Instead, he had a briefcase. He was well-built and if his greying hair was cut better, he could have been an important businessman or even a news reader. The music and chatter suddenly ended, and the whole castle seemed to fall quiet for a few moments.

Linda jumped as a solitary church bell loudly signalled the start of St Alekseev's day of celebration.

CHAPTER TWENTY TWO

The Traveller

The church bell faded away and the traveller raised his hand, daring to command silence from the King. He spoke in hushed tones barely above a whisper.

"Who am I? My name is of no importance. I come in friendship to negotiate, to offer power beyond power, in return for certain favours."

Mörrah's heart pounded with excitement and she had no intention of allowing her husband's temper and lack of social grace to spoil the moment. She slipped her arm as far around the King's waist as she could manage, and whispered to him.

"My darling Metriev, would you suggest we go to a more private place to discuss such matters? I believe this to be most strange, perhaps a golden opportunity, perhaps an elaborate joke, and is therefore not to be shared with.. others. Perhaps you might propose to lead us somewhere?"

The King repeated most of her words, and lead the way from the hall. Mörrah clapped her hands sharply as she followed them out, signalling for the entertainers to continue with their mindless distractions. She stopped to instruct the guards to return to their posts, and to leave any bodies alone for the time being. As always, she wanted the peasants to see any corpses - it helped to keep the fools in their place. She hurried up the stairs, barely noticing the momentary chill as she brushed past the blue banner.

The King, his Queen, Father Czaslas and a guard sat along one side of a long oak table, in the room usually reserved for drawing up battle plans. The traveller sat facing them.

"Speak, or I'll have your tongue removed," snapped the King.

"Of course, but I request your guard leave us," he replied calmly.

"That he will not. Now speak while you still can."

Mörrah melted as the man ran his hands through his greying hair.

"Very well then," he began, "I am not of your time. I do come from this land, but this land far in the future, a time where you.."

"Future? What is this word?" flared the King, impatient with the sedate manner of the prisoner. Mörrah squeezed his hand, and explained in a manner that let him feel he was still in charge.

"A time that is yet to come, my love. A time that can be influenced by yourself.. if that's what our guest implies?"

"Precisely," added the traveller, courteously.

Mörrah could tell that the man's command of the language was a little poor, but that was understandable and even forgivable if what he said was true. She shifted excitedly in her seat, and tried desperately to make eye contact again. Father Czaslas was less impressed, and crossed himself first with his hands and then with his crucifix, which he then pointed at the traveller.

"What madness is this?" he spluttered, "What talk could greater rival that of chattering birds? That we should hear this on the day.."

"Hush, monk! Our guest must continue!" snapped Mörrah, "Now then, you were say.." she continued, before Metriev interrupted.

"A future man? A man who claims to journey from.." he said, standing up and ready to declare the prankster as good as dead. The traveller calmly raised a hand, as if he had been embarrassed by a huge compliment.

"My good people, I understand your suspicions. Allow me to offer proof of my origins, for it is only right that proof should be needed," he said, finally throwing a glance to Mörrah.

He opened his briefcase and stood an empty grey picture frame on the table, and passed his hand through it a few times to show that it was indeed empty. Then he touched a small white symbol in the top right corner, and an image appeared within the frame showing the castle viewed from the point high in the forest where he and his associates had first arrived. The King leaned forwards.

"A painting from nowhere? Out of air? And this.. this is my castle?" he said, peering closely.

"Very astute, Your Highness. This is your exalted castle, viewed by a remote 'eye' for want of a better word. Please, observe.."

He pressed a button on his wristband, and the small remote viewer sped closer to the castle, soon racing through the gates, past the people in the Trading Courtyard and then into the Entrance Hall. The eye moved onwards, up the stairs and along the corridor, and then through the end window. Had Mörrah not been so stunned by the miracle taking place before her, she might have noticed another person who was dressed as incorrectly as the traveller, crouching beside a table practically outside their room. And she was so engrossed that she even dismissed the small chill that once again passed through her.

Instead, she watched in awe as the remote viewer left the castle and settled a few feet above the Second Courtyard. She reached into the image to try and push the peasants over with her giant hand, but the screen flickered and the scene disappeared, leaving behind nothing but a grey frame. She laughed uncontrollably and had to sit down, while Father Czaslas turned his back on the room.

"Your Highness Queen Ephra! This is no laughing matter - a Demon stands amongst us, a bringer of evil who shall raise nought but hatred for you within your people!"

"Oh, oderint dum metuant.." *(Let them hate me, as long as they fear me..)* she said dismissively, tapping and knocking the frame in an attempt to make the pictures come back. The King had no idea what to say.

"I told you not to speak Latin - all them ridiculous complexities infuriate me! Now then, Great Traveller, you have shown something I have no words for and I am duly impressed, yet also wary. What power is to be gained from such trickery?"

"From this? Nothing.." he said, leaning forwards to switch it off and stand it upright again.

"See?" exclaimed Father Czaslas, "..a worthless Sorcerer, a jester of Satan! Send him on his way, Your Majesty!"

The traveller casually looked at him and lit a small cigar. He couldn't help but grin as his cheap lighter gained even more gasps than his old See-Far 950. He blew a cloud of smoke at the Priest.

"Father, I am a good man, and I believe myself to be a man selected and trusted by God to change history. Today, we four can avert a thousand years of tragedy, prevent the suffering of millions, and save countless lives. By a few minor actions carried out in the name of King Metriev and his beautiful Queen Ephra, we can leave countless atrocities behind, lost and forgotten in a world that history shall never have known."

He turned his attention to the dumb-struck Metriev, who was trying to make the small fire appear from the Magic Vessel again. Mörrah temporarily forgot her dignity, and tried vainly for a few seconds to wrestle it from him.

"Your Majesties?" said the traveller, politely, "Your Kingdom can be the vast Kingdom of Metriev, a far mightier Kingdom that shall bear your name in the new chapters of history, and will be filled with millions upon millions of loyal citizens. I offer you the chance to remove the blood from over a thousand years of history! And as for the riches you shall so rightly garner.."

The door shook as if it had been hit with a battering ram, making everyone in the room jump. The King gestured to the guard.

"Goury, see who's there and ensure they don't remain there any longer. Then you remain outside, and.. and.. then stay there. Go on, now! And Ephra - stop staring at the guest!"

Mörrah ignored the King. She was intrigued by the prospect of greatness, and leaned forwards onto the table.

"My, aren't we fortunate, Traveller. However, are we to assume this is of no benefit to you, a mere exercise in sleeping easily at night? After all, nulla mensa sine impensa (*..there's no such thing as a free lunch..*), I do believe? "

Metriev flinched, and placed his hand firmly against the table.

"Will you stop doing that, woman? But she's right. What's in it for you, traveller?"

"Perhaps something, perhaps nothing. There are those I know of who will win, and there are those who will justly lose. My own riches shall be won many years from now in the lands of my own time, where I belong. And I enjoy winning so very much, as I'm sure you do, de bene esse, my lady." (*..subject to certain conditions..*)

She eyed him suspiciously, and sat back in her chair. The traveller gave a small laugh and blew a dense ring of smoke. A very low and deep roar came from somewhere outside, and Mörrah laughed to herself at the thought of what must be going on out there. Perhaps the performers' bear was feeling hungry - it wouldn't be the first time an animal had become unpredictable in her presence.

"I promise you both wealth beyond imagination, and I assure you of power matched only by your greatness. A tempting offer?"

"Yes, you do arouse my.. our.. interests," she said, slowly coiling a length of jet black hair around her finger, "..but how is your promise to be realised? And how is it that you bring this Future Knowledge here? By means extraordinary?"

The King nodded.

"Yes, how.. why.. how.. what she says?" he added. Father Czaslas slammed his hand against the table.

"Your Majesties, the man is a travelling fool! Cast him out to.."

Metriev nodded his agreement, and stared at the man. His evasiveness was becoming deeply irritating.

"Choose your words carefully, traveller," he warned.

For the first time the traveller looked angry and allowed his cool persona to slip.

"With or without your help I will remove those who plague me in the future. I merely offer the chance for you to assist me and to therefore occupy history with a dignity that you would otherwise fail to achieve. You are forgotten in the depths of time, and that need not be the case! You wish for more proof of my integrity?"

The traveller put the frame back into his silver case, slipped on a pair of silver gloves and brought out the Stone. It was a dull grey, and lay on the table looking very unimpressive. Silence fell as Mörrah's heart sank - the man was obviously no more than a rich fool from a distant land. Metriev slid the lighter back to him across the table.

"You bring us a stone? Carved and faceted expertly, but a stone none the less," he observed.

"On the outside, perhaps. But put in simple terms, there are people who can ask great favours of this 'stone', and those favours are granted in every detail and without fail - but dependent upon their.. 'abilities', let's say. But unfortunately Requesters are rare, and there are no recognisable traits from one to the next, as far as I can tell. Their abilities vary quite dreadfully, and alas, I'm not gifted in this respect."

"Are you mad? It's a dirty grey stone, not even worthy of being called a gemstone!" barked the King.

"Touch it, Your Highness," the traveller asked, having completely regained his composure. The King reached across the table and touched the Stone, immediately sending a blood-red cloud swirling violently through it. He drew his hand back, quickly.

"That.. that's no stone.. no gem.. and it near burns to the touch?" he said, shocked by its peculiar heat.

Mörrah leaned closer, enthralled.

"The most sublime energy floods and torrents from its every facet," she breathed, wiping a trail of saliva from her chin. This was suddenly becoming far too exciting and fascinating, and she wanted Metriev and Czaslas to be anywhere but here with her. She wiped her chin again, while the King looked at her and sighed. The traveller smiled to himself and took a long draw on his cigar.

"Now then, as I was saying. Generally, the Requesters are unwilling to assist me, and therefore do not survive for long. One lies butchered outside these very walls - a victim of your highly enthusiastic guards. Unfortunately, that particular Requester was responsible for opening a doorway through time which enabled my presence here. With the right servant, I shall have the future world as my Kingdom.. and this world shall be yours."

"And actions now would create such a world for you? Surely the activities of these mere Ground Cr.. citizens is all but worthless over time?" curled Mörrah.

"Consider a mighty oak tree," he began, pausing to tease Mörrah's interest, "Such a tree is a great task for one man to remove in its entirety, is it not? The roots reach far beyond vision or expectations, to say nothing of the cumbersome body standing above ground. In time it gives rise to other trees, equally mighty and an even greater task for one man to remove. If a thousand or more years pass by, that man would be facing an entire forest reaching out as far as the eye can see. Could he even begin to clear the land? Could he ever finish? No, of course not. But if the man were to attack the first insignificant acorn at its planting, the mighty oaks and the endless forest would never be! The problem of eliminating every single trace of the trees would never arise."

"Trees? What are they to do with any.." mumbled the King. Mörrah patted his knee and turned a playful eye to the traveller.

"Do elaborate further. My husband - and I, of course - find your symbolism confusing."

"Yes we do! Tell my wife what you mean," Metriev said, scratching his head and nodding towards her. The man tossed his cigar into the fireplace and took his time lighting another one before continuing.

"If your Kingdom were to prevent a certain other Kingdom from ever existing by annihilating its founding generation, the future world will be a very different one for me to.. work within. That is all you need to know, and all you can possibly comprehend. I need your word that you will follow the actions I have listed in this document."

He handed a thin pile of papers to the King, who glanced briefly at them and passed them to Father Czaslas. Reading was always best left to those who were good at it.

"Have these written out three-fold and returned to my hands by the morning," he said, glaring intently. "And then you can tell me what's.. we can establish what's in them. Seal them all, save for this one. We're not to take chances of loss on these matters. Need I point out that your life is in your own hands, Father Czaslas?" he said flatly. The Priest folded the papers, and looked away.

Mörrah was overflowing with excitement again, and lunged for the Stone but the traveller was too quick. His hand shot out and he calmly put it back in his case.

"Let me hold it!" she cried, knowing that once it was hers, she would never let go of it. The prospect of being more powerful than Lady Morganna and all the other Dark Spirits combined was too much to cope with. She sat back, prepared to bide her time until she could brush aside the fools around her.

"Ah, greed, greed, greed.. the eternal human failing, a relentless pest which blights us all from birth to death," said the traveller, recognising the look in her eyes. Mörrah laughed loudly and clapped her hands.

"You have no idea how true that is, oh traveller, you have no idea at all," she said, smiling wickedly at him and blowing a discrete kiss, after veiling herself from the King with her hair. The man blew her a smoke ring which disappeared around her face, making her shiver with delight. She knew that she would enjoy disposing of him, eventually. He tapped an inch of ash onto the floor, and addressed the Queen.

"Indeed, my work here is almost done and I believe yours is now starting. I'll be needing a Requester to get me back to the time I came from, of course, which you might help with.."

"An edict!" she announced, "We must put out a Royal Edict bringing all who reside in the Kingdom to my.. our.. castle where they shall be assessed for their suitability! Rich or poor, if they are alive they will be tested. And even if they're not alive.."

"Eh? But yes, my thoughts exactly!" added the King.

Father Czaslas stood up, raising the papers above his head.

"What devilry is this? You bring a play-thing of Satan's hordes to our table on this very day of Our Lord? I wish for no part of such evil. Your talk is madness - devilish, malevolent madness!"

He threw the papers into the fireplace, and rushed to the door.

"I leave, and pray the Lord watches over your Souls as he watches over mine! Dei gratia, decrevi.." *(By the Grace of God, I decree..)*

The door slammed shut behind him, turning his rants into soft mumbles.

"Deus vobiscum! Deus vobiscum!." *(God be with you!)* she called after him, and laughed wildly as a mood of triumph filled the room.

"Kindly ignore him," she commented, trying to appear as stable as a Queen ought to, "..barba tenus sapientes *(..he only looks wise)*. Besides, he's afraid of his own shadow - occasionally with good cause, might

I add. Now do write your plans for my Kingdom.."

The door edged open a little, and a shiver ran straight through her, yet again. Today was proving quite a day for shivers. She dismissed it, and carried on.

"..sorry, your plans for my husband's Kingdom, once more. My husband and I have much to prepare!"

She held her hand out for him to kiss, and he promptly did so - and it was his turn to shiver.

"Your Highness is beyond enchanting. I will have them completed by this evening, if you would wish to collect them and.. discuss them, perchance? Or am I being presumptuous? Am I right to assume that hospitality will be offered in this magnificent castle until a Requester be found?"

The door swung open with a tremendous force, and Father Czaslas stood in the doorway pointing a gleaming knife at the traveller, and then at the King.

"You leave me no choice, for you have succumbed to the vilest Devilry!" he shouted at the top of his voice as his men ran in.

A dozen guards and monks filled the room, hacking down the traveller, the King, and the Queen. Czaslas withdrew his sword from the traveller's chest, and stood above the King's body, to finish him. The door of the room across the corridor from the Meeting Room swung open a little further, but fortunately no-one seemed to notice the girl standing there.

CHAPTER TWENTY THREE
Intruders

Linda jumped as a solitary church bell signalled the start of St Alekseev's day of celebration. The banner seemed to tremble with the reverberations as the chimes drifted around the castle, eerily passing from wall to wall until they echoed away to nothing. The Banqueting Hall had fallen silent following the arrival of the traveller, and except for the sounds of an irritated guard removing Linda's goat-hair blanket, the entire castle seemed to have become quiet. A few minutes passed, and the guard wandered back outside.

"Avie, can you go and see what's going on?"

"Now?"

"Big now."

"Okay.. you'll stay here though, you won't go away somewhere?"

"Uh oh, forget what I just said.." whispered Linda.

She caught a glimpse of the traveller being lead from the Banqueting Hall by a Priest and an odd man wearing a small crown. A huge guard marched behind them, nervously glancing around and looking rather shaken. Linda let go of the edge of the banner, praying she wasn't too late and that it would stop swaying before the approaching group could notice. They began climbing the stairs and she pressed herself against the wall, sure that the world was about to end. Her heart almost stopped as Sceleste started wriggling and bristling again, and she prayed her cat would behave herself for just long enough.

A few seconds later, a woman's footsteps hurried from the Banqueting Hall to catch up with the group and she raced by Linda, muttering and tutting as she went, and even brushed against the banner's folds with her arm. The material swayed and rippled as the footsteps went further away, and Linda felt able to breathe once more. And then the music started playing again.

"They all went right by us just now! Blimey.. and the Stone as well! Can you see where they're going, Avie?"

Avalon flew off to follow them, and came back looking excited and very pleased with herself.

"Along a long the 'long a long along a long along longa long.."

"Shhh.. shh.. slow down and start again, with different words. Nice and slowwwwuh this time. Deep breath first."

"They all.. went along.. a long.. long.. corridor. And it's up there on the left. And they went in a room at the end but the door's closed now. It's all gone quiet, so if you're going to make a move, do it whenever you want because it's up to you, really it is."

Linda hurried up the stairs, ran across the huge first floor landing and kept going past room after room. The very last one had the kind of door that was designed to keep absolutely everybody out. There was no keyhole for Avalon to go through, and was obviously intended to be locked from the inside only. Its heavy, dark wood was so thick that Linda couldn't hear anything at all on the other side.

"Can you hear anything?" asked Avalon.

"No, not a word.."

"I don't mean through the door, I mean in the air. High pitched kind of buzzy whistle, getting near ever so quickly?"

Linda strained to hear anything on either side of the door, and wasn't sure what to do. She joined Avalon underneath a small table which stood next to the door's massive hinges. With a little advice, she became completely concealed behind its cloth - all except for her feet, one leg, her back, a lot of hair and an arm, and also Sceleste's tail. Finding somewhere a little safer moved to the top of her list of priorities, even higher than finding the Stone - so once Avalon had said that the weird noise had passed by and gone out of the window, she began to try a few of the doors along the corridor. They all appeared to be locked or maybe just too heavy to open, and she soon arrived back where she started.

"You could always try that one?" said Avalon, pointing at the one opposite the Meeting Room. Its wood was paler and there were far fewer iron strips running across, and it had an elaborate cross carved almost through its centre.

"That's good! Then we can keep an eye on them and the Stone."

Avalon looked bewildered.

"But The Stone's not in this room, is it? If we're going anywhere, we need to be going in the other one, where The Stone went, shouldn't we?" she said, miming the actions with her hands. She ended by flying over to the Meeting Room door, and giving it a kick which almost shook it off its hinges. Fortunately it stayed shut, but most of the metal strips buckled and a few deep cracks appeared in the stonework all around it.

"No, Avie! Not that one!"

"Yes, it is this one.. I saw them all go in there, remember?" she said, innocently. Linda felt the adrenaline version of an atomic bomb explode in her stomach.

"Hide!" she yelped.

"Where?"

"Far away not here!" she babbled while running as fast as she could along the corridor, across the first floor landing, past the main staircase, and on towards the very far end. Her socks were hopeless for running in and even more hopeless for stopping in, and she slid the last few yards like an express train on ice, hitting the end wall with an almighty clatter. Sceleste was not impressed, and gave a dizzy meow. Linda sat facing the wall for a moment, at the foot of an uneven wooden staircase leading upwards. It lead a short way back along the corridor before disappearing into the ceiling, and once she had managed to get her breath back and the world had stopped spinning, she shuffled over to it. She scrambled up them as the Meeting Room's heavy door shut with a thunderous slam.. and she froze half way up the blackened steps.

"Uh oh.." she whimpered.

There was no next floor. There must have been an intention to build another floor at some stage, but that was probably going to be a long way off. For the time being, the steps ended at the white-painted ceiling, allowing just a few inches of space above what would be the first landing.

Heavy, slow footsteps began echoing along the corridor. Avalon flew into the gap, and Linda pushed Sceleste in after her and then pressed hard against the ceiling, hoping something might give way. Nothing happened, so she lay as flat as she could against the stairs, knowing that she was in huge trouble if the footsteps didn't stop and go back very, very soon. The guard steadily walked the length of the corridor, pausing no more than a yard or two before the stairs, his head just within Linda's view.

He tapped his sword against his foot a few times, flicked some dried mud from a deep groove in the floor with its tip, and stood for an eternity without moving. Then he turned around and went back along the corridor. Linda almost cried with relief, and slowly and silently started putting her trainers back on. Crashing into walls was a bad way to get away from people, and she didn't fancy doing it again.

"We're a bit stuck now, aren't we?" said Avalon as she returned from a brief flutter.

"What-do-we-do?" mouthed Linda, helping Sceleste from her hiding place and giving her an apologetic hug - after all, Sceleste was a cat and didn't actually need to be hiding, least of all somewhere so uncomfortable. Avalon had a think, and decided to take matters into her own hands. She flew out from the stairs, singing in a way that very few songthrushes had ever sung, and made her way towards the man at the far end of the corridor. Sceleste followed, and managed to leap up to sit on the square pillar at the top of the main stairs.

Goury looked at the Meeting Room door. He wasn't happy at all. He wanted to be inside the room, seeing the unimaginable miracles that the traveller had brought. But now he was stuck outside with a stupid bird bothering him. He struck out at the annoying creature with his hand.

"Want to play, feathered fool? Well let us play then!" he muttered, following the bird along the corridor and swishing the blade of his sword towards it. The songthrush settled by a cat at the top of the stairs, who dared to stare at him.

"You have a friend? An accomplice in irritation? Well the mightiest sword must taste blood once more today!" he said dramatically, and laughed.

Sceleste licked at one of her paws, unflustered. He swung his sword in a full circle above her head, missing by barely an inch. Incredibly, she wasn't troubled in the slightest and calmly moved her attention to another paw. The sword came around again, this time missing her by half an inch. The guard laughed at the cat's apparent stupidity, and cursed her as she nibbled at her shoulder. He swung again, this time close enough to ruffle the fur on one ear. And then she sat upright, staring straight at him. Playtime was nearly over.

"Oh no, ohnonono.. don't do that, big Person, you run away now, just like me.." whimpered Avalon, and flew as far down the corridor as she could manage, and hid herself in a display of marigolds. The guard gave another mighty swing, and the sword removed a few millimetres of fur from the top of Sceleste's left ear.

"Aha, perhaps the brave small beast wants to play outside? Your ears shall get there first, then your flea-bitten tail, then each of your legs, and.."

Sceleste's yellow eyes narrowed, and she glared at him. Instead of meowing or hissing, she summoned a roar from the depths of Hell.

Linda was shaken down the steps and rolled out into the corridor, where she watched the guard drop his sword as the force of the noise threw him backwards. He struck the wall hard and froze for a moment before stumbling forwards, and falling down the stairs. He became tangled in most of the banners as he went, and smacked into the wall at least twice before falling over the stone banister, dropping ten feet onto the floor where he landed with an armour-plated crash. To his credit, he did manage to stand up a minute or so later and he even tried to walk, but he promptly collapsed into a groaning heap in the very centre of the vast hall. Linda arrived next to Sceleste and peered over the balcony.

"Some people, I don't know.." she mumbled, before noticing that Sceleste was glaring upwards, intently. Linda followed her gaze to where a thin column of dust was trickling from the hall's high-arched roof, and unless she was very mistaken, part of the ceiling was wobbling. A block of masonry the size of a fridge suddenly plunged forty feet and landed with a foundation-shaking smash near to his head, making his entire body bounce with the impact. Sceleste turned her back on the scene and went back to the more important task of licking a paw. Linda winced, and looked at Sceleste for a bemused moment before putting her arms around her.

"Oooza good girl then? Yes woo are, come to mummy!" she cooed as she picked Sceleste up from the pillar, and gave her an extra-special hug. A few guards had already started inspecting the damage and were helping Goury to his feet, so she hurried back along the corridor towards the Meeting Room. Avalon emerged with a sneeze from the flowers and sneezed three more times, and made an important note in her Journal on the Must Not Do page to never hide amongst Yelloworange flowers again - and then she made another one about never, ever waving sharp things at Sceleste. And no blunt things, either.

The pale door opposite the Meeting Room didn't have a handle or keyhole, but it did have a suspicious-looking blackened metal plate. Linda gave it a poke, and it swung in like a letterbox, revealing a bolt which smoothly slid across to the left. The door opened inwards to reveal a large, formal room, which Linda figured was probably used for big important gatherings of big important people. More significantly, it was empty except for a few tables and chairs so she carefully closed the door, leaving a crack of just a few inches to keep an eye out for whenever the traveller might emerge. She jumped when one of the door's lower hinges gave a clunk and a rod fell out, clanking loudly on the floor. It allowed the iron strip across the door's base to rest against the stonework, wedging it open.

"That can't be good.." Linda sighed.

Suddenly the Meeting Room door was thrown open, and a portly man in dark vestments stormed out, shouting in a red-faced rage about something. Whatever it was, he was fuming. Laughter and Latin, two words which didn't normally go together, came from the room before its huge door closed again. The Priest shouted as he made his way down the corridor, calling to anyone who would listen and exploded with anger as he came across the dazed guard in the Entrance Hall. A few moments later, his voice had faded away and all was quiet again.. almost.

Linda inched her door further open, trying to stop the scraping noise of metal against stone. That wasn't easy, but she knew she had to find out what was going on behind that other door. She squeezed through the gap, daring herself to cross the corridor and kneel down to see if there was now a crack between the door's damaged wooden panels and the floorstones. The ground was cold against her face as she pressed close to see or hear anything at all. She leaned her hands against the door, and her heart turned to ice as she felt it move a little. No-one had locked it after the Priest's exit, or perhaps the encounter with Avalon had left it a little less secure than it should have been, but either way it began drifting away from her. She stared almost paralysed as another inch of the room appeared, then two, then three. Avalon gave her braid the biggest tug she'd ever managed, and that did the trick. Linda yelped and suddenly noticed the raucous noise as a mob began shouting and stamping their way up the stairs, and she scrambled back into the safety of her room - just as they turned into the corridor.

Her trainers squeaked and slid on the stone tiles as she tried to close her door more, but the ironwork was well and truly jammed against the floor. The best she could do was to stand with her back against it, hoping no-one would be too bothered by the narrow gap.

The horde arrived in a riot of shouting and clanging swords, and her door shuddered and edged further open as they pushed against it in their impatient charge to the Meeting Room. If there were any protests from the victims, Linda didn't hear them. All she could hear were the sounds of everything in the other room being hacked to pieces, and she held Sceleste close in a futile attempt to block it all out. Her door yielded another inch, and then a few more as furniture was knocked hard against it, and suddenly she wasn't trying to close the door anymore - she was trying to stop it swinging wide open.

And then an unnatural silence slowly descended, steadily replacing the cheering and chanting of the mob. Linda sneaked a look into the corridor, to see if it was safe to leave yet. The blood-drenched Priest and two other men stood just feet away from her. He held the black Stone out in front of himself, looking with disgust at it while the two monks babbled near-silent Latin chants. Linda was too numbed with shock to notice her door creeping further open, slowly at first, but then gaining momentum as it swung under its own weight all the way back to the wall, screeching as it caught on an unevenly raised slab. The group turned away and began to hurry along the reddened floor.

This was not the time to be normal. She couldn't be scared, she couldn't be sick, and she couldn't stay where she was. But she was normal, and she was scared, and she felt like being very, very sick.. and she could also see the Stone being taken away by the Priest.

"Someone will have to do something about that, but not me no way is it me.." she thought, in shock. She watched Avalon flying after the Priest, and wondered how marvellous it would be to just fly through one of the broken windows and leave everything behind, to just take to the air and..

"Oww!" she squealed as Sceleste gave her hand a small nip, prompting her to step into the corridor, avoiding a large wrecked bench immediately outside. The door to the Meeting Room was half open and lurched ominously on its hinges, gaping further away from the wall. Sceleste meowed, as if she was desperate to have a look - or maybe Linda was desperate for a look, overpowered by morbid fascination and just wanting to blame Sceleste. She squelched across the rug and poked her head into the room, agreeing with herself to only open her eyes for a fraction of a second.. but they wouldn't stop opening. And then she wished she hadn't come anywhere near the entire castle at all.

The traveller's body lay blocking the door from opening any more, and drew her eyes into the rest of the carnage. The other bodies lay partially hidden under the splintered table and the savaged remnants of ornate chairs. A silver briefcase lay as empty and twisted as the grey picture frame next to it, and the walls were covered in so much red.. and the world seemed to stop. Linda wasn't sure, and she didn't want to ever be sure, but her eyes had flashed to the fireplace for just the tiniest fraction of a second. Perhaps she only saw some crudely chopped logs looking a bit strange, perhaps it was just her eyes playing their worst ever trick on her, but there was a definite chance that there had been three heads lying in the roaring flames. Maybe.

Sceleste hissed and meowed loudly, struggling to leave Linda's arms and have a closer look, but that couldn't be allowed. She could scratch and bite if she wanted, but nothing was going to keep Linda there for a second longer. She hugged Sceleste and dragged the door as far as it would go, then hurried along to the top of the main stairs to where Avalon had perched. She stood on the stone pillar, anxiously hopping from one foot to the other.

"Don't tell me what was in there.." she said, placing her hands over her ears before coming back to Linda's shoulder.

"No, no chance of that, no chance ever," she replied, stilted but resolute, and moved all of her hair protectively over Avalon.

"Good. That round Priest went down there and I think we should too," Avalon added, struggling to point through all the hair while drawing him in her Journal.

Linda picked up one of the torn blue and yellow banners off the stairs and wrapped herself in it, then raced down to the Entrance Hall. The Priest had marched through an elaborate archway far beyond the Banqueting Hall, and was being applauded by other monks and guards as he made his way past them. Linda stayed a safe distance behind, with her heart fixed on the Stone, and channelled all her shock into the only place where she could possibly deal with what she had seen. She forced herself to imagine that she was flying in the beautiful sunset high above the clouds, ready to swoop down and seize the Stone, easily taking it away to a far, far better place.

She followed Czaslas and his growing entourage along two tall corridors full of arches and sharply-carved Biblical verses. The voices of the ones who chiselled the words into the walls echoed through her head, reciting every letter, and she had to stop for a moment to try and push them all away and claim her mind back for herself.

The last of the Brothers and guards disappeared into the elongated doorway of a decorative building to the rear of the church. Linda took a deep breath and slipped her shades on, then dropped her banner and ran towards the entrance. She stopped the door from swinging shut and tried her hardest to look very, very cool indeed. Operation Freak-Out had begun.

"I demand the return of the Stone!" she announced, trying hard to sound full of authority, but her voice was shaking far too much. The dozen monks and guards stared at her, noticing her peculiar clothes. Avalon had a word of advice.

"Try speaking their language. They don't know what you're.."

"Huh? How?"

"You just do - like you do with meee. It's so easy, if you'll only relax your mind and imagine you're flying.."

"This is hardly the.. look, do your subway-thing and spook them?"

Avalon flew in front of her, and put on a display of Not Me-ing that could win prizes. Sister Mariephred, Emma, a large bear, Dee with a hideous beard and then a strange combination of all four did the trick, helped by Sceleste hissing and writhing on the floor as if she was possessed. Linda found herself laughing uncontrollably not so much because it was funny, but because she couldn't stop herself.

One by one the men either ran away, passed out or suffered a major heart problem. Linda picked her way through the prostrate bodies, removed the Stone from the Priest's cassock and gathered Sceleste in her arms. A few of the monks who hadn't seen Avalon's performance threw anything that came to hand, while those who merely fainted began to stir - and Linda ran. The only place she could think of was the room where she'd been hiding, the one opposite the Meeting Room. She held it in her mind, imagining her mother's picture on one of the tables, maybe Aggy on the stool near the empty fireplace, warm sunlight coming through the windows..

..and then she turned into the corridor that lead into the Entrance Hall, with no idea at all how she had arrived there. She raced past the fallen masonry and launched herself up the stairs, oblivious to the bemused people who were staring at the oddly dressed girl with a cat, and maybe a bird. By the time she arrived in the corridor her feet seemed to weigh at least a ton each and she had the startings of a truly grotesque headache.

The corridor's thin rugs had become darker and stickier, and Linda carefully stepped through the mess determined not to risk falling over. That was far too disgusting to think about. And then she froze for a heart-stopping moment. Shuffling sounds were coming from the Meeting Room, which made her wonder if the sound of her footsteps might have attracted the attention of whoever was in there. She needed time to think, but there simply wasn't any. She hurried back into the Prayer Room and madly tried to pull the door away from the wall, but it had wedged itself wide open against the floor.

"Avie! Can you close it?" she said, from a safe distance in the room.

"Hmm.." Avalon hummed as she flew behind the door to assess where to kick. Linda heard a pathetic tap. A split second later it had swung shut with a wall-rocking slam which could probably have been heard on Jupiter. For a moment it appeared to be a job well done, but then the door slowly toppled forwards, landing in the room with a resounding whumf and sending up a storm-cloud of dust.

"Sorry.. big oops just there," she called, darting back to Linda's shoulder. They hurried to the empty fireplace at the far end of the room, and hid behind a chunky wooden table. Avalon was getting stressed, and flew in small circles, tying herself up in the braid.

"What do we do now? What do we.."

"Uhh.. let me think. Maybe we could just aim to go anywhere but here.. how about going to when we left Odessa in the future?"

"Yes yes yesyesYES! Why?"

"Well.. my stuff's there, for a start. And it won't be so bad anymore, will it? No-one'll be after us."

Avalon looked blank.

"The Stone won't have been hidden away for hundreds of years because it'll only be a legend won't it? One tiny appearance now is going to be long-forgotten by the time we get back. Nobody really knows what it can do and hardly anyone's seen it - so there'll never be a Cult, no dodgy Government types, no nothing. Just us three."

"I like that! That's just us, yes, good thinking!"

"And that doesn't happen very often. We'll have changed things for the better, and we might be able to do good things all over the world with this Stone!"

Sceleste gave a meow, and Avalon nodded enthusiastically.

"Brilliant! Do it, do it do it doowitdoooowit.."

Linda closed her eyes while Avalon settled back on her shoulder.

"Okay.. Odessa, beautiful Odessa.. I'm thinking of 1313 Shuiskaia Stree.. whatever's Ukrainian for street. Our room on the top floor, with the iffy floorboard by the wide window.. it's nailed over the wide window, actually.."

Linda spoke clearly and confidently, and gave as many details as she could remember, especially the time and date in order to avoid any more self-duplicating or Stone-vanishing predicaments. But nothing was happening because.. because.. Avalon was distracting her too much, patting her nose and calling.

"Li-i-hin-udahahhh.." she warbled loudly for the fifth time. Sceleste hissed and jumped from her lap, causing her to open her eyes. And then Linda wondered if she'd ever close them again.

The Queen had stumbled through the doorway, grimacing and covered in blood, adjusting her head back onto her shoulders. She stood in the centre of the room, wiping the wounds from herself and flicking the blood from her hand. Finally, she pushed her jaw back into place and wiped away some of the burns from her face. Her eyes fell upon Linda and she began striding forwards.

"My, those were such interesting words from.. another traveller? Have I found another in my castle, trying to return from whence she came? An escape to a time and a place unfamiliar to my ears.. oh, how intriguing. But what's this? She's with a dirt-faery, and a.. a.."

The Queen's expression changed to deep uncertainty as she looked down at Sceleste who was standing just in front of Linda, arching her back and hissing. Avalon looked from Sceleste to the Queen, sensing something familiar in the woman's eyes. The Queen pointed at Sceleste, then into Linda's very heart.

"You bring a Bearer of Sacred Curses as well? One who walks within Death? Such contemptible intruders.."

Linda tried hard to believe what she was seeing and made an effort to tune her mind into the blood-covered woman. Her fear and the shouting coming from the grounds outside weren't helping her to concentrate and she missed every third or fourth word, but she got the general idea of what the Queen was saying. The Stone glowed warmly in her pocket, and she found the strength to stand up.. and even speak.

"You.. you were dead! I saw you lying in that room and your head was.. yes it was in the.. you're dead.. what are you?" Linda called, her voice faltering far too much.

"What am I? You ask what, rather than who, child? Perhaps I might forgive a fool's slip of the tongue. I am the Queen Ephra, made of flesh and blood, and I most certainly care to know who you are, intruder! Speak, child!" she commanded, as the rips in her clothing repaired themselves.

Linda couldn't say a word. She felt an invisible hand closing around her neck, squeezing and losing its grip over and over again.

"Hah!" Mörrah spat, "Your voice has betrayed you as much as your eyes! You saw nothing!"

The hand moved down through Linda's shoulder to form an icy

cloud around her inside pocket.

"Ah, the vile thief has something of mine.. don't make me take it from you! To steal that which has already been stolen would be.."

Sceleste walked a tight figure of eight, and then twice again in the opposite direction, never taking her eyes from the Queen. The woman shuddered as if she'd been struck by lightning, and fell back towards the doorway. She stood up, in agony and breathing hard, and her face twisted as she tried to step closer again. Avalon left Linda's shoulder for a moment, hovering close to Sceleste and pointing up at the Queen.

"You can't cross a Curse Bearer.. you can't cross her.. and People can't kill you.. you're a Ved'ma!" she said, returning quickly behind Linda's neck.

"She's a Ved'ma? What, like Mörrah?" said Linda, without thinking. The whites of the Queen's eyes changed to a deep, burning red and a fury raged inside her. Her fingernails grew long and black like talons, and she pointed them all at Linda.

"Child! What Demon Blood runs through your veins? Speak, damn you!" she screamed at Linda, who's legs finally gave way. She crawled out of sight behind an overturned table close to where Sceleste was still firmly standing her ground. Mörrah pointed a deathly white hand at the table, and Linda felt the sharp nails scratching at her face as if they were trying to tear into her. Sceleste hissed and pounced forwards, making Mörrah stumble away, brushing wildly at the air between them as she fell. She writhed on the floor and began screaming at Linda while her skin blistered and burned. With each word her voice rose closer to hysteria.

"You dare utter the name of Mörrah? My name is beyond you! I demand you tell how your kind should know of me, lest I bring every Spirit of Darkness to.."

A monk rushed in, striking her with an ancient black spear and knocking her hard against the ground. Five more immediately followed, surrounding her with crucifixes and silver emblems while Father Czaslas threw great handfuls of Holy Water over her, chanting loudly after each one. An elderly, senior monk arrived, already repeating verses from a worn old book, and quite oblivious to the chaos around him. Mörrah screamed incomprehensible words to curse their souls, and then all the monks descended upon her.

Linda grabbed Sceleste and crawled out through a doorway near the fireplace, not daring to stand up until long after she had turned a corner and been tugged and told repeatedly by Avalon that it was a better idea to be running rather than crawling. And then she did run, faster than she'd ever managed before and wondered if she was somehow using the Stone to help her along. The wide corridors went past in a blur until her head pounded and her lungs began to feel as if they were full of acid, so she slowed for a while to look for a place to hide and get her thoughts together.

Linda turned corner after corner along the quiet corridors, and finally staggered up a flight of stairs - to arrive at a dead end. The short corridor ended in a huge stained-glass window, a small entry to a staircase, and very little else. Avalon flew up the stairs and came straight back down, happy that no-one had been there to surprise her, and even happier because she'd just been really useful.

The stairs lead around in a tight spiral up to a short, gloomy corridor that had been blackened with coal dust. The first two doorways lead to what appeared to be individual Maid Rooms, and the other two doorways were just staircases leading down - and Linda heard, or sensed, a lot of shouting drifting up from them. But the final room of the corridor was ideal. Its solid door swung open easily, revealing a large, plain bedroom with a huge four poster bed on the far side. Linda quickly set about piling as much furniture as she could manage to block the door, but couldn't get the bed to move. She gave up pulling and shoving, and left it at a strange angle which would normally have driven her mad, but at that particular moment she didn't even notice. Finally, she slid the door's heavy bolt across and its heavy thunk almost made her feel safe, for the first time since arriving.

She looked out of a shattered window at the guards running to and fro in the Trading Courtyard far beneath her, and stared at the frantic monks in their different coloured vestments. They all seemed to be carrying anything at all that was even remotely religious. The world down there was going completely berserk.

Sceleste lay on the bed as if nothing at all was going on, scratching at the gold-embroidered sheets and widening a big hole that she had caused, while Avalon hovered to find her Serious Thinking Level. She flew over to Linda, staying at exactly the right height all the way.

"So make sure I've got this straight, Lindy? Even if we'd never come here, Mörrah's always known about The Stone?"

"Uhuh, looks like it. And that's probably why there were so many curses and hexes around it back in the underground Chapel where we found it, too."

Sceleste gave a weak meow, and then started another hole, in a peculiar triangular shape.

"Don't worry, Sceleste sweety - we're not going back there ever," added Linda. "And I reckon The Silent Keepers weren't just keeping it from bad people, they were keeping it from her as well, and that must be why 'the second Queen Ephra' was banished from here. I'm not surprised."

Avalon nodded her agreement, and looked relieved.

"So we haven't messed anything up?" she asked, straightening some of Linda's wilder waves.

"I don't think so.. I mean, the Priest and the monks killed them all and took the Stone, and that had nothing to do with us. And then the Queen came back to life to get the Stone and the Brothers figured she was a Ved'ma and they must have gone curse-mad to protect themselves and the Stone as well. And they would have done that anyway, whether we were here or not. So.. I think we're completely in the clear. If anything, we've improved things because once we get back to our time.. the cult would never have existed! Wow."

"So Brother Dalovich was totally right, wasn't he?"

"Umm.. apart from missing out one or two little useful bits, he was completely spot on," said Linda, to keep life simple. Avalon cheered and settled down over on Sceleste, and began attending to the short fur on the top of one ear. Linda sat next to them on the bed hoping that her headache had gone for good, and tried to get everything straight in her mind before risking a return to Odessa.

"And I bet that's why she trapped you in the Matryoshka Doll - she wasn't just being mean, she did it because she didn't like you knowing that the Stone was real, and she didn't want Kupula or anyone else in Hesperides to know it was real either! She must have spent centuries dreaming up a million failed ways to get her hands back on it before her life was due to run out. Wow, I feel like Sherlock Holmes' scary sister, the one none of them ever talk about."

Sceleste's ear looked fine once again, and she gave Avalon's leg a big 'thank you' lick. Avalon suffered a silent agony, rather than risk annoying her.

"Eww, cat lick!" she mouthed to Linda and giggled, "..but none of that matters now, does it? We've got it, and she can't ever have it!"

"Yup. Mission accomplished, and I think we're.."

Furious shouting and screaming broke out in the courtyard, and Linda looked from the tower's window to see a heavily wounded Mörrah rushing from a doorway. Her feet didn't seem to be on the ground as she raced and glided to the centre of the square, where she came to a sudden halt. She slowly turned around, trying to sense where her prey was hiding. And then she looked up to her bedroom window, fixing her red eyes on Linda. She smiled to herself, and raced across to another door.

"Uh oh.. she's sorted out the monks for the time being!"

Linda picked up Sceleste, stood beside the bed and closed her eyes. She found it hard to imagine flying anywhere, and knew she wasn't likely to feel calm enough to even try.. but she had to. Avalon hummed to her, and Linda slowly forced her mind to be above the clouds, soon soaring her way to somewhere better.. somewhere that was already giving her a headache. She ignored the pounding sensation and started talking about their room in Odessa, while Avalon settled on her shoulder and wrapped herself in the braid.

"Okay.. back to Odessa.. 1313 Shuiskaia.. Street whatever, to our room on the top floor with my mum's picture, and Aggy, my suitcase, and Sceleste's dinner plate by the bed, the split floorboards.. an hour or two after we left so we don't duplicate ourselves.."

Linda sensed the room changing, the temperature altering a little and the air becoming filled with the smell of old wood, tobacco, damp.. and she knew she was back, back to a world where nobody would be after them.. and her headache drifted away. She opened her eyes, blinking in the sudden, impenetrable darkness of night. Avalon whimpered and unravelled herself from the braid.

"Avie? What's wrong? It's only night time, there's nothing to.."

Avalon had moved down onto Sceleste and was trembling all over, staring out into the darkness. Even Sceleste was growling in Linda's arms, her every muscle fraught and tense. Linda stared into nothing but blackness. 113 candles lit themselves in a circle on the floor around her, and Linda shivered as the sharp, penetrating clacks of a woman's footsteps broke the silence. A figure emerged from the darkness, vaguely revealed in the orange glow.

"Welcome back, child," she breathed, "I've been waiting a long, long time for you."

CHAPTER TWENTY FOUR

Lehane Eidahr

Mörrah walked around the circle, drifting in and out of the darkness, her footsteps not always coinciding with her appearances.

"How many years have I waited for this moment?" she said, slow and full of gloating, unable to hide her loathing of the three before her. She opened a thick, old book and stood just within the flicker of the candles, losing her features in the shadows.

"So many years, too many years. Your theft has plagued me, filled every moment of my life with the tormented memories of that which might have been, that divine object of beauty you clutch.. that for which you have no right!"

"Why were you there?" spluttered Linda, struggling to keep hold of Sceleste while attempting to sound confident at the same time. Mörrah laughed, sending an icy chill blowing across Linda's face, even causing Sceleste to shiver. She slowly turned another page of her book, enjoying the crackling sounds of the aged paper.

"You ask why? Can you possibly imagine how tiresome life can become when walking an ageless path, knowing it's to continue for a millennium? One has to step into positions of authority on occasion simply to make it all pass by somehow. Such games and diversions are there to be taken."

Avalon kneeled up from behind Sceleste's head.

"You're not supposed to do that - you'll be in so much trouble with Lady Morganna!"

Mörrah looked shocked that a faery as low as Avalon had dared speak to her.

"Silence, moth! I took my risks and yes, I took my fates. I suffered the Repentance for such transgression. But the Gemstone you denied me will be worth more than any retribution a Spiritae could ever face. These past centuries will count as nothing!"

She ran a finger down a page of sharp writing, and lightly tapped at a manically scrawled line in the middle.

"Ahh.. yes.. even now I remember the day as yesterday, that day upon which The Stone was brought unto me and delivered to my Castle, placed before my very hands.. and how I resent the memory of the truly vile Traveller who carried it to me. Never had I met a Ground Crawler so enticing and yet so worthy of destroying. But he had that Gem, that which could make me powerful beyond all others, to live beyond the reach of those who would dare dream of reaching me. But it was taken, cruelly snatched by a Gifted One, leaving me to face the agony of banishment within my own land."

Linda tried to think of being back in England, back in the grounds of St Teresa's, near to the Quiet Area where hardly anyone ever went. She tried to picture the tall holly bushes, the conker tree, the wobbly bench where she thought she half-saw her mother once.. but nothing happened. The headache returned with its first full throb, and Mörrah laughed.

"Difficulties? The Stone disobeys you? Look around, foolish one, look around. You think I would be unprepared for this moment?" she whispered.

Linda's eyes had adjusted enough in the darkness to see thousands upon thousands of strange symbols and incantations written all over the walls. She could almost understand their meanings, and sensed that her mind was being blocked by powerful lines of magic.

"If you were banished then why are you still alive? You need people to feed on!" called Avalon, before shuffling well out of sight behind Sceleste. Mörrah reappeared on the other side of the circle, lost in her own thoughts for a few seconds. She turned two more pages of her decayed book, and a few cracked strips of parchment fell from it. They burned quickly in the candle light, and her eyes fell upon Linda again.

"The banishment.. was dreadful at first, and I hated returning to the existence I had known before my time as Queen.. but humans are so weak, and their sufferings let me grow again. With a little effort, rumours and tales spread of the miraculous Gemstone and all the riches, the power and the wealth it could bring.. and of the three putrid creatures who carry it, of course. Some chose to believe, and others were encouraged with suffering or occasional gifts of Magics - and that kept them in my hand, or each other's. But their greed for unearned rewards has passed from generation to generation, and kept me strong. Very strong. Perhaps I should thank you?" she said, and snorted callously.

"Did you like my story? Do you know who the three putrid creatures are?" she added, her voice hanging in the darkness.

"But.. but we were only there an hour or two at the most - and hardly anyone saw us," Linda choked.

Mörrah held a hand up, and thirteen of the candles went out.

"Think of the madness on that day, and think of the excitement you brought into their dull lives. Such people are want to talk, and they talk a great deal - and repetition is so rarely accurate. A tale can grow and change many, many times.. and who better to listen to than those blessed with Magic?" she laughed.

Another thirteen flames disappeared, and the remaining candles began flickering as if draughts were catching them from every direction. Linda felt cold air rushing past her as if she was standing in a stream on a winter's day.

"Belief in the Stone ensured belief in me. I've been content to remain out of sight of your kind, preferring only to be known by my Believers, and there to offer guidance to the most trusted ones when necessary, to ensure that faith in the Stone's great power would spread. Now there are Institutions and Cults, there are Believers behind doors, all aware that today is to be their great day. But their great day is mine, for now I have no need of their petty faith!"

Linda felt a shiver run down her spine. Mörrah drifted backwards, and reappeared further to the right.

"So perhaps times have changed since you were last here, thief? Perhaps the Odessa you left is not the Odessa you have returned to, and your game has affected history? Would you like to find out?"

A door slammed shut somewhere downstairs, reminding Linda that she was standing in a room that held her mother's picture somewhere in the darkness, as well as Aggy and a pile of Abba cd's. A series of candles flickered back into life, briefly. Mörrah stepped on them one by one, laughed and closed her book.

"And thus my Book Of Abhorrence is complete.. every thought of you that has ever burned in my mind, all the tortures that I have contended with every day and night of my life.. the hundreds upon hundreds of years spent waiting for you.. each of my persecutions is engrained here, each one scribed in the blood of.. of.."

The book trembled in Mörrah's hands as her words trailed away, and she lost herself for a few final moments of obsessive loathing. She glared down at the pages and wallowed in their venom, drawing her fingers across the words to feel the bitterness of each one. She breathed in with enough force to lift and pull the pages upwards, and then breathed out for so long that the room filled with her breath's aged stench. She looked back to Linda.

"And now it's all over. I'm loathe to burn these, for each and every vexated page holds such strength and such feeling.. but that, child, is the true victory of this day. I have overcome the torment, and now that you are here.. you must pay for the ills you have caused me."

She bent down and held the book above a candle until the small flame leapt across the cover. She smiled in the bright crimson glow as the volume burned away, page by page, and she seemed untroubled as the flames engulfed her hand. Linda kept herself attuned to Mörrah's voice, her body language and her emotions, but sensed almost nothing. Seeing her in the stronger light, she bore only a passing resemblance to the Queen. Her eyes were perhaps similar, her hair was still jet black, but her slender features and even more slender shape were new, no doubt fashioned in whatever way would wield more power over the latest generation of her Believers. Linda kept watching her in the diminishing light, trying to read her, trying to sense.. anything.

Mörrah stood up and brushed the ashes and burns from her skin, and pointed at Linda with a curl, or twist, of her fingers.

"Your silence amuses me, but I grow tired of being with you. Hand over my beloved Gemstone, and perhaps I will consider sparing your Soul. Do NOT trouble me further.." she grinned.

Mörrah waited for a few seconds and folded her arms while more candles disappeared, steadily sinking the room further into darkness. Thirteen remained, evenly spaced around the circle. Avalon stood on Sceleste's head, and whispered to Linda.

"Tell her she'll have to take it.. she might not be able to cross Sceleste even with all these years of thinking how to! And tell her she's a miserable cave-dog.. and she never washes either.. and.. she lives in a cave and.. and she never washes, and.. she likes smelly things.."

Without knowing if she actually spoke, Linda dared her to take it. Mörrah threw her arms wide, and in the dull light seemed to grow taller as bright red veins flashed across her black gown like scarlet lightning. She threw her head back and screamed.

"I command you to surrender my Gemstone! Let me take the world that was and always shall be mine! I have waited too long for this day and I will not wait any.."

The doors opened and Linda held Sceleste even closer while a procession of shrouded Believers in black vestments quickly filed in, working clockwise around the room until they stood three-deep in a circle. Two of them carried burning torches and stood either side of Linda whispering quietly and rhythmically to themselves. Mörrah didn't even look at them.

"Ah, my closest Believers!" she said, raising her hands either side of herself. "The vile creature has declined my offer. Take the Gemstone from her, lead them to the Burial Ground and commit them to earth.. but ensure the child is last - her final moments must be filled with her companions' suffering. Do it now!"

Her orders were met with an ominous silence, and nobody moved.

"Did you not hear? I command you to take from her that which is mine!" she screamed, and her voice shook through the floorboards.

A pair of hands lightly rested on Linda's shoulders and drew her backwards into the mass of black robes, and suddenly the torch-carriers' whispering turned into loud chanting. Thirty or more voices immediately joined them, all reciting the old Czaslas Texts that had lain secret and unused for so long, forcing Mörrah into the corner of the room. Her voice soared into a hysteria of anger and panic.

"You dare betray me? You DARE to be.."

Linda was guided from the room feeling confused and scared, too relieved for words to be leaving the madness behind. She was lead into the well-lit hall and stairway, where despite everything that was going on around her, she found herself wondering if the walls and staircase had been in such good condition last time she had seen them. A man in decorative golden robes and gloves stepped in front of her and took the Stone, much to Sceleste's annoyance. Linda stroked her, knowing that there was practically nothing she could do - for the time being. People in blue and white gowns stood at the end of the staircase casting rose-petals at her feet as she neared them. She stared as she went by, unsure whether to say 'thank you' or not, so Avalon said it instead.

The street outside was definitely different. It was still a grim street with a crossing at either end, and still had the rows of dilapidated and run-down houses, but the pavement was perfect, the intricate street lights beamed out strong yellow light, and the houses either side of 1313 were anything but neglected. Linda stared at them, turning around trying to work out how much had changed, or if her imagination and memory were just ganging up on her again.

A bearded man in white robes and a gravestone hat opened the doors of a waiting Bentley, and politely prompted her into its cavernous and lavish interior. He followed and sat opposite her, looking alternately nervous and pompous. He made a sign in front of himself, then removed his peaked cap and bowed his head, as did the man next to him and also the chauffeur. Linda looked at Avalon, and they both shrugged. The car started moving, and Linda watched as a more people in black vestments raced into Number 1313. The bearded man finally spoke.

"Lehane Eidahr, it is my privilege to welcome you. We are at your command. Your arrival had been long foretold, and we are honoured.." he said, bowing his head again and losing his words into the depths of his beard. Linda stared at the bushy explosion, and wondered what could possibly make someone want to walk around with all that growing out of their face.. and she felt pleased that her father didn't have one anymore.. but he wasn't actually her father any more, was he? And in fact he wouldn't even know her if he met her, and neither would her mother, or the fam.. a few pokes from Avalon put her mind back on track.

"Uhh.. Leeharnuh who?" she said, "I'm Linda. Linn-dahh."

The man looked impassive.

"Lehane Eidahr, that is your name as the writings have shown us. Your sacred title means Bringer Of Enlightenment And Power. Our very oldest scrolls inform us that you are the Gatherer Of Light, the Reclaimer Of The Stone, the Glorious Gifted One. And as promised in the Verse Of Truth in the First Chapter Of Prophecy, you have come to us, bearing The Stone, guarded in Sacred Trinity," he said, respectfully gesturing to Avalon and then Sceleste.

Avalon giggled and Linda went red. If cats could laugh, Sceleste must have come pretty close with the strangest meow Linda had ever heard. The man still looked remarkably serious, though.

"No, you don't understand," she continued, "You've come to me. About four or five hours ago me and Avalon and Sceleste went back to 1186 to stop the Stone being stolen from the traveller who'd brought it, and that was one big mess like you wouldn't believe - although you probably would, come to think of it, but this is hardly the time for all that and anyway we managed to get it and then we came back just now.. but I think Mörrah's been up to no good since those olden days and.. you do know she's a Ved'ma don't you? You see, the people in the castle didn't seem to know that and neither did I for a while and there was so much trouble when.."

The man nodded appreciatively.

"You're tired, I see. We have prepared living quarters which we trust will be worthy of your Blessed presence. We hope your Palace Of The Stone will please you."

"Palace of the Stone?"

"You will see. It is not for me to explain."

Linda sat back, wondering if she'd misunderstood everything he'd been saying. For no good reason, a question appeared in her mind and felt as if it turned her brain upside down.

"Are you speaking English, or am I reading you without even knowing I'm doing that now? You see, I think I'm losing track of what I do and when I do it, like my mind's all over the place."

He looked puzzled and had to think for a while before answering.

"Do my lips match the words as you understand them?"

"Uhh.. yes, they do," Linda replied, watching closely.

"Should that make any difference?" he added.

"I don't know."

"And perhaps it's better that you don't."

Linda decided to stop talking. This was becoming more weird than all the other weird things put together, and there had been far too many of those already. Avalon sat up on the ledge of the Bentley's window, leaning against the glass and looking out at the passing streets of Odessa. She knew almost every inch of the entire city, but now noticed that some buildings were different, and one or two weren't where they should have been. And occasionally people would look at the car as they drove past, and some even fell to their knees. She hovered to Linda, poked her on the chin and went back to the window.

"It's different out there isn't it, Lindy? Mörrah's changed things.." she said, pointing out a new tree.

"Avie, I dread to think what yarns Mörrah's been spinning over the years to keep her Believers so obsessed. I think we're just going to have to watch what happens for a while," she whispered, as much with her mind as with her voice.

"And then you'll figure out what to do?" yawned Avalon.

"Yup, I'll figure out what to do. We're in a mess.. and you are too, Sceleste, aren't you.. yes you are," she said, giving her a hug. Avalon jumped down and joined in.

CHAPTER TWENTY FIVE

The Palace Of The Stone

After half an hour of silence, the car and its lengthy entourage arrived at the high-walled entrance to the palace. Three security guards struggled to open the heavy iron railings, gradually drawing them aside to reveal a distant spot-lit building which resembled a collection of inter-connected stately homes, rather than somewhere like Buckingham Palace. Linda watched as they drove past clusters of cheering people who lined the mile-long driveway. The main building was magnificent, and the Bentley pulled up outside the white entrance while the other cars went further along the looping drive.

The man beside the driver stepped out of the car and hurried to open her door, while another appeared from the Aston Martin parked behind them. He raced up the steps in order to be standing in the gaping doorway ready with her suitcase and a jewelled chest, from which Aggy and her blankets poked out. He was waved away by a butler who stood at the head of a line of important-looking people. Each of them bowed in turn as she walked past, and more than half seemed overcome with emotion. The bearded man, who Linda classed as being Facially Afflicted or maybe Follically Indulgent, lead her along a wide corridor. Everything was highly decorated, shining, and probably expensive. The portraits weren't exactly pleasant, but at least they weren't the disturbing kind that had been in the Chapel. The thought of the Chapel suddenly made Linda feel better. It had never existed, so none of the sick portraits of forlorn Gifted Ones had ever been done, because there was no-one to be painted. And that made her feel so good - confused, but good.

She came to a halt at a pair of white double doors which reached high up to the ceiling. The man knocked twice on one side and only once on the other, and after a few seconds Linda imagined doing the extra knock to even it out.

"I'm slipping there," she thought, knowing that there was a time when she would have done the extra knock for real. A few minutes passed and he began to look embarrassed.

"You are to be greeted by our Masters," he said quietly, "I thank you for your time, and I hope I have not caused any undue stress or confusion on our journey from the city," he said in a sombre manner.

"No, umm.. it was fine, really. Very good car-work and all that," she said, searching for anything to say. She was tempted to mention his beard-issues and door-imbalance, but was starting to feel too tired for anything. Instead she gave a smile and waited for him to open the doors, and was eventually shown through into the kind of room that stretched the word 'ostentatious' twice around on itself.

"Woah, look at all this.." she whispered, feeling rather lost as she settled into a huge leather chair, facing a desk. She was alone except for the obtrusive ticking of three clocks, one in each corner of the room. The fourth was silent, but its hands were making small bouncing movements as if they were nearly-stuck at the midnight position. Sceleste decided to go for a walk, and Avalon took the opportunity for a sleepy circuit of the room, paying no attention to anything at all. She came back to Linda and wrapped herself up underneath a few waves of hair on her shoulder.

Linda turned around to see where Sceleste had gone, noticing the thousands of books lining the walls and the strange kerosene lamps which hung from ornate struts between each one of the walls' narrow jade columns. Sceleste appeared from under the chair, and settled back in Linda's lap, quietly demanding some attention.

One of the bookcases swung open, and two elderly men walked in. Their robes were cream, which Linda assumed meant they were incredibly important. They bowed to her, raised their white and gold skull caps, and sat behind the desk on ludicrously high-sided chairs - which were also in cream.

"Hello, and I'm pleased to meet you. I'm not sure I recognise you?" asked Linda, using one of her father's lines for gaining the upper hand with new people. He would always speak first and put the other person on the backfoot, regardless of how famous, important, scary or intimidating they looked. Apparently, this was a good idea in any given situation unless the other person was holding a gun, in which case it was much wiser to let them do all the talking. The man with the wider and less-grey moustache spoke in a voice entirely void of emotion or personality.

"It is an honour to meet you Lehane Eidahr, we are truly proud to be present at this historic moment. We trust your journey was acceptable?"

Linda stared at him, not entirely sure what to say. Her stomach loudly rumbled a reply, and Sceleste meowed in sympathy. Linda realised that she was tired, hungry and really needed some time to think - and maybe to play an Abba track or two. This was rapidly becoming the wrong time of day for her to be dealing with two excessively-serious types while being treated like a three-headed visitor from a distant galaxy. The man gave a subtle gesture for her to give a more acceptable reply.

"Uhuh, the journey was fine, thanks. I.. err.. didn't catch your name?" she said, hoping not to appear pushy. The other man smiled at that, and his colleague shifted in his chair.

"I am Lehane Primus, and this is Brother Syrus Lehane," he said, not taking his eyes from her. Linda noticed the Lehane word again.

"About that Lehane bit.. you see, I think Mörrah must have mis-heard my name in the castle ages ago, so although it's okay for me, it's hardly an appropriate one for two such uhh.. unfemale gentlemen of your umm.. respectable years, you know."

He stroked his moustache, and looked down at her through his overhanging eyebrows. She stifled a yawn, and felt its bigger brother coming on.

"Gifted One, only those in the highest authority bear your title. I am in such authority. My role in your Palace is to govern the lives of those who believe in you, and to oversee the accurate teachings of the words of The Eternal Lady Mörrah, and nurture all that is.."

Sceleste wriggled and Avalon sighed loudly, prompting Linda to make an interruption.

"That's nice and everything, and I don't mean to be pushy but it's been such a long day for us, especially these two," she said, gesturing to Sceleste and then to Avalon, "..and I have no idea what's going on or why I'm here or anything," she said, realising that she probably did sound very pushy. Primus took his time before replying, in the same way her father would pause whenever he was either being particularly annoying or attempting to take control of a conversation. Or both. Linda wondered for a moment if he still did that, and what the family would all be doing right now, thousands of miles away in Happy Land.

"This gentleman is Brother Syrus Lehane, who is my counterpart in Educational Research, and happens to be the one who will help you to settle into your new environment. He will.."

The white phone gave a politely subdued ring, and Primus waited until the fifth before picking it up. He listened and said nothing, then slowly put it down.

"Do forgive my brevity, but I am called away. It appears events around you this night have brought changes in our hierarchy. If you will be so kind as to excuse me, I must bid a temporary farewell," he said, bowing his head as he walked backwards to the hidden door. It closed after him with a firm double-click.

"Is he your new friend, Lindy?" whispered Avalon, leaning against her ear.

"I don't know.. I haven't got a clue," Linda whispered back.

Brother Syrus Lehane blew his nose, and apologised with a glance. He shuffled his chair closer to the desk, and smiled.

"As you may have noticed, I am Brother Syrus," he said, already sounding far friendlier than Primus.

"Hello then, Brother Syrus. Are you going to act like a Dormitory Head for me?" Linda asked, and gave up fending off the yawn.

"Hmm.. that's a little impersonal, but yes, I will if you'd like that," he said, in the kind of warm voice that Linda imagined a grandfather should sound like.

"I'm the one you can call upon for life's luxuries and essentials. Anything you want, you ask for me. Anything bothers you, ask for me. Anything at all. We could try now.." he suggested, and cleared his throat in a mock attempt to be formal. "Is there anything you would like, Your Most Sacred Highness?"

His eyes were a soft grey-blue, and she couldn't help but feel some of her tension drift away. She even managed a smile.

"Well.. we're all hungry. Like I was saying, it's been a long day already, and it seems to be getting longer and also a lot weirder by the minute. Avie loves hazelnuts with a dollop of strawberry jam, and for a side-order she'd like a capful of mineral water, but not the fizzy stuff or she'll fall over.. and Sceleste's a one for full-cream and the usual catfood stuff of course, but she might like to try some salmon, maybe. And I'm just plain famished. A gallon of flat Diet Coke would be nice, if they've got a bottle that's had its lid left off for a while.. that'd be lovely. Maybe not a gallon, though. And could you check they got my mum's picture?"

"Ah, an easy task to start with.." he smiled, and picked up the refined telephone. He ran through the items, added a few here and there, and stood up.

"Your picture is with all your possessions, don't worry. Now, I think my Study would be easier for talking - it's much less formal. Would you prefer that?"

Linda nodded and he lead her through another hidden doorway and they eventually arrived in a neat room which was lit only by a small and very warm fireplace. Books and dozens of charcoal sketches of running animals covered every wall, and an enormous old-fashioned globe took up almost an entire corner. He gestured towards the well-padded settee alongside it, and sat down in a chair opposite her. The soft smell of tobacco soon filled the air as he began trying to light an elegant pipe, and the food arrived by the time he managed to get it going properly. Linda noticed that the person pushing the trolley didn't dare to look at her, keeping his eyes firmly on the silver dishes, then the floor, and finally the door.

"I must say, Your Most Sacred High.." Syrus began.

"Limna, jus' Limna's ohkay," she said, through a mouthful of chicken sandwich.

"Thank you, Linda. I must say, I would expect that you're finding it rather hard to understand any of this, perhaps?"

"Mmm, and then some. I don't know what's going on anymore. All we did was go back to 1186 to stop the Stone being stolen so that a really bad cult wouldn't exist and horrible people wouldn't ever be able to try using it wrongly - and we actually managed to get it, for a while. But then we came back to Number 1313 and everything's different, and now I'm here and everyone's being so.. umm.."

"Odd?"

"That's the word," Linda nodded, as Sceleste fell asleep with Avalon snuggled into her fur.

"Well, a great deal may have altered in your absence - a brief trip for you would have resulted in enormous changes through the intervening years - but ones that are only apparent to yourself, of course. Indeed, your simple visit to a land long ago has caused centuries of waiting and planning by many generations, solely for this great day."

Linda could see the sense there, but it was hidden extremely well.

"Huh?" she managed to ask.

"You are someone we've been expecting."

"Ohhh. So now I'm here, what's next?"

"Next? Well, our Lady Mörrah has many great plans - but she gives little of her true thoughts away, and that does concern me at times, I must say. She can be a frightening creature, I find."

"Over in the other building she got sorted out by people in black, and then I got taken to the car and someone took the Stone off me.."

Syrus sat upright, and grinned widely.

"Aah, I wondered if there was trouble afoot. That explains why you're still alive," he said, and re-lit his pipe.

"Huh?"

"Don't be scared. She's an aged Ved'ma - and her age is catching up with her. The fear and faith of her Believers has given her great strength over the years, but she has her natural life duration and that can't be flouted too much - or at least, that was the case until your arrival. If she could seize The Stone her life and powers could be immeasurable. A few of us wondered if Our Gracious Lady would seek to control you, or simply destroy you and claim The Stone for herself and take another Gifted One to do her bidding. She might even have been tempted to destroy the rest of us, because we would all be irrelevant."

"Charming."

"Yes, charming indeed. But she appears to have been overruled, doesn't she? When one has lived as long as she has, the ability to surprise people diminishes greatly, so most eventualities for this day had been considered. We mortals may be foolish, but we're not fools, and it's no surprise to me that she's become a victim of her own Followers.. and that's good," he said, emphasising the point with a match. Linda nodded, to help keep him in a talkative mood.

"Who does everyone think I am?" she asked, reaching for a coffee.

"Oh, there's no need to be concerned with all that tonight. Tomorrow you'll be put in the picture. I'm merely welcoming you here, and matters relating to 'who' and 'what' are not my area at all."

"Oh, right.. but now that I am here.. how come my things.. why was the room.." Linda's brain managed a double-knot.

"That's sounds like my area, and that's the reason I'm the one chosen to be with you. Time Dynamics. I want to hear all about your experiences, and maybe put your mind at rest with any pressing questions. I would be quite bewildered, if I was in your position."

Linda hoped her coffee was at least 99.9% caffeine, and started trying to convey something that had only just started to bother her.

"When we arrived outside this place," she said, "..someone was holding my suitcase and Aggy for me. She's my bear but that's not too important at the moment. How come my things were still at number 1313, if it wasn't exactly the same building that I'd left when I went to 1186? I mean, Mörrah had written all over the walls, there were candles on the floor, and someone had put a carpet on the stairs! And then outside, the entire street wasn't as grotty anymore. So how come my stuff was still there?"

Syrus tapped his pipe, and looked at it with a hint of despair. He fiddled with some more tobacco, and gave Linda a rueful look.

"Ah, a perplexing question which unfortunately requires an even more perplexing answer, and no-one can adequately do that. All I could say is that when you interfere with time, you interfere with much, much more than you could possibly imagine. You become independent of the myriad rules that govern movement and even existence which.." he said, striking a new match and pausing to take a few puffs to get the pipe going again.

"..which apply to everything else in the universe. The most significant one, of course, is that you merely have a location in time to aim for, and no journey, as such, to get there. An instantaneous traversal, no less."

"I thought so."

"Did you?" he said, genuinely impressed.

"Well, maybe not. No."

Syrus gave a low chuckle. Linda tried to look intelligent, and thought she was managing it quite well until he threw her a question.

"How long would you say 'now' lasts for?" he asked.

"Now? Umm.. I.. err.. it's.. I've no idea," she mumbled, trying not to fuse her overloaded brain. She could feel another yawn starting.

"Quite, and yet that's where we always are, aren't we? And you have been to a 'now' in the past, the present, and in a way, the future. Mind boggling, no?"

He gestured in a half-circle with his hand as if that would help, and Linda raised her eyebrows and nodded as if she had understood every word so far.

"Uhuh.." she began, ending with an expression that didn't hide her yawn at all. He leaned across to an upright tin on the corner of his desk, and flicked a switch. A light came on inside it, casting soft patterns and shapes onto the walls and ceiling.

"That's nice, what is it?" asked Linda, promising herself to buy one sometime.

"Delightful thing, this. I do find a simple kaleidoscope offers mild refuge for the soothing of a mind. Always have done. But I'm not answering your question, am I? Why would your possessions be waiting for you in the room. Hmm.. let's see.. earlier today you were at a Point A, the modern Odessa that you knew of. Then you left to visit Point B, which happens to be a place in history, in this case the pre-Odessa of 1186 - thus interrupting and crossing the impossibly complex passage of time.."

"I interrupted it before then as well, for my mum. She's alive now, and back home with everyone."

"Ahh, umm.. let's overlook that for the time being, shall we? There's only so much my poor old grey-cells can deal with all at once. Now then, where was I?"

Avalon mumbled in her sleep, giggled, and drifted back into silence, while Sceleste's ears gave a twitch.

"Something about a Point A and a B.."

"Oh yes, yes.. so you then finished your business at Point B and returned to Point A, but you had inadvertently caused Point A to have changed, due to your actions at point B. So therefore.. perhaps all that remained of the first Point A were your memories of it, as real as the world around you, because they were indeed real prior to your journey - a journey that involved no journeying, as it were."

Linda tried to think of a polite way to get him to stop talking. He seemed to be enjoying himself, so she nodded and made an intellectual 'Hmm-hmm' sound.

"I would say that your suitcase and bear, a Ms Aggy, materialised when you did, presumably because of the manner in which the Stone operates. Who knows? All we do know is that Odessa and Shuiskaia Street were created during the natural course of time, regardless of the fact that you would be arriving there. Not everyone knew you would be arriving, just the Believers who reside here, due to the prophecy of Our Lady Mörrah, the Guide Of Our Light."

Linda's eyebrows went higher than they'd ever been.

"She's the ex-Guide now. But how come anyone knew?" she said. Syrus almost leaned forwards in his chair, but decided not too.

"Indeed. The Lady Mörrah heard you speak the location of a future-place shortly before you fled her Castle, and thus line one of the First Prophecy was transcribed. Therefore all that our previous generations had to do was monitor the development of Odessa and ensure that when such an address existed, it was protected and watched until your arrival - without raising any suspicions from other parties. Otherwise, who knows what would have happened? Perhaps nothing, and you would have remained in the glorious Castle of 1186 until you chose to appear somewhere in time that did exist. Call that place Point C, if you like."

This was nearly making sense to Linda, in a tip-of-the-iceberg kind of way.

"It wasn't her castle, you know, and she only had the Stone for a few minutes," she said, sure that she was dropping a bombshell.

"Our historic archives show different, but if there is one person who should know.. well, that would be you - so I'll take your word for it."

"Good. I wish it had all been like going somewhere on a bus. Nice and easy."

"Yes, I certainly wish it were. Thanks to your short appearance in the Castle, I am now the tenth generation of my family dedicated to unravelling the mysteries of Fourth Dimensional Hypotheses, but now that you're seated here before me and are as real as I am, I fear we've barely scratched the surface. In fact, I doubt if the mind is capable of comprehending such issues, I really do."

"Sorry about all that, then," she apologised from behind her mug, and Syrus laughed.

"But now that I've met you, the Gifted One, the one who has actually mastered time itself.. well, my remaining years will be more contented, knowing that the unanswerable riddles that have surrounded my life and those of my forefathers do have answers, even if I can't find them. Time will tell, I'm now sure of that."

Linda was pleased to be with such a warm person, and let him in on a secret.

"Well add this to your list, then - I'm a duplicate of myself! How does that work? And that's nothing, you'll love this one - the Stone disappeared when it got near itself. Any thoughts there?"

Linda's eyes flashed to the clock just as its hands reached one o'clock. A delicate chime rang out, and continued far longer than chimes normally did.

"Ahh, saved by the bell! How fortunate, for I have no idea - and nor do I wish to, at this late hour. I'm much too old for such weighty puzzles, even in the full brightness of day. Besides, this coffee's far too nice to spoil with brainery.. would you care for another biscuit?"

He smiled to himself, and Linda settled back in her chair with a couple of wafers, and watched the faint stars and moons revolving on the ceiling.

"To conclude.." he said, finishing off something crunchy, "..you are proof that the inexplicable can be explained, one way or another. Wonderful, yet beguiling, proof."

Linda quite liked being 'wonderful yet beguiling' and felt special for a good reason - which made a very nice change.

"And much as it grieves me to point this out on such an historic day.. it's bedtime for you, young lady. Tomorrow holds much in store - and if I might say, you do look tired."

"I am, I really am.." she yawned.

He guided her from the room through a velvet-covered door, and they went along a corridor so richly carpeted that neither of them made any footsteps. Even their voices sounded leaden.

"These are your Quarters, and I'm sure you'll find that they're rather pleasant. Either myself or one of the Hospitality Brethren will be around should you need us - just pick up your phone."

He unlocked the door and Linda stepped into a room worthy of visiting royalty. It was vast, even larger and more ornate than her room back at the Pecherskij, and only seemed to be missing a tv - but there was always a chance that it might be hidden in a wall. Her suitcase, the chest and Aggy were waiting for her on a long table next to the wardrobes.

She unpacked her mother's picture and put it on the table beside the tall four poster bed, Aggy took up residence on the elegant chair by the window, and what little remained in the suitcase could wait until tomorrow. A slow double-chime marked half past the hour and Linda nervously pulled the bedspread over herself. She lay awake feeling like the world's biggest charlatan, convinced that tomorrow everyone would see her as an idiot and a waste of space who wasn't much good at anything other than doing weird things that didn't involve being clever. She fended off her tiredness for a while longer, and watched Avalon and Sceleste sleeping quietly next to her, both of them silver-grey in the moonlight.

CHAPTER TWENTY SIX

Persuasion

The next morning Linda was already awake as the door opened. Four people in black and silver robes sat silently while she ate a light breakfast, and then they escorted her along a series of high-ceilinged corridors, and into a vast and spacious hall. Avalon pointed to a circular stained glass window occupying almost the entire end wall.

"Oh, I am not a moth! Mörrah's so mean! And I don't fly anything like that, either, do I? Will you tell them Lindy, when you speak to them, will you tell them ALL, puhleeaze?"

Linda stared at it for a moment, trying to understand what it depicted. It showed a girl with long hair and an angelic expression holding the Stone high above her head, casting light around the world. A huge black cat reached up from the flames along the base, trying to draw her down to join the suffering spirits, while a Disney-esque moth burned in a dragon's mouth. A bird depicted in an equally ridiculous style was shown plummeting from the sky, shedding feathers and looking terrified.

Linda didn't have time to think of something comforting to say. A man with eyebrows which joined in the middle lead her across the marble floor, and by the time she reached an elegant high-backed chair, she had figured out how to walk without making embarrassing squeaky footsteps. It may not have been very lady-like, but it was effective. She sat down and the man went and took the last place in a dozen or more chairs that fanned in an arc either side of her.

Primus sat a few yards in front of her, on the other side of an impressive gold and marble table. Syrus was to his left, and a heavy-set man with greying hair and a scarred face sat closer, on Primus' right. He was either the most intimidating security guard of all time, or he was stupendously important. The sinister man stared at Linda and whispered behind his hand to Primus, who nodded and whispered a reply. They both looked at her, and she tried to tune into their thoughts or feelings. She was far too nervous to manage that, which made her feel even more nervous.

Syrus stood up and lifted a red and gold cushion from behind the table, which had something dark on it. He handed it to the first of the people around her. She watched, silently, and realised they were all being shown the Stone. She'd never seen it so black. She tried to imagine it in her hands, and then thought of being back in the park near where she used to live, watching Sceleste scare the ducks while Avalon counted leaves. By the time it arrived back on the table, it was almost clear again. Avalon leaped from Sceleste's head, pointing both arms towards the Stone.

"There it is! I've found it for us! It's on his table, Linda, over there!" Primus wasn't pleased.

"Kindly ask your simple-minded pet to stop squawking - or perhaps we should stop feeding your cat and allow her feline nature to take care of the matter?"

A ripple of laughter travelled around the circle, and Linda shuffled uncomfortably in her chair. Primus stood up, and made a sign in front of himself before speaking.

"Father Markov Lehane, Brother Syrus Lehane, Senior Members - the Prophecy is fulfilled."

"Who's Father Markov?" whispered Avalon.

"That scary one who isn't Syrus or Primus.." breathed Linda. Primus stopped his address and stared at her to be quiet.

"The Stone has been delivered, as you have seen. The Gifted One is here, accompanied by the Creatures Of Custodianship, precisely as foretold. Faith serves its own rewards, and after many centuries and many generations, we now have that reward. We are honoured to be in your presence, Lehane Eidahr, and we anticipate the success of your great works which lie ahead."

A round of applause broke out, only ending when Primus raised his hand. Linda looked around, going red as she noticed everyone staring and smiling at her. These people were genuinely weird. In fact, they took 'weird' into new and uncharted areas of weirdness. Primus granted himself a grin.

"We must present her to the Believers before our work can begin. You are all aware of your duties - now carry them out."

He sat down again, and the room emptied to the rhythmic claps of the Senior Members. The man next to him whispered behind his hand again and their muffled conversation dragged on for long after the room had fallen silent. Sceleste began to wriggle with boredom.

"Might I suggest we move proceedings forwards, Masters?" mentioned Syrus, politely, "The crowd outside might grow a little impatient, I feel,"

Primus clicked his fingers, and two women in white and yellow robes emerged from a narrow door and escorted Linda through into the Robing Room, leaving Avalon and Sceleste behind. One woman painted Linda's face in thick pale-grey make-up, while the other helped to shuffle a long white and gold robe over her head. Their hands trembled while they did it, and neither took their eyes off the floor, apart from the one doing her make-up who (fortunately for Linda) glanced up occasionally. They tucked her hair into a bizarre hat shaped like a pyramid and then, apparently, she was ready.

"Hello?" said Linda to the hairdresser for the third time, "I'm Linda. What are your names?"

They ignored her once again, and then hurried out after bowing. For a few minutes, Linda felt very alone. She sat on a small foot-stool, rather than risk marking the expensive furniture. One of the other doors opened, and Primus strode across to her, casting a near-perfect reflection in the shining wooden panels of the floor. He stood before her, examining the quality of the Formal Dressers' work.

"What's all this in aid of, Mr Primus?" she asked, completely bewildered.

He stared down at her, moved a little too close and spoke in an intense whisper.

"You are ready to meet your people."

"Meet them?"

"You stand on the Palace balcony, the adoring masses see you, and you leave when I tell you," he harshly instructed.

"I do that? Why would anyone need to see me? I'm no-one."

"You must appreciate that there are those of us within the inner circles of Lady Mörrah's elite Believers who are fully aware that you are not from God. You are no more than a wretched thief. You are Gifted but you are still wretched none the less, unworthy of your talents, as written in the second and fourth Book Of Truths."

"The books of what?"

"The first writings by Lady Mörrah, prior to her revised interpretations. She wrote of her many conversations with the Creator, the one who brought the Stone to her and entrusted its powers with her. You defied her, betrayed her, and now I fear she has been betrayed once more and is in no position to reclaim what is rightfully hers. But she will return, oh yes, she will return. Those of us loyal to her will ensure that happens."

"So if I'm just a thief, what's with all this dressing up?"

"Many centuries ago, my own forefathers decided that by claiming you to be a carrier from God, belief in the Stone would be stronger than by claiming you to be a common vagabond. Outside, there are crowds who stand as living testimony to the wisdom of that judgement. So when you step out onto the balcony and face the adulation of the Followers, you'd better act like you're sent from Heaven or I'll make damn sure you get to Heaven a great deal sooner than you'd like. Understand, thief?"

Linda nodded, and felt sick. He pointed to a wide door, and gestured for her to get out of his sight. The room beyond was much better. It was bright and spacious, had peculiar thin windows, and a set of glass doors in the far wall leading out into the centre of a long balcony.. and somewhere outside there was an awful lot of cheering and chanting going on. She hurried over to Sceleste and Avalon, and sat down on the grand chair with them. She moved Sceleste onto her lap while Avalon flew around her a few times, analysing every detail.

"I prefer the Previous You. And Sceleste does, too," she said, making a small handprint in the make-up.

"So do I. Can you believe this get-up? Lucky it's only once for the crowd out there 'cause I feel ridiculous. Do you think they'll laugh?"

Avalon nodded, then shook her head while her glow turned pink. A solemn man in appropriately drab garments placed a red cushion on the floor at Linda's feet. It was covered in strips of countless small spikes. He began speaking to the room about Deliverance or something similar, and then bowed before Sceleste, which Linda found amusing until she picked up on the sentiments of his speech.

"The pernicious Black Fiend, she who bears no name, she who courts Satan, she who unites Heaven and Hell in mutual loathing of her very existence, shall be presented to the Believers upon the Sacred Linen.." he said, and then made a big mistake. Linda's eyes widened as he actually placed his hands around Sceleste.

"No don't do that, whoever you are, very bad idea, that's so bad," warned Linda, while Avalon giggled.

"..to be slain as foretold by Father Ivasko Lehane in the Second Book Of Penitent Delive.. ow! Oh, you wretched beast.. I mean, how honoured I am that you scratch me.."

Sceleste did not want to be picked up, and did not want to go near the cushion. She lashed out in a single swipe, and three short scratches appeared on the back of his hand, which then steadily widened and grew longer until they all joined up across his palm -

and then they started widening. He stared in horror as his robes became covered in blood, and was quickly lead away by two distressed Brothers.

"She has a name and she's not going on the cushion. Always ask her first, because she's very sensitive," Linda advised everyone, and gave her an extra-special hug.

The double doors opposite her swung open, and for a heart-stopping moment she thought Mörrah had returned. But Sceleste hadn't responded to her sudden appearance, and Linda could see that the woman was adjusting a black wig over short blonde hair, while having the last tweaks made to a very slender, full-length black dress. She also lacked the air of menace that Mörrah exuded, but apart from that she was a good stand-in. Linda beckoned Brother Syrus to come over, and he approached with a smile.

"Syrus, is there something you're not telling the Believers?"

"Ah, you can't begin to imagine what they're told and what they're not told. Lady Mörrah required their faith, we their money, thus.."

Somewhere a clock chimed nine times, and a fanfare from a line of strange curved trumpets announced Linda's eminent appearance on the balcony. Primus stared coldly at her, and lead the way.

The crowd was stunned into silence. The cheering and babbling voices ended as Linda took her place on a podium and looked down at them. She wanted to climb under the red carpet as she realised that three or even four thousand people were all staring up at her, transfixed. And then she noticed herself in a close-up on two huge screens either side of the balcony, which made her feel even worse. She took the Stone and held it high above her head, just as Primus instructed her to do, and the masses went wild. A small ripple of applause at the front had quickly spread into cheers, clapping and stamping, and then chanting. The woman who looked like Mörrah quickly took the Stone from her, and held it in one gloved hand, like a nightmare version of the Statue Of Liberty. There was no close-up for her, of course, and the cameras remained fixed on Linda. Primus nudged her, discretely.

"Wave, you common mountebank, that sea of fools expect it.." he muttered, through a wide smile. Linda couldn't believe the sight before her, and looked to Avalon.

"This isn't.. it can't be happening, can it? I'm nothing special!"

Avalon began waving her arms in front of Linda's face.

"Hold on, don't say anymore, I know this one.. I'm nothing special.. dah-dum.. in fact I'm a bit of a bore.. de-dooh dahdooh, if I tell a joke.. you've probably heard it before, dah dah dummm.."

"Avie, I'm not doing an Abba Challenge, I'm saying this is total madness. Look at them down there, they're bowing to me! And listen to them calling my wrong name as well. How weird is this?"

Avalon agreed, and sat on the balustrade swinging her legs and humming the rest of the song to herself. Sceleste looked completely unimpressed, and even yawned.

After a few minutes of self-conscious regal waving, Linda was lead back inside, glad to be leaving the repetitive music playing for the Believers to chant along to. The woman holding the cloudy Stone took her wig off and was ushered away, while the unpleasant-looking Father Markov carefully placed the Stone onto a purple cushion. He nodded to a group of lower-ranking monks in the corner, and they seized Primus and a few others who were in the room. Armed guards immediately ran in and took over, holding them in a line. Father Markov walked along in front of them, as if inspecting his troops.

"You, the weak-minded, have failed us. Your devotion to Mörrah renders you incapable of serving the New Succession, the Guild Of The Stone."

"Guild Of The Stone?" Primus grunted, "Is that what you call yourselves? You'll pay for your treachery - our Eternal Lady Of Righteousness has faced worse than you, and when she returns.."

Father Markov nodded to four guards by the double doors, who drew guns from their robes.

"Take the Gifted One away. The fate of these subversives is not for her eyes."

Linda's heart pounded as she was guided towards one of the doors. She turned back to Markov, and called to him.

"Where's Syrus? He's not in trouble is he? He didn't like Mörrah, 'cause he told me!"

"He will be safe, I assure you. His judgement is perhaps not always consistent, although there is an undeniably wise head on his shoulders - for the time being. Now return to your Quarters."

Linda was lead silently back to her room, and the door was locked firmly behind her. She sat on her bed, waiting for Avalon and Sceleste to be brought in. And waited. And waited. She counted off the chimes of a distant clock as the late morning became early afternoon. A tray of lunch was delivered in complete silence, and she listened to the afternoon ticking into evening..

She woke up to find herself still in the heavy make-up and robes, and still alone. This was bad. She looked at her ludicrous face in the mirror and began wiping off the pale layers, sighing as she noticed that her skin underneath didn't look particularly different in colour to the pale gunk. She left the robes on the floor, edged a biscuit from a trouser pocket and felt as if she had regained part of her identity.

"Why can't they worship me in jeans and stuff?" she said to herself, suddenly realising how quiet the room was. She leaned against the only window, staring out just a few feet to the side of a building. If she pressed her face against the first layer of glass and looked to the left, she could see.. another brick wall, with thick pillars. There was a small gap high above it, near the top of the window, where the building ended and a small section of sky began. She figured that she must have been asleep for a long time, because the light outside was the early morning kind. Suddenly the series of locks on the door rattled one after the other, and a woman wearing green robes walked in. Linda was in no mood for small talk.

"Uhh.. hello.. morning. Where's my friends?" she asked.

"All will soon be known to you. Here is your breakfast, and also some Day Clothes which are most similar to the kind you wear now. We'll get you more like this if they're of a style that appeals to you, because we want you to be happy here - but we'd prefer you to wear robes. Robes are more befitting someone of your status. Father Markov will see you after breakfast."

She bowed twice and offered a curtsey, and left a tray that had been loaded with a collection of wooden bowls filled with the kind of food that would bore a squirrel.

Linda soon found herself sitting in Father Markov's grandiose office, seated before him.

"Where's Av.. my friends?" she asked, noticing that they didn't seem to be in the room. Markov stared at her.

"If you want to see your pets, then read these sentences aloud. That's all," he said, then leaned across his desk and handed Linda a sheet of indecipherable nonsense. She looked at it, nervously.

"But what do the words mean? They're all short and there's hyphens everywhere," she said, turning it around a few times.

"They are transcribed phonetically."

Linda had no idea what he meant, and shrugged as she handed the sheet back. She looked at the Stone, and wondered if she could conjure Sister Mariephred - she'd sort this freak out. Or maybe she could just think about somewhere like her room at St Teresa's.. but that would be pointless because she'd never been there, so there would be normal girls in it - and anyway, if she conjured somewhere now, where would that leave Avalon and Sceleste? And what abou..

"Are you listening?" Markov snapped at her.

Linda nodded, bemused.

"At the risk of repeating myself, the words are written as they are pronounced. They are of a language compiled from many others, and if you really are a Gifted One, you will 'read' the intent behind each syllable and your recitation will instruct the Stone to enable a minor task to occur. This is your test. Time-travel may impress some of our group, but it does not impress me. Serious Requests and their complete fulfilment are how I will judge you. And even if you fail, you can still see your creatures. Is that fair?"

Linda felt sick.

"No, not for a minute. I don't know what the words mean, or what they'll do. I can understand loads these days, but this is.."

"Tell me, do you care if your pets can breathe?"

"What?" she replied, convinced she had mis-heard him.

Father Markov pressed a button on his desk, and a monitor flickered into life. He turned it around so that she could see the screen. The image showed Avalon and Sceleste spotlighted in a dark room, both confined within circles of hieroglyphics. Avalon had a glowing chain leading from an ankle to a gold nail, for extra effect. Linda went cold.

"Wh.. what have you done?"

Markov laughed, and patted the top of the screen.

"Nothing, yet. And neither have you. Now would you care to carry out your test, or would you like encouragement?" he said, and then spoke quietly into a small phone.

Linda watched as a masked attendant placed a large plastic dome over Avalon, and then another over Sceleste. A different attendant fitted a tube on the top of each one, and flicked a switch. Avalon began looking around herself, and started pushing against the dome, fluttering in a panic. Sceleste lay perfectly still, staring directly up to the camera. Father Markov smiled at Linda, and turned the monitor away from her.

"It appears that air is becoming scarce for them. Now I ask you again, do you care if they can breath?"

For a few seconds Linda's voice left her, and she nodded wildly until it came back.

"Yes! I'll read the things! Give me the sheet!"

"I advise you read quickly, and do try hard for their sakes. You may wish to hold the Stone? No tricks, if you don't mind - but I seriously doubt there will be time for such folly."

Linda held the Stone which immediately went from black to shining transparent, and she read the five lines of strange words. Somewhere in her mind she could see what they meant, but the prospect of harm coming to the two she loved blocked everything out. She dropped the Stone with the final word, and pulled the monitor around again.

The domes were being raised, and Avalon looked as if she was crying. Linda certainly was crying, uncontrollably. Her face was covered with tears, and she fell to the floor longing for it to swallow her up.

"Well done, well done. I hope you were successful - and I'm sure your little pets do as well. I will see you tomorrow. Go."

He pulled a bell-chain and a woman entered the room. She took Linda firmly by the hand, and lead her back to her Quarters and locked the door as soon as she was inside. Linda crawled back into bed, and pulled the covers over her head.

And the next day she did exactly the same. And the day after that. And then she didn't really care what day it was, because she knew that as long as she kept doing as she was told, nothing bad would happen to her loved ones.

But on the sixth night, everything changed.

CHAPTER TWENTY SEVEN

Linda's Sixth Night

Midnight.

The clock inside Linda's room began chiming very, very slowly.

She waited until the voices beyond her door had faded away, and then slid quietly and carefully from between the sheets, down onto the floor. She crawled underneath the bed, quietly shuffling over to the tall window where she curled up in a faint rectangle of silver-white light on the floorboards, in just the right position to see the moon high up in the sky above her. She thought of the time she met Avalon, a beautiful, delicate faery glowing in the Lunaressence on the bed in the Pecher.. Pekshej.. whatever that hotel had been called. That was all such a long time ago, probably. Everything had been so different back then, so wonderful and magical and.. and somehow she'd caused her faery all kinds of suffering in ways that she hadn't a hope of understanding or doing anything about. And Sceleste, too. She wondered if maybe all three of them were better off dead.

Her thoughts drifted to the other Linda, who was probably asleep in a perfect home in a perfect street, surrounded by her perfect, sleeping family. She prayed that her other-self couldn't see any Half-There's or silhouettes or Ved'mas, and wouldn't ever come near to encountering anything as loathsome and vile as the Stone. Had Other Linda undone the knots in her trainers by now? Were all those bears and books still lying all over the place? Was she going to see Andie sometime soon? A tear rolled over Linda's nose and landed on the floor.

She lay perfectly still, wishing with all her heart that she'd never found out that Half-There's were Really There. Avalon would still be free and happy in her own innocent world, counting leaves and looking for something she wasn't ever going to find, and Mörrah would be even weaker by now and less trouble to anyone, and Sceleste.. well, maybe her life wasn't as bad in the Chapel as it was now. Another tear fell.

Her head throbbed a little, so she just stared upwards without thinking, watching the dark clouds lazily drifting by far away in the night sky, safely beyond her wretched world and all her problems.

The clock finished chiming midnight and the cloudy sky cleared a little.

At long last, her mind allowed her some freedom. Ever since she had arrived in this new Odessa, she had been too distressed and upset to take herself anywhere near the dreamworld places Avalon had shown her. But now she was simply too worn out to be hurt anymore. Her heart was aching so much that she could no longer feel the pain.

She sensed the moonlight on her skin and imagined swimming up through its beams, high into the sky, onwards and onwards and onwards towards the beauty and the freedom that lay far above the clouds. She imagined herself being as free and as strong as an eagle again, gliding and soaring through the air. She thought about Avalon's words when they had both flown into the world of Brother Oldmonkperson, and soon she could feel those words around her as she soared higher and higher, growing in confidence, afraid of nothing. The night faded away below, surrendering to the warmth and power of wonderful sunlight, and time meant absolutely nothing for so, so long. A shadow of darkness fell across the blanket of clouds far beneath her, but it was nothing to concern herself with. It was trivial, a nothingness, and she soon left it far behind as she soared further and further away into the sky, basking in every wonderful golden sunbeam around her.

She tried again and again to imagine the Stone in her hands, and could almost feel it as real as the day she had first released it from the Golden Claw. But then a wave of anxiety hit her. For no more than a heartbeat she felt Avalon crying out as if something was desperately wrong, and suddenly the Stone was gone. She looked down and saw it tumble from her grasp, spinning and shining as it fell into the clouds. She knew she was stupid, and this proved it beyond doubt - what kind of fool couldn't even imagine things going right? She began falling from her dreamworld, plummeting through icy air, watching the Stone racing further away from her as she left behind the sunlight and became lost in the harsh darkness of night once more. The Stone had been so close, but she'd messed everything up again and burning tears streaked back across her face.

The lights of Odessa spread out far beneath her, and she knew she was returning to her body in the Palace Of The Stone, back to her room, back to her miserable existence, and back to hurting Avalon and Sceleste. More tears stung her eyes as her helpless fall became even faster, and she barely noticed a black mist drifting across the city. She blinked her tears away for a moment, and watched as the great waves of mist poured out from the palace. This had to be something evil, and it had to be something involving Mörrah. But she couldn't stop herself falling. She'd never fallen this far before, and couldn't think how she'd ever managed to stop herself before. If only Avalon was here to help her, Avalon would know what to.. Avalon.

The name stayed in Linda's mind, filling every thought, drawing her faster towards the palace. She sensed Avalon's pain, her desperate need, and understood why the Stone had fallen from her hands. Not because she was useless, but because Avalon.. no, Sceleste, Sceleste was calling to her, reaching out to her. A tidal wave of pure rage swept through Linda's body as she struggled to focus on where she needed to be.

And then she knew where to go. The mist was so dense, so unforgiving, but she could sense the source of the evil even if she couldn't see it. She closed her eyes, trusting her destiny and her guidance for the briefest of moments to Sceleste, who leaped beneath her, leading her forwards through this blackest place. With all her might, Linda imagined striking out with all the strength she could find in her heart, smashing and ripping through.. through..

..she found herself back in her room, sitting bolt upright beneath the window, crying, perspiring, and shaking. Whatever she'd been dreaming about was already less than a memory. The three Nocturne Assistants To Lehane made the first of their regular nightly checks on her, righted the fallen chair beside her, and put her back to bed.

The room was left in a silence which was broken only by two gentle chimes of the clock outside.

Linda was soon lost in a deep sleep. The assistants sat on guard outside her door, ensuring as always that no-one came near, and listening intently to her movements so that she didn't become too active again. They sat in the dim light of the corridor, untroubled for the rest of the night - except two of the three, who were plagued by a small and very irritating fly.

CHAPTER TWENTY EIGHT

Mörrah's Sixth Night

Midnight.

A clock outside Mörrah's room began chiming very, very slowly.

Mörrah looked up at the glass-panels in the palace ceiling, and studied the engraved symbols as they trapped the weak moonlight. In a way, she had to admire the Containment Curses. They were complex, long and highly effective. They even changed, depending on how the light caught them.

Her treacherous Followers had obviously spent a long time preparing for the thief-child's return, and Mörrah had occupied her mind during the previous few days and nights by calculating the revenge they deserved. She stared out to the night sky, far beyond the lines she could never cross, and seethed. Then she glared at each one of the ten cameras that watched her, hating the clicking and whirring sounds as each sensitised lens zoomed backwards and forwards, matching her every movement.

During the past few days she had studied the symbols rendered in the powdery Blessed Clay of the floor around her, and strained her eyes to read and re-read every single blood-chalk marking on the distant walls. The nights had allowed her to see the thin beams of intense light running upwards from the alexandrite lasers in the floor, caging her like a wretched bird. This time she was very nearly stuck. Not completely stuck, but very nearly.

The clock finished chiming midnight and the cloudy sky cleared a little.

Her eyes narrowed as she looked up at the crescent moon in the sky, and she smiled to herself. This night was different to the others. Tonight held her lunar-birthing sign, as it did three times each year. She stared at the near-quarter moon under which she was first granted life in the world of the Ved'ma. No-one other than herself and Lady Morganna could possibly be aware of its significance, and the Ground Crawlers who had scribed all the curses around her certainly had no cause for suspicion. Now she had one night to act, one chance to claim her freedom and serve her revenge.

She tried time and again to calm her mind and draw down the strength from the crescent, but it wasn't easy. She was too angry and frustrated that her lifetime of patience had so nearly been rendered worthless. But revenge had to be hers, as did the Stone. But before that could happen, she needed the moth, that wretched low-faery. She closed her eyes again, and finally grew calm.

The weak Secondary Spirit that only her crescent moon could allow her to create, began veiling her and then shrouding her in a faint black vapour. Then it steadily drifted from her, down through the floor, passing into the very heart of the earth and then emerging a breath later as a shadow, safely beyond all the restrictions around her captive form. She moved silently across the walls of her palace, crossing unknown over guards, and passing through the rooms of the sleeping deceivers. Their punishments could wait.

She looked in at the Gifted One, unnerved that she was sleeping on the floor in the moonlight.

"..so very Gifted, so very flawed.." she sneered. She knew the girl was aware of her presence, and yet the child refused to acknowledge it. Was that arrogance? Was it strength, perhaps? Or was she simply too stupid? But trivial questions of that nature could wait until later. Mörrah had no time and no will to linger so she moved on, passing unhindered through walls, floors and ceilings. She quickly found the moth, and the despicable Beast.

Darkness fell across Avalon, and she woke suddenly from another troubled sleep. The room had gone very cold, and the marble slab beneath her felt like ice.

"Sceleste? What's you looking at? What's up there?" she called across the gap to the larger podium. Sceleste's yellow eyes were glaring into the darkness somewhere just above Avalon, yet she wasn't hissing or doing any of the things she usually did when she stared in that manner. Avalon swallowed hard and turned around. A vague pair of smouldering red eyes swayed snake-like before her in the darkness.

"She needs our help, little one, she needs our help.." a voice whispered. Avalon tried to hide underneath her wings.

"Who's you? Are you Mörrah? Leave me alone.. you're so bad," she whimpered, and shuffled away a little.

"Damn your impertinence!" Mörrah breathed, and emerged on

the other side of the table. The eyes moved with an easy, hypnotic rhythm, captivating Avalon until a hiss from Sceleste held them steady. They briefly glared over to her, and returned to the faery.

"We have to work together, you and I. You want her, I want The Stone.. and neither of us wish to be surrounded by these creatures of deceit. Am I correct?"

Avalon nodded.

"But you made this place, you and your stories and lies! And I know they're making Linda do bad things.. I don't want anything to do with you!"

The eyes backed away, and sank low against the floor. Avalon crawled as far across her small platform as she could, to see where they had gone. They slowly rose again, and came a little nearer.

"Are you sure, littlest one? How disappointing. Very well then, you shall stay here and force The Gifted One to stay where she is, doing her bad things. Let the Living continue to suffer under her blood-soaked fists. So many unfortunate incidents, so many worthless lives lost.. yes, you are right to reject my offer of collaboration, to spurn my hand of friendship. You and I, we could have a pact between us to save her. But no, you are right to stay here, as you wish."

The eyes grew fainter as Mörrah's Secondary Spirit began to fade into the darkness.

"No! Come back! Please come back, pleeease.." cried Avalon.

The eyes emerged again, a little brighter and stronger than before.

"I want to help, I do ever so much!" she pleaded.

"But how can I trust you now, little one? I have to trust you.."

"I promise you can trust me! Really I do!"

"Very well," Mörrah replied. The eyes moved higher, looking down upon the circle of crudely chalked symbols around Avalon.

"A solitary Magic and a Phaedrus Chain binds you? So pathetic, so weak.. you are truly of no value, are you?" she sighed, "Repeat these words.."

The chain binding Avalon's leg turned to dust, and immediately spread over the chalkmarks as if blown by small, sharp wind currents. Avalon squealed with delight, and shook her wings until she fell over.

"Now go to the Bearer.."

Avalon did as she was told and hovered above Sceleste, where she said everything she was supposed to say, all at the right time. The linear hexes faded, the spikes were soon kicked across the room and at last, Sceleste found herself with enough space to have a stretch. The red eyes melted away, leaving behind only a faint whisper.

"Come to me.. come to me.." softly echoed around the room, and Avalon followed the cold heart within the voice. Sceleste followed at her own pace a short way behind, protectively watching the Harmless One's every move. The voice lead them through corridors and rooms, and finally to a narrow passageway. The end door was missing, but in its place the floor was marked with a huge, angular symbol daubed in the blood of a dozen eagles. Even a faery as low and insignificant as Avalon couldn't dare fly across such a sign, so she closed her eyes, held her breath and clung onto Sceleste - who trampled all over it, quite unconcerned.

Mörrah lay in the centre of her room and soon felt her Secondary Spirit returning. Her guards were no longer capable of watching their monitors, and she allowed a small laugh to escape as the cameras continued to click and whirr to themselves. For the next two hours she hid her frustrations and pointed to the appropriate curse for Avalon to wipe from the powdery white floor, and then patiently whispered over and over again the words for her to recite as the stupid creature wiped away the writings on the wall. The correct order was essential, so relying on a low-faery whose concept of left and right changed from minute to minute was always going to be a test of endurance. Eventually, all the Constriction Curses were gone and the violet flames of the Maleficus Candles were extinguished, leaving only the cage of light. Avalon flew around from one beam to the next, kicking small piles of clay powder over them until they were dimmed and weak enough to allow Mörrah to step through, without too much pain.

She stood in her new freedom, and immediately had to sit down again. Being isolated and surrounded by so many inhibiting forces had left her unsteady and unable to have drawn on the nourishment of weak-minded fools for six long days. She breathed deeply to try and make herself feel stable again. Her eyes turned to Avalon.

Avalon was certainly feeling happy with herself and looked around for Sceleste, but she didn't seem to be anywhere. That didn't matter too much though, because Mörrah had become so nice, and wasn't even half as scary as she used to be. Avalon even had a question for her.

"How come everyone can see you? When we.. hold on.."

She paused for a moment, to think how to phrase a really tricky question correctly.

"..right, I've got it now. In the other version of what's happened, when you put me in the Matryoshka doll, there was only Linda in the whole world who could see you. You were so old and weak.. but in this now, everybody can see.."

"Come here, my little one. There is so much we have to discuss."

Avalon fluttered near, pleased that she was becoming a friend. Mörrah's long white arm darted out like a streak of lightning from a split in her black sleeve, and plucked Avalon from the air. She held her tightly, watching her desperately kicking and trying to breathe.

"I despise not knowing what you are talking about, but I do know this. These Believers have made me strong, and granted me all I need. And now I need that which you and the thief took from me!"

She squeezed tighter until Avalon couldn't cry out any more.

"But yes, I grow old and I desperately desire The Stone. And I won't need you once I have your friend exactly where I want her."

Mörrah looked down as Avalon's wriggles grew weaker, amused but unable to laugh. Teasing a low-faery was no challenge, and killing one was so unrewarding. She watched as Avalon's legs slowly stopped kicking, wondering whether or not she was worth granting any further life to.

"Goodbye, dirt-moth.." she smirked, and squeezed a little tighter.

Sceleste had waited patiently in the darkness of Mörrah's room, crouched beyond the Ved'ma's weakened awareness, watching Avalon free the troublesome Evil One.

Shortly after midnight she had sensed the spirit of the Gifted One soaring somewhere in the safe world between the living and the dead, free at last but filled with anger and confusion. The girl was alert but in need of a moment's brief guidance, and that would be so very easy to offer. While the Harmless Faery and the Evil One were pre-occupied with spell-breaking, Sceleste had searched for Linda in the same way that she had searched for her during the Incantation Of Zalozhnye, by allowing her feline Spirit and Aura to spread far and wide, reaching out to find her. She was so close.. so close.. but she had to stop.

She watched as the Evil One had turned her loathing onto the faery, and time had run out. Sceleste raced out from the shadows, as fast as her body would let her, intent on leaping between Mörrah and

Avalon to save the faery and serve brief justice by inflicting a few moments of unimaginable pain on Mörrah. And as she ran from the darkness, she called out for the final time to her Gifted One.. and felt the arrival of the girl's powerful Spirit screaming into the room.

Sceleste leaped across Mörrah in a single bound, brushing her tail across the Ved'ma's face for a little extra punishment. She turned around even before landing, and watched as Mörrah dropped Avalon to the floor. Sceleste held the Ved'ma's desperate gaze for a split second before she was swiped hard from the midriff through to the top of her head by something too fast and vicious to comprehend. In Sceleste's mind, the Evil One had been ravaged by a monstrous talon of rage, anger.. and phenomenal power. She hissed with delight as the Evil One was thrown backwards, hurled violently like a rag doll into the darkness.

Mörrah lay against the furthest corner of the room, writhing in the agony and torment caused to any Ved'ma who might cross the path of a black cat with Sceleste's credentials. Her dazed mind tried to understand what had happened, but she was too shocked to think straight. The Bearer Of All Curses had leapt from nowhere, launching its vile self out of the shadows, and had bounded clear across her arm. Its tail had scraped and burned across her face and her very soul felt scorched, but then what had happened? Could a Beast really be that powerful? She looked at the damage to her human form.

Her right arm was already blistering and smoking, that was no surprise, and she knew that what remained of her face was probably doing the same. But three wide ruts had appeared from deep within her waist through to the top of her head, and very few parts in between remained where they should be. This was going to take a long time to sort out. She could repair her body without any great trouble, apart from the burns to her Spirit from the Cursed One, but the shock of being hit so hard and unexpectedly would take a long time to recover from. Her eyes rolled wildly as she scoured every corner of the room, searing through the darkness and the shadows, trying to find where the vile creature lay. She screamed and choked on her rage.

"You'll be.. you'll be first, Cursed One! You'll be first! Before the Ground Crawler, before the low-spirit, you'll be mine first!" she roared into the darkness, pointing in the few directions her arm would allow. She glared over to Avalon, who had almost managed to sit herself up in the circle of moonlight on the floor, and was crying. She laughed at the pathetic faery.

"She'll pay as well.. oh, how she will pay," Mörrah wheezed, almost silently.

Sceleste strolled over and gave her Harmless One a maternal nuzzle, then settled protectively in front of her, daring Mörrah to come and incur her wrath again. Mörrah's laughter turned into a wild, uncontrollable scream of vengeance as she slowly disappeared, still pointing and spitting curses at the two of them.

The room was left in a silence which was broken only by two gentle chimes of the clock outside.

CHAPTER TWENTY NINE

At Sunrise

Sunrise brought a huge headache for Linda. She felt as if she had slept with her head clamped in a vice all night, and groaned to herself when she heard the sharp clattering of the five locks. She sat up in bed holding the palms of her hands against her eyes while her Primary Nutritional Assistant brought in a tray of breakfast. She'd been having the most magical dreams during the night. In the first, she had been flying through clouds and feeling wonderful, and then started falling because she was panicking about something, or maybe she'd done something important and brave, but whatever it was she couldn't quite remember anymore. The dream had been one of her intensely real ones, and those kind always guaranteed a headache.

The Nutritional Expert was offering today's Nutritional Advice, but Linda ignored her and instead stayed in her own warm world behind her hands, and tried desperately to cling on to the memories of the second dream. That one had been perfect. She had dreamed Avalon had flown in through the bedroom door's top keyhole and then hovered above her, shining in that special way of hers, filling Linda's world with the fragrance of a summer meadow and all the warmth and beauty of a sunbeam. Avalon had seemed so happy to be with her again that she couldn't stop crying and giggling while trying to hum the chorus of Hasta Mañana properly. Being with Avalon again, even if she was only in a dream, had made Linda feel wrapped up in security and love. She tried to join in on the second chorus, and that brought the dream to a miserable end. The Nocturne Guards unlocked the door, waking her abruptly, but probably hadn't come in. The next thing Linda knew was that another boring day had started with another headache, and the uppity fat woman was bringing her a boring tray of boring breakfast.

Sunrise had also brought a huge headache for Father Markov. A lot had changed during the night, and he began the Emergency Meeting by sighing loudly. Not only had Mörrah escaped a few hours earlier, but she had released the Hell-cat and bird-faery-creature as well. However, the Stone was safe, the Requester was safe, and as far as he was concerned, the Requesting should continue for as long as possible. He rose to his feet and addressed the twelve nervous Guild Superiors seated around the table.

"I am disappointed, very disappointed.." he said, staring intently from one face to the next, "..that despite the rigid adherence to the writings laid down, it appears that the Ved'ma has left us. Either we underestimated her, or she was assisted. I will assume the former is the case, and no-one here need feel unduly worried that they are currently under suspicion and investigation, etcetera."

The Superiors tried not to look at each other, and especially not at Father Markov.

"As such," he continued while walking around the table, "..we must initiate a modified defence plan. Hex all the buildings against her, and issue a command that all persons of significance must carry the Emblem Of Divine Protection, and then distribute Secondary Meanieries amongst all Believers."

Three of the twelve nodded and stood up to begin the preparations, but he raised his hand for them to wait.

"No, hex only the Central Zone buildings and supply EDP's only to Superiors. Offer no such benefit to the Believers. To Hell with the gullible fools. Make initial plans to execute them all - I want them dead and turned to dust by the end of the week. It's their faith, adulation, etcetera which sustains Her and we must be free of Her presence and Her threat. The Believers are as nothing. Now you can go. Now!"

Markov remained with his most trusted Followers, and began contemplating how to adapt to their new and unforeseen situation. There was a lot to plan for, and a lot to talk about.

At 10pm, a full twelve hours later than usual, Linda was escorted from her room to the grandiose Hall Of Light. As the days had gone by and Father Markov's confidence in Linda's abilities had grown, he had twice moved their sessions to larger rooms, and sometimes invited dozens of other people along. She had even been given new robes to wear, but she still felt as if they were from the outer-reaches of awful.

Despite having been through another day filled with reading tedious books about tedious people doing tedious things, Linda was feeling good. The previous night had made a big difference to her, and today she felt like a person again. Her dream about Avalon had strengthened something deep inside, and reassured her that she could still feel close to her faery and Sceleste, if she tried. And that felt so good. She hummed the tune from the night before under her breath as she walked along the grey stone corridors and almost sensed Sceleste on the way, but dismissed it as a wishful left-over from the dream. Maybe Avalon had been there too, behind a large vase near the Columns Of Whoever.. and that made her feel even better. Maybe they had both really been there, or maybe they hadn't. So.. that would make them half there, wouldn't it? And all her life she'd known that something being 'half there' was a million times better than something being 'not there'.

"I said Good Morning, Lehane Eidahr. Do you not wish me a Good Morning as well? Does even Brother Syrus not receive your Blessings for the day?"

She sat in a different chair facing Father Markov's grandiose desk. This one was old and covered in gold-threaded symbols, and felt a long way from being comfortable. The fact that it was positioned on a security grill just made it feel worse, as if Markov might be able to press a button on his desk and make her disappear into a bottomless pit. She looked at Syrus who avoided eye contact like an expert Eye Contact Avoiderer. He hadn't attended any of the previous sessions, but for some reason he was at this one.

"Odd.." Linda thought to herself. And then she thought it again as she watched Markov flattening the hair down above his ears, and noticed that he hadn't gelled it all back for a change.. and although he seemed his usual irritable self, he was also more than a little distracted. And yet even that wasn't all that was peculiar. The monitor was gone from his gold table, and there were no telephones at all. She smiled to herself as she realised that he couldn't instruct anyone to do something bad, or if he did then it would take quite a while to happen.

He handed her the day's parchment, with the customary long list of hyphenated words for her to repeat. Syrus trudged over to her, looking tired and weary, and handed her the Stone on a new cushion. It had taken on a cloudy redness recently which stayed even when she touched it, and sometimes she could feel quite ill by simply being near it. But she could cope with feeling a bit sick, as long as she didn't think about it too much.

"Well? We are late today, so kindly hurry along with your work," commanded Markov, more gruff than ever.

Linda held the Stone, and looked deep into its cloudiness. It felt bad to hold, passing its dulled colours into her mind even more than it had on the day before. She had to change that feeling, and make it go away. A thought drifted into her mind as if Avalon was speaking to her, and Linda felt ready to do some work - but on her own terms. She met Markov's gaze.

"When it gets cloudy like this," she said, holding the Stone up to make sure he understood, "..it's not so good, and it won't respond much. I.. I need to cleanse it."

He leaned forwards, suspicious and cold. Syrus offered some support, which Linda had hoped he might.

"I do believe The Gifted One may be right, for if anyone would know the best treatment of The Stone, surely such a person would be her? A few moments would not be wasted, I feel."

"Very well," he grudgingly conceded, adding, "But be aware that you are.."

"..being watched intensely, etceteraaah. I know, I know," Linda finished, knowing a quote would annoy him.

In her mind she hummed Avalon's giggled tune, and thought of the cloudiness fading as much as possible, taking away whatever had caused it to go cloudy in the first place. A little reversal was called for, and in her heart she asked for it to do whatever could be done to redress any imbalances between good and evil that she had caused over the previous few days.

A feeling of understanding in her heart told her that far too much had been done to ever put right, but she wasn't too late to ease a lot of suffering. She asked for anything that could be done to be done - or perhaps she instructed or even commanded, because it was so hard for her to know the difference. Without opening her eyes she knew the cloudiness had faded a little, and then it cleared a little more, and then.. she realised the enormous power that had to be unleashed to achieve anything of significance, and she held nothing back. She focussed every good and positive emotion she could muster through to the Stone, letting it build and grow and grow..

..a huge beam of soft light rose in a column, filling the hall and bursting through the walls, the ceiling, the floor and the windows until Linda could feel it reaching the very edges of the clouds. She could feel the night sky being illuminated brighter than any daytime. It spread further and further, reaching all around the world, unrelenting and growing in power, her power, and.. Father Markov struck her across the face and she fell from the chair, sending the Stone spinning across the floor. The light disappeared as suddenly as it had arrived. He stood glaring down at her, and drew a knife from his sleeve.

"Impudent fool! If I thought for one moment that your intentions were anything other than EXACTLY as you'd said, I'd make you wish you'd never been born. Guards! Take this devious beast.."

Syrus intervened, placing a hand on his arm.

"Father Markov? I'm sure the Gifted One means well. Might you consider that she has been so busy recently.. and so beneficial to us, I'm sure you agree? If she is cleansing the Stone, we shall find out in the days ahead, and if she were behaving surreptitiously.. well, again we will find out, surely? I suggest we're not too hasty in our actions, your Majesterial Holiness."

A dozen armed guards had Linda in their sights as Syrus pointed for her to go and pick the Stone up. She placed it back on its cushion.

"And see?" exclaimed Syrus, "The clarity is returning, no doubt a critical and noteworthy improvement?" he added.

Markov looked from Linda to the Stone, and back again.

"Yes, yes.. we will see, tomorrow," he murmured, and hid the ceremonial blade back inside the folds of material.

"I apologise profusely and profoundly, etcetera, Lehane Eidahr. Guards, return her to the Quarters."

Despite her face stinging, Linda was escorted back to her room feeling much better than she had done for almost a week, and more than a little confused about Father Markov. He had definitely been apologetic to her, hadn't he? Shouldn't he have been putting Avalon and Sceleste through agonies, to teach her a lesson? But the hour was far too late to wonder about that, and Linda could feel the distant pounding of a headache coming on.

By the time the three Nocturne Assistants had locked her door, she lay on her bed feeling exhausted and also a little triumphant. She looked over at the moonlight on the floor, and prayed that she'd managed to undo some of the bad things that she'd been causing. She stared and stared, until sleep eventually overcame her.

The fat woman shook her awake and pointed at her breakfast. Linda was annoyed with herself for not dreaming about Avalon again, but changed her mind when she realised she was on top of the bed and still wearing the ridiculous robes from the night before. That was a good sign. That meant she must have been extremely tired, which meant that she must have achieved something extremely important with the Stone.

On the final chime of 10am, the three Morning Assistants walked her to the hall as usual. Her chair had been changed for a wooden stool, and had been moved to the centre of the huge marble floor. Three of the Guild Superiors sat immediately behind it, each holding a long sword.

"I do hope you will not be tempted as you were yesterday. The consequences would be.. predictable, justified, and so and so forth," sneered Markov as Linda nervously sat down. Syrus was there again, and brought her the day's list of Requests, which ran to five pages. Markov leaned forwards, pointing at her.

"You have some catching up to do, and I am in no mood for waiting. The Stone remains here on my table, where it can be seen by us all. Would you care to begin?" he instructed, not taking his eyes off her.

Linda looked at the sheets, but something beyond them caught her eye. She hadn't seen a genuine Half-There for so long that she'd started to wonder if she could still see them. She cast a quick glance up to the top right corner of the ceiling, high into the far stone arch.

"Avie?" she whispered, and knew in her heart Avalon was up there. Then for no reason at all she looked down at the long row of old and not-so-old suits of armour. Her eyes settled at the feet of the tall one which towered third from the end, and she instantly knew Sceleste's eyes were upon her. She couldn't see them, but the feeling was as strong as if Sceleste was lying in her lap and she was looking right at her. Linda stood up, attempting to buy some time to figure out what to do. The tips of three swords pressed against her shoulders and neck, and she sat down again. Her heart pounded. If only she could think straight, if only she could do something clever, if only Sceleste would..

..Sceleste strolled into the centre of the room, and sat midway between Linda and Father Markov. Instead of glaring at him or gazing at Linda, she stared at the long left-side of the hall, transfixed by the armour and crest-laden wall. She hissed loudly.

"What is the meaning of this?" snapped Markov.

"Well hello, Sceleste," Linda said, as calmly as she could manage while trying to understand what was so interesting about the wall. "Is

Mörrah around today? Is that nasty lady bothering you again? Never you mind her, sweety, you come to mummy!" she added, and held her arms out.

Father Markov stood up, and gestured to the Superiors behind Linda. Suddenly the cold steel of all three swords pressed hard against her neck again.

"Be quiet! The Ved'ma is gone! Banished from these.." shouted Markov, drawing his own sword. Syrus placed a hand on his arm, gesturing for him to sit down.

Sceleste wandered over to Linda, not taking her eyes off the wall until she had jumped up onto her lap. Something was definitely bothering her, but for the time being she seemed prepared to let it wait. She stood up on her back legs to look over Linda's shoulder, and fixed her gaze on the three Superiors, searching their souls one by one, finding their most intense fears and nightmares, and passing them from one person to the next. Avalon flew down and settled on Sceleste's head which completely spoiled the moment, but not the effect. The first dropped his sword, fell to his knees and started babbling incoherently, while the second tried to run out of the room. He missed the doorway completely, collided with the wall and rendered himself unconscious beneath a display of shields. The third merely collapsed, clutching his chest and gasping for breath.

"The man in the subway did that, and the monks too! Why do People do that so much?" shouted Avalon, completely over-excited for a hundred different reasons. Sceleste looked over to the wall again and a mild tremor went through the floor, but Linda couldn't have cared less. She wrapped her arms around Sceleste and felt Avalon hugging the side of her face, crying all over her cheek. Another tremor, much stronger than the last one, shook the floor and didn't appear to be fading away at all.

Suddenly an explosion ripped through the left wall launching rocks, masonry, glass and a huge cloud of heavy dust throughout the hall. More explosions immediately followed, coming from all directions at once as if the entire palace was under attack. Huge splintering wooden beams fell from the ceiling and for a moment Linda was too shocked to do anything. Avalon re-tied her braid in a split second, tugged it to get her attention and shouted something in front of her as the first of the Government's black-masked troops ran in through the gaping holes. Linda fell to her knees and started crawling through the mayhem.

Sceleste had settled on the security grating in the floor, and pawed at its intricate ironwork. Avalon darted down to her, and desperately waved for Linda to come and join them, and open it up. But Linda had her mind on something else. She could see the Stone. It was still on Father Markov's table lying dull and blackened next to his bullet-riddled body. She ran and screamed her way through the gunfire, thinking of nothing other than holding the Stone and taking it anywhere, anywhere that was far away from everyone.

But she had to stop. A soldier stood at the table, pointing the kind of gun at her that could probably blow holes through planets. He unleashed a blast over Linda's head that sent her rolling backwards until she hit a smashed table, and lay breathless in the rubble. She watched him knock Markov to the floor as he snatched the Stone and ran outside, flanked by two others. They were soon lost behind more troops and the approaching tanks.

Linda felt layers of dust and rubble covering her as she lay dazed in all the madness, and squealed as something pinched her ear. She turned around to see Avalon fluttering and pointing over to Sceleste, who was still sitting on the security panel, casually examining a paw as if nothing at all was happening. Linda got to her knees.

Two soldiers were clambering over fallen stonework, either to take her away or ensure that she didn't survive the onslaught, so she ran for Sceleste. She slid onto the grating and grabbed her as the ironwork gave way, and they landed with a harsh bump a few feet below. She cradled Sceleste in her arms, and scrambled along as the entrance above them filled with wrecked armour and stone blocks.

"Now that was close.. close," she breathed, pausing for a moment. Avalon was still crying as she hugged Linda's hair and Sceleste at the same time. The walls shook violently, but at that moment nothing outside the security tunnel mattered at all.

"Avie, Avie, I'm so pleased you're okay.. they were going to hurt you both if I didn't read stuff out and I was scared and I hated me more than anything ever! Did I hurt you? Say I didn't.."

"You couldn't if you tried! But don't try again, all the same.."

Sceleste meowed disdainfully, more aware of the chaos than Linda or Avalon seemed to be. A crack appeared all the way around the walls as another explosion rocked everything about them, and Linda crawled on her knees in the darkness until the noise abated slightly. Avalon hovered ahead, shining brighter than ever, and turned around looking puzzled.

"Do you think Mörrah's caused all that? We helped her get away, and she was so bad even though we'd been really good to her. Can we stay here 'till all the noise goes?"

The walls shook again, and hundreds of falling stones sent crashes echoing along the narrow tunnel.

"No, no I don't think so. That army might want to wipe the whole place out even with everyone still in it, I reckon. Do you know where this goes to?"

"Uhuh. These go under everywhere in the whole palace, and in the walls by staircases too. Sceleste and me have been looking around for ages! The dents on the wall say what part we're in, and what direction we're going in.."

Linda fell flat as a huge explosion rocked the entire floor.

"Well, we need to be somewhere safe, but more to the point, we need to.. get the.."

"Not again?" said Avalon, raising her arms in despair.

"Well I nearly had it, but a big army type soldier got there first.."

Linda could see that Avalon was close to being either upset or annoyed, and that Sceleste was looking under-fed and much the worse for wear. The madness above could wait for a minute or two, despite every part of her brain telling her to keep moving and get out of there. She shuffled through the pockets of her usual clothes underneath her vestments and found some old broken hazelnut biscuits and the odd-shaped remnants of a packet of HappyKat YumYum. They didn't last long, and Linda awarded herself a silent round of applause.

"Look at this robe.." she said, gladly pulling it over her head, "..it's a billion times worse than the last one, and that was the worst thing ever - even worse than that goat-hair-thing I had at the castle.."

"The burial shroud?" asked Avalon.

"Huh? It was a..? Ewww, gross.." she said, before realising something important.

"I know this sounds stupid, but before we leave here I have to go back to my room, I want my mum's picture - it's all I've got of her. Do you think we can manage that?"

Avalon nodded, shook her head and then nodded again.

"Come on then.." she sang, and Linda crawled behind her as the noises drifted further away little by little, soon replaced by sporadic bursts of gunfire instead. They re-emerged in the main corridor of the palace's Central Secure Zone, two short corridors away from her

Formal Quarters. Avalon lead the way to her room, giggling and saying how she'd been there the other night.

"So that wasn't a dream? That was really you?" gasped Linda as they rounded the final corner.

"Uhuh, but you were asleep and when you're asleep, nothing wakes you up. You sleep like a.. like a.. you."

They stood outside her room, where the walls bowed outwards, and long cracks had opened up around the door. Linda gave it a push, and nothing happened. Even if it wasn't locked, the lop-sided stonework had secured it like a tomb. Avalon took a long flying approach to the door, stopped an inch or two before it and delivered a small kick. Nothing happened for two or three seconds, but then the door hurtled across the room taking the dressing table on its way and demolishing most of the bathroom. She flew straight to the cd player while Linda ran for her treasured picture, then gathered up Aggy and the cd's. She threw whatever else she could find into her suitcase and fiddled with its irritating little catches while the gunfire came nearer.

The room shook as she lifted it off the bed, and new columns of dust poured through the widening cracks in the ceiling. More explosions rocked the whole building, and vast chunks of plaster and stone cascaded around her from the room above. A gaping section opened up from one side of the wall to the middle, and Linda screamed at Avalon to go out and fly away to somewhere high and safe. She stumbled across the floor to fetch Sceleste, and suddenly found herself lying at the foot of the bed staring at two Scelestes, two floors, two suitcases.. three.. four.. too many of everything.

She dreamily wondered if the entire ceiling had just landed on her head, or maybe she'd been shot by a particularly large bullet, or maybe even knocked over by a toppling bedpost. The room grew hazy and drifted far away while she pondered whether or not a three-poster bed was as good as a four-poster one, and then nothing really mattered much at all..

CHAPTER THIRTY
Government Circles

..and then she tried to blink, but couldn't quite do it. Her head felt as if an entire family of hippos had moved in and were shifting the furniture around. She tried to blink again. One eye opened properly, and then the other decided to have a go, allowing a brief glimpse of a new place. The world around her was blurred and wouldn't stay still, but that didn't matter. There weren't any explosions or guns going off anymore, and everywhere seemed wonderfully quiet. She closed her eyes again, and listened. She could hear the fluttering of delicate wings, and felt the air moving gently over her skin, making her feel as if she was lying in tall, feathery grass on a gorgeous day in a world where everything was warm and nothing short of idyllic. And the breeze was whispering her name, gently calling and effortlessly guiding her away, taking her back, gently, gently..

Avalon hovered a few inches in front of her face, smiling and singing a cleverly adapted Healing Song. She had changed its melody to Dancing Queen, and over the course of the morning she had changed all the words to Dancing Queen as well. She hummed and sang until Linda had woken up enough to speak.

"Avuhl.. ah yoowokay? Wayr'z we now, Avlunn?" she mumbled, and tried to rub her eyes but missed completely.

"Safe place. Big Hos Pital with things that bleep, and People who know what to do. Stay dreamy, Lindy, that's best now."

That made sense to Linda, and she did as she was told.

A few hours passed before the world became clearer and a lot more stable. Sceleste jumped up onto the bed, meticulously picking each step before settling near the pillows. She stared at Linda without blinking for an age, and then gently trapped Avalon under one of her paws to make her presentable. Linda breathed a slight laugh, and looked around.

The room was clean and clinical, with a flight-deck of monitors running along one side of the bed. Her mother's picture sat prominently on top of a trolley on the other side, which had been crammed and overloaded with small jars and bottles of pills. Aggy had a nice chair just beyond that, and even had her own cushion. The cd's had been taken out of their cases and stood along the window ledge in a shining row, all perfectly balanced on their edges. Linda figured that had to be the work of Avalon.

"I think she's clean enough, Sceleste.. you are a good girl, aren't you?" she whispered, and stroked her head.

Avalon wriggled free and shook herself four times before hovering just in front of Linda.

"Hello sleepy! You're awake!" she exclaimed, staring into each eye to make sure.

"Hmm.. just about. I'm so glad you two are okay. Did I miss much?"

"Not really. You fell over a cereal bowl in your room and bumped your head on the floor. Then everything started collapsing and the Soldiers burst in and Sceleste got a bit cross and gave them one of her looks, so they decided to shoot each other, not you. Then there were more explosions and fires and the Palace isn't there anymore, and some different Soldiers took us all here. Yesterday, I think. Apart from that, nothing's happened. Oh, there's wires and things coming out of your hair."

Linda felt a headband running from one ear to the other across the top of her head. It seemed to be connected to some of the monitors, but it wasn't hurting and didn't appear to be doing anything, so she left it alone.

"Wow. You two aren't kept away from me, are you? You're here with me all the time?"

"Uhuh. All the time. They might have to look at your head though. You've got a big bump.. just there."

Avalon poked where the bump was, so that Linda would know which part to be really, really careful about.

"Ow. That is so utterly me, isn't it? World War 3 breaks out all around us, and I get wounded by a bowl of muesli. So embarrassing."

Avalon nodded, and Sceleste purred for some more attention. Linda obliged, but Avalon didn't want to risk another clean.

"I wonder how long we'll be here?" Linda asked, looking around.

"Only a few days! The doctor said so. She said you'd be finished.. no, they'd be finished, after that. Either you or them - I'm not sure.. I heard her in the Coffee Room. And look - press this! Press this!"

Avalon shuffled a small, narrow grey box across the sheets, and pointed at its red button.

"What's that do, Avie?"

"It's a Magical Summoning Thing. A Person comes in, checks

you're alright, and goes away again! She's like some sort of Healing Spirit, a powerful kind who can.."

"A nurse. She's a nurse."

"She checks your temp-atch-ure and looks at the bleep-things. Press it now! I've been doing it all morning and it's worked every time! That's why you're getting better!"

Avalon jumped on the button and darted behind Aggy, trembling with excitement while Linda began trying to think of an apology. The door soon opened and a trim matron walked in, analysing a clip board loaded with Linda's charts.

"He-hello.. is that.. someone there?" Linda wavered, with a voice intended to be so sympathy-inducing that even Genghis Khan's heart would have melted.

"Ah, you've pressed it yourself this time! You do have a very mischievous cat, don't you? You wouldn't believe the number of times I've had to come in here expecting to see.."

Sceleste meowed her innocence, while the friendly woman made her tenth check of Linda's monitors.

"Open up.." she said, tapping Linda's chin.

"That's a biro, isn't it?"

"Excellent, your vision's fine! Now open up.."

The matron swapped her pen for a thermometer and waited patiently for the red line to stop moving. She held it up into the sunlight and added the latest reading to her list, and then proceeded to ask a few simple medical questions. How was her head? Did her ears feel tingly? Did she like chicken and pasta? She finished with small talk about cats, and appeared to have no idea who her patient was. That was a relief. Linda felt too tired to be Linda anymore.

"I'll tell Dr Thulin that you're back with us. She's been very keen to meet you. Stayed here all night! She slept on the couch outside. You must be famous, or from a rich family - or maybe both? Well I can't talk all day, work to do, jobs to be.."

Less than two minutes after the nurse left, a slight woman with prematurely greying hair hurried in. She spent a moment or two casting an eye over Linda's charts and monitor readings, listened to her heartbeat for a while, and then sat down on the bed near Sceleste. She smiled down at Linda, and seemed to be friendly.

"How are you feeling, Linda? Or do you prefer what the cult called you?"

"Linda's fine, please, not that weirdy stuff. How come you know my real name?"

"Clues. There are five sticky name-labels on your cd player, five on the top edge of your picture frame, five on each cd case, five on the back of your bear's head, five.."

"Well.. you see, my dice.."

"It's alright, little quirks make us who we are, don't they? Some of us more than others, granted.. now then, how are you feeling?"

Linda had a think for a while.

"Pretty much okay now, but I'd love to know what's going on."

"Yes, of course. I'm Dr Thulin but you can call me Besha, unless there are military people around who look important, in which case do call me Doctor - it sounds much more formal.. you know what men can be like. You're in the Hospital Wing of the Alliance Military Facility, which is rated as a Level One Cross-National Security Site."

"Oh. Is that good?"

The doctor nodded and flipped a few pages over on her clipboard.

"Yes, I should say so. Level One means that nobody outside these walls knows what we do, apart from the American Government, the Russians, the Chinese and our host Ukrainian one, of course. They all finance us for various military development projects. In the eyes of the rest of the world, we're a humble engineering research centre.. and that suits us and everyone else very well."

"Huh?" was the best reply Linda could think of.

"In other words, you're safe. Very safe. There aren't any pseudo-religious bullies to bother you. Do you want a coffee? Maybe tea? It's better that we keep things nice and light for the time being, because once you're back on your feet, we really do have so much we need to talk to you about."

"Yeah, I'll bet you do. Like the Stone?"

Dr Thulin sighed and looked mournfully to the window.

"Yes, there is that, and one or two other things besides."

"I can tell you loads, just don't ask me to explain any of it. Or prove it. And I'm not sure I can even remember it all in the right order anymore."

Dr Thulin laughed, and stroked Sceleste's head. Sceleste glared at her while purring at the same time, so she took her hand away.

"Well, we don't need you offering any more proof to us about that thing - just an outline of how a girl like you crossed hundreds of years to arrive exactly as predicted by an obscure 12th Century cleric. How and why, that would be nice. Well, it would be a start, at least."

"That's easy - Mörrha. Don't get me started about her."

"Who?"

"Mörrha. She's also known as the second Queen Ephra, not the first. She's a Ved'ma, and she's good at it."

"A Ved'ma?" laughed Dr Thulin, "..why that's just folklore, barely fanciful mythology. Peasant stories to explain human nature and to scare naughty children into being good children!"

Linda tried to shake her head, but the wires and strapping wouldn't let her move easily. A monitor gave a loud double bleep, and the doctor held her hands up for Linda to relax.

"You're still exhausted and groggy, so I'll wait until you're better-fed and back on your feet before making any notes," she said and put her pens back in her top pocket, still laughing. "We're far more interested in the fabled Odessa Stone than in old folk-tales. You know, something like that Stone really shouldn't exist. Such power.. it's quite frightening. Officially, it doesn't exist and never did, of course. The Government line is that the palace was a training ground for terrorists, and needed destroying once enough evidence had been conveniently found. So at long last that wretched cult's gone.. people can be worse than sheep, can't they? They'll follow anything."

Sceleste gave a high meow, and rolled onto her side for some serious scratching, and Linda set to work again.

"The palace and everything's gone? All of it?" she said, mid-scratch.

Dr Thulin nodded and moved the wires from one monitor to another. The new one had yellow lights instead of green ones, and looked like it belonged in a cheap games-arcade.

"I'm pleased to hear that, really pleased," Linda added. "How come they didn't finish me off?"

"You? Because we know who you are. You can't be the Holy Icon poster-girl for religious fanatics stretching back hundreds of years without other people getting to know about you as well. But if you hadn't been in your room, you certainly wouldn't be here now.. and you'd be a whole lot thinner as well. The forces knew where you ought to be because the palace was watched all the time. Almost every room, in fact. Regrettably, the Government took a few days to realise that you had actually turned up, and they wanted to wait for proof that the Stone worked before they'd do anything. And you've been giving us a lot of proof, haven't you?"

Linda felt a knot in her stomach.

"I didn't know what the words ever meant, it was awful there.."

"The light display the other night was the final straw. They got NASA to explain to the world that it was some kind of solar storm, which also explained a few other.. recent events. Of course, the Russians agreed, and the Chinese were on-side with it, and then the press agencies towed the line. So the troops went in. The CIA wanted the place nuked, but that would have been hard to explain."

"I didn't know what was going on.. they were so bad to us. Father Markov said.."

"Relax, we know all about him. Former military chief, discharged twenty years ago for being war-damaged and psychotic, to put it mildly. Now then, speaking very confidentially, no-one holds you responsible for your actions over the past week, but that could change. Having something as powerful as that Stone.. well it's got to be a temptation, hasn't it? There's a lot of top-level activity here."

Linda nodded, watching Dr Thulin's lips closely as she spoke.

"Just so that I know, Besha, are you talking Russian or English?"

"Pardon?"

"See, I'm speaking English, but I don't know if you are."

The doctor looked bemused, and jotted a few words down on her clipboard.

"Umm.. well.. I'd say you're tired, and that bump's not helping."

"I'm serious, really I am. Avalon showed me how to read things and people, and now I never know when I'm doing it. I do all kinds of stuff without realising.."

"Who's Avalon?"

"My best friend ever. She's a faer.. bir.. depends. Never mind, bit of a secret. Anyway, the first time I came to Odessa we found an old book and I put my hand on it, and it all made sense like we were flying through the words and that's how this all started really. But now I talk to people who shouldn't understand me, and yet they do. And me too them, as well."

She finished writing, put a few ticks on another page and then scratched her head with the wrong end of the pen.

"Hmm.. in my opinion.. as long as you understand what you're talking about, I think we can all be happy."

She reached across and turned one of the dials down, and a small ball of light bounced around its monitor screen a little more slowly.

"Before you go, what's up with my head?"

"They're only electrodes, so you don't need to be worried. We're recording different parts of your neural activity at the moment, and after that we'll start some tests and scans to find out what the Stone responds to in your brainbox. Stop me if I'm getting too technical. Once we know what influences and affects the Stone, we can all start figuring out how to get rid of it. You see, it's completely unaffected by heat, cold, radiation, pressure and so on and so on.. jargon and more jargon. It's a strange one, that's for sure."

Sceleste purred loudly.

"Anyone tried getting it to do anything yet? Sounds like they just want to find out how to use it themselves," said Linda, indignantly.

"Don't speak like that. Now then, I'd say you need another injection before this evening's tests.."

"I don't, really! There's nothing wrong with me.. I don't have to go to sleep," she said, and Sceleste settled on Linda's front and prepared her claws. Dr Thulin's hand paused over her small white case, and she appeared to change her mind.

"Yes, well, alright then. Maybe you don't need one, perhaps. You're healthier than we thought. I have a few rounds to do, so I'll say 'bye' for the time being, but I'll look in on you in thirty minutes or so, I hope. Honestly, there's new staff everywhere. It's all your fault, you know!"

She gave a final laugh and went out, locking the door behind her. Avalon emerged from behind Aggy and settled on Sceleste's head.

"That's the Doctor who hooked you up to all this, and she let us stay with you. Is she your new friend?"

Linda stared at the door for a long moment, and then gradually worked the band of wires upwards until it slipped off her head. Most of the monitors stopped moving.

"No, I don't think so. I trust her about as much as the rest of.. can you smell anything?"

Avalon followed the air currents up to the vent in the ceiling, directly above the bed.

"Yes, there's bitter smells.. coming from.. up.." she spiralled down to the bed, landing on Linda who was already asleep. Sceleste couldn't fight it, and growled defiantly as the world drifted away from her.

A few hours later Linda woke up in a new room. Her mind was swimming in treacle, and she spent a long time slowly looking into the darkness, trying to focus on anything at all and piece together her new surroundings. Weak moonlight occasionally filtered in through the window, but not enough to offer much help. The monitors around her were all switched off and the electrodes had all gone from her head, which was a relief. Her mother's picture was there beside her, and so was Aggy which made her feel a little better. But Sceleste and Avalon were gone.

She breathed steadily and deeply for a while, trying to wake herself up enough to figure out what was happening. Eventually she managed to sit upright, and soon felt able to trust her legs sufficiently to get out of bed. She walked over to the secured window, and looked out from her first floor room across a huge expanse of fields, fences and trees stretching far into the night. A soldier with a gun marched a few feet below, and halted directly at the bushes beneath her. Linda's heart stopped, and she wondered if he knew that she had dared to get out of bed. After a few seconds he started walking again, traipsing his night-watch path, and soon turned a corner and wandered out of sight.

A series of small red lights came on as she walked into the main part of the room, which meant nothing to her until a narrow striplight along the length of the ceiling started flashing. Hundreds more bright red dots began blinking intermittently all over the walls, stinging her eyes and creating a disorientating contrast with the darkness. She hurried back to the bed, and as soon as her feet were off the floor all the lights went out. Then she noticed a small box with a button on it, similar to the one Avalon had perfected using earlier on. She pressed it, hoping the friendly nurse would come in and tell her things were fine. A few minutes dragged by, and Linda gave up waiting. She pulled the sheets up to her chin, and stared at the window for a while. Her mind began to drift, and the sleepy feeling came back.

"Feeling.. lonely?" said a calm voice. Linda turned to her, but the woman stayed in the darkness, just out of the moonlight.

"Whuh.. sorry, I was.. I didn't hear you come in. Yes I am feeling lonely. Are you the nurse from this afternoon, or a new one?"

The woman paused before answering.

"You think she would spend every minute of the day waiting on you? To do such a thing.. who would wait even one day for you?"

Linda was taken aback by her harsh attitude, but her mind wasn't working properly enough to pay attention for long - after all, what kind of person would work a nightshift in a top-secret place?

"Oh, I'm sorry, I forgot it's this late. Where's Avalon and my cat..

are they in the other room? I want to be with them."

"I understand, really I do.. you must be so concerned, away from your companions. I can change that for you. I can change a lot of things for all of us."

"Who are you?" Linda whispered to the darkness.

"Don't you know?"

"No.."

"Then think of me as your Night Doctor. I look after you through the dark hours. We'll speak tomorrow, I'm sure."

"You've not got injections and stuff have you?"

She paused again before answering, and Linda tried hard not to fall asleep.

"Hell would freeze before I resort to such crude measures. I know that you are here now, and I will come again for you. We have work to do, but not tonight."

"Is Dr Thulin around?"

"Not for much longer."

"Is she leaving?"

"In a way. I must leave you now."

The woman slowly click-clacked to the door, and she was gone. There was definitely something a little familiar about her manner, or maybe her voice, maybe her walk, but heavy sleep quickly returned and took away any thoughts running through Linda's mind.

The next day was bright and sunny, but Linda didn't know too much about it. Dr Thulin had arranged a series of scans and tests for her, and she was wheeled from one room to another, each more intimidating and mechanical than the last. Over the course of the day, a dozen doctors introduced themselves and even explained what they were going to do, but they needn't have bothered. Most of them had at least one injection for her, or a special medical cocktail to make sure the scans would show up clearly. If she hadn't slept through most of it, the day would have really dragged.

But that night, as her clock flicked around to 2am, something at the edge of a dream made Linda wake up. Maybe a sound, maybe a brief current of cold air, or maybe someone saying her name.. she couldn't tell, because it was gone as quickly as it came. She blinked in the darkness, feeling groggy but glad to be awake and able to think fairly straight. A woman's footsteps approached the bed. The Night Doctor must have been doing her rounds.

"Good. You're awake at last. We have work to do."

"Huh? Who're you? The Night Doctor person?" she mumbled, squinting into the darkness.

"Yes, undoubtedly. We don't have much time. Now get up and get dressed. Be very quick!"

"The lights'll go crazy.."

"I've taken care of the lights. You have nothing to fear."

Linda liked the sound of that.

"What are we going to do?" she asked, feeling sick after sitting up too quickly.

"This night we must get the Stone. The filth in here want you to carry on doing what you're so good at, but this time you'll be acting as the puppet of Governments instead of religious fools. Do you want that? And once they deduce how you command such power, they'll cast you aside like ashes to the wind. Imagine what you will have unleashed upon the world! Quite a legacy, wouldn't you agree?"

"Uhuh.. but why d'you need me?" Linda asked, still unable to separate the woman from the night.

"This isn't a job for one person or even two - but two is all we have, and once you control the Stone again.. but we have very little time, so you must hurry!"

"But I don't even know where it is, though."

"Quiet, fool, and get ready! Delay, delay, delay.."

Linda was shocked to be snapped at in such a way. She quickly dressed, and dutifully followed the Night Doctor into the impenetrable blackness of the corridor. All she could do was follow the sound of the footsteps and hope nothing was in her way. At the end of the first corridor she had woken up enough to feel something deep inside telling her not to be alone. She stopped, and whispered loudly to the woman, out to wherever she might be.

"Where's Avalon and Sceleste? I'm not going anywhere without them first."

"What?" she hissed back. Her voice appeared to be immediately in front of Linda, unlike her footsteps, and when she continued speaking she was even closer.

"Don't be worried about them! We have little time and if anything is to be 'first' it shall be the Stone! You can get them afterwards!"

"No. I'm always being pushed around. I need them now. We have to get them first," said Linda, surprising herself with her firm tone.

The woman breathed loudly, as if she was trying to suppress her anger. Her footsteps lead to a moon-lit room containing perspex boxes and an array of technical displays and apparatus, which Linda didn't like the look of at all. Her heart sank as she noticed that the room had the same bitter smell that had invaded her own room the previous day. She felt drawn to a corner on the far side, beyond a wall of silent monitors. A small container held the faintest of silvery glows, and Linda ran to it. She unscrewed the entry-disc on its top and lifted Avalon out, whispering and blowing softly on her, coaxing her to wake. The Night Doctor stayed in the corridor, loudly pacing back and forth and muttering incoherently to herself.

"L'nndy?" drawled Avalon, barely able to keep her eyes open. She soon lay across Linda's shoulder, wrapped in the braid and shuffling herself underneath the waves of hair until she felt safe.

"Yeah's me here, Avie, we're all okay now, I think.." she said hopefully, and wondered where to look for Sceleste's container.

"Downdowndowwwwnn.." Avalon slurred, and Linda saw the lid of a container set firmly in the floor. She unscrewed it and reached inside, gently waving her hand in the darkness before brushing against Sceleste's fur. Inch by inch she brought her up through the narrow gap, and found that she was in a deep sleep. She held her in a position that was hopefully comfortable, and crept from the room. The Night Doctor's echoing footsteps were lost in the darkness a long way ahead, and Linda hurried after her. Avalon was practically awake after a few steps, shook her head a few times and shivered as she felt a cold wind pass over her. Sceleste stirred far more slowly.

"Stop! Here, now!" instructed the doctor as Linda unwittingly walked straight by her. The door swung open to reveal a vast laboratory, only illuminated at the far end by the pale light of the emergency back-up system. Linda warily entered, and immediately found herself standing at the main control desk, at the start of a series of rows of computers and monitors. She climbed up onto the desk and looked across the top of them. The Stone was lying a short distance away in the centre of a wide slab of white quartz, surrounded by broad lightbeams and lasers, all of which were deflected and interrupted by countless tiny spinning mirrors. The Stone itself was encased in a rotating circle of light which kept changing in colour from bright red to an almost invisible blue. Linda watched transfixed as two metronomic columns of green light slowly moved backwards and forwards on either side of the Stone, buzzing and blurred, adding to the hypnotic effect. A pulse of neon blue went through the Stone and the Night Doctor smacked a large monitor in frustration, snapping Linda's attention back to her.

"So very, very fascinating, isn't it? After two whole days of testing, it's revealed not even one of its secrets. The authorities are intent on getting it to work without you, and therein lies the very essence of the problem. Now then, we must rid the world of it, and we have barely two more minutes before the main power supply gets fixed and the guards endeavour to determine why we're here alone."

"Uhuh.."

"So I'll kill the emergency power, which should only leave a few lasers operational - I don't know how to remove those, so you'd better not walk into them. Now leave your friends here - hurry and fetch it, and I'll get us all out of this.. this.. place, understand? We have to work together! Age quod agis, as the better of us say." *(..Do what you do carefully..)*

Linda left Sceleste half-asleep on a desk near the front and then made her way towards the Stone. The emergency power went off surprisingly quickly, leaving behind just darkness and the low buzzing sound. Linda approached the quartz. She looked at the black Stone, and the lattice of red beams around it.

"Avie, it's still surrounded by laser things! What do we do?"

Avalon fluttered ahead for a closer look, careful not to drop the end of the braid, and sniffed at the air.

"I think that's Alexandryite light, from special light-stones," she whispered back.

"Alexandrite light? That could make sense. Are you sure?"

"Maybe. Harmless and pretty. Watch me."

"No, Avie!"

Avalon fluttered through the beam twice, and then once again so that she could perch on the Stone. She waved to Linda, who grinned and reached in for it.

"That's good," called the Night Doctor, "..you take it, child. The beams are.. presumably for sundry research purposes.. hurry!"

Linda's hands closed around the Stone, and Sceleste suddenly jolted awake. She struggled to understand where she was, and tried to make herself stand upright to face the evil lurking in the darkness. She looked around, bewildered and confused.

Linda felt a sudden wave of dizziness, but didn't have time to try and understand why. Her heart was pounding too much and she expected every alarm bell in the world to start ringing in a huge chorus of accusation. But nothing happened. She turned to bring the Stone back, surprised at how easy it had all been, and suddenly felt deeply troubled by something. Sceleste was sitting upright on the desk, peering into the darkness. A door clicked open somewhere in the line of her gaze, but Linda didn't pay any attention to it, for now that she was holding the Stone she was intent solely on thinking of somewhere safe to take Avalon and Sceleste.. as soon as she could have a moment to sit down and hold a few thoughts in her foggy mind. She was too distracted, too tired and still feeling rough from a day full of injections and metallic drinks. The door clicked again as she went to pick Sceleste up.

Suddenly all the lights came back on, flooding the laboratory with an unbearable brightness. Linda slipped the Stone into her inside pocket and covered her eyes, only allowing small slivers of light between her fingers and desperately willing her eyes to adapt more quickly. Steady, sharp footsteps came nearer and nearer, and walked around her twice before coming to a halt somewhere in front of her. Sceleste's claws made small scratching sounds as she dropped to the floor and hurried to Linda's side.

She lowered her hands from her eyes and looked straight into the emotionless face of Mörrah. Her skin was roughened and drawn, and her red eyes were deep-set and burning with intent.

"You?" whispered Linda.

Avalon's eyes finally started working again. She squeaked and shuffled behind Linda's neck.

"And you were expecting someone else, child?"

"How can you be here?"

Linda felt invisible fingernails dragging lightly against the side of her face. She shivered and covered her cheek with her hand but it made no difference, and they began moving back upwards. Sceleste stood at Linda's feet, swaying her tail from side to side. Mörrah held back a flinch, and the nails drifted away. She stared from the cat back up to Linda.

"I have many roles, such is my privilege. For a Being of my importance, relying on a Cult could never be my only option. There are many paths for one such as I to walk, and I have been visiting this Institute from the day it was first planned - sometimes an official, sometimes no more than a shadow.. or for you, a Night Doctor. And now my time has served me well."

Linda felt numb, and knew she had to say anything.

"Did.. did you cause the palace to get wrecked?"

"Cause? No. I assisted their demise, as they deserved. That disloyal body had been my life's work since the woeful day that you infected my existence.. they were deluded, felt they had grown too strong for me.. betrayed me. I merely guided other fools to do that which I could not, but I fear they took it a little far. And now without the beating heart of so many of my Followers, I can't allow any more unforeseen situations to arise.. with the Gemstone the end of life need not blight me, for oh, the power within reach! The High Priestess herself will bow before me.."

"What if we don't.." Avalon emerged from the left side of Linda's neck, peering from under her hair, "..don't want to help you?" she said, and Linda nodded.

"You won't defy me for long. I will never leave you alone. You'll want to die, but I won't allow that to happen until I choose your time. Your nights will be oh, so very long. And the days? You will do anything to please me, unleashing your misery to nations.. and you're so very good at that, child. Perhaps you need to be shown what you've been doing? No, this is not the time, and certainly not the place.. there would be too much for you to see!"

Linda could feel her heart pounding harder than ever as Mörrah spread a sheet of thick black cloth onto a table. A heavy mist rose slowly in its centre, causing the edges to ripple.

"You are to indulge me a brief ceremony. Place the Gemstone, my Gemstone, upon this.. cloth."

"Don't Linda, no! That's a Unification.. Wyth-ern.. W-thing! Bad!" squealed Avalon, falling over her words and tugging at Linda's ear.

"Ahh, the little one has a brain after all!" Mörrah derided.

"What's that b-black thing?" stammered Linda.

"You give the Stone to it, and we then recite these verses which have taken a great deal of painful preparation during our long time apart. Would you be so kind?" she added with a contemptuous grin, and unfurled a scroll.

"Why, what are they for?"

"They grant me a little influence in your Requests. I will command through you, and we have a little power-sharing, at least for a while - I shan't pretend otherwise, as I don't intend needing you for long. There are others to be found.. ones more willing!"

Linda's legs were shaking so much that she had to support herself against the table. Mörrah looked straight into her.

"What would you prefer? Spend the rest of your miserable life being dissected in here and plagued by me, or an unspecified time as my associate? I might even grant you freedom, if you prove amenable. Freedom for the Bringer! You'd like that wouldn't you? Now place my Gemstone here, NOW!"

Linda's mind wasn't up to this kind of dilemma, so she didn't even try to think of an answer. Besides, she had no idea what 'amenable' meant. She did know that she hadn't a hope of calming herself enough to use the Stone to create a safe place to escape into, so she needed a cunning alternative, and needed it very quickly. Mörrah pointed to the swirling mist, and Sceleste meowed sharply. At precisely the same moment that Mörrah cast a disgusted glare at Sceleste, Linda had the kind of idea that normally wouldn't go anywhere near her. It was more of an attitude than an idea, and something deep inside her wouldn't allow any self-doubt to creep in and take over. She took the Stone from her inside pocket, and made her hands tremble even more than they were already.

"I need.. I need to hold it," she said, putting an extremely pathetic shake into her voice.

"No, I believe you do not. I've seen you command it at distance - and I know precisely what you can do. Avoid lying to me."

"But I'm weak, I'm so weak, Mörrah.. Father Markov and then the doctors.. they've been very uh.. demanding. Perhaps we both hold it?"

Linda held the Stone out towards her, knowing that she would never be able to resist such a temptation. Mörrah's long, cold fingers entwined Linda's, until her hands were completely wrapped around the upper half of the Stone. The touch of her skin sent a bolt of ice straight into Linda's heart, and a splitting pain through her head. A smile spread across Mörrah's face like a mask of demonic ecstasy, as a lifetime of desire and torment lay in her clutches. Her red eyes turned as black as the Stone.. but Linda's side took on a faint, almost imperceptible blueness.

"Tell me.. what to say, please Mörrah.. and I'll do my.. best for you, really I will," she pined in weak, short breaths.

Mörrah forced her attention back to the girl. Her pencil-thin lips curled into a smirk, and she slowly whispered the first of the verses.. and Linda slowly nodded.

"Please, my Lady Mörrah.. please can I hear them again? Your words are all.. they're all so new to me.."

Mörrah could hardly contain her glory at exerting such control over the Gifted One, and laughed wildly as she tightened her grip around the Stone. She repeated the words loudly enough to fill the room, and finished by looking down into the child's eyes - and found that the girl was already staring straight up into hers. And the Gifted One even dared to speak?

"Cast this foul and aged Spiritae into realms of darkness! Captive of the weakest!" Linda screamed, not questioning or doubting for a moment that the Stone would do as she wanted.

In her mind, she saw the empty Faery Dust bag hanging loosely from Avalon's thin gold belt.. but nothing happened, and for a few long seconds, a crypt-like silence hung between them. Her eyes stayed locked onto the narrowed black slits in Mörrah's porcelain-white face, and saw them flicker with utter disbelief. Mörrah laughed again, but this time in a short and forced snatch. Linda held the image of Avalon's bag in her mind, and pushed.

At the precise moment that Mörrah began summoning her vilest curse, her body turned into a cloud of swirling shadows, and formed a screaming whirlwind that grew narrower and narrower until only a near-invisible thread remained. It bowed in the middle, from where it was drawn towards Avalon.

"Oh not me, no, no, nooo.." Avalon warbled, wanting to fly up to the ceiling in a bid to get away from her Medicamentum pouch. She quickly realised that even if she got there the pouch would still be with her, so she didn't try. Well, not much. Once the shadowy line had disappeared inside it she drew the silver thread tightly, and tied an elaborate bow. The small bag twisted and shook with Mörrah's violent struggles, throwing Avalon in all directions.

"I can't do this! I'm not strong enough and she's still scary-mad!"

"Avie, just keep the string tight, and maybe we'll let her out one day. Come down to me now, it's fine.. I'm getting such a headache.."

Linda picked Sceleste up, gave her a hug and slipped the nearly-clear Stone back into her inside pocket. Avalon took an unavoidably scenic route to Linda's shoulder, and became much happier once she was holding the braid tightly and had settled down on Sceleste.

They hurried into the dark corridor and Linda closed her eyes and thought of her room, her picture, and Aggy. She held Sceleste tightly and started walking just as she had done in the Chapel, knowing the walls were passing her by in the darkness. Somewhere far away an alarm bell had started ringing, and its faint traces echoed along the corridors and spurred her onwards. It was soon joined by another, and then another, each one a little bit nearer and louder. Linda ignored them all. She kept on running faster and faster, turning when she felt she ought to and leaping over the prostrate bodies of guards without even realising she was doing so. Avalon knew the corpses were there, and felt sick wondering what Mörrah had done to them all. A series of emergency strip-lights came on, illuminating the centre of the corridor floor with a dull green path for her to follow, but she was oblivious to them all. Her eyes stayed closed until she was back in her room.

"Okay, nice and calm, where to now, where to.. where to?" she said to herself while taking her mother's picture out of its frame and putting it safely into her inside pocket, next to the Stone. Sceleste suddenly meowed and stood alert on the pillow.

"Got it! Avie, we're going to Andie's place, or near there, anyway - it'll be easy to conjure up, and she'll believe I'm me, hopefu.."

The lights flickered on, and before she knew what had happened a nurse had rushed into the room and stabbed a syringe deep into her shoulder. Linda screamed and fell to the floor, desperately trying to reach around to it. Avalon managed to draw the needle out, but almost half of its contents were gone. The world began swimming, and Linda couldn't do anything other than crawl towards the bed, already unable feel her legs or her right arm. She looked up at the hysterical woman who was pointing down at her, screaming while backing away to the door.

"What have you done to the guards, you evil witch? You're a devil! We all knew you were! There's hundreds of soldiers and they're all coming to get you! They'll get you!" she screamed, and lunged across the room towards her again, clutching a larger syringe like a dagger.

She looked at the woman and shook her head, trying to think of the right thing to say, but it all seemed so confusing now.. and then the woman stopped. She stared at Sceleste, who hadn't moved from her place on the pillow. After an eternity, the nurse grabbed at her own throat before being slammed hard against the floor, where she lay staring blindly at Linda from the other side of the bed. The syringe bounced a few times and rolled out of the door, and a long way down the corridor.

"Oh no, I don't need this right now.." said Linda, as the sedative began taking a stronger effect. She pulled herself onto the bed and sat next to Sceleste while the air around her seemed to become heavier. The world started moving as if the hospital was far out at sea, being lifted and dropped by huge rolling waves.

Avalon knew there wasn't much time to get out. She flew over to the window, chose the largest of the security bolts which held it into the wall, and gave it the best kick she could manage. The window, the bars, and a major part of the wall were launched far out into the grounds below. Someone down there might have called "Whuh?" just before it landed, but that didn't bother her. She had to get Linda out, and nothing else in the entire world mattered.

She turned back to Linda, who was lying on the bed, slumped against Aggy. Sceleste stood nervously beside her, not sure what to do. Avalon took a deep breath and pinched and prodded her until she became a little more alert.

"Uhm so tired Ahhvee.."

"Come to here, Linda! Walk to me, not far, come here.. good Linda," called Avalon, pulling the braid and hovering a few feet in front of her. She dropped it and steadily backed out of the gaping hole in the wall, to hover directly above a dense mass of bushes. They looked soft, and she felt they would be good for someone who couldn't fly to land on, hopefully. Linda did as she was told, and stumbled to the window where she kneeled against the damaged brickwork, finding that the breeze helped some of her senses to come back. Unfortunately it didn't bring all of them back, and she fell forwards, more or less where she was supposed to. She landed Aggy-first and rolled onto the grass, leaving her bear impaled on a series of broken branches, concealed spikes and looped razor wire.

Avalon flew to her and began trying to get her to stand up and start walking again. Sceleste emerged leafy-but-demure from the undergrowth and walked a short way ahead, keeping low to the ground, leading the way through a sparse line of trees. Linda followed, trying desperately to shake off the leaden tiredness, stamping her feet and waving her arm back into life as she meandered along an obscure entry road. Avalon sat on her shoulder, shouting advice in her ear.

"Think of our hotel! Think of that nice one we were in with the telephone? We can get there if you think of it, we like that hotel!"

Linda stopped completely, and tried hard to think of the hotel, or any hotel. She slowly shook her head, and leaned a long way forwards. Then she fell over, much to Sceleste's annoyance, who meowed loudly until she slowly found her feet again.

"Okay, think about moving fast instead, Lindy.. try that? Along the road! We like the road such a lot. Think about moving fast!!"

Linda preferred that. She was already on a road, and that made it so much easier to think about being on one. She imagined that the road lead to the waterfront, to where Avalon had seen a boat, no, bow-tuh, going past. That was so nice.. such a nice place. Sceleste jumped up to her arms, and had to cling onto her jacket for a while until Linda managed to hold her.

The trees passed by slowly at first, but as her thoughts became clearer they began passing with more and more speed. She didn't notice as the road grew wider and more formal, and she certainly didn't notice the trucks full of troops roaring towards the Institute's buildings. But that didn't matter - the troops didn't seem to notice her either.

She passed the first of the flood-lit Check Points without causing a stir from the guards, who carried on waiting for the arrival of the next truck. But then everything began to slow down for her. A headache similar to a grumbling volcano was threatening to blow her head apart, so she left the road and soon found herself running somewhere deep into the forest, and then crouching in a protective gathering of sighing fir trees. She vaguely knew she was collecting armfuls of anything broad-leafed, and covered herself as much as she could. Her effort wouldn't win any awards, but considering how fragile she felt, it was fine. Exhausted, she settled down against one of the trees, and let the world drift away.

A few hours later, Linda felt something hard against the back of her head. It might have been a wall, although it was curved and bumpy like bark on a tree trunk, but why would she be lying against a tree? And for that matter, where was she? She opened her eyes a little, for a careful look. She was outside. The sun had risen, so it must be early morning, but that didn't help her very much. She never slept outside at St Teresa's except once a few years ago when Brenda had locked her out of the Dorm. Therefore, she had to be somewhere else. She couldn't be home, because she never went home because her father didn't want her there anymore because of his new Dee-friend, or something. And she couldn't be at Andie's because Andie never made her sleep outside. Andie was too nice for that kind of thing.

Odessa. That word was right. Odessa. It was early morning in Odessa, and her new friend Avalon would be coming back any minute now, unless she'd managed to catch a moonbeam last night, in which case she'd gone home, if she ever really existed in the first place.. in which case, Linda figured, she was just a loony who thought she'd met a faery-fairy in her hotel room. Which was outdoors.

"Avalon was nice.." she thought to herself.

"Lindy? Are you alright now?"

Avalon had seen her starting to wake a little, and flew over to her. She hovered in front of her face, humming a medley of very catchy Healing Songs.

"Avellllon? You came back! Didn't you find a moonbeam?"

"No, but that wasn't now, that was ages ago.."

"Was it already ages? Oh.. that's right.. ages."

Linda slowly remembered being in bed on the settee in her room at the Pech-foreign-name Hotel, talking to Avalon all about moonbeams before, but quite when she'd done that was too hard to work out. Sceleste meowed and lightly stepped onto her lap, staring at her. She nuzzled her head against Linda's chin and an avalanche of memories came back.

"Ohh, the hospital place.. we were stuck there, I remember that now. But how did we get all the way out here?"

Avalon gave her an update in no particular order, which didn't help matters at all.

"Thanks Avie, I think. Ugh, you know that feeling when a herd of elephants has walked all over you, and then they have to come back for something so they walk all over you again? I've got that, right in my head. And my shoulder, too.."

"Maybe you know too much, like your head's all full up?" she said, and Sceleste purred loudly as if agreeing. "And what's an Allyfunt?"

"That's right, I don't expect you get many round here.."

"I forgot to tell you. You had an injection," she said, prodding where the needle went, "and it made you all sleepy in your head."

"Did I? Maybe it's wearing off now - I can actually feel the ground beneath me.. yeah, that's ground. See? That's good, it stops me from falling too far. But what are you standing on?"

Avalon was still hovering in front of Linda's face and looked into her blue eye, and then moved to the brown one. They weren't quite right yet.

"We need to go somewhere safe, Lindy, till you're all better. Bad ones might come, and they'll take us away again! They've been firing guns and they sound nearer all the time!"

"Okay.. you think of somewhere while I get my brain out of bed." Avalon scratched her head, trying to find her Big Thoughts Level. "How about Odessa?"

"Aren't we there already?" Linda mumbled.

"No, I don't know where we are. How about Hesperides?"

"Hups-where-edeez?" she yawned.

"Umm.. what about Other You's home?"

"Other Me.. another me?" she laughed, and Avalon decided to wait until Linda was feeling a whole lot better before attempting anything with the Stone.

Sceleste twisted around and stared through the vast cover of undergrowth, briefly disappearing into it. She returned with a thick line of fur bristling along her spine. It was time to move on, so she clambered back onto Linda and looked at her indignantly until she stood up and started wandering again, taking them ever deeper into the forest.

Linda stayed crouched for most of the next hour, scurrying and flinching as occasional gunshots carried through the air. There seemed to be a lot of trigger-happy soldiers around, and whenever she started to feel safe, another distant crack would break the silence. Her legs still weren't working properly, and she seemed to spend most of her time falling over. Even Sceleste chose to walk rather than be chauffeured. Every now and then Linda tried conjuring up anywhere at all with the Stone, but concentrating on anything was painful and completely beyond her.

Eventually she stood at the beginnings of a long incline, which lead down to an exposed wire-mesh fence running alongside a railway track. They stayed parallel to it for a few hundred yards, as concealed as possible in the safety of the ash trees and fir trees, before spying a break. A 'V' shaped section where two lengths of the fence had come adrift offered the only obvious point to cross, so Linda waited until a freight train shuddered and clattered past before she ran from the cover of the trees, to get closer. Her heart almost exploded as she noticed a soldier walking out from behind an abruptly-banked hillock off to her left, and she dived into a mass of bushes. Her brain felt as if it was still bouncing around for a long time after the rest of her body had stopped moving, and she curled up, praying for the pain to go away. Avalon gave Linda five of her most trusted Healing Songs and two of Abba's most trusted as well, before the aching slowly began to leave her.

One solitary guard patrolled the rail line. He had wandered alongside the fence for two hours, gradually making his way ever-nearer to the Bilhorod Dnistrovsky train station where a nice mid-morning coffee break would be waiting for him, followed by an afternoon spent just like the morning - ambling around looking out for some girl or another. He was already a long way from the guard centre, and looked up at the sky. It was definitely getting cloudier, and he hoped to himself that any rain would hold off until he'd finished wasting time in this obscure outer-most part of the Institute's grounds. He sighed, and wondered why a stupid kid was worth being so bothered about. Still, orders were orders and if he could spend a morning doing nothing but walking by a railway, that was just fine by him. He lit a cigarette, and cursed as the first drops of light rain began to fall.

Linda watched him as he paused to light up, no more than twenty yards away. Had he heard her? Maybe he hadn't. Avalon flew over for a closer look, and settled on top of the fence. He ignored her, of course - or maybe he couldn't even see her? Either way, Linda spent an eternity peering through the branches and urging him to walk away. But he didn't. He eventually lit another cigarette and began sauntering alongside the fence again. Avalon flew back.

"He can't see me, and his name's Viktor and he'd rather be at home with lots of Nice Ladies."

"Well done, Avie.. that's good to know. Are there any other soldiers around?"

"There's two a long way behind who are following him and they might be here in a few minutes. Viktor's got three guns, and a big spot on the side of his nose."

Linda couldn't think clearly enough for any great plans to emerge.

"How can we get him out of the way? If he can't see you we can't do the subway thing to freak him out.."

Sceleste stretched, and then stretched again. She trotted out with her nose and her tail high in the air, as if she was an entrant at a demonic version of the Cat Of The Year show, and sat a little way in front of him - staring, with her head at an angle. Viktor kicked a clump of earth at the annoying cat, and then narrowly missed her with his cigarette end. And then he seemed to freeze for a few seconds. For reasons known only to himself and Sceleste, he decided to scream and climb the fence, looking back at her all the time. He fainted (or something similar) as he clambered onto the barbed wire circles running along the top, and lay sprawled across them as if he'd been parachuting without a parachute.

Sceleste slowly returned, looking a lot weaker. Linda held her, realising that she had never been so active before and that it was all becoming too much for her. Avalon stroked her head while Linda tried to make all the right kind of noises to make them all feel that everything was going to be fine. That wasn't easy, because Linda knew that once the other soldiers discovered the body, they would probably bring the entire Ukrainian, American, Russian and Chinese armies with them. So she held Sceleste tightly, made sure Avalon was securely on her shoulder, and made her bid for freedom. She ran for the cut in the fence, and froze as a volley of shots flew through the air behind her. The other soldiers were still a long way off, but they must have heard Viktor's scream and were already racing towards the area.

Linda started to run again, but felt something like a brick smash into her leg. Before she could even try to look, she had dropped Sceleste and was rolling down the embankment towards the fence, where she came to a painful halt in a bank of wet gravel at its base. A thick dart poked out of her calf, and Avalon struggled to remove it before she even had time to think what it might be. But she didn't need long to wonder.

By the time Sceleste arrived, Linda's left leg felt as if it had been hit by a truck. She pulled herself up against the fencing and limped a few steps along until she fell through the gap, sliding head-first down another steep embankment, hitting the railway track hard. Avalon was shouting things to her, and maybe there were more gunshots from somewhere, but that didn't matter. She knew she had to get up and she had to keep moving, and more importantly, she had to clear her mind as much as possible and just do whatever her heart told her. That would be the right thing, the only thing.

She sensed there was a railway station ahead, maybe a mile or two away, and intuitively knew that she could make it with a little help from the.. from the.. it wasn't a Stone, it was a.. was a.. she despaired. The words stayed just out of reach, lost in the numbing chaos around her mind. She knew that she had never been so close to seeing and understanding the Stone, and tried to force herself to reach a little further.. but the harder she tried, the more she seemed to be pushing the Stone away. A sharp pain pounded inside her head, matching her next dozen heartbeats and hurling her attention back to the world around her, back to the railway, to the ones she had to protect.. to the Stone..

For a while she felt as if she was watching herself and that her body was little more than a puppet. She could look down and see herself standing on the railway track, with Avalon flying frantically around her while Sceleste laboured to catch up. Linda concentrated as much as she could, and made her near-yet-distant self pick the poor cat up. And then she could start moving. She moved her useless body, sometimes from the usual view-point behind her eyes, and sometimes from above like her own puppet-master, covering twenty paces with every calm step and hurrying away from the soldiers and the research centre, leaving behind all the vileness it held.

As the station approached, Linda's grip on herself weakened. Her mind was becoming too fuzzy, and the world was becoming so unreal. She hadn't the energy to stay outside herself any longer, and as her vision returned to her body's eyes, she sluggishly wondered if she had actually been outside herself at all. But that didn't matter, now. She stood by the railway line, and squinted through the rain at the gentle ramp which lead up to the station's platform, and wondered if she would be able to climb such a mountain. She staggered out from the bushes, laboriously dragging her heavy feet through each and every step.

A train arrived as she reached the middle of the platform, and she practically sleep-walked on board. The military tranquilliser was beginning to overpower her mind and her body, and she collapsed onto the hard wooden seat. The few passengers in her dismal Low Economy Class compartment decided the weird girl was either an addict or a head-case, and all ten moved into the next carriage - except for one elderly man. He would have left as well, but for a moment the bird that had followed her on looked wrong to him. It was chirping at the drugged-out girl, which was a peculiar happening anyway, but for the slightest moment it looked nothing like a bird whatsoever. He wasn't quite sure what it resembled, but he'd seen the same kind of Something-Or-Nothing throughout his whole life. And he hated that. He threw his newspaper at it, making it fly away. His paper hit the girl, but she didn't seem to notice or even care - and neither did he. The noisy bird had defiantly perched on a small open window instead of flying out, and that annoyed him more. He hurried over and waved his stick at the wretched thing, and that did the trick. He closed the window firmly, and went back to his seat for a while. The girl's cat caught his attention, glaring with its sickly yellow eyes, and he decided to leave the compartment. Quickly.

Sceleste sat in Linda's lap, wondering what to do. The old man had left just in time - he was due for a scare, and had narrowly managed to avoid it. Perhaps she might visit him in a dream, one night very soon. She looked around. The Trusted Faery was now gone, the room was moving and shaking, and her Gifted One was falling into a dangerously deep sleep. She bit Linda's hand, which made her respond a little. Sceleste sensed that she had stopped falling for a moment, so she did it again. And then she dug her claws through the material and into the girl's leg. Linda responded again, hovering at the very brink of darkness. Sceleste kept biting and scratching, again and again.. and the train approached the first station.

The doors opened and a blast of cool, fresh air rushed into the compartment, causing Linda to stir a little more. Avalon flew in, exhausted and crying, and immediately began tugging the braid and shouting to try and get her waking again. Linda's eyes followed the source of the noise, because it seemed to be one that was inside her head as much as outside, and that felt good. Quite why it felt good eluded her, and she couldn't understand the words anyway. She stared at the fairy, no, faery, and the faery stared back. Sceleste sunk her teeth deep into Linda's hand, causing her to wake up enough to make a little sense of what the flying thing was saying.

"We have to get off at the next stop, okay? We have to leave because.. uhh.. umm.. you rolled your dice and your dice showed a two and that means the second stop and that's the next one! You have to do that!"

Linda stared at her, and almost managed to wonder what on earth she was shouting about. But nothing had made sense, and the strange little thing's emotions were too chaotic and panic-stricken, and besides, the entire world was too softly crushing for her to be bothered by complicated things like that.

The train doors closed, and Sceleste turned her attention to the other hand.

CHAPTER THIRTY ONE
Strange Looks

Saturday 28th June 10.00am

Linda stumbled onwards, almost blind through the grim streets of a town near Odessa. Or maybe it was far from Odessa? That wasn't important to her. It was the second stop on the railway line just like the dice had said, and that was all that mattered, that was all she could deal with. Her rain-soaked hair lay clinging to her pale skin, and her head rocked slightly with each vague and unsteady step. Her joints screamed at her to stop moving, to stop right now and curl up and sleep for a while, sleep forever, sleep would make everything better.. but she couldn't. Someone was shouting at her from inside her mind or maybe a little outside, and wouldn't let her do that.

She looked up at the not-quite-a-bird as it frantically dived at her over and over again, screeching as if it was possessed by the devil and wickedly intent on tormenting and bullying her. But somewhere in her heart she could make sense of its noises, in a way.

"Linda! Keep listening to me! Don't fall asleep again! You have to keep going.. please Linda, keep going a little further that's all, and I promise we'll be safe!"

She barely responded. The pain in her joints ebbed away a little, dulling more of her senses as it went. Her eyes were so heavy and the daylight hurt them so much, and her feet seemed to weigh more and more with every single step. She imagined reaching out to anyone in the world, desperately screaming for help, pleading for someone to come to her. There were people nearby. She couldn't see them, but she could feel their presence and sense so much about them.. she felt their names.. their lives.. one had a cold.. maybe flu.. the other was just about to catch it. Linda imagined reaching out to them, longing for them to look at her, and begging them to come to her..

Galina Ahmatova stood across the road patiently waiting for a bus. Her attention was suddenly drawn to the deathly girl who was close to her own daughter's age, and she sighed with despair at yet another bad sort who was throwing her life away and tutted at how the world seemed so full of them these days. She watched the bird screeching and charging at her, and raised an eyebrow at the ugly black cat acting nervously around the girl's feet. The vile thing seemed to be scratching at her ankles. Galina blew her nose for the hundredth time that day, and threw the tissue into the gutter.

"See that girl, Olya? What a waste, what a waste.. if she was mine, I'd be as angry as the bird," she commented to her friend standing next to her. Olya nodded her agreement, and wondered why Galina was talking about a bird. She couldn't see a bird, but she did think there was something very odd about the girl's cat. Galina and Olya both looked away, preferring to stare down the road for the bus, and let the girl stumble on.

Tarkovsky's unrated hostel occupied the entire corner block at the end of the street. With plenty of encouragement, Linda managed the three stone steps and kept on moving all the way to the reception window. She could make out a vague shape in front of herself.. his name was Stanislav Someone.. he was going through a divorce.. he always smoked filterless cigarettes because he didn't like being told not to smoke them.. he hated his job and he hated the wretched small town.. and he got cramp in his legs a lot..

The clerk didn't like being stared at, and especially not by scruffy low-life. He looked at her with contempt while she clumsily cast a wad of notes onto the counter, and he grimaced at the blood left on the money - and then shivered when he saw the masses of bite marks on her lacerated hands. He could imagine where someone in her condition got money like that. Dirty little thief. And on top of all that, she'd brought a wretched bird into the place with her, as well. Dirty messy creatures.

"How long d'you want?" he grunted, waiting a few seconds until he realised that she wasn't going to answer. He gave her a key with a cracked 18 hanging from it, which was for a filthy room on the second floor - one entirely appropriate for her sort. He watched as she attempted to make her way up the stairs, and decided to leave a note for whoever was on the next shift to check on her early in the evening, just in case a mortician needed calling - there was no way someone like that was going to be his problem. He carried on watching as her disfigured black cat clawed its way a few steps ahead of her, where it paused to look back as if making sure that she was still following. Stanislav sighed and went back to his tv.

Linda turned the corner guided by a braid, and crawled up the second flight. Somehow she managed to half-stand at the top, trying to fight her way through the blurred and distant world around her. She had nothing left. No strength, no energy, no idea where she was, no understanding of how or why she was anywhere.

"Linda! Come on, just a little more! I'm begging you, a little more that's all! We're nearly safe!" cried Avalon, lifting her eyelids and then tying more braids to pull her with.

Somewhere she could hear the voice shouting and shouting at her, drifting deep in and out of her head and turning her mind upside down. She carried on following it, unable to even wonder if she was actually moving.

Stanislav hurried up the stairs and changed her key to the one for Room 22, which was up on the next floor. There weren't any other people on that floor, and it would be far better for trade if nobody knew she was there. Avalon stayed close to Linda as he helped her up the stairs, and changed her opinion of him when he offered her some advice about mixing with the wrong people. He didn't really say who the wrong people were, but maybe he'd heard of Mörrah and knew that she was definitely the wrong sort to mix with. With that thought in mind, Avalon decided to trust him for a moment and flew to the far window at the end of the corridor. She landed on its sill and looked out. The street was almost empty except for a few cars and even fewer people going past. That was good. No soldiers, no Viktors, no anyones.

Stanislav guided Linda to the bed for her to hopefully sleep off whatever she'd taken, and cursed at her under his breath when she simply stood beside it as if she had no idea it was even there. He gave her a nudge and she toppled forwards across the horsehair mattress, lying face-down as if she had been knocked unconscious.

"Stupid kid.." he muttered, figuring that her position would be a little suspicious if a doctor had to be called in later on. She needed to look as if she'd simply fallen asleep and not woken up, and that way he could claim that she seemed fine when she had arrived. He moved her around until she looked almost natural, and then started rooting through her pockets to find a few extra Hryvenas for all his time and effort.

"Damn it! What the.."

His fingers touched something far down in her inside pocket which made him wince and stifle a yelp. Whatever was nestled in there amongst all the wrappers and biscuits had sent a sensation through his heart that made a cold sweat break out over his entire body. He grabbed at the roll of banknotes which had edged out from a side-pocket, dropped one or two for her to keep, and made a quick guess that he was holding at least four week's wages, maybe five. Sceleste hadn't the strength to deal with him as he deserved, so she struggled up onto the edge of the bed and lashed at his other hand, almost missing as she toppled back onto the floor.

"Oww, you miserab.." he cursed, looking at a small, clean scratch. He hurried to the door, pausing at the room's only table to throw an ashtray and an old mug towards the vile creature. The weird cat didn't move or even blink as both brushed past her fur.

Perhaps it was just his overactive imagination, but even before he had reached the stairs, the small scratch was becoming quite raw and irritable, and was probably going to be a lot worse than the burns on his fingers - and they were bad enough, already approaching his knuckles.

"Burns? Where the.. where've they come from?" he wondered. He swore back at the room and staggered down the stairs before collapsing outside Room 18.

Avalon heard Linda's door creak as it began to swing shut after the clerk left, and she raced into Room 22 before it could close. She saw Linda lying on the bed and felt pleased that the nice man had helped her into a comfortable position. She flew around to check for candles, hexes or curses like the last time they had arrived in a small and unkempt room, but luckily this one was fine. Sceleste sat on the floor beside the bed, and looked anxiously from Linda to Avalon, knowing that there was nothing that she could do to help. Her Gifted One was somewhere in a bad and unnatural place that couldn't be reached through spiritual means.

Linda breathed in small shallow breaths with long gaps between each one, and her eyes stared straight upwards into nothing. Avalon started trembling, and fluttered down to hover erratically a few inches above Linda's face.

"Linda! Linda! I'm still with you! You have to listen! Can you hear me? Lindahh!"

She turned to Sceleste.

"Oh they've done something bad this time, really bad haven't they? What do we do now? What do we.."

She flew in panicked circles around the room trying desperately to remember her best Adapted Healing Song, but Mörrah began stirring, throwing her from side to side and quickly casting her into a dive. Avalon couldn't hold her any longer. She pulled the golden cord from her waist and raced up to the safety of the ceiling to watch the silver pouch drop in a slow, irregular spiral to the floor. It settled near Sceleste who immediately jumped up onto the bed where she stood protectively on Linda, digging her claws into the denim jacket, arching her back and hissing down to where the pouch had landed.

But nothing happened. An ominous silence fell over the small room, broken only by the sound of Linda's weak gasps as she struggled for another breath.

A thin trail of dense grey mist ventured out onto the floorboards. Small fingers of vapour spread out from its sides, pausing after just a few inches. Another emerged from the pouch, much denser and thicker, moving like a snake as it disappeared under the bed. Another joined it, quickly followed by another, and then another. More and more raced free of the pouch, soon covering every inch of the floor in a dark, writhing mass of misty tendrils which quickly grew deeper and deeper, easily reaching the top of the mattress.

Sceleste hissed and dug her claws deeper into the denim as the sheets became lost beneath the impenetrable murkiness. Every strand of her jet-black fur bristled with fear and devoted, protective aggression. The sea of mist rose defiantly higher, edging around Linda's body.. and then it fell, flowing backwards in waves as it returned to the small pouch. Silence reigned for the briefest of moments, and a freezing darkness engulfed the room.

Suddenly a storm of anger roared upwards in an explosion of raging, twisting columns of shadows and light, writhing like thousands upon thousands of snakes, entwining, merging and separating in a wild frenzy until they became one single, powerful entity. Within seconds the mist, the dust and the burning light began fading away, drifting somewhere far beyond the confines of the room and allowing daylight to slowly return.. revealing Mörrah standing beside the bed.

She glared across to Avalon who trembled and tried to fly even further away, and then turned her jet black eyes onto the girl.

A cold and callous smile spread across her face, and her ageing skin cracked a little more.

CHAPTER THIRTY TWO

The Inner Lair

Mörrah stood towering over Linda, watching her life slipping away and smiling as a trace of blue crept into the thief's face. It was all so amusing. Avalon's fear and distress suddenly turned into an unbearable anger and she finally reached boiling point. She flew down from the corner of the ceiling.

"What are you smiling about? Don't you get it? If she dies you don't get the Stone at all! You know Sceleste would take you to Hell rather than move out of your way, and even if you could get hold of it what good is the Stone to you without Linda? You want to spend the next thousand years looking for someone as Gifted? Well you're old and you won't last until autumn! Look at you!"

Avalon was more angry than she'd ever been in her life, and didn't like feeling that way. She turned away from Mörrah hoping the feelings would all pass her by, but they wouldn't go. Instead, she grew scarlet with rage and returned to within an inch of Mörrha's face - and conveniently found her Great Big Shouty Level.

"YOU GREAT BIG PILE OF SICK!" she screamed, "For once in your rotten life do something good! This is why every living thing's hated you ever since you were a Ground Crawler like her and always will hate you especially ME! I hate you! I-hate-you hate you hateyouHATEYOU! And I really do too," she added, perhaps tagging the word 'bitch' onto the end - but if she did, it was so quiet that nobody could have heard.

Mörrha looked shocked, and watched Avalon back away a few inches. There was an element of truth in what the moth was saying about the girl, but oh, the way she was saying it.. that would never do, and would have to be dealt with - perhaps now, perhaps later. She casually swatted Avalon away, making her bounce off a wall and land down on the floor, closely followed by a cheap painting of some fruit.

Mörrah held out a porcelain-white hand, and a grey mist slowly formed in her palm. She pursed her lips and blew it into a small whirlpool. It soon disappeared, leaving behind two elegant glass vials, both of which contained a sparkling clear liquid. They stood upright, floating barely an inch above her hand. Avalon wriggled out from under the picture and flew dizzily to Sceleste, who purred softly to her while she regained her senses.

"Oh, little troublesome one," Mörrah said in a voice full of controlled loathing, "let us see if you can be an aid rather than a hindrance. Which shall the Gifted One take?"

She spread her arms wide, a vial on the palm of each hand, and looked down at Avalon.

"Of these Waters, one will grant her life, whereas the other.. well, you have to choose the correct one, don't you?" she whispered.

Avalon hated this more than anything, but Natural Laws could never be flouted.

"Uhh.. uhh.. the left one. No the right. Yes. The right. No. Yes, the left. No. The riyyy.. no the left one. The.. the.. the left one. Please?" she faltered, and covered her eyes with her hands. The one on Mörrha's right palm faded away.

"You're too late to change now, small creature. Shall we see what fate you have brought her?"

She gestured for Avalon and Sceleste to leave Linda immediately, and then slowly removed the gold stopper from the vial's long neck. Linda froze in mid-breath, held in a balance between life and death. Avalon shook helplessly and held onto Sceleste's neck, burying her face deep into her mane. Mörrha traced a hand in a snake-like sideways motion above Linda, and chanted the first set of ancient verses to release the powers held within the Water.

A shadow of a crescent moon appeared across Linda's heart, becoming darker and wider until all thirteen verses had been completed. She poured a few drops onto the back of her right hand and held it a few inches above Linda's face. The drops rolled down to hang on the ends of her black fingernails, until Mörrah chose to release them across Linda's forehead. A cool, grey vapour formed above her skin, quickly hiding her features.

She repeated the process above Linda's heart and continued down to her feet, spreading the faint blanket across her body until the last of the Water had gone. Avalon dared peek between her fingers to watch while Mörrah deliberately waited before ending the ritual by returning the glass stopper to its vial.

"Patience.. patience.. patience.." she said in a mocking whisper, enjoying the faery's torment. She teased the stopper back into the neck of the vial, and stepped back. After an eternity, the vapour shrouding Linda slowly turned pure white.

"Ah, the Waters Of Life.. you chose well."

Avalon hugged Sceleste's neck, crying with joy and relief. Mörrah's lips curled into a smirk.

"Of course, insolent one, I assume that you meant my left, rather than your left?" she said. Avalon had a think, and realised that she didn't. Her left was Mörrah's right.

"Thank you.." she gulped, realising that Mörrah had actually bent a rule in order to save Linda.

"Hmm.. I sense visitors.." Mörrah said, folding her arms, "Many Unwelcomes approach. I need time to execute the Siva Rites. I suggest you move your small self and delay our guests. The girl will be perfectly safe with me in your absence. Begone!"

Sceleste leapt back onto the bed, settling like a sphinx next to Linda's head, fractionally beyond the swirling white mist. Avalon looked out from the window and saw dozens of cars pulling up outside. She took a long look at Linda, and flew outside to cast more Not Me's than she'd ever tried before.

She settled across the road, and concentrated hard on recreating a whole Not Linda. For two or three seconds she managed to hold it, long enough to be spotted near a sidestreet. The Officials and troops began shouting, and took the bait. Avalon flew high to appear in windows along the ramshackle street, appearing for a second or two at a time, long enough to cause confusion and buy more time for Real Linda. The air was soon full of gunshots, and the chase went on.

Linda twitched on the bed and sat bolt upright. Before she had even opened her eyes, she was aware of the Stone. It was safe, it was hers and hers alone, and.. and she had no idea what had lead her to wherever she was now. She suddenly found herself looking directly at a strange window in a strange room. She held Sceleste closer, feeling safe, confused, and perhaps different, somehow? Sceleste purred reassuringly in her arms, and a light rain fell against the dirty glass. The world outside looked patchy and dull, but that didn't matter to her at all - she hadn't felt this good in a long time. The overpowering tiredness of the last few days had lifted, and.. and.. and who's reflection was that in the window?

She turned around to see Mörrah standing a few feet away, and wondered why Sceleste was only being slightly hostile instead of being ready to rip the Ved'ma to shreds.

"Mörrah? What are y.. where are we?" she said warily, stroking

Sceleste and choosing to trust in her cat's judgement.

Mörrah said nothing. She was more jealous and angry than she had ever been throughout her entire life, which was an incredible achievement. She watched the cat deliberately pad at the girl's pocket and had to look away as the child brought out the Stone. Warm light came from its centre to fill the room, making her shiver with contempt. Sceleste looked over to her and purred, knowing the agonies she must be going through. Mörrah clenched her fists, furious at being tormented by the cat. The Beast was too despicable for words.

"It's okay, Sceleste, I've still got it, see? And my mum's picture's still in there too! That's so good. Oh.. my sleeves and everything!" she wavered, looking at all the blood, "Where.. where did all that come from?"

Sceleste gave each unblemished hand a lick.

"Well, I haven't got any cuts and neither have you, so.." Linda stopped as if she'd been struck by lightning. "Where's Avalon? What have you done to her, Mörrah? If you've hurt.."

Avalon returned through the cracked window, forgetting her exhaustion as soon as she laid eyes on Linda.

"You're not dead! You're not dead, you're not.." she sang, and hugged the side of Linda's face, crying.

"There you are, Avie! Me, dead? You're so stressed, you are. And how come we're here - and have we run out of money already?"

Mörrah sighed loudly in a bid to halt the pointless emotion.

"And have you noticed Her Majesty over there?" Linda whispered. Avalon nodded, but couldn't quite manage words yet.

"The Unwelcomes draw nearer, moth. I believe they have entered this.. building."

Avalon shook herself and sniffed a few times, and tried to get her thoughts straight before speaking.

"Here's everything.. okay.. there's bad ones coming any second and you need to get us out of here and somewhere safe and I don't know where that is," she said, shrugging her shoulders.

A bullet tore through the door and left a broad gash in the plaster and brickwork next to Mörrah. She stared impassively at the damage, and then down at the debris at her feet. Avalon flew through the missing section of the door, and immediately came back.

"I'll only be a minute, Linda.. you wait for me!" she called, and disappeared from sight again. She flew across the corridor and went outside the end window where she waited until the first trigger-happy soldier had climbed the stairs and could see her, and once again became Not Linda. The two troops ignored Room 22 and fired towards the window instead, then clambered out onto the roof of the neighbouring bakery. They were determined that their target wouldn't get far, and shot at everything. Avalon flew as fast as she could around the side of the building, and back to Real Linda.

"We have to go we have to go-we-have-togowehavetogowehave.." she said, from under Linda's hair.

"Okay, I think there's only one place left, isn't there?"

"Yes there is! Where?" said Avalon, wrapping herself up in the braid. Linda held the Stone, and looked over to Mörrah.

"You have to help me, Mörrah. We have to think of the traveller who brought this to you, so I can try and get us to somewhere near him - whenever it was created."

Mörrah eyed her suspiciously, but had a plan or two of her own. If only she still had her Followers she wouldn't feel so weak, and this could be so terribly easy. But for the time being, she would play along for the Crawler. The floor shook as dozens of heavy footsteps pounded up the stairs, and Linda shut everything out of her mind except for a small channel with Mörrah, allowing her no more than the briefest glimpse of the power of the Stone. In an instant she sensed the Ved'ma's hateful jealousy, and couldn't help but laugh to herself. Her thoughts passed far beyond Mörrah's reach and once more she saw the traveller arriving in the Entrance Hall, sensed him striding across and then into the Banqueting Hall, felt Mörrah's attraction to him and her irritation with him in the Meeting Room, and her overpowering desire for the gifts of the Stone.

Linda concentrated on the man, speaking clearly in her mind that the moment of creation was her aim, to be near him before his arrival in Obrovechen. The sensations of the castle were strong, and she knew Mörrah was trying to invade the moment, trying to push her and take her back to that day in 1186. So Linda surprised herself and effortlessly shut Mörrah out completely, and centred her entire attention upon the traveller. She could sense where he was from, how far in the future he lived, the darkness of his lair, and..

..and the entire hostel rocked as the first of hundreds of shells and explosives tore through it. The whole street came under a massive bombardment and Tarkovsky's quickly folded along with all the buildings around it, leaving nothing but piles of rubble and..

..and Linda opened her eyes. She was in a dark place, a miserable, oppressive and frightening place.. but Avalon was still clutching her neck, and Sceleste was still in her lap. That felt good, and so very comforting.

"Where's The Stone, Lindy? Has it gone again?"

Linda held her hand out and ran her other hand a few inches above it, seeing little in the room's poor light.

"No.. it's not gone completely. I can sense all of it, but only the middle bit's still really here.. so we must be in the right place.. and he's not finished creating it yet. Does that make sense?"

"Yes. No. Yes. Sense about what?" Avalon asked, shaking her head so much with each word that she started turning herself around.

"Where's this? Where have you brought us?" spat Mörrah. She stood silhouetted against the dim light of the doorway, trembling as if she was caught in the middle of winter. She rubbed her arms, and quickly moved to her hands.

"I wanted you left behind - why are you still here?" said Linda.

"Wretched ungrateful filth! You think I didn't know you would do a devious act such as that? I imposed a Binding Enchantment as part of your 'return to life'. I go where you.. where the Stone.. goes."

Mörrah took her gameplan further. She wavered and fell to her knees, folding her arms tightly and trying hard to conceal her rage. She gave a deceptively weak moan and slumped a little more.

"Return to life? Avie, what's she mean by that?" asked Linda, watching Mörrah carefully. Avalon tugged her ear, distracting her from Mörrah's glaring eyes.

"You were nearly almost dead, but you're not now because we changed that and she helped with those Waters Of.. Hers, even though it was all her fault in the first place, and now she's really old and scared. Well, I'm not. Not old, that is," she explained.

"Quiet, lowest one!" Mörrah hissed, "Your prattling is delaying us and I will not tolerate.. the Gifted One must hurry and claim the Stone," she said, sounding a little too strong for someone so weak.

Linda could feel the anger still writhing within Mörrah and knew she was concealing something, and couldn't allow her to gain the upper hand. She chose some morale-denting truths to set the scene.

"We must be somewhere in the future now, but where and when is beyond me.. so you don't have anyone to feed off, do you? No

Followers, and I bet no-one here's even heard of you. I'd say you've Spelled yourself into a spot of bother - maybe you could try selling trinkets? Now, if you'll excuse us.."

Linda walked past her, hoping that her heart wasn't pounding as loudly as it felt, because that would give the impression that she wasn't quite as confident as she was trying to sound. Mörrah watched her leave, and grudgingly rose to her feet, suddenly no longer suffering as much. She wasn't finished yet, but the others didn't need to know that. She followed them into a roughly-chiselled corridor, illuminated by flaming torches and thin, red strip-lights. Its dank atmosphere carried a sense of evil and foreboding, making Sceleste continually look around herself, staring into shadows and clawing at nothing. Linda stopped as soon as they had turned the first corner.

Tall shapeless voids hung in mid-air throughout the corridor, and some even extended into the walls. They reflected everything around them, drawing light in until each briefly disappeared.

"Are they gaps? Floating ones?" asked Avalon as she flew nervously around one. Linda waved the braid for her to come back.

"No idea.. this is all too weird.. it's like science gone mad.. come and stay with me, Avie," she whispered, captivated by one that mirrored her in three dimensions. They kept on walking, listening for people and watching out for dimensional voids, and soon entered a long and under-lit passageway that appeared to be comparatively safe. The uneven walls had silver blocks embedded in them, each about the size of two bricks, embossed with strange gems and even stranger markings. Sceleste wandered a little way in front and gave a shudder every few steps, as if she was blocking certain areas and not allowing Linda to step over certain symbols.

Mörrah allowed them a slight lead, preferring to stay back in the shadows away from the Beast. She waited for the cat to stray too far ahead, and hurried to catch up with the child, and held back a scream as the red-hot knives of a Predator's Curse ripped through her - but she ignored the searing pain in order to drift closer than a breath to the girl. She wondered if she could plunge her hand through the Gifted One's back, rip her heart out and be fast enough to search her Soul for the power of the Stone, taking the Gift for herself before the Crawler's life was gone. But she fell behind again.

The evil around her was overpowering, far beyond anything she had ever felt or could ever hope to take advantage of. She looked at her hands, and wailed as the skin showed even more jagged and cracked lines of age. She knew the end of her life was approaching and making her too weak to cope with the kind of hostility that she had once thrived on. This time, she shivered for real and desperately tried to think of the way to reclaim her life. The answer lay in the girl's hands, and the route lay through her heart. Playing on her gullibility and sympathy might work, and that would take a degree of humility.. and honesty.

"Child.. please come to me, I.. I need you here.." she moaned. Her contorted eyes looked up at the Gifted One while she rubbed her hands, frantically trying to make the black streaks go away.

Linda walked back to her, and stood beside the dark and hunched figure, watching her shake.

"Look at me.. so weak, look at me, oh, something is so very wrong here, Gifted One. The evil is far beyond redemption.. this is a bad, bad place. Once, I could have dealt with this.. taken it, even controlled it. But not now, see my ageing? Curse this wilted Spirit! I gave you life, a precious gift you could never pass to me - so you must leave me here, leave me as I am, I must face my end at the mercy of the Spiritae around me.. forever a tired and defeated creature trapped within these cursed walls, never to pass into the Black Sea of the Lady Morganna. My beloved Sea.."

Avalon cheered quietly to herself, but Linda reached down for her hand. Her skin felt more like a dense fog than the ice-cold leather of the woman in the Research Institute, but a shiver of revulsion still ran from Linda's toes right to the top of her head. Mörrah looked disturbed, but grateful.

"I don't care if you stay here or not. If you follow us you might find others to nourish you, and they might sustain you long enough to allow you some dignity now your life's nearly over - not that you deserve any dignity, but I'm no-one to judge you, am I? I've probably harmed more people in a few days than you could ever have hoped to harm in your entire life - and that makes me a whole lot worse than you, doesn't it? But I'm also better than you.. far better."

Mörrah shuddered, and Linda could tell she was undermining her. A little more kindness and platitudes straight from the heart could only swing the balance further.

"So we won't leave you here. I know there's nothing for you to take from us. Yes, apparently you did give me my life back so I can't give you any real malice or resentment in return, can I? And Avalon's heart was never capable of that in the first place, and as for Sceleste - your kind can't touch her. So, I say you can follow us, if you wish, because I just don't care. How d'you like that?"

Mörrah weakened further and became transparent enough for Linda to see the wall through her. She turned and walked away, hoping to seem forthright.

"Linda? Have you gone all Mudbump crazy mad? What are you doing?" whispered Avalon, flying backwards in front of her.

"Keeping an eye on her. I trust her about as far as I can throw her, assuming she was hexed to a rock the size of a.. really big rock. And the way she is right now, even that's probably trusting her too much. Oh no, look! The Stone's getting even smaller!"

She hurried on, not sure of where to go, and soon had to come back anyway - Sceleste had grown tired of walking and refused to go anywhere without being picked up. The corridor narrowed gradually, and gained a definite slope until it had lead them around to a differently styled passageway altogether, which looked as if it belonged on an old ship. White wood panels, low beams, dozens of small brass lamps.. and dozens of doors.

"There's always doors, loads and loads of doors.." sighed Linda.

"What sort are we looking for?"

"The sort that lead us somewhere nearer the Stone, or maybe just somewhere that shows us where we are in this place."

Avalon took off, visiting each door in turn, running her hands over the surface of each one - except for a few which made her dart away as if they were electrified. Linda watched her criss-crossing the corridor and tried to read her, to feel what she was sensing behind each door - and surprised herself with how easy that had become. She soon established in her mind which one was most likely to be of some use. Avalon flew back looking pleased with herself, and spoke in a flurry.

"Some rooms are bad and some have People in them, and some aren't used for anything, but all the doors are really thick.. and that's not very helpful, is it?"

"Yes it is, that's really good.." said Linda, and encouraged Avalon to lead her to the largest one, midway along the corridor. She pressed its horizontal bar which lit up with a soft glow, but the door stayed firmly closed. Linda placed her hand against it, ready to give it a push with her mind, but didn't have long enough to try. A small 'tap' came from the left side and the door shook for a few seconds before swinging open to hang from a twisted hinge. Linda stared into a long room lined with rows of cluttered desks, each supporting piles upon piles of papers and books, interspersed and illuminated by dozens of tinted computer monitors. The walls were covered in charts and maps, linked by different coloured strings and sharp beams of light.

Sceleste wriggled until Linda put her down, wanting to go for her own look around. Linda followed her for a while, passing through the candle light and the weak blue glow from lights embedded along the desks and ceiling. She wandered along a row of maps entitled Pre-Odessa, and stopped at the one of Obrovechen, neatly marked 1186. A red marker-line circled a small black cross.

"Hey, second Queen Ephra? Here's your old castle - remember hubby?" Linda called in a hushed voice. Mörrah loathfully drifted into the room, and they both followed the red string across the room to another map, dated 1485, which was linked to the one next to it, 1512, then 1712. That lead across the room to 1896, 1932, and in turn 2159. Mörrah breathed loudly with sharp intakes as she looked around herself.

Avalon sat on one of the longer linking-strings, bouncing.

"What's these for, Lindy? All these pictures and strings.."

"They're maps with timelines, I think. It's the same place on every map, but with all the different countries shown as the centuries have passed, right up to this point here.. maybe we're in 2159? Just there.."

Linda scrutinised the erratic handwriting, vaguely making sense of the language by running her fingers over the words.

"The different colours are religions and politics, and I dread to think what else. See the areas in red? He's really annoyed with them."

Mörrah slouched near the wall, rocking slightly. She spoke in a cracked voice, hoping to draw the girl nearer..

"Back then, he wanted us to annihilate our neighbours.. wanted to prevent other countries from ever being created by destroying their founders. So long ago, it was all so long ago.. his plans for a mighty kingdom in his time were being challenged by.." she gestured to the red countries, "..those cursed in the Deicuralium, I believe."

"Deicur.. what?" thought Linda, hoping Avalon would hear. She did, and flew close to her.

"It's the red of coral, mixed with the blood of.. very young ones.. of your kind," she explained, and quickly moved away from the map.

Mörrah grew fainter. She had lost any trace of colour and now existed in only a few dark shades of grey.

"So by wiping out a few towns and ports, a whole nation wouldn't be created? Why do that?" asked Linda.

"Think, foolish child! Perhaps their leaders dare endeavour to prevent him from creating the Stone.. perhaps they are blind to the genius of his Gift, they harbour jealousies, fears, and countless other Human failings?"

That seemed reasonable to Linda, but she needed to know more, to find out where she was, and where this person was as well. She looked at the masses of paperwork around her, closed her eyes and allowed herself to be drawn to whatever would help her the most. She ran a hand against the stacks as she walked between them, briefly sensing and dismissing them, time and again. And then she stopped. She pulled a thin file out from a tower of green box-files, sending them crashing to the floor. Her eyes flashed to the doorway just in case anyone unpleasant happened to have heard. No footsteps, no guns, no cannons, no rockets, nothing. She breathed again and flicked through the file, looking at none of it but understanding almost everything.

"All of these files are histories, like monarchies and politics and everything.. and it's not just Mörrah's old place, he's got loads of others lined up for visits. It's like he's trying to cultivate the world as a nation in his own name, and then step in to take charge of it once he's returned here! He knows he's created the way to become a living god, or at least his version of one."

Mörrah sighed. Her dreams and desire for having such power had driven her for so long, and now it was so desperately, bitterly unfair - and it was all the thieving Ground Crawler's fault. She wondered for a while if she had enough strength left. Could she.. dare she..

"Look Avie," said Linda, holding her hand out, "..the Stone's even weaker, it's getting less! We really, really need to find where it's being created.. how can we do that?"

"Why don't you tune-in to wherever it is?" Avalon suggested.

"Yes, but how? I don't know where it is to even try and tune-in to it, do I?"

Avalon almost followed what Linda said.

"Umm.. well.. why not treat this whole place like a book? Fly into it and through it and all that."

"You'll help me, won't you?"

"Can't, not with Mörrah here.. she might do things to me if I don't keep away from her," she shivered.

Linda glared at whichever shadow felt like Mörrah, and picked Sceleste up. She sat down on one of the tall stools and stared at the dusty herring-bone tiles of the floor, searching for the purest essence of the Stone, feeling as if she was dream-walking through her senses to locate it. For a while the mocking laughter of Mörrah took her away, but she easily left her behind. She let herself fly higher, returning to the dreamworld, and soon felt as if she could touch everything for miles around her, all at the same time. An understanding passed through her as she opened her eyes, which lasted for less than the first blink, but revealed great swathes of where she was. She smiled at Avalon, who had nervously made her twelve new braids.

"This is just a rich man's fortress - I felt it all.. part of it's a fake castle, above the entrance to a massive science place stretching under a hillside.. and I don't think we're the only visitors.. but there's so much unrest.. I don't know.. like evil's everywhere.."

"Umm.. what d'you mean?"

Linda shook her head, and wished that she hadn't. A tight pinching sensation ran straight across her forehead.

"I'm not sure. I can't explain what I felt.. it was too fast for me."

"Oh.. uhh.. did you get where The Stone is?"

"Sort of.. I mean, I can feel where it is.. this is bringing on a headache like you wouldn't believe and I've.." she trailed off as her eyes fell on the door at the far end of the room. That was where she had to start. It looked antiquated and wouldn't have been out of place in a manor house, but had modern security running down one side, full of lights, sensors and dials. She wandered over and placed her hand above the palm-scanner, triggering a bright green bar to run downwards. Nothing happened. No alarms, no running guards, no shouting.. and no open door. That was good. She took her hand away so that she was barely touching it, and willed it to open instead, as if she was asking without asking. Everything made more sense that way. She opened her eyes, and it gently swung open.

Linda hurried along the corridor, following wherever her feelings lead her. Each room that passed by silently revealed its purpose to her, and as each corridor lead into another, the locations became clearer in her mind.

"..East Wing, that's no good.. Early 18th Century research.. Eastern European something, no good.. Political Analysis Centre..

Alternate Uprisings.." she whispered, confusing Avalon completely. Sceleste hissed occasionally, but only when Mörrah dared venture a little too close. She was fainter and harder to sense than ever, which Sceleste took no comfort from. They soon reached a small series of stairs, and quickly arrived at the start of a medical part of the building. Linda had to pause at the swing-doors leading into the Creation Centre's B Wing, and delicately held the side of her head. She tried to massage and coax the constant ache to go away, and Avalon tried to help by stroking her hair and humming one of her most effective Healing Songs, but even that made no difference.

"Don't worry, I'll be fine Avie - I think we're getting there.. it'd be so good to have a plan, what to do, what to do.." she mumbled, trying to get her heart to stop racing so much. A series of gunshots faintly echoed along one of the corridors.

"Not again," sighed Avalon, and changed into Not Linda. The other Linda looked at herself, before one of them turned back into Avalon.

"Avie, what're you doing?"

"I don't know, but it worked really well last time," she said, scratching her head. There wasn't enough time to find out what Avalon was talking about, so she let it go. She put Sceleste on the floor and placed her hands against the tiles of the wall, opening her mind as much as she could. She had to try and sense anything at all about the route ahead and the dangers around them, without bringing on the most colossal head-splitting migraine of all time.

"They're quite a way off.. they're shooting anyone they find.. they know what he's trying to do and they're trying to stop him.."

"Who's they?"

"I'm not sure.. something to do with other Governments. He doesn't like other Governments.."

Linda peeked through the circular window in the door. People in medical clothes were wandering to and fro between the rooms on either side of a white corridor, clutching clipboards, talking to small monitors in the walls, and generally being very busy.

"This isn't good," she thought to herself. "Mörrah? You still here?" she asked, looking around. A grey old woman, a faint apparition, stood close by and darkened her tone just enough to be seen. She reached out a limp hand to Linda's face.

"Oh yes.. but so weak.. don't be harsh with me, sweet Gifted One.." she moaned. Her hand drifted down towards Linda's heart, but Sceleste ran from behind Linda's legs and lashed at the shadowy form, and Mörrah drifted away a little.

"Can you do anything with that lot?" she whispered to the shadow, "Like disturb them or something? We have to go right through there and real quick!"

Mörrah grinned, but her features were lost in the light. Avalon tugged Linda's ear, and hovered round to look into her blue eye.

"Lindy? You don't need her help, you can do all kinds of Specials, can't you? You hardly ever needed my help, even right from the start - and you never roll your dice anymore or do any of that crazy stuff! I trust you, Sceleste trusts you, so YOU can trust you."

Linda thought for a moment. Avalon was right, she hadn't rolled her dice for ages and she hadn't thought twice about connecting lines - and when was the last time she bothered about odd-or-even dilemmas, or felt as if she was triggering off any accidental calamities? She suddenly realised that a huge part of her life was missing, and she hadn't even noticed it was gone.

"Yeah.. you're right, Avie.. I know you are.." she breathed.

She looked back through the glass panel, and forcefully imagined everyone going into their nearest room. They didn't, so she tried again, harder this time - but still nothing happened, apart from a stabbing pain around her head. Mörrah laughed as loudly as she could, but only Sceleste heard her. And then Linda changed her approach. Instead of trying to influence each and every person at the same time, she tried to affect the corridor instead. She imagined it becoming a cold place, the sort of place that nobody would choose to go into. It would feel bad, it would be filled with unease and fear, the kind that could creep into a person's subconscious and make them stay away without quite realising that they were staying away.

She opened her eyes and saw the long white corridor had cleared, and the doors to all the rooms were firmly shut. She felt no surprise at what she had done, and picked up Sceleste and ran, pushing the unease and fear ahead of her, trying to balance being fully alert with walking through a dream. The first painful throbs of her headache began forcing their way into her mind.

"Ohh, not now," she prayed, holding her head and shutting the world out.. and kept on moving.

By the time she really knew where she was again, the corridor had changed from being clean and clinical and had lead into one with a pseudo-Medieval style.. and the Stone had become even smaller in her hand. A feeling of cold trepidation crawled all over her skin, making her shiver so much that she could barely stop herself from shaking. She looked around, to make herself think of anything else - and chose to scrutinise every detail of the walls until the feeling passed. She stared at the glimmering stonework blocks and the blue lighting-panels that had been shaped into a series of small coats of arms, and watched them flare and stutter themselves out as she passed by.

She arrived at a large metal security door blocking the end, to find the last light flickering itself out and leaving the corridor in darkness. She drew her hand over the cold surface, suddenly feeling the malevolence which lay on the other side. Its power hit her like a tidal wave of misery and hatred, coursing through her heart and forcing her to realise that she was in the last place where someone so weak and inadequate should ever be - and she was there at the worst possible time.

"I can't do this, it's too.. I'm just not.." she cried, stumbling against the wall to keep herself from falling.

"It's alright.." said Avalon in a squeaked whisper, "..we'll all be in there together, won't we? All together.. just us.." she said again and again, gently stroking the braid while Sceleste purred her reassurance.

Linda breathed deeply for what felt like a long time before she tried to imagine the door opening, dreading any more tremors that might run through her head. She leaned against the wall, and sent a wave of unease rushing in front of her, clearing away whoever lay beyond. The numbing pain that had subsided for a while became a little more constant, freezing her mind for two or three heartbeats at a time. She bit her lip and barely touched the metalwork, and the door inched silently open, closing softly again as soon as she was through. Sceleste purred loudly.

CHAPTER THIRTY THREE
The Winner Takes It All

The new passage was dulled but not dark, and the walls were made of large rocks and boulders piled high on each other. Avalon flew ahead a few times to check that the coast was clear, returning for long enough to say 'Yes' before darting off once more. As they went further in, the trace of a low hum gradually became a powerful buzzing drone, rising in its intensity until the ground began to resonate. For a few seconds Linda watched the layers of sand and gravel minutely shaking more and more rapidly, and suddenly found herself staring into the depths ahead of her. Had she heard a scream from somewhere, or was it in her mind? Avalon came back very slowly, trembling.

"Avie? What's wrong?" she whispered.

Avalon shook her head, refusing to take her hands away from her eyes. She drifted forwards until she bumped into Linda's forehead, and felt her way down to the safety of her shoulder where she wrapped herself up in as much hair as possible. Linda closed her eyes and tried to sense what was ahead of her, but the vibrations in the air seemed to merge with the aching in her head, blocking her ability to even think. Her heart started pounding as she tried again, but she simply couldn't do it. Everything that had seemed so easy and natural just moments ago now felt completely out of reach.

Mörrah had stayed a few feet behind, struggling to avoid the wretched cat's attentions, but now she glared at Linda and laughed to herself. She drifted as near as the cat would allow, and turned her attention momentarily to the Beast. The time would soon be right, it would soon be perfect.. if only her strength could last a little longer..

The ground began sloping downwards, and a gap opened up between the rocky walls and the ceiling which rapidly grew wider and higher. Soon the passage had become no more than a sheltered path leading into an immense cavern, with masses of boulders and rocks spreading out high and far on either side. More gunshots carried from somewhere, still distant but less subdued - and certainly closer than before. Linda immediately left the passageway for the comparative safety and anonymity of the rocks, and worked her way through the narrow gaps and over the curved sides until she reached a point where she could hear echoing voices carrying in the air. Her new vantage point was about as close to the activity as she dared go, and she stayed perfectly still and hidden for a while, taking a moment to wait for both the droning and her heartrate to drop.

She edged upwards until she could clamber over the top of a manageable mound of rocks, trying her best not to squash Sceleste in the process, and crept further forwards to settle behind a series of jagged blocks - and looked a long way down at an enormous, cavernous open area. The very far end was brightly lit and filled with rows of computers, flashing lights, and dozens upon dozens of uniformed people hurrying around, all talking into handsets or taking notes from thin screens. But in front of that zone, in the wide area between the first line of computers and the start of the incline of rocks at Linda's end, lay the work zone. And Linda spent a long time just staring and staring.

For a reason that made absolutely no sense to her at all, her first thought was that despite being oval-shaped, the area was bigger than the three tennis courts at St Teresa's - and then her school's name suddenly raised a million questions and emotions all at once. When was she last there? How was everyone? Who would be at her desk and would they like whoever she was? And her thoughts turned to home, and her two sisters, her brother, her mum.. and then she suddenly lost track of all her thoughts, her grip on where she was, who she was, and why she was even in this place..

..until Avalon steadily brought her back, stroking the side of her head, nervously singing about soothing a headache. Linda tried to speak, but Avalon gestured a 'shh' and wiped both her eyes for her, and after a few calming minutes she pointed back to the work area.

The zone was dominated by two huge mechanical structures which resembled a pair of metal crabs lying on their backs. The curved arms of the larger one must have been at least forty feet high at their peak, before immediately turning inwards, pointing to a terrified man strapped onto an operating table at its centre. Linda felt his panic for a moment, and her whole body shook until she forced the feeling to leave her. And that hurt inside her head so much that she wished she hadn't tried.

The next victims had been masked and restrained a short way beyond the apparatus, penned behind narrow beams of intense yellow light. Linda stared at them, hypnotised. Sceleste bit her wrist to force her eyes away and break her link with their fear. Sceleste was staring at something far more important, and Linda followed her gaze to it. Avalon squealed.

The smaller apparatus stood far over on the right side, connected to its partner by a series of thick cables, and separated by five widely-spaced walls of green neon light. Instead of a person lying on the platform at its centre, something small and very bright hovered high above a clear podium, and pulsed alternately with white light and complete blackness. Linda's eyes widened as she realised she was looking at the partially complete Stone.

Twenty or more uniformed assistants attended to the man and the equipment in strict order and rotation, each group carrying out their own part in the preparations, while guards marched all around them.

Sceleste wasn't interested in that anymore. Her gaze was fixed far closer, down on a dark, concealed entrance in the walls which stood just to the left of the oval area, at a passageway where the rocks ended and the work zone took over. Linda tried to see what she was so concerned about, but other than two motionless guards there was nothing unusual there. She turned her attention back to the Stone, and tried desperately to concentrate again, but simply brought the pounding back into her mind and had to close her eyes and ignore everything around her. Avalon anxiously tied three more braids, and whispered in her ear.

"I don't want to go and look down there, but I will if you want.." she said, and immediately wrapped herself up in even more hair.

"No, no, s'ohkay.." breathed Linda. She opened her eyes again and made herself look, forcing herself not to question what was happening. Thinking would only bring the aching back.

Over in a sealed glass area on the furthest side of the cavern, three assistants in radiation suits removed a wide disk from the wall, drawing out a long cylindrical carrier, and then carefully replaced two long rods inside. They pushed it back and locked it in place, while one of them finished lowering a series of levers before gesturing to a man in the main work zone. Linda knew who he was before he had even turned around.

The traveller, dressed in the clothes she recognised from his arrival at the castle, walked past the green neon walls and stepped up onto the larger platform. He clapped his hands loudly, and looked down at the man on the table.

"Afraid?" he taunted, "That's good! You have to be afraid - for that means you're ready! Attention everyone - we are ready once more! Initiate Extraction procedures!"

He quickly walked a few yards away and stood behind a red line on the ground, adjusting a pair of dark goggles. The whirring started slowly, and began rising again to its unbearable pitch. A dense white beam emerged from each of the larger apparatus' six arms, burning slowly down through the air, towards the victim. The rays focussed at the centre of his body, arching him away from the table as if he was being drawn towards each of them. The seventh beam was much paler and thinner, and flashed constantly from his head to his heart. Linda covered her ears as hard and tightly as she could, and screamed to block out the madness with her own. She wanted to look away, to leave the image behind her and never, ever look back, but she couldn't.

And then she stopped screaming. Screaming was no good anymore. All she could do was watch, terrified and unblinking. She stared beyond him, as she had done the very first time that she had looked at Avalon the bird and saw Avalon the faery, back in a hotel restaurant so very, very long ago. And now he stopped being just a person. Linda watched as a faint, white aura seemed to be rising up through his skin, quivering, twisting and struggling to remain a part of his body. The intensity of the noise grew higher, drawing the.. the.. Linda knew she could see his spirit, and it was being taken.. she had to turn and run, she had to faint, she had to do anything that would take her away from the most evil act imaginable.. but she couldn't. She had to.. he looked at her. It was only a fraction of a second, but he had looked into her, and she knew in her heart that she had drawn his eyes to her. His spirit, the energy, the very life force, rose relentlessly higher, convulsing until the divisive strength of the six beams lifted away its last contact with him, and his body fell lifeless against the table. Linda heard no sound, felt no emotion or pain as she watched his spirit disappear into the machinery, through the seventh beam. And the second unit began its low buzzing.

Small white lights ran in a bright sequence along each of its four arms, arriving at their pointed ends, faster and faster until each point shone with an unbearable intensity. The widening buzz combined with the high whirring and made Linda feel as if her head was being torn apart. The points of each arm began firing short bursts of an intense laser beam at the Stone, and the entire apparatus became lost for a few seconds in an overpowering blue light.

Linda realised what she had been so close to knowing all along. The Stone was a living entity, a key.. no, more than a key.. it was a forbidden link between the worlds of the living and the dead, a gateway between dimensions created from an obscene marriage of science and spirituality. She collapsed into a ball on the ground, pushing herself against the rocks until the noise eventually grew quieter, leaving the entire cavern silent. The echoing voices, the footsteps, the clanking of machinery and the sound of someone loudly clapping their hands all returned, dragging Linda back to the world outside her mind.

Avalon stumbled in the gravel and sand in front of Linda's face, and lifted her hair up. She had hidden behind her neck and hadn't seen what had happened, too scared to dare look. But now she looked past Linda's tears and into her blue eye, and saw everything that she needed to. She tried to say something that would bring her any comfort but couldn't think of anything, so she shuffled onto her shoulder and hugged her neck instead. Linda gradually stood up and forced herself to look over the rock once more, and shuddered to see the next person being strapped onto the table. The woman was shaking uncontrollably while a few of the assistants carried out their onerous task, much to the traveller's amusement. They soon left her, and the whirring noise began again.

Linda picked Sceleste up and held her close to try and find some solace for the nightmare ahead, unaware of Mörrah's presence just a few feet away. Although she was so weak, she had managed to stay near enough to Linda to gain a little strength from the child's every trauma, and had grown a little stronger from all her anguish. The wretched Beast had sensed her faint resurgence of vitality, so she had stayed back, out of its reach.

Mörrah stared down in awe at the evil beneath her and yearned with more desire than ever for both the Stone and its creator. She savoured his disregard and the abject terror he demanded. For her, the man was no mere traveller. In her eyes he had become the ultimate Ground Crawler, one worthy of status as her male equivalent, a Vedun, one to rule the Dark and the Light for eternity alongside her. But she had to reach him and declare herself to him, to stand before him as he had stood before her all those centuries ago.. but she needed more strength to do that. Her eyes turned to the girl. The fool-child possessed all that was needed..

Linda took a deep breath, and reached into her pocket for the Stone. She held its last small section as tightly as she could, shielding herself, Avalon and Sceleste with an imagined forcefield that could block out all the screams, the suffering, and the vicious whirring. But she couldn't. The pain was too much for her to bear. Either her ability had gone completely, or the noise was too intense.. or perhaps the Stone simply wasn't hers to command any more?

She stared into her hand, powerless to stop it melting away, watching helplessly as it became smaller than the alexandrite crystal of her mother's necklace, going further until nothing was left. The loud buzzing and humming stopped instantly. The lasers had finished burning, the equipment shut down, and the Stone floated above its podium. Linda had to see it. She stared, unthinking. It was a thousand shades darker than jet-black, and seemed to be suspended in a blood-red aura.

The silence ended with the traveller's footsteps. The green neon walls disappeared with a series of loud clicks as he crossed the floor, and he stood beside the Stone, spreading his arms in a self-reverential display of glory, taking the rapturous applause of his guards and assistants. His gloved hands trembled as he reached forwards and picked it up, so much so that he almost dropped it as he held it close for inspection. He walked over to a brightly-lit circle of crystals embedded in the floor, and stood on a symbol to the side of them. A guard brought a few Gifted Ones forwards, and the traveller chose the most frightened. He grabbed her blond hair and held her inside the circle, while his group of armed assistants took their places around its edge. She clutched the Stone in one hand and placed her other on a stone relic from the wall of the Boriso Glebov castle.

"Speak, my first Requester, the greatest honour is to be yours!" he declared in a voice that verged on hysterical.

And then everyone froze.

The entrance which Sceleste had been watching so intently was suddenly filled with a rapid burst of gunfire, and Government soldiers began spilling into the cavern. The guards gunned down the first few, and a fragile stand-off took over. Silence filled the cavern, until the Requester squealed as the traveller twisted her hair, and she began speaking the only words she had been allowed to say for over a year.

"Ahh.. June 24th 1186 Anno Domini, Leshii Forest, Boriso Glebov Castle.. 24th of June, 1186 Anno Domini, the Leshii.." she screamed.

Linda felt sick, and had to close her eyes. The girl reminded her a little of Andie, which brought on an overpowering wave of loneliness, exaggerating her feelings of being a complete failure. Everything was going so terminally wrong. The first headline for a long time crashed into her mind, adding to the burgeoning pain and intensity of her headache.

"Lindagate: Idiot Messes Up Again - World Changed Forev.."

Avalon stopped singing a nervous Healing Song while stroking Linda's forehead, and tapped at an eyebrow until she opened her eyes again.

"Lindy? Look there!" she said, pointing up into the cavern's high ceiling. Linda stepped back to see, but there was nothing but darkness there.

In less than a blink Avalon had darted into Linda's inside pocket, and came out holding her treasured picture. She hovered just out of reach with it, and ripped it across the middle, separating Linda and her mother. And then she ripped it again. And again. And then faster, until a snowstorm of minute pieces floated down to the ground, and she even managed to rip up most of those before they could settle. Mörrah moved nearer, barely daring to believe what she was seeing. The faery had lost its weak mind, the Beast was low with exhaustion and distracted by the chaos.. and had left the child vulnerable, rendering the gates to the Gifted One wide open. She seized her opportunity to control the girl, and moved into the shadows that surrounded Linda, and then beyond them to embrace her, casting a cloak of despair all around her.

The traveller shook the Requester, who started over again. This time a familiar blue glow began to appear, very faintly, and he let go of her hair. His assistants fired a few warning shots to keep the troops contained in the tunnel, and the image faded away.

"Again!" he shouted to her, and faint, indistinct trees and long grass began to appear around him. He clutched at her shoulders, and laughed quietly.

"Avie? What have.. how could you?" gasped Linda, too shocked to even cry. Avalon settled down in the middle of the colourful shreds, and blew a handful up to her.

"If you want it, you can put it back together again - just close your eyes because I know you can make it happen. The Stone's here, and so are you. You have to believe you can, Lindy.. because I do."

Linda crouched down and ran her fingers through the pieces, and saw the first of her tears land on them.

"Try, sweety, that's all.. just try," whispered Avalon, holding onto a braid.

Deep in her heart, Linda knew Avalon could never do anything to hurt her this much. But a voice drifted through her mind, whispering words of betrayal, mocking such a trusting nature, and bringing questions which were heightened in their power by the shreds that lay in front of her. Why had the low-faery done it? How could the best, closest friend she could ever have, be the one to do something so unspeakable? Why? How?

More tears fell as Linda lost herself in countless heartbreaking questions. How much hatred can even a worthless faery hold for her? Was it deserved? Why did she do such a thing? Why, why, why.. she scooped the pieces into a pile and sat before them, absently smoothing them back out, unable to think of anything. The entire world seemed a million miles away. In her mind she ran away from this evil place, spreading her wings and racing fast enough to take off and fly, leaving everything and everyone behind. A darkness drifted by her feet, trying to slow her down and keep her wrapped in bitterness and pain - but she couldn't give in to those feelings. No, she wouldn't give in. She had to get away from the hurt and confusion, because there had to be a better place, a place where impossibly difficult questions were answered, and a place where love was all that mattered. And as she imagined soaring above the clouds, feeling the golden warmth of sunshine upon her, she knew that such a place existed. It existed in her heart.

She glided high and low in safety and security, and thought of holding the picture in her hands, as warm as the sunshine, and felt herself looking at it. She had spent her whole life knowing every single detail. Her mother's eyes that were so full of love, the dark mauve jumper with the snag, the woolly white blanket with the small lambs, the earring at an odd angle, the alexandrite necklace and the millions of other wonderfully important things, all the perfect imperfections that made it so beautiful.. and no-one could take it away from her again, not even.. even.. Linda sensed a shadow falling across the picture, penetrating every colour and every shade and bleeding away the love it had always held. A vile darkness lay around her, dulling her sun, her clouds, her very self..

..but darkness had no place with her. A rage burned in Linda that she had never felt before, and immediately the darkness moved away, hiding, waiting for another chance to seize control of her. But where was it? What was it? She imagined holding the necklace in the photograph, bigger and more powerful then ever, spreading its rainbow colours through every shadow that dared to be in her special world. Nothing could take away the beauty that her picture carried, nothing could ever be capable of such a crime, no person, no Spiritae - and nothing as unworthy as such a loathsome being as Mörrah.

Linda felt herself laughing. Mörrah? The darkness was that of an aged Ved'ma? In her mind, Linda cast every vibrant colour around herself, giving the darkness no place to hide, and leaving the weak Spiritae nowhere to go..

Sceleste lay on a rock, and watched her Gifted One easily destroy the Dark Spirit. The darkness that the Harmless One had unintentionally allowed to fall over the girl had lifted, and gone forever. She hissed with delight as Mörrah grew fainter than the last shadows of twilight, ending her evil life alone and unknown even to Lady Morganna. A voice filled with self-pity cried out to no-one, too weak even for Sceleste to hear. The Spiritae faded away into less than a shadow, to be lost and drifting through darkness for eternity.

Avalon tugged the braid again, a little harder this time, and Linda opened her eyes. The picture rested in her hands, perfect again, even down to the ridged crease in the top right corner.

"See?" said Avalon, in a very told-you-so way, and gave Linda a quick round of applause, and her best face-hug. She flew up to the vantage point again, and anxiously gestured for Linda to join her.

Linda slowly stood up. She knew she had been flying around in her mind, loving everything held within her picture, and then.. something to do with feeling bad, and feeling better. A lot better, actually. But it was all a vague blur, and she couldn't even try and think about anything - every heartbeat now seemed to be amplified a hundred times inside her head. But Avalon kept waving so she slowly crept over to her, and looked down at the blue and white world which had grown a little stronger near the traveller, and shivered. She left the picture on the rock next to Sceleste, and leaned close to Avalon, looking into her silvery eyes.

"You.. you have to stay here and look after this for me, Avie, and keep Sceleste with you, you promise?" she said, tapping the picture.

"Okay. No. Why?" Avalon replied, carefully placing the picture back into Linda's inside pocket.

"Because if everything all goes wrong.. you two can still get out of here, can't you?"

"Why would we want to be anywhere without you? Besides.." she said, winding herself up in three long braids, and hiding herself beneath a blanket of hair, "..what if what goes wrong?"

"I'm going to get the Stone, but I don't know what to do, and that's why it might all go wrong," she said. Sceleste rubbed a shoulder low against Linda's arm, and planted her front claws into the denim.

"Oh great, you as well? Okay, okay, you can both come along. So no heroics from me then.." she sighed, and picked Sceleste up who purred warmly in her arms.

Linda forced her way over and through the next few gaps, nearing the work zone. She felt convinced the entire world could see her leaving the concealed safety and shadows of the rocks as she clambered onto a smoother and less haphazard area. She stood up in full view of the cavern, looking fifty or sixty feet ahead at the ritual unfolding a long way beneath her. Nobody looked up at her. No-one had any reason to. The Requester was having more and more success, showing everyone the rewards of their labours, creating the first distinct sight of the scientific miracle. Linda trembled as she watched them, feeling more scared than ever.

"You can do anything," breathed Avalon, "I know you can," and stroked Linda's hair, trying to ease away the agonies inside her head.

The forested scene before the traveller grew a little clearer, and his select band of guards moved close to him, taking their places within the circle. He allowed the Requester to put both hands on the Stone, and the monotone trees grew sharper and more solid.

The uneven surfaces and gaping drops at Linda's end of the cavern spread out in front of her, and a huge knot formed in her stomach. She didn't have the time or the strength to climb and falter her way over them, so she did her best to bury her feelings deep inside, where common sense and logic didn't matter. She closed her eyes and forced herself to fend off the pain, not allowing anything to get in the way of simply thinking of the Stone, and of her need to be near it.

"I can do this, I can do this.." she said silently to herself, keeping in time with Sceleste's gentle purring. She dismissed everything else around her and stepped forwards, not questioning where her foot might come to rest. Her step would take her where she wanted to be.

She immediately felt solid ground, and looked around in the intense glare from the lights at the edge of the work zone. The Government troops to her left shouted at her in their authoritative, angry voices, but she ignored them all. She walked between the crab-like structures, across the area where the green neon walls of light had been just a few minutes earlier, and tried hard not to shake with every step. The guards pointed their guns at her, but in her mind, they simply didn't exist. The pain from her eyes tore through her entire body, but she had to keep them open, fixed a short way ahead of herself - and firmly on the traveller. He stared back at her. All of his assistants trained their guns on her, and she stood alone, midway between the troops and his entourage. The shouting grew louder as more and more voices joined in, and small groups of armed workers began making their way towards her from all sides.

"Silence!" she shouted, as loudly as she could manage. Fighting against everything around her as well as pushing away the demands on the Stone of a lesser Gifted One was like walking through the raging fires of hell, but had to be endured, it simply had to be. Her voice echoed for a long time around the cave, maybe naturally or maybe because she wanted it to, making her feel small and yet large at the same time. A pain worse than a burning knife plunged into her head, making her cry out and stumble to the side.

She stood perfectly still for a long moment, waiting for the agony to subside a little, and lowered her eyes to the Stone and the four hands that held it. Seeing it so black unbalanced her for a fraction of a second, and a volley of harmless clicks went off from all the guns pointing at her. And then another. And another. Sceleste looked around, nervous and trying to decide who to take first, but Linda stroked her, knowing that nothing would harm the ones she loved.

Linda looked to the Stone, rocking a little on her feet. The trees had faded and the traveller violently shook the Requester, demanding she continue repeating the location. The blue world began to return, and he waved a fist towards his guards, before pointing wildly.

"Kill that intruder! Whoever she is, kill her NOW!"

Sceleste fixed her eyes upon him, searching his soul, ready to take him to the lowest depths where he belonged.

"Kill them both NOW!" he roared.

But Linda wouldn't let them. Nothing could harm her now, and she didn't fear anyone. She kept her eyes firmly on the Stone, held her free hand out in front of herself, and whispered at the only level that didn't send storms of pain through her.

"Come to me.. as I come to the Stone, so the Stone shall come to me.. as I come to the Stone, so the.."

The small vision of trees and grass faded away completely and a hazy white bridge of light grew from the Stone to her hand. She felt the most incredible sense of power filling her and surrounding her as the Stone slowly appeared, complete and resplendent in her grasp. She guided it high above herself, feeling its heat soaring as the intensity of its pure light increased far beyond anything she had experienced before. For a few seconds she was lost in awe, enraptured with its beauty, fighting through her pain to see and feel its vile glory. She screamed as she felt as if more burning knives were slicing into her head, and it all became too much for her. She knew that she still had to do something, perhaps say something.. but she couldn't cope, the pain and the burgeoning power in her mind wouldn't allow her to think anymore.

Avalon.

Somewhere in her heart Linda heard her, or vaguely sensed her, for the tiniest split second - but it was enough to guide her to a place of calm for the briefest of moments. Linda searched in her heart and found the words already waiting to be said.. so clear, so honest, and so simple. She looked up into the Stone, opening her eyes wide, challenging the tumult of agonies within her and defying them all.

"I command the release of Souls within! I free the power of their lives and of their Spirits, and I command the return of all the pure-hearted to where they belong, to whom they belong!"

A blinding white light roared out in every direction from the Stone, infinitely hotter than it was bright, and as unstoppable as it was powerful.

CHAPTER THIRTY FOUR
Arrival

Linda felt nothing. She could see nothing, and she was aware of nothing. And yet she could feel everything, and she could see everything, everything that ever was or ever would be. Silence surrounded her, and darkness surrounded the silence. She was nowhere, she was everywhere, and it was beautiful.

The faintest of heartbeats began to grow, softly at first, then stronger and gently louder. It came from far away, it passed through her, and it stayed with her.

The heartbeat belonged to her.

CHAPTER THIRTY FIVE
Awakening

Linda slowly blinked, barely opening her eyes. She could feel herself drifting in a wonderfully secure and warm place, somewhere perfect between a dream and the real world. She blinked again, opening her eyes just enough to allow the tiniest sliver of daylight into her beautiful world. Unknowingly, she let the dreamy place drift away from her or perhaps she drifted from it, and her head swam with a gentle new awareness.

She slowly sensed that she was lying in a strange bed, which somehow felt vaguely familiar. A soft breeze danced against her skin and she opened her eyes to see Avalon hovering just inches away, humming a Morning Song for her. She flew over to the slightly open window, and perched herself on the top edge of a picture frame, which was nestled between two small bears on the windowsill.

Linda's head felt heavy and full of lead, which was a vast improvement compared to how her body felt. She eventually managed to raise herself up onto an elbow, and looked around. Early morning sunshine filled the bedroom with a warm glow. Aggy lay at the end of the bed, a dressing table stood over by the door, countless teddies lay strewn around, a computer and a tv took up a whole corner, and a dozen trendy popstars adorned the walls.. and a badly knotted pair of trainers still lay on the chair. This place was very familiar.

"Avie? We can't be back here, can we? How could we be here again? This isn't my home.. I don't belong.. what about the white light, and there was a flash and all the shouting.. what's happened?"

Avalon didn't even try to answer, and waved instead while munching on a hazelnut. Linda was already out of bed and making her way around the room, examining each and every picture on the message board again. She turned back to Avalon.

"This isn't mine, Avie, is it? I'm the other Linda.. the wrong one, who doesn't belong anywhere.. especially here."

As she made her way back to the bed she caught her reflection in the dressing table's large oval mirror, and hurried to take a closer look at herself, lightly bumping into it. A can of hairspray fell over and triggered a series of decorative small bottles to do the same, but Linda didn't notice. She could only see the girl looking back. She had neck-length hair which sat very nicely even though she'd just got out of bed. She was wearing a baggy Winnie The Pooh nightshirt, and.. her skin was so smooth, and she had two piercings - in both ears. And there was a good chance she really was a little taller. Her eyes were still blue and brown, so she was definitely Linda. For the briefest of moments it all made sense to her, but the understanding passed as quickly as it came and suddenly she was back feeling bewildered. She clambered across the light blue duvet and leaned against the windowsill, accidentally nudging one of the small bears off. Avalon was still sitting on the picture frame, and smiled up at her.

"Hello sleepyhead. Are you feeling alright now?" she sang, as her wings waved slightly in the breeze. Linda nodded and looked out of the window at the suburban world beyond. For a split second Avalon became a songthrush before becoming Avalon again. Linda noticed, but only just.

"What's happened, Avie? How can we be back here? And where's Sceleste?"

"Sceleste? She's waiting down in the driveway for me, there by that gatepost, see her there?" she said, pointing. Sceleste was nonchalantly licking a paw and looked remarkably unconcerned with life, but Avalon seemed to be in a hurry.

"Lindy, you have to listen to me because.. because we don't have long anymore. This is your home now."

"What are you talking about, Avie? And why do you keep flickering like that?" she garbled, feeling her heart start to race.

"That thing you said to The Stone - pretty clever, it really was you know. You are so clever, you are!"

"Huh?" she said, expecting to wake up any second and find herself back.. back.. she couldn't think where.

"You told The Stone to release all its Spirits, so it destroyed itself by doing what you wanted! I think all the energy of them leaving blew it up, or something like that.." she said with a shrug.

"So shouldn't we be dead then?"

"Yes, but the last part of your request was, 'Return the pure-hearted to where they belong and to who as well', which was very, very good. And that put you here, where we belong!"

"And then it destroyed itself?"

"Well it had to.. you'd said so."

"And now we're here?"

"Uhuh," she nodded, "You created this Linda's world because of your love for your Mum and your family, and you wouldn't change it for the same reasons. You gave up everything for this, so it's where you belong."

"Like an escape clause?"

"Uhuh. Maybe a few others got out? But we'd be the only ones with anywhere in the past to go to. How about that? So we're here now, and there's no Stone to bother with!"

Linda wasn't just stunned with where she was, but also with how much Avalon knew.

"There's no Stone?"

"Nuh-uh," she declared, "It can't exist anywhere because you destroyed it pretty much at the moment it was created. So it was never taken back in time to that big castle, and it never went anywhere. Kupula told me to write that bit down, in case I forgot. See?"

Avalon held up a page of carefully rendered squiggles from her Journal, and gave a huge smile. And then an equally huge sniff.

"Kupula? You've been back to Hesperides?"

"Uhuh. Because that's where I belong when I'm not with you. Nothing was going to wake you up last night, so I tried finding a moonbeam and there were millions of them, all everywhere!" she exclaimed, spreading her arms wide.

"But if there was never a Stone.. she'd never have asked you to go looking for it, would she? Did she believe you?"

"She had to, because lying's not what my kind do, is it? And she's so pleased with me, she really is."

Linda picked a question, almost at random.

"Hold on.. aren't there two of you now?"

"Yes.." she said, scratching her head, "..but Extra Me's in Odessa where she's always been, and I'm put here from now on. And if I ever meet Extra Me in Hesperides, we'll just look the same. Some of us do. Especially Rhalla. She looks just like R'alla, and Rallah.. oh, and Rahlla, as well. We get around, you know."

"That's so weird.."

"Yup. And for a little while longer, I belong here with you. That's why I'm here now. You and me, and Sceleste too - with no curses!"

Avalon flickered for a moment between being a songthrush and herself. Linda was fending off a million questions that were racing around in her mind and went to nervously fiddle with her hair, but there was nothing lying near her elbows to fiddle with. Avalon noticed and grinned up at her, while Linda found a bit behind her ear that would do instead.

"Shorter hair's nice on you.. not good for a braid, though.. see?"

Linda felt for Avalon's handiwork, and the braid was definitely too short to be much use at all.

"But things aren't that easy for me though are they, Avie? How can I fit in here? I don't know anything about this Linda or what she does or anything.. I can't be This Me, I'm Me Me, the wrong one! We've already been through all that - ages ago.. haven't we?"

Avalon shook her head, before nodding.

"Yes, but you are her - she's the only Linda who exists now. This is where your heart belongs, so that means you're her, now. You belong here and that's why we don't have much longer. You have to forget m.. you'll have forgotten me and remembered her.. probably by the time we finish speaking, maybe earlier.. but I hope not."

Linda felt as if everything bad in the world had just landed on her.

"Forgotten you? No, no way.. no WAY! What's the point in being here if I.. if I forget you? Please don't say that, Avie, please.."

Avalon sniffed and waited a moment before carrying on. Her voice wobbled slightly.

"I promise I'll be in your heart forever, Lindy, and it's your heart that makes you who you are.. so you'll always be special.. but you can't walk between a life that no longer exists and this life, the one where you belong. That wouldn't ever be right. How could you belong in one when your memories are from the other? You'd never really belong to either, would you? So.." she said, pausing to wipe her eyes, "..so that means you can't have everything, Lindy, and.."

"..and you're everything! Avie, you're all.."

Avalon flickered back into a songthrush and then a faery again. She tapped the top of the picture frame. Linda's gaze followed where she was pointing, and she looked at the family in the picture.

"See here? This one's your Mum, as you probably figured.." she said, using a leg to indicate who to look at. She waved her other foot towards a man who was smiling widely while trying to keep two very alert toddlers on his knees.

"And there's your Dad with no sign of a scary beard.. or temper.. or Dee.. and she's Katie and that's Sarah and this one being held safely by you is.." Avalon looked expectantly up at Linda, whose eyes were fixed on the picture.

"..is William.. the baby's called William, yes.." she said, finishing Avalon's sentence for her. Now that she had a chance to look closely, that made sense. Their names really suited them. She looked back to Avalon who had become a bird again, and watched her struggle to become a faery. She managed it, and sniffed quietly. Linda cast a quick glance around the room.

"I'm remembering things.. I.. I don't want to remember all this if it means forgetting you.. we can be together anywhere, I don't have to be here, Avie.. so you have to stop changing, you have to stop it Avie, pleease?" she begged, and felt a desperate wave of panic rising from her heart which seemed to become stuck in her throat.

"I can't help it Lindy, it's how it has to be. Kupula said.."

"But you can't leave me, you're everything to me! All of this is because of you, and I'd die if you aren't with me! You have to.. you have to stay and never leave me, you're a part of me, you're my life!"

Avalon sniffed again and wiped a huge silvery tear away from her cheek. It was immediately replaced by another which rolled all the way down to her foot.

"You.. you have to forget. How would you ever cope with the things you saw? Or when the day comes where you realise that you once had the power to have stopped a million bad things from happening? No wars, no famines.. no accidents and all that stuff, and you didn't change any of it?"

Before she could stop herself, Linda turned around to the sound of her mother's footsteps softly padding up the stairs. She grinned and looked over to her bedroom door, and waited for the inevitable two knocks. There was only one thing that her mother could possibly want at this time of the morning, and that involved babies and bottles. Or maybe the dreaded nappies..

Linda shook her head and felt cross with herself. There was something she had been doing just a moment before.. something important. She turned back to the window and saw Avalon, who was looking back up at her. She had to concentrate now, more than she'd ever concentrated before. She had to keep her mind on Avalon and not let anything stop her from thinking.. but one of the babies had started crying, somewhere. It sounded like Katie. No doubt she was more than ready for her first feed of the day, or maybe she needed changing already. Probably the latter, knowing Katie.

Linda looked back over to her door, and then shook her head again to rid herself of the other thoughts, and turned back to Avalon, who flickered erratically between faery and songthrush, struggling to hold either form. Or maybe Linda was struggling? Avalon soon managed to stay as herself, and her eyes glistened, heavy with two huge tears. Linda felt as if the whole world was coming to an end, and moved close to her.

"Pleease, Avie.. please don't leave me.. don't.. don't.."

Avalon held her hand up and touched Linda's top lip, and looked deep into her blue eye for the last time.

"I'll always be near you Lindy, always Half-There.. because you'll always know in your heart that I love.."

The bedroom door swung slowly open and a yawning woman poked her head around. She brushed a wave of dark brown hair from her eyes, and tried not to step on a bear. Linda looked over to her, and for a moment went completely blank.

"Morning, Lin darling, everything okay?" she said, and noticed the toppled hairspray and bottles on the dressing table. She sleep-walked in, and began standing them back up while absently dabbing milk from a baby's bottle against the back of her hand.

"Well, sweetheart," she continued, "I'm so glad you look nothing like how I feel. I was up all night with the dynamic duo, so could you be an absolute angel and feed His Lordship for me while I sort out Sarah? She's really on form today, practising since four o'clock - she'll be in the choir by this Christmas, you see if she's not.."

Her mother lost her trail of thought and lifted up a necklace that had been draped over Linda's no-expensive-jewellery-yet box.

"Ooh, well look at this. Is it a new one? Looks so nice! Actually it's like one I lost a long time ago.. that's alexandrite, you know.. my absolute favourite gem. You should see it in moonlight, and.."

She stopped suddenly and stared into the mirror, and then turned around to look somewhere a little to the side of Linda's head.

"Oh, a bird.. don't start encouraging feathered friends in here sweety, they're even messier than Sarah. Shoo it out and.. oh no, William's crying again, I give up. Remember to sort out Sarah? Or Katie, whichever one you want, I don't mind. Thanks Lindy, you're such a sweetheart.."

Her mother smiled a weary kind of smile, blew a small kiss and stumbled sleepily off to William's room. Linda wondered what on earth she was talking about. Feathered friends? Maybe the strains of motherhood had finally caught up with her? It was bound to happen sooner or later, all things considered.

Far away outside, the faint bells of St Mary's began ringing.

"Oh, for a quiet Sunday," Linda thought, and a very light scuffling sound drew her attention to the windows. A songthrush stood on top of her favourite photo. The bird scampered along the frame to the end nearest to Linda, where she sang three loud and very shrill notes before hopping over to the open window. She stood on the ledge and looked back with big silvery eyes, and spent a long moment barely moving, as if she was frozen to the spot. Linda leaned against the windowsill, a close-but-safe distance away, and rested her head down on her arms. For a while she stayed as still as the bird, happy to just watch her feathers moving slightly with every tiny breath, ruffling gently in the breeze.

"Go on sweety, there's a whole world for you out there," she whispered, and watched the most beautiful songthrush take to the air.

Linda Beaufort, who was about as 13 as it's possible for anyone to be, watched as the bird flew in two huge circles high above the houses and the gardens, filling the June morning with the most wonderfully bright song. She watched as a black cat wandered along the road as if it was trying to follow, and laughed to herself. Animals could be so funny. Maybe the cat didn't belong to anyone? She decided to go and find her after breakfast, as the poor thing didn't look too healthy and could probably do with a good home. And then Linda turned away, and wondered which of the terrible trio she was supposed to be preparing a bottle for.

She picked the necklace up and squeezed the dodgy loop on the clasp so that it would work properly again, and attached its awkward catch behind her neck. She stared at her reflection, and tried to figure out why she had taken it off. She never ever did that - after all, it belonged to.. it was her only.. her only.. actually, what was it? She wondered for a moment.

And then nothing more than half a thought, like the fleeting memory of a dream, made her turn back and watch as the bird gradually flew further and further away, until she disappeared somewhere towards the horizon.

And for no reason at all, Linda felt a tear roll down her cheek.

CHAPTER THIRTY SIX

A Few Days Later

My Secret Friend

by Linda Class 2A   Friday June 27th
     Beaufort

I thought I saw a faery
     sitting on my knee,
She smiled and laughed and waved her arms
     and giggled up at me!

She came back to me late at night
     to say that she could stay,
And had a Note to prove it
     signed with a squiggle, and a 'K'.

She loves my cat and isn't scared
     to come and say hello,
And show us things or dance a while
     before she has to go.

You see, she's really busy,
     disguised in her Not Me's —
She repositions daffodils
     and counts the leaves on trees!

I really love my faery,
     she's always here and there,
And never leaves for very long
     because she knows I care.

8/10

*Bizarre even for you,
Ms Beanfort.*